C000255618

October Eclipse

F. J. Blooding

WHISTLING BOOK PRESS

Whistling Book Press, LLC

Alaska

Printed in the United States of America

Published by Whistling Book Press

Contents

Dedication

To the most powerful being in the universe. My husband who can lift heavy things, takes out the trash after being asked eight times instead of nine, makes the bed warm before I get into it, fixes cars, takes care of the kids, and does everything I ask.

Thank you. You're my best friend.

I love the life we're building together.

Acknowledgements

O ctober bonds to an oracle deck that is amazing and wonderful. In the real world, I found Alberto Villoldo and Collette Baron-Reid's *The Shaman's Dream Oracle* deck.

I got this deck specifically for October, and it works super well for her. It's not the deck that bonds with how I use tarot, but I love watching how she uses it. It is one of the most beautiful decks I've ever seen, and the meanings of the cards work amazingly well for daily life, meditations, and visualizations. Their deck was used as inspiration and when I'm stuck in a scene, I shuffle the deck and see what appears. It's amazingly accurate and shaped several of the scenes in this book.

The tarot deck I, personally, use is Joseph Ernest Martin's *The Quest Tarot* deck. Everyone it touches calls it the chaos deck because it rips through the chaos to find what's hidden inside. It's another gorgeous deck with amazingly deep insight.

I love tarot.

Foreword

T he Whiskey-verse uses both spellings of the word magick, both with a 'k' and without it, depending on the main character and their magical practices.

There is a generation of witches who grew up where magick was something our neighbors feared, and that 'k' meant we were safe. Without it, we had to watch what we said and what we allowed others to see. We had our windows smashed, our belongings torn, our tires slashed, and sometimes we were physically attacked by people who were afraid of us.

With that 'k', we were safe to be ourselves.

October is young enough, and she was raised outside the protections of the magic(k) society, so she spells magic without the 'k'. That's not a slight and it's not a typo. It is a representation of *her* path.

Never slight someone else's path because you weren't forced to walk theirs.

Be blessed, my witches.

Chapter 1

Despite everything that had happened, we were still alive.

The sounds of the city held me like a lover offering comfort in a storm. The few vehicles on the road murmured like a healthy stream. The people calling out to each other below my apartment made me feel like there was still hope, that life was still worth fighting for.

And it was. Of course it was.

It didn't always feel that way, though.

I clipped my helmet on and grabbed my classic red bike, then pushed out my apartment front door. Standing in the poorly lit hallway, I locked it behind me. The lock wouldn't keep anyone out, especially the PPE officers. If Paranormal Population Enforcement suspected you were para, nothing would protect you—you were guilty until proven innocent.

So, we all did what we could to stay off their radar.

"October," a frightened female voice called to me as an apartment door opened.

I turned to Dana, already halfway to the stairs. If I reacted each time she was angsty, I'd be exhausted. "Hey, I'm on my way to work."

"Yeah." Red blotched her face as if she'd been crying all night. She clutched a tissue in her hands and gripped her dark grey cardigan in front of her. "I know." She closed her eyes and took in a deep breath before opening them again. They glowed a bright blue. "Jeff's missing."

I stopped, my heart pounding in my chest. Dana was paranormal, but she wasn't powerful enough to be high on the PPE's list. After The Wipe, which had stripped everyone's names, social security numbers, and bank accounts, most of us had taken that as a fresh start. We'd used it to build more layers between us and the PPE, changing our names, our addresses, our careers.

As long as she kept her emotions in check, Dana could pass as human without a problem, and that was *good*.

But Jeff was struggling. She'd thought he would be fine, that he could remain in hiding. Getting out of the city—getting out of the *country*—was too dangerous. We'd heard the stories. Not the ones they told on the news. No, the ones that made it back to us from the border, of entire families being shot for trying to escape.

Shot while trying to get to a place where being para wasn't a crime.

I hated ParaWest and everything it stood for, and I loathed Paige Whiskey, the woman who'd destroyed us. Our country. Our society. She'd put a bullseye on everyone.

And now, all we felt was constant fear.

"I'll keep an eye out for him while on my rounds."

"Bless you, October."

I didn't need her blessing or anything that came with it. I liked breathing free air.

She held up her fingers and took a step back. "I only mean—"

I knew what she meant, but I couldn't help the rattle of fear burbling up either. The only thought I had was that I hoped he hadn't been caught by the Witnesses because then she'd be next, and there was nothing I could do to stop it or help her. Otherwise, I'd be next too. "Sorry."

"I know." Dana looked away and retreated into her apartment.

I practically ran with my bike down the single flight of stairs, but it wasn't because I was late. It was because I hated this person I'd become. It took everything I had just to keep breathing, to keep living.

Before the Para Wars had split the world, I had been fearless. If someone had needed my help, I'd been there. I'd fought beside them, using my ability to understand the future to help in any way I could. I'd always had my tarot on me—my gift was rather stupid as far as things went. Without my cards, I was useless, but it didn't matter.

I'd been out in those streets. I'd fought Paige Whiskey's war.

But we'd lost. She and her people had won and left us behind. Paras trapped in the Northern United States of America were criminals just by virtue of being alive.

Something red flashed just on the edge of my field of vision.

I stopped at the glass door leading to the street, ignoring the red light with the wispy trails that told me it was a vision, a warning of something to come. I didn't know what it meant, but I wasn't going to chase it, either. Doing so could give those watching the idea that I was different. I'd asked Jamal to bury my gift for that very reason, but sometimes it still tried to push through.

I just wanted to live and let live. So, I gathered myself, pushing my hate and fear and rage aside. I couldn't allow myself to be sidetracked. I was a normal person. My tarot cards were hidden in my apartment in a place no one would find, not even Paranormal Enforcement—hopefully. I ignored my gift now. Well, as much as I could.

I was *normal*. I was not para. My "sight" was just my ability to see connections where others couldn't, like Sherlock Holmes. I was a weird kind of smart. That was all.

That was the lie I told myself, repeating it over and over again until I almost believed it. I had to. The checkpoints between the suburbs were getting better at finding paranormals, and I didn't know what made one person human and one person not. I didn't have another set of teeth or gills or fur or pheromones. I just had a brain that was wired wrong.

All I could do was hope, and keep my head down like a living, breathing, walking, talking person.

But people were disappearing off the streets all around me, and I didn't know how much longer I'd be able to ignore that in my vain attempt to hide, to remain alive. How much of myself was I willing to sacrifice in order to live a "normal" life?

Shaking my head and pushing my shoulders back, I shoved a smile on my face, opened the door, and hopped on my bike, pedaling to Speedy Couriers one burb over. It had previously been called Pony Express, LLC, but Jamal had been forced to change the name because too many people believed he was employing actual horse shifters.

He *was* employing paras, of course. The people who worked for him were trying to hide under the radar, like me, but the checkpoints were making it harder and harder, even there. Originally, we'd needed to stay moving in order to remain hidden. Now, even that was quickly evaporating. We'd have to rethink things soon. Very soon.

Johnny shouted out to me, waving with an apple in his hand as he put out his storefront. "New shipment!"

I smiled and shouted back, "Save me one!"

"You got it."

Torrez stopped and watched me pedal by. Her car door was open, one foot on the ground. She was a beat cop in plain clothes, which was meant to make us feel more comfortable. It didn't, for the most part. "Keep it safe, Martinez," she called out to me.

I'd changed my name after the Wipe, but she'd known me before. "You, too," I yelled back. But then I had an idea. It wasn't a great one, but...

I pulled my bike toward her, and her expression grew interested. I never asked her for favors or pushed her for help. I didn't want to put her into a situation where she'd be forced to out me or others because someone caught on that she knew too much. "Hear about Jeff?" I asked quietly as soon as I felt reasonably certain she could hear me.

She gave a slight shake of her head, stepping out of her door and closing it. "What happened?"

"He disappeared."

Torrez bowed her head and rubbed her eyebrow, wincing up at me. "What kind of para was he?"

I shrugged. "Some sort of empath."

"He could be okay. Simple paras have been disappearing and coming back days later." She shook her head. "I'd hope for that."

"Yeah. Thanks." What she didn't say was that the police force wasn't looking into any of these missing person cases because they didn't care. She might. That was why I'd taken the chance. I did what I had meant to, helped as far as I could.

Now, I moved to continue to work.

"Hey," Torrez said, stopping me with a hand on my handlebars. "Be extra careful out there today."

I narrowed my eyes at her. "Yeah? Why?"

She looked around and then came in closer to speak quietly in my ear. "Seers have been disappearing all over too. Someone's targeting them."

I looked at her in surprise. I hadn't realized she knew what I could do.

She shrugged as if reminding me she was a "good" cop. "Just be careful." She let go of my bike and opened her car door.

I slipped through traffic, ignoring the wafts of rotting trash mixed with freshly made bread, pastries, and other breakfasts I couldn't afford. I moved slowly toward the border checkpoint that separated Littleton, the suburb I lived in, from Kins City, the beating heart of our sprawling metropolis. Drones buzzed in the air above us, recording everything for peacekeeping.

I didn't just have to hide from the government, and that made things even scarier, in my opinion. There were other organizations led by other people who were trying to get in on the para game. The Sect, the Witnesses, the Supes, and the Red Queen were just a few of the ones I knew of. That didn't count the friends and neighbors who just decided to *take justice* into their own hands to protect their illusion of safety.

Every once in a while, I'd see a flash of red, like brake lights in the corner of my eye.

My gift was trying to break through, to tell me something even though I was doing everything in my power to ignore it.

I could care. I could try to follow the leads. But it also meant that I might duck before a bullet was shot, or that I might dart right when the trackers knew I should be going straight.

And without my tarot cards to give my gift some focus, that red light could be anything.

So, I continued to ignore the occasionally blipping color at the corner of my vision.

Riding a bike had its advantages in a post-war city. I didn't have to wait in line, for one. So, I raced past the nearly parked vehicles at the checkpoint and made my way to the guard shack. "Hey, Roger," I called, waving my courier credentials.

He raised his chin and pushed the button that released the yellow-and-black-striped arm to let me through.

I knew most of my guards' names, and I kept little bits of information on each to the degree that I could. Roger had a kid in school. He was in the process of moving to Lista Point because it was the safest suburb in the city, with all the latest in para detection equipment.

The bar above me flared red and beeped.

Was this what my gift had been trying to warn me about? The red light? My heart raced.

"Hey!" Roger yelled, his tone forceful. "Hold up!"

My hands went clammy inside my bike gloves as a waft of rotting garbage filtered past my nose from the alley beside me. A possible escape route?

No. This close to the guard shack? Unlikely.

I'd never set off a para detection point before. I stopped my bike and twisted to look back. "What's up, Roger?"

He jerked his thumb up to the bar that was no longer flashing red, his expression professional but not overly stern. "I just need you to step over here for a minute."

"Seriously?" I didn't want to. What if his wand detected what I didn't want to believe, that my gift was more than a brain wiring thing? "What'd it detect?"

He shook his head and shrugged, drawing out his thick surveillance wand. "It's new and, as far as I can tell, it doesn't actually detect anything right."

That reassured me—a little.

The wait was longer than a minute. With my heart in my throat, I tried to lighten the mood by asking about his kid, and he shared information, though not enough to get him into any trouble if I decided to take my revenge on him. Nothing he shared could identify his family.

That was smart, and I respected that.

I stood to the side as several cars cleared the checkpoint, the drivers all careful not to stare, not to even notice I was there. I could be taken right here and now, and no one would see a thing.

That pushed at my need to hide, anger rising in me like a tranquilized cat coming out of the haze. What about Jeff? Had he been on his way to school? Had he triggered a checkpoint and been taken right in front of other people? And no one had said anything?

Would I have said anything?

Roger stepped back finally, stashing his wand, a flicker of relief washing over his dark face, his pale lips curling up on one side. "Be careful, October."

I hadn't even realized he knew my name. "Yeah." The tight string holding me up released. "You, too."

How much longer would paras be able to hide as couriers? We were all going to have to find different employment soon, and that in itself could set off PPE alarms.

Jeezum!

The light at the checkpoint went off again, but this time the alarm chirped and stayed on.

The man who'd gone through froze. He looked at me, and his pupils slitted before he took off down the smelly alley.

Roger ran after him, eventually grabbing him by the shirt collar.

Eight months ago, I might have helped this stranger. Now? I just grabbed my bike and slung my foot over the bar to move on.

Then a masked figure in a white outfit swooped down, punched Roger in the face, and pulled on the man who'd tripped the sensor.

I jerked, ready to come to Roger's defense.

He glanced at me and shook his head.

Right. Not my fight. Roger didn't know anything about me. I didn't need to look out for him.

And what was wrong with me? I should have been fighting Roger and what he represented, not coming to his aid.

So I left. I pedaled to the maroon concrete building with three blue garage doors. Several people were gathered in there, most with regular bicycles, a few with motorcycles or dirt bikes. Bicycles could get around faster because we weren't stopped for hours at the checkpoints. That was the downside with cars and motorized bikes. It meant we were fit, too, because Kins City and her suburbs weren't small by any means.

"Did you see the latest upgrade?" April asked, coming up to me as I stashed my bike on the rack, her curly red hair up in small buns on either side of her head.

She meant the new sensor I'd set off. "Yeah. What is it?"

"Smell. That's what Ginger said, anyway. Some kind of sensor that reads your pheromones or something."

Ginger was the guard April was being nice to. We all had our ways of staying out of jail. When was it going to be a better idea to change careers than to chance the new sensors? "Well, it tagged someone. A Supe saved him, though."

Matt came up to us, stashing two boxes in his backpack. "Which one 'as it?"

I didn't think he had an accent as much as he was trying too hard to be someone cool. Before the Wipe, my guess was that he'd been a grocery clerk or a math teacher, and now he was attempting to come off as interesting. "I don't know. A guy, I think. Wore white."

"White Wolf," Matt said, slinging his bag on his shoulder, his blue eyes lighting up—with excitement, not para powers—behind his red frames.

Just frames, to be clear—there was no glass in there. He didn't need to wear glasses. He just thought it looked cool.

"Yeah, okay." I didn't know the names of all the Supes. No one knew where they lived or stayed. They were sprinkled all over, protecting the paranormals and keeping a certain sense of law and order on the streets. We were all fairly certain they were paras, but they wore masks and suits to protect their identity. You know, like in the superhero movies.

And this was our *life*.

They practically thumbed their noses at Paranormal Enforcement, daring them. I envied them a little, but I also remembered the steep price of that life. It wasn't one I wanted to pay again.

"March," Jamal called from the counter, blinking his thickly lashed eyes and tipping his bald head to the side. "Get moving."

Matt shook his head. "M'name's still Matt."

"I'm collecting the whole damned calendar, Baby March," Jamal said, his glistening full lips pressed flat as he staged boxes along his counter, the light catching a glint on his blue, sequined jacket. "Get going."

That was the other thing about our new world. It almost felt like we were creating a comic book existence. Things sucked so hard that people were like, fuck it! And they created new personas for themselves as if to say, "You haven't killed me yet, fuckers. So, I'm wearing guy liner and high heels until you shove a bullet in my brain, you big asshole!"

"October," Jamal called, and pointed to a pile of parcels to his right. "You got Lista Point today, baby doll."

"What? No way!" Lista Point was miles away, usually kept for the few with motorized transportation. But more than that, it had the best security around.

"Lady doll," Jamal said, putting a raggedy-nailed hand on his slim hip.

I didn't have the power or stamina of shifters, which would make sense if Matt or April had that route. I still hadn't worked out how or why Julie had it normally.

"I have an appointment," Julie said, coming up behind me and taking another stack of envelopes, her dark hair in a severe ponytail. She glanced at me with her heavily kohled eyes and winced, the light shining off her lip ring. "With my mom." She released a puff of breath, rolling her eyes.

Her mother was the leader of the sirens, so whatever was going on, I didn't want to know. "'Kay,"

"Thanks." She rolled her brown eyes. "I can't wait to hear what she needs this time."

"Are they trying to get you to do things?"

Julie was here because she didn't want to be a part of the siren politics, always framing the world around them through a continuingly deteriorating political storm.

"Probably." She shoved her stack of deliveries into her bag but kept out her list and route map. "She won't take no for an answer."

"Well, she's your mom."

"And she should know me by now."

"Yeah. Tell Mildred hey for me."

Mildred was my least-liked person on my normal route, infamous for making any day horrible.

Julie's eyes widened, and she turned to Jamal, who waved her away. "You picked your poison, sugar. Take the lumps."

I took my packages and prepared for the long trip to Lista Point. This was going to be an all-day trip on bike, but mostly because I needed to stop and take breaks. I wasn't out of shape by any means, but I wasn't para strong either.

Jamal gave me an extra bottle of water and a food voucher.

"Thanks." Because those two things were going to make a world of difference.

He grabbed my hand and pulled me close, his dark eyes latching on to mine. His voice was low as he growled, "If you think you're gonna get pinched, you hightail it back here. Do you hear me, baby girl?"

Say what you wanted about Jamal, but he cared about us. "Yeah," I responded, my voice low.

His eyes searched mine. "Use your gifts."

He knew I couldn't. I'd asked him to magically hide my gifts months ago when I'd nearly gotten caught the last time.

He gave my hand a shake. "Baby doll."

"Yeah." I pulled away. "Okay. I will as much as I can."

He sighed in relief and then waved me away. "It'll trickle back in. Shoo. Get going."

I waved to April, who was with a group of our friends. "Meet up at The Cup."

"You better," she called back.

And then I was out the door and headed toward the most secure suburb of the city.

The trip actually wasn't that terrible. I didn't try to slip into my gift on the way, knowing it would be a complete waste of time. Without my decks, I was useless.

After three stops in a tall office building, dropping off four letters and a small box, I spotted a poster of a blond woman with a professional smile that seemed to grow brighter as the letter Z flashed and grew.

Was that my gift again? If so, it really needed to wait until I could figure out how to get my decks out of hiding and then carry them without being arrested for contraband.

Throughout the rest of the morning and into the afternoon, every letter Z I saw on a poster or sign went bold and became bigger. I didn't know what it meant, per normal. I didn't have the *helpful* seer ability, but I did keep my eye out for anything that might have something to do with the letter Z.

Lista Point was clean. Kins City had trash and smells, and the people looked rough. Like Jamal wearing his sci-fi punk outfit—his nails were ragged, his make-up was half done, and his sneakers had holes in the tops and the bottoms.

But here in Lista Point, people were polished. Their shoes matched their clothes. Their hair was properly done. Their nails always looked nice.

And there weren't many cars. Not a ton of noise.

On the flip side, no one talked to anyone else. No one smiled at one another, and no one made eye contact. It was a colder place.

I made it to the next stop, another nondescript skyscraper. The Mozz Building.

The Z's in its logo refused to pop out at me.

Huh. Interesting.

Stashing my bike at the entrance, I walked through the rotating door with my attention on alert and headed toward the security officer. I glanced at the address on the envelope, just to be sure. "I'm looking for Suite 210."

He took my credentials, gave me a wand sweep, and then escorted me to the elevator.

The office that opened up when I stepped off was wide and open. No cubicles, and no minions wandering around. The receptionist escorted me to a room at the back, which was rather odd. Why didn't she just take the package?

Then the door opened to reveal a face I knew from my past, my life before the Wipe, and I froze.

Senator Victoria Armstrong looked up from her paperwork and smiled. "Sky, I'm so glad you could come. Please, have a seat."

Chapter 2

I felt like a rat caught in a trap. Like, what should I do? Play dumb, act like she'd mistaken my identity? The problem was, she knew my face, and she knew my abilities. She'd used them before for months.

"October Blaze." Senator Armstrong winced and shook her head as she sat back and swiveled her chair to the side, crossing her fingers in front of her abdomen. "That sounds like a porn name."

What did she want? "It's what we're all doing now."

"What was wrong with Sky Martinez?"

Sky Martinez had only been *part* of my real name. October Sky Martinez Blaze. "It's my real name." It really did sound like a stripper name, though.

The senator paused, then blinked, raising her eyebrows. "Well, I'm sorry. And you went with it because . . ."

She knew why. After a couple of seconds, she nodded as if taking the silence as my answer.

The door behind me opened, and the woman who'd shown me into the office arrived with a cup of coffee, offering it to me.

I took it, confused.

"Please sit," Senator Armstrong said, pointing to a chair.

"I'm on a schedule." I didn't know if the coffee was drugged, or if it might be a new test and I was the guinea pig. This was a surprise, and I didn't have the luxury of enjoying those anymore. Surprises were dangerous. I set it on the desk.

The senator held up her hands in surrender, stood up, walked around the desk in her thick brown heels, and took a sip of my coffee before setting it back down. "I didn't ask you here to poison you."

"You *didn't* ask me here." Julie had needed to swap so she could meet with her mother.

"Didn't I?" Senator Armstrong walked back to her chair, her brown fingertips trailing along the polished edge of her overly busy desk. "I looked for someone who seemed to be one step ahead of our changes. There were a few, but your name came up on several lists. Then drones caught you on video. Not many, and not for long, but it *was* you."

My belly twisted with fear. Even with my gift behind magical lock and key, she'd been able to find me? With her knowledge of my abilities, she could do whatever she wanted with me.

"I went to a great deal of trouble to bring you here." Sitting down, she crossed her brown sheer legs, then leaned an elbow on her desk and placed a well-manicured nail on her cheek. "I gave you the ability to come on your own."

Was that a thinly veiled threat?

Before I could consider it further, she added, "I have something I need you to do for me."

I stroked the handle of the cup on her desk. "No."

It was that simple. She'd used me before the war, before the Wipe, to help her with negotiations. With my tarot cards and my gift, I read people's intentions, saw glimpses of information no one else knew. I didn't see visions of the future like my sister did. I only saw deeper into the psyche of the people around me.

Right now, that gift could actually come in handy.

Senator Armstrong used people, so if she wanted me here, it was to use me again.

"No," I repeated.

"You're going to want to listen to my offer." She pulled out a drawer near her knee and held up a small white-and-red card between her fingers. "This will get you through any border checkpoint without question. You won't trigger any alarms."

My mind went quiet as my heart raced. That . . . that was tempting.

The senator met my gaze and then gestured to the chair again.

My gut told me to leave. My head told me that having that card might be my only way to keep breathing. I eased myself back down and reached for my cup. Since the war, coffee was hard to come by, at least anything good. I needed to know which side she was on.

"You used to fight for good," I said.

"I still do, but now I do it while keeping my enemies much closer. It's a gamble." She swiveled to face me directly, her full lips frank. "I back measures I'm certain will never make it through or that are harmless enough, and then I remain on the committees to ensure that what does pass isn't as bad as it could be. They believe I'm one of them."

"They?"

"Those who want to take things too far."

I didn't like it, and I didn't know if I could trust someone who was so flexible with her moral truth. "Why not just be honest?"

She snorted a puff of breath of disdain. "Don't be so naive."

The senator had a point. Being honest about backing paras got many people killed. Or worse.

"I need you to find a bus," she continued.

Every yellow spot in the picture behind her head flared. Yellow, huh? "A school bus?"

Senator Armstrong nodded. "We've been using them thanks to the drop in population."

"That's bound to happen when you kill people for something they can't control."

She smiled, her dark eyes crinkling. "I was wondering if that was gone. Your fire, your zest. You've kept it hidden a long time."

Sure, if almost a year was a long time. I sipped my coffee, enjoying the smooth, dark flavor that coated my tongue. We lived in a scary world, and being fired up about how broken it was and how you could be disappeared for having an opinion was enough to break anyone.

"This bus was full of paras, children mostly. We meant to secret them out of the country to safety."

So, she might have been the one to take Jeff, Dana's kid. "And how was that supposed to happen?" I didn't for one moment think the news showed reality, but . . . "Getting out of the country is impossible."

"Not *impossible*, but difficult, yes. There are people up north helping. They've got a secret road of sorts."

In a place like this? How long was that going to last before they were found and dealt with?

"I've been organizing trips like this for a year, ever since the agreements were signed and the new nations formed." Senator Armstrong shook her head and then let it fall back to her chair, a tired look entering her dark eyes. "We've moved our locations, scrambled our people, kept things quiet."

I settled into my seat and felt for a moment like the old normal, when it was her and me, fighting the good fight. I had to be careful though. At her core, she was a politician. "But it's not enough."

"No, and I knew it wouldn't be." She rolled her head to the side. "I need you. If we'd had you, the bus might not have been taken in the first place."

The air shifted, and the fire of her words burned away the pounds of fear weighing me down, slowly melting the walls of garbage I'd built around myself.

She leaned forward, an open, honest expression on her light brown face, her black hair falling forward slightly.

"Sky—October, it's scary out there. I know that, and I'm doing everything I can to help."

"It doesn't look like it," I whispered, pulling up a mental news feed with her name written all over a bunch of anti-para bills.

"I'm the wolf in sheep's clothing."

"So you think. But what happens when your gamble doesn't pay off?" Some of those bills she'd backed had put some of my neighbors away. They weren't all safe.

Fear leached into her eyes as she folded her hands together. "That's why I need you."

Exactly what she'd said the last time. I didn't know if I wanted to get involved again.

Every nerve in my body screamed. Some for me to help her. Some to run, to get out of there.

I hated the person I'd become who could listen to Dana tell me about Jeff being missing and just run out to get to work. I didn't want to be her anymore.

But getting involved meant losing people.

"I'm going to give you a bodyguard this time."

I hadn't even agreed yet. "A what?"

Senator Armstrong shook her head and gestured for someone behind her to come closer.

Closer? How had I missed someone else being in the room, period? I twisted in my seat as the smell of lilies and leather wafted to my nose with a subtle, dangerous promise my mind didn't understand. A shiver ran from the base of my spine to my shoulders as my breath hitched.

A tall woman in a black leather jacket, her blond hair pulled into a ponytail, stepped toward me. She wore biker boots and dark jeans, with several knives strapped to her thighs. She was fit—her legs went on for days. My hands itched to reach for her, to touch her skin and test how soft it was. Attraction stirred inside me, making my heart pick up a beat.

As I met her blue eyes, she locked on, daring me to look away.

An emotional silence filled the space around me, like the constant buzz of bees had just been silenced. I mentally stumbled, realizing I wasn't getting any feedback from her. I didn't have a clue as to her intention. I didn't know what she needed from me or how she was going to use me to manipulate the situation. It felt like standing on a beach by myself, just listening to waves rolling in and rippling on the sand.

"October Blaze, meet Ryder Van Sant. She's a good fighter and can help guide you."

Ryder's eyes lit with a golden glow as she shot a daggerous glare at the senator.

"You're para," I said, keeping my voice soft as the noise came crashing back in. I could feel Senator Armstrong's need to push Ryder toward me. She was looking for something bigger than the bus. That much I could glean, though if I had my cards, I might be able to read why—and what trouble I'd get into by helping her.

"I'm a Valkyrie," Ryder said, her voice low and hoarse like she'd been yelling for a week straight. She appraised me, her arms crossing over her chest.

The weight of her words hit me like an anvil. "A Valk—" She would set off every single alarm at all the checkpoints and in all the warded buildings. I coughed a ghost of a chuckle. "How are we going to make it through the stops?"

Senator Armstrong held up the white card in answer to my objection. "It works, Sky."

Ryder clicked her tongue in disgust. "I don't need that. I don't trip the sensors."

"How?" I asked.

She raised a blond brow and gave me a smug smile.

"Valkyries aren't para in the same ways we are," the senator said. "They're more celestial."

Celestial. Maybe that was the reason for the silence? A silence I'd thought I'd had this entire time. Was my gift even turned off?

I took in a deep breath, waiting for the fear to rise inside me and tell me what a terrible idea this was, that the safety net I was certain had been around me hadn't been working and the world was going to end in another bloody mess.

That thought didn't stir the fear it typically did. I didn't feel . . . *any* energy, really. No unease. No hesitation. It was almost as if the hamster wheel of fear was exhausted and dead inside me.

I was, however, a little frustrated that my gift was only giving me the barest traces of intent. I needed to know how Senator Armstrong intended to use me before I got into bed with her again.

Emotions rumbled inside me as I considered my options. I shook off the attraction I felt toward Ryder. Falling into that at this point would only get me killed.

So, what were my real options?

I could leave. I could go back to being a courier for the sake of being a courier, but the noose was tightening every day, each time the security checkpoints got a new upgrade, or the government passed a new law. I didn't know how much longer playing it safe was going to help any of us remain hidden.

"I get how terrifying it is out there, Sky, but we need you." Senator Armstrong leaned forward. "There are more paras out there than we ever imagined, and we're starting to realize that more people have the para gene than we thought possible. There's a reason some people become paras after being born to normal parents. I don't understand half of the science, but . . ." She dropped her head, her dark hair hanging down to shield her face. When it rose again, her expression was pained and exhausted. "We might not have a city left—a nation left—if we don't stop this now."

I believed what she was expressing to me. It felt genuine, real. But I'd already lost one war *with* my gift. How was I going to win this one? I shot a glance at Ryder. I didn't feel like hiding any more. I wanted to unlock my gift. I was excited to get it back again, to see where it would lead me, but not before I understood the stakes a little better. I turned my attention back to the senator.

"You need me to find this bus."

"Yes."

"Because of the kids?"

Her expression pinched tighter as if to tell me to stop pursuing this line.

Which meant that the real reason was important. "Do you want me to find out on my own?"

Senator Armstrong released a frustrated breath. "Someone very important to continuing our underground railroad was on that bus."

That made a lot more sense. She wasn't a terrible person, but she also wouldn't allow herself to get bent up over a bunch of kids. "And those things"—I pointed at the card—"really work."

"They do."

We'd needed a solution, and here it was, staring me blank in the face. "How many more of them can you get?"

She narrowed her eyes, pursing those full lips. "Why?"

"The couriers."

The senator's eyes somehow grew even narrower. "What are you thinking?"

I wished I was tuned in enough with my turned-off gift to be able to tell if this idea was a good one, but I couldn't wait. This was an opportunity we needed. "For this, I need more eyes, and the couriers are the best network we have." Not to mention they needed this in order to stay alive. I could take this job for that protection alone.

And Ryder, a little voice inside my head whispered.

A breeze from the open window brought the scent of leather and flowers to me again, and more than a shiver rent through me. She was a distraction I didn't need.

The senator shook her head. "I don't have more to give."

I didn't believe her, but I also didn't think she was just trying to make things harder for me out of spite. Whatever these devices were, they probably weren't easy to get a hold of. So, she was just treating them like the gold they were.

Clamping her lips, she pulled a package wrapped in brown paper out of a drawer. "This is all the information I was able to gather."

I took the package and stashed it in my backpack, wondering for a moment why I was so willing to just go with this. I was tired of hiding, of course. And I wanted to do more for the people I cared about. I desperately wanted to want to make the world a better place again, even though we'd failed so terribly the first time.

Yet all of that didn't make sense out of why I had just taken the box and shoved it in my bag as if I'd already agreed to help. This morning, I'd run after hearing Dana's story, knowing there was nothing I could do. Jeff was missing, and he was likely dead. So, why was this suddenly okay now?

The chip. I could get through any security screening, and this was the price. That made the kind of sense that settled my nerves.

I had to give this my time.

"Do we have any idea who took your bus?"

"What I know is in that box, but the short answer is no. It could be a lot of people." She looked disgusted. "It's probably not the people intent on killing the paras. At least, I hope not. But it could be someone trying to stop my railroad."

"That makes sense." I chugged back my coffee. No way I was going to let that go to waste. "I'll contact you."

"Use this." She pulled a black flip phone out of her pocket and slid it to me.

I pushed it back to her. I hadn't seen a phone of any sort since right after the Para Wars had started. We'd lost a lot when Paige Whiskey had taken down our infrastructure. "This is too dangerous."

"If you get caught with it, you're my *personal* courier."

That protection came at a cost. "I'll take the pass, but not the phone." And then I was going to have to figure out how to reawaken my gift. I didn't want to walk through a gate if she ever decided I hadn't earned her protection.

"Sky," Senator Armstrong said, rising to her feet. "Keep her close to you. You're much too valuable to go unprotected."

I snorted.

Her eyebrows rose, a shade darker than her brown eyes. "What happened last time can't happen again."

It made me feel a *little* better that she understood my hesitation, so I nodded and turned to leave.

Ryder followed, then pushed forward to lead the way.

Half of me wanted to allow her to brush me as she passed, to get the briefest of touches. But that was stupid, and I tugged the thought away, taking a half step to the side instead. I needed a clear head as I followed in her wake.

And it was a wake. People cleared out of her way as if afraid she'd beat them.

Yeah, she wasn't exactly low profile.

She also wasn't much of a talker, and the silence was already awkward. It wasn't a comfortable just-sitting-and-chilling kind of quiet. It was a we-should-really-be-talking-because-you-obviously-have-something-you-want-to-say-and-aren't silence.

Though, part of that was probably me. I was uncomfortable because of my attraction toward her. I didn't do relationships. Potential partners struggled to stand beside me for long. They complained that my ideals were too high and that they didn't feel like they could measure up.

That was stupid. I had high standards for myself, but I didn't force that on others.

The door dinged open on the elevator, and I followed Ryder into the lobby.

When we reached the wide foyer, she headed to the right toward the garage.

Well, I had a bike, and I wasn't giving that up. I headed to the left.

She grabbed my arm and jerked me around. "We're taking my bike," she said in her raspy voice.

Shivers rippled down my spine. Was she going to throw me over her shoulder and have her way with me? "I'm taking *my* bike." Though a motorcycle would be cool. Oh, the things I could do with a motor.

Getting through the cities faster, I meant. Not the . . .

Okay. There were a lot of other things I could do with a different kind of motor, too. Fuck!

That, too.

I brushed that aside as Ryder closed the distance, towering over me, her blue eyes almost physically chilly as she stared me down.

My breath caught in my throat as I bent to look up at her, taking in the silence that enveloped me again, welcoming me like a lover as it calmed my nerves.

She licked her lips, her cheekbones standing out with the slight movement. Her nostrils flared as if she was taking in *my* scent now.

I didn't know what to do. This was terrible timing.

"You are the only way to get what I need." Her words feathered along my lips.

A shiver ran over me as I studied her lips, wanting to taste them. "What's that?"

She didn't answer.

So, she did want to use me like everyone else. With considerable mental effort, I jammed my fingers into her elbow and twisted her wrist, forcing her fingers to relax. "Meet me at Speedy," I said.

Her eyes flashed as she gritted her teeth.

I shot out of there like a bullet as the noise of the world crashed down around me again, invading my head, heart, and soul with chaos.

Things had just gotten way more complicated than I had any desire for.

But a flicker of flame sparked in my heart, and for the first time since we'd lost the Para Wars, I was excited.

Chapter 3

I let the ride back to Speedy clear my head. Mostly. I was still struggling with my attraction to Ryder, and with the fact that I'd made a gargantuan leap from fear to fearless.

Ryder was a very attractive woman, but I struggled with relationships. With my gift, I saw a lot more than they typically wanted me to see, a lot that didn't make them more attractive. This excitement and my inability to remain focused with her around were probably nervousness and inexperience more than anything.

The silence she offered was something I'd never experienced before and something I'd never realized I needed.

Did that have something to do with her being celestial? If so, maybe my attraction to her wasn't even real attraction. Maybe it was something outside of my control. Maybe it had something to do with the way she never set off alarms or sensors.

The fear-to-fearless thing was throwing me off, though, but only because I was a hero. I was stupid and reckless and believed in fighting for the side of right and doing everything I could do to make things right and, well, that made me the type of person who got others killed.

One of the reasons I'd clung to that fear was because it was the only thing keeping me from being a moron. I just naturally, stupidly trusted that things would work out. My brain just instinctively knew that if I followed the path of "right," everything would work out.

But I'd proven that wrong already. Without that fear, my old self could come back, and I'd be reckless all over again. I had new friends, a new life. I didn't have the old crew—War Hawk—to protect me.

I had my drive back, and that terrified me. It was the exact thing I'd been looking for, but now that I had it, it was like holding a fireball in my hand.

It was easier to think about Ryder and wonder what I was going to do about her. Nothing was the right answer, but I couldn't get her out of my mind.

Speedy Couriers was empty by the time I arrived and let myself into the back. It was late, and with only normal-powered legs on a nonmotorized bicycle on one of the longest routes, I was the last one in.

I stashed my bag and two parcels I'd been unable to deliver.

What did I want to do about Ryder? There was no doubt I was interested in her, even though she'd admitted she was just one more person who wanted to use me. She stirred a fire in me I hadn't felt in a long, dry while, and she offered a silence I'd never experienced before.

How long would it be before I drove her off, like everyone else? Even for a celestial, I was a difficult person to get close to. I just was. So, silence or no, fire or no, getting close to her was a bad idea. The end.

Now, the only remaining question was what *she* needed from me. I had to be careful of how many people I allowed to use me. I was the type who said yes to everyone—Dana, Senator Armstrong, Jamal, Ryder, some random stranger in search of a puppy. Being stretched too thin had just been one more reason I'd failed so horribly the last time.

I headed over to The Cup, expecting Jamal and the gang to already be there. I needed my gift back. Things were getting too chaotic, and too many people were starting to see me. I couldn't walk this path blind.

The roar of a motorcycle rumbled down the nearly empty, rainy streets. It wasn't a downpour yet, but a slight haze drifted around the streetlights, creating shallow puddles in the pockmarked sidewalk.

I looked up to see who would be driving around at this hour. Excitement rushed through me at the sight of Ryder.

She turned her bike around and headed back, sitting tall, owning the vehicle in a way that made my breath shallow and my head hazy as her back tire kicked up water from the road.

I ducked back behind the corner of the building. I didn't need her involved with me reacquiring my gift until I knew what she needed from me. A group of people came out of the noodle shop beside me, laughing and pulling their collars up against the drizzle.

The Valkyrie parked her motorcycle beside one of Speedy's blue garage doors and stepped off, walking with a sexy ease I couldn't pry my eyes from. Her dark jeans hugged her legs, and her knives gave her an air that said she knew her business.

Every part of me felt pulled toward her, which was the wrong way, so I slipped around the laughing group and jogged around the block to The Cup.

This was our normal hangout. During the day, it served really crappy coffee and teas—mostly teas, because they could grow those. But around three, they switched everything up, and it became a bar with great fries and equally crappy drinks.

Crappiness had settled over our part of the world, and the owners of The Cup did their best to just own it. They even advertised that they had the worst coffee in town and the shittiest margarita of New Kins.

They weren't kidding on that last one. I seriously didn't know if Cindy ever even put tequila in one.

"Hey," April shouted over the noise from our normal table toward the middle, her two buns let down into poofy, red pigtails. "You made it back!"

Julie slid off her barstool, carrying an empty pitcher, and gave me a one-armed hug on her way to the bar. "Sorry for the ditch."

"How was the meeting?" I gave her a slight hug and continued to the table, a little upset. How had Senator Armstrong managed to *arrange* for today?

Julie glared and ran her tongue along her teeth in irritation. "Not great. Kalindi wants me back, and she's pretty insistent."

"How so?"

Rolling her eyes, she shook her head. "I don't want to get into that part of it." Julie propped herself up on a bar stool at their table. She grabbed a glass and poured herself a beer. "She's creating a mess, though, and I don't want to be a part of it."

Julie had a weird family dynamic, coming from a siren family of highly influential women. She didn't have to worry about being nabbed at checkpoints because she could talk her way out of anything. That was one of the reasons why she had Lista Point—anyone else would get caught entering the city.

"She's always had big goals," I said, tilting my head, "but what she's doing now?" I was more than a little curious, but part of me hesitated to ask, as I also had a growing plate of crap that needed my attention.

Julie leaned forward, a frown burrowing between her brows. "She's blackmailing politicians."

I realized that was a bad thing, but I also realized this was how the senator had coordinated everything. She'd used her pet siren matron to make an appointment with her daughter so I'd be allowed to meet with Senator Armstrong without it feeling forced. I hated that woman. "Is she making a difference?"

"I guess?" She looked surprised at the question.

"Why don't you like it?"

"Why don't I like blackmailing people?" Julie asked, fully incredulous now.

"Blackmailing horribly evil people."

She sat back and seemed to think it over. "Doesn't that make *me* evil still?"

"Well, what would be your reasons?"

"The same as theirs, O," she said, stabbing me with her conviction. "They're trying to protect themselves."

"Against horrors that don't exist. We're trying to protect ourselves against being murdered on the street, arrested for no reason, tortured because we're not even people."

She swallowed and looked concerned.

I didn't like the direction this conversation was going either. "It might not be as bad. I mean, we're just fighting back."

"By being evil."

She had a point. "You've got to do what's right for you, but at some point, we should probably stop dying in order to be right."

Her brown eyes met mine, her lips twisted in disbelief. "I didn't think I'd hear you say that. Ever."

"Me either."

"Baby girl," Jamal said, appearing with a big smile. He was wearing blue heels to go with his blue, sequined dinner jacket and tight white jeans. Wrapping me in his well-muscled arms, he squeezed me tight. "You made it."

I loved that man's hugs. "I did." Pulling away, I whispered in his ear, "I have something to help get me through checkpoints."

Jamal turned his head to look at me, one of his eyelashes falling toward his eye. He blinked several times, then pushed it back on with a frustrated sigh. "Please share," he said, keeping his voice low to match mine as the noise in the bar rose, different conversations cascading over each other.

I kept my lips close to his ear as I took off my damp jacket. "I got my hands on a pass that bypasses the sensors."

One of his eyebrows lifted. "Can you get more?"

"Not yet."

Noah appeared with a clatter, carrying a fresh pitcher of beer. "Where's Matt?"

"Can it be trusted?" Jamal asked me, barely moving his lips as he tipped his face to Noah. "March's been nabbed," he said louder. His words were clipped, his voice tight.

"Yes," I answered under my breath, but then what he'd said to Noah hit me with a painful pang of alarm. "When? Where was he?"

April stared at Julie, her green eyes wide.

Julie froze mid-pour.

Noah let his head fall into his hand. "That's why he never picked up."

"Picked up?" I asked in disbelief. Most of the phones on the black market were paratech since the government couldn't monitor them, but paratech was highly illegal. The other phones—like the one Senator Armstrong had tried to give me—were expensive, hard to get, and legal with a permit, but they were trackable, which was a different kind of dangerous.

He rolled his eyes at me. "I already know, but what are we going to get if we're caught? Be more dead? It's worth the risk."

"Where?" April asked in a quiet monotone, her hand on her chest.

"Coming in from Rockrage," Jamal said, leaning in. "That new sensor got him."

"Scent," Julie said with an understanding nod.

And it did make sense. He was a wolf shifter, and dogs gave off an odor that was probably some scientific cocktail of "gotcha," especially at the end of a long day with hours of pedaling his bike.

Still, he should have been safe in Rockrage. It had older tech security, like Littleton.

"I should go after him."

Jamal looked at me in alarm.

I didn't even realize I'd said the words at first, but then I realized I didn't want to take it back. I was done hiding in the shadows, doing nothing. Jeff was missing, probably dead. A bus full of people was gone as well, and one of them was the key to getting paras out of the city safely. Now Matt was missing? The noose was around our necks, and it was time to stop wishing it wasn't there and do something about it.

Besides, Matt was one of us. He wasn't a neighbor kid I barely knew, nor a bus full of people I'd been hired to investigate. He felt like a good place to start.

"Was he taken by the guards?" I asked.

"As far as I know," Jamal said, blinking furiously, like his anger was a nugget of dirt caught in his eye.

Music blasted at the back of the bar, as if someone had realized it'd been too quiet with only table talk keeping up the ambience.

Part of me wanted to yell at Jamal for coming here and drinking beer with a smile on his face when he'd known one of us was missing. But what else was he going to do about it? Drink beer with a frown on his face?

"Baby girl, you are not going with your"—Jamal raised a painted eyebrow and leaned in with a snarl—"eyes closed."

Julie glanced over at Noah, who tipped his head and nodded at April.

They all knew what I could do. It wasn't a secret to them. "Then I need to open them."

A hesitant smile crept over Jamal's face. "Are you sure?"

No. I'd shut off my abilities for a reason. Mostly because I'd misinterpreted them, and that had gotten friends killed.

I just had to do better this time, though, and I knew I could.

That right there was the reason I'd needed the fear. Without it, I would've gone in reckless all over again.

I was sick and tired of quietly waiting for *my* noose to drop. "Yes," I said aloud.

Jamal flicked his hand in a circular motion, signaling that he needed a distraction, and pulled something out of his pink fanny pack, palming it.

Noah and Julie took his direction and entered into a spirited argument about Star Trek vs. Star Wars, standing to make a bit of a screen.

April leaned against the table, shaking slightly.

Jamal plastered on a smile and took my hand, raking a sharp blade along my palm and drawing blood. "Just remember, this wasn't my idea in the first place."

He'd been the only one able to help me at the time. "I know."

He put something in my hand and curled my fingers around it, my palm burning at the cut. Then he poured some cheap whiskey into a glass and handed it to me. "Take that. Trust me, you'll want it."

I shot it back and shivered in disgust. It tasted like fiery dirt, leaving a trail of burned tissue as it traveled from my mouth to my stomach.

Taking my hand with the satchel in both of his, he closed his eyes, the one eyelash about to fall off again, and chanted something I didn't understand. The only thing I got was the soft lull of his voice as it rose in a gentle wave, rolling over me like a thick and comforting blanket on an icy winter night.

Then the pitch changed, turning up.

Pain lanced my ears. I tensed to clamp my hands over them, but he refused to let go of the one, while my other sat frozen in my lap. Was he trying to get us caught? Did he not think we should do this somewhere more private? Also, there was no reason to do this without my card decks. I still had to retrieve them in order for my gift to even work.

Jamal stopped so suddenly, it felt like I'd been left dangling over a cliff of silence, my feet without purchase, my ears without direction. I opened my eyes and saw—

Well, the people, sure. But they were all bathed in darkness.

Had I just jeezed up?

A blinding white light walked in the door and stalked toward us.

I moved to scramble away . . . or tried to. I managed to scoot awkwardly on my bar stool, swaying a little as my head swam.

The white light stopped beside me, and Ryder's face formed from it, her eyes blazing like two blue swords, her expression angry and pinched with concern. "You were supposed to come with me."

"Oh, who is this darling?" Jamal asked, inserting himself between us.

Ryder leaned over and looked at me around him. "Are you okay?"

"Uh, yeah." I wasn't. The room spun slowly, but it was gaining speed. I gripped the edges of my seat and felt the saliva build in my mouth as my stomach prepared to heave.

"Oh, no you don't." Jamal's hands gripped my upper arms, keeping me steady.

I didn't know what had happened to the satchel he'd given me. All I knew was that it wasn't in my hand anymore.

"Oh!" Noah whooped and sing-songed. "She can't hold her liquor."

A couple of other patrons cat-called, then turned away and ignored us once more.

Noah dropped to the table, his elbows supporting him. "What's going on? Did it work?"

"Oh, my sweet November, it worked." Jamal turned back to Ryder. "Who are you?"

"She's with me," I said, grabbing his arm weakly, still holding back a heave. The darkness that bathed everyone started to brighten in increments, and with it came symbols like I'd never seen before.

The woman in the jean jacket at the table to my right was surrounded by toy babies in varying colors. The man beside her practically glowed in playing card faces, all jacks of diamonds.

As I focused, the world settled, my saliva reduced, and the bar slowed its tilt.

Another woman was surrounded by white cats, a single diamond sword hovering point down over her head. A kid whose gender I couldn't tell sat in the middle of monarch butterflies. A man walked up to the kid, a single ten of diamonds plastered and glowing on his right shoulder, beating red.

Jamal and Ryder were continuing their conversation without me, which was fine as long as they didn't bump into me.

A white rabbit jumped through the room, reminding me of *Alice in Wonderland.* He wore a small jacket and paused every once in a while to scan the room on his hind feet before scampering off again.

I noticed something else, then, too. There were a lot of playing cards in this bar.

The woman across the bar from me was a nine, all diamonds. The man at the table not far from her was a two. His cards glowed around his hands. Beside him, another woman had nine cards shining in red around her hands and arms.

The rabbit glanced at me, then tipped his head.

I looked away, but why? He was a vision—it didn't matter.

"What are you seeing?" Ryder whispered in my ear, her voice like a rope I didn't know I needed.

I latched onto it and pulled myself out of my vision to discover that she was *very* close to me, her body shielding mine, one arm wrapped protectively around my shoulders. Her body heat cascaded over me, providing a bit more than just warmth. My heart raced as I looked up, her features worbling slightly like drunken heat waves. "Just symbols."

She gave me a lopsided frown and narrowed her eyes, scanning the room above my head. "Do any of them make sense?"

They really didn't. If this was how my gift was going to reappear—it was too much like when my gift had first appeared, before I'd been introduced to tarot and could study symbols. There were just too many ways to interpret what I was seeing.

She sighed shortly and leaned to murmur in my ear, "We have work to do."

"Yeah, well, I'm working on it."

Ryder grunted. "What did you do?"

I swallowed hard and closed my eyes to the visions for a moment, waiting for the silence she'd offered to return, but it didn't come. "I turned my gift back on."

"You'd turned it off?" That surprised her. "Why?"

"It seemed safer."

"For who?"

I looked up to meet her gaze, and the silence enveloped me as she latched on. "Everyone around me."

Ryder's eyes searched mine. "But you got it back? Why?"

"It seemed safer." The truth of that repeated statement stabbed.

"For everyone around you," she finished.

I nodded. Ryder looked away, and the buzz of the visions crashed around me again.

"How much longer do you need?" she asked.

"I don't know. It's different now." I needed to find Matt before he ended up dead. Jeff was probably dead already. The bus full of people? Chances weren't good there either, but Matt? He'd only disappeared today.

My visions were abundant, and they were *loud*, giving me insights I didn't quite understand about the people around me.

My gift had never been this strong before.

"Okay. Well." Ryder took her arm off my shoulders and leaned on the table with both her hands. "I have a lead I need to check on."

As soon as she moved away from me, the world went back on full tilt.

"Are you seeing anything that could lead us to Matt?" April asked.

I tried to breathe, thinking that would help. Hoping, really. But it was in vain. A headache built behind my eyes, and saliva pooled at the back of my mouth again.

"Who's he?" Ryder asked.

"One of us," I said, "and he got pinched today." I was too warm—I needed cool air.

Ryder frowned at me and then settled her fingertips back on my arm. "He's probably dead."

The physical relief her touch brought was immediate. The room righted with only a slight spin. I took in a deep breath and focused on . . . I had no idea what I was doing, actually. I could just feel that my mind was doing something without me. "Maybe not."

April scrambled to her feet. "But you got your gift back. Let's go find him."

Ryder held out her hand. "She's got another job."

Now Jamal stood, taller than the Valkyrie in his heels, though only barely. "We come first. Baby girl," he said to me, ignoring her, "I was happy to drink when there was nothing we could do, but please tell me you see something."

Ryder didn't look pleased.

"Curfew's coming," Jamal continued. "So, if we're doing something, now's the time."

The rabbit popped his head up, catching my attention.

I blinked and nodded at him.

He gave a hesitant wave.

I waved back. "I think I may have something."

Ryder frowned even deeper, if that was possible. "What is it?"

"A rabbit?" That wasn't the question. My question was, what did it want?

He—I suddenly knew it was a he somehow—waved at me to follow him and then headed toward the door on all fours.

"I think we have a guide."

"You're serious."

I looked up at her, rising to my steadier feet. "Might as well test drive this on us."

"And if the real mission is killed while we're playing around?"

"The real mission is probably already just as dead as our friend."

"What's this?" Jamal asked, forcing himself in and looking first at me then at Ryder. "Do I want to know?"

I shook my head at Jamal. "I'm going," I told Ryder.

The Valkyrie growled low as she pushed off the table, bringing me with her. "Let's go."

Chapter 4

S ilence greeted us as we slipped into the damp night. We were dangerously close to curfew, and most people didn't like the rain. That was good and bad news. The upside was less people. The downside was less people to hide behind if surveillance drones showed up.

Ryder kept her hand on my shoulder as if she understood that it somehow helped. Maybe her celestial magic had a mild healing aspect.

That gave me the freedom to focus on the visions. Before I'd turned it off, my gift would speak to me through murky visions that were clarified when I brought out my cards. The visions I saw now weren't murky—they were as clear as day. They were bright and looked solid, at least for the most part. Wisps streamed off of most of them.

Not the white rabbit who led the way with hoppity steps, though, looking back frequently to ensure we were still following, his floppy ears shifting with his movements.

"You're sure we're going the right way?" April whispered, fidgeting with one of her seven tails that had sprouted in her anxiety.

"Yeah." I sidestepped a puddle and kept my eye on the bunny. Rabbits were symbols of good luck, so that had to mean we were on the right path.

The animal glanced back in alarm and then smashed himself against a door, finding a shadow to hide in.

"Hide," I hissed, and ducked behind the only car parked along the street, water slipping into my collar from the mirror. It was about the worst hiding place imaginable, almost in plain sight.

Jamal looked at me like I'd lost my mind and then ran down the street, his high heels making little sound. He disappeared down the alley.

April jumped up the fire escape and disappeared onto the roof.

Noah literally became a shadow and hid in a recessed doorway protected by a cage gate.

Glancing around, Julie narrowed her eyes and then crouched down beside me.

Ryder just shook her head in disgust and grabbed me tight to her.

I squawked, not sure what she planned, until a pair of white, feathered wings sprouted from her back. She beat the air with her large wings and ascended.

My stomach twisted, and my butt clenched as the ground disappeared.

The white rabbit twitched in place, moving his head from side to side, his ears perking as he listened. The whir of a drone fan buzzed slowly along the street below us.

"Go get her," I whispered to Ryder.

She moved to launch herself off the roof and then stopped, ducking behind the wall and peering over.

The drone was within sight now. I stared at Julie, telling her silently to get underneath the car. Those drones didn't just go in a direct path. They searched in all of the easy hiding places, like behind vehicles.

A shadow deepened around Julie, and then she disappeared from sight.

That was new.

The drone flew right over her hiding spot, spun in place a few times as if the controller wanted a look around, and then took off again.

We remained hiding. Sometimes, those things doubled back unexpectedly. There were cameras all over the city, and we had no idea which ones worked and which didn't.

The rabbit came out of hiding and waved for me to follow.

"We're safe," I whispered.

Ryder nodded, then gathered me with her arm.

I closed my eyes as she took us over the edge of the roof, my butt puckering again, but less this time since I hadn't even come close to dying the first time. I released a shaky breath as soon as my feet touched the ground, and I pulled away from her.

She watched me carefully, maintaining a steady grip on my arm.

That comforted me and made me feel uncomfortable at the same time. I wanted her to be interested in me, but I suspected she was only keeping me close so she could get what she needed.

The shadow protecting Julie disappeared and slipped toward the alley where Jamal was hiding.

"What was that?" I asked.

"Noah," Julie said quietly. "He's a shadow walker."

"That's a thing?"

She shrugged.

April used the fire escape and landed lithely on the sidewalk. "That was too close."

Where had she been hiding? I hadn't heard or seen her up there.

"We're fine, darlin'," Jamal said calmly, though his eyes were wide and rounded. Noah stood by his side. "You're sure we're going to find March?"

I had no idea. "The only thing I know is that we're following a rabbit, and they're supposed to be lucky."

"All this and we're following a rabbit?" Julie asked.

"Sing me a better solution," Noah said, his voice quiet enough that it blended with the rain. "Where next?"

The white rabbit disappeared around the corner, the tips of his long ears the last thing I saw.

"Around there." I chased after the creature. The incident with the drone had been scary, and it shook most the cobwebs from my head. I didn't need Ryder to hold my hand to keep me stable.

Which was good, and a little disappointing at the same time.

Still, this wasn't the time to be distracted.

The next street was dark, with no cameras or lights. We abandoned all pretense and ran as flat-out fast as we could. I just hoped this rabbit was as lucky as they were supposed to be symbolically.

Three blocks later, the rabbit slowed, glanced back at me, and then disappeared.

Crap. "I think we're here." But I didn't *know*. Without my cards to ask directly, I had no idea how to tell which building we were supposed to go into.

"Where's 'here?'" April demanded, spinning around, looking up. The air around her lit with electricity.

Ryder frowned at me. "What symbols are you seeing?"

This was another reason using my gift to save people was a bad idea. "None. He just disappeared."

She flexed her hands in irritation and spun, looking around in a slow circle. "Did it disappear in any direction?"

The street was like any residential block in New Kins. The buildings were three stories tall, with flat faces, and fire escapes laced the front of each one. Most of the windows were dark, so the street only had the light of April's kitsune glow.

Ryder tipped her head at the ground, then looked around again as if getting her bearings. "Is this where it disappeared?"

"Yeah."

"I think this is it." She gestured to the metal road circle I was standing on. "It's a manhole cover, leads underground."

Well, the rabbit had been standing right there and had simply disappeared, so. . . maybe? "Doesn't that lead to the sewer?"

Ryder went to a knee in front of me with a frown, then shook her head. She inserted her finger into the hole on the cover and pulled as I took a step back. The lid sounded heavy as she set it beside her on the empty street.

So, she could fly—wait, where did her wings go?—and she was strong. What else could she do? Hunger grew inside me, demanding to learn more about her. What was her background? How old was she? Where did she come from?

April stopped beside me and peered down. "We're going in *there*?"

At the bottom of the hole was the white rabbit, waiting impatiently, his foot tapping, eyes staring.

"The rabbit's right there, so yeah." Rabbits were good luck, I reminded myself again. But what if this wasn't my vision? I'd just gotten it back. I had no idea what was going on in this city anymore. What if someone was luring us somewhere?

That didn't seem likely.

The rabbit frowned at me, cocking his head to the side as if irked with me.

I started to head down.

Ryder grabbed me and pulled me out of the way. "Me first," she said in that commanding voice.

Gooseflesh rippled along the arm she'd touched. I rubbed it, picturing us in a room with more privacy. The goose bumps spread.

"What are we going to do here?" April asked, her tails flicking behind her like a live wire dancing on a broken street. "Can your visions give us any clue?"

Noah looked at me and raised an eyebrow, flicking his gaze toward Ryder in a question.

I frowned at him in exasperation and shook my head. "No more clues," I said so only he could hear. "I don't even know if we're after Matt or something else. My gifts weren't super reliable before I turned them off."

"Maybe you weren't super reliable when it came to listening," Jamal said, sounding a lot more confident than he looked.

I hadn't heard anything, but I was done standing in the empty street, so I lowered myself to the ground, prepared to go down into the hole, wondering how I was going to manage when I didn't have the greatest of upper body strength. And how were we going to get out again? Did these things come with ladders? My feet floundered, trying to find a rung, hitting nothing.

Noah stopped me, his expression telling me to wait and listen.

I scrunched up my face, telling him I had no idea what he was saying.

He smirked, cocked an eyebrow, and gave me a suggestive nod followed by a pointed look down into the hole.

Toward Ryder.

He thought *this* was the time to talk about that?

As if in answer to my mental question, Noah tapped a finger on the tip of his nose with a gotcha smile.

I rolled my eyes and waved him off. I didn't know what I was going to do with Ryder—if I should do anything at all.

Noah just bit his bottom lip and grinned, shoving his hands in his pockets. Then he nodded to me with a good-for-you look.

"What?" Jamal asked us.

I didn't want to have this conversation out loud. Ryder was directly below us, not out of hearing range. "Nothing," I growled.

Jamal thought about it for a moment and then rolled his eyes, the problem eyelash falling off. "Good for you, baby girl. But stay focused."

Good call. I punched Noah in the arm to relieve some of my nervousness.

He took it with a grin.

April had watched the whole exchange, and then her entire face lit up as she looked down at my dangling feet.

"It's clear," Ryder called. "Come on."

April let out a soft laugh and then shimmied down first, maneuvering around my legs.

I followed, eager to be off the streets.

The sewers were wet and smelled gross, but not as bad as I'd imagined. Cold, musty water mingled with . . . more gross. Jamal managed to wrestle the manhole cover mostly back into place behind us and then grimaced as his heeled foot touched questionable water. "Where next, baby girl?"

The rabbit seemed to be asking the same thing. He kept looking first in one direction, then the other, his ears rising a little, one at a time. He hopped twice one way, then turned back and went a few feet down the opposite path. He paused, nodded once, and gestured for me to follow.

"He seems confused." But I followed him, careful to stay out of the water as much as I could. There was a concrete curb of sorts, and I walked on that.

"Your vision is confused?" Julie asked, her tone tense. "Great."

Symbols blazed on the walls the farther we went, glowing with neon colors in my vision. They weren't anything I recognized, though. A triangle with a squiggle on top like a corkscrew antenna. Two dots with thin lines running between them. A band of nine diamonds.

I had no idea what they meant.

The rabbit led us into a large tunnel that wasn't a part of the sewers. It could have been part of a subway, but there were no tracks.

Also, there wasn't much of a divider. The doorway was just open.

"Why are we stopped at a wall?" April asked. "Is your vision lost again?"

"It's a . . ." I narrowed my eyes in thought as I realized what was going on here. Illusion. "It's a door." I stuck my hand through. "See?"

Noah's mouth dropped as he came to check it out, sticking his head through the illusion. "Do you smell that?"

"Do you *hear* that?" April asked, taking a step forward.

I couldn't smell or hear anything.

Ryder led us through and to the right. The rabbit scrambled out of her way. "It sounds like a damned party," she said.

The rabbit mouthed something at her and then ran onward, taking the lead once more.

Julie just shrugged as we both moved to follow Ryder.

It didn't take long for me to hear the pounding bass, followed shortly by other interesting sounds, like some kind of dark techno music. "Is this a rave?" I asked as lights flashed along the concrete walls, illuminating a large intersection ahead.

April skipped forward, finding the beat and matching it with her steps. "If it is, how've *we* missed it?"

We hadn't been invited, and none of them had been able to see through the illusion.

The other side of this though? If we really were following Matt, then he was probably safe, and maybe even alive. This might be a secret group of paranormals that we hadn't known about. There might be resources we didn't know we had.

That begged the question, though—if this place was hidden, then how would people respond to us suddenly showing up?

A gritty voice growled occasional words that I couldn't make out over the increasing volume of the bass and beats. We kept going until we spilled into a large cavern of a room.

It wasn't a party like I'd expected. It was, instead, more like a rave farmer's market, with booths lining the walls and making a haphazard maze. People milled around, dancing, talking, and exchanging goods for other goods.

Beams of light raked around the room like we were on an airfield. Strange marks covered the booths and walls. Most people wore them as well, each one glowing with different colors.

Were they glowing in real life, or was that my gift seeing things that weren't there? I didn't know. I was certain they meant something either way, but what?

The rabbit just continued on, leading us through the maze of booths.

April let out an exclamation over something I didn't see, and then she disappeared.

I twisted to see where she was.

Ryder pushed my arm. "She's fine."

The rabbit hadn't stopped. I didn't like the idea of plowing forward without my friend, and I didn't know who was controlling the rabbit. Was that me, or was that thing real, and I just happened to be the only person to see it, like the entrance to this place?

The music changed to something with less bass and more of a zinging, higher-pitched beat that rankled my nerves. A girl with pink hair and fox ears turned and bumped into me, her fingers landing on my waistband.

Ryder grabbed the girl's hand and pried her away without even looking down.

"Hey!" she cried out.

"Don't. Be somewhere else," Ryder said, her voice so low it almost growled.

The girl slinked away and folded into the crowd.

The rabbit finally stopped and looked back before waving for me to continue as he disappeared into an orange and yellow tent.

I stopped two booths down.

Ryder went still beside me. "Where is it?"

I pointed to the tent.

Jamal stopped on the other side of her. "What are we doin'?"

"I'm going in," Ryder said.

Noah stepped forward, gave us all a look like we were stupid, and then shifted into a shadow and slipped into a large pocket of darkness. He hid easily, skirting the booth to the back.

We waited as people moved around us, no one paying much, if any, attention to more paras.

A group of floating playing cards rose in the crowd to our right, and people shifted out of their way as the music changed again.

I didn't think interacting with these guys would be great, so I backed up. It was less of a warning from my gift. Plus, I'd seen a lot of playing cards so far that night. The *Alice in Wonderland* vibe was just getting weirder.

April came bounding back up, her smile blazing. "This place is amazing."

Julie followed, also with a bit of pep to her step, but a frown on her face. "It's somethin', that's for sure."

Jamal scanned the crowd. "What are we doin', baby girl?"

I didn't know. The only visions that made sense were the rabbit and the playing cards. If I fell on the symbolism of *Alice,* then I had to assume that . . .

We were being led to the bad queen? And that her playing cards were her army of sorts?

That didn't make me feel great. And what were the other symbols? The ones that didn't make any sense at all? The triangles and the dots and the other shapes? They were almost more like runes or hieroglyphics of a sort, or . . . I didn't even know.

I needed a distraction while waiting for Noah to come back. "Why are you here?" I asked Ryder, my voice hidden under the beat of the music and the volume of the conversation around us. "How'd you get tangled up in this?"

She stepped into my space in a gesture that felt wildly intimate. Her fingers trailed down my arm as she spoke into my ear while maintaining an eagle eye on the crowd. "That's my business."

"You're going to use me, though, right?"

Ryder frowned and shook her head before raising her blue gaze to our surroundings. "You have a gift. Victoria said it was useful. So, yes. But I will not endanger you."

"Victoria?"

"Senator Armstrong," she said, looking down to meet my gaze before scanning the crowd again.

"It's just a woman," Noah said, appearing beside us again and giving me and Ryder a knowing grin.

Julie stepped away from April and Jamal. "Like, a creepy woman? A normal woman? What?"

Ryder managed to move closer to me somehow while also shifting to the side to better see Noah.

He shrugged. "There're a lot of people coming in and out, getting orders from her. Well, there were two while I was there, but I definitely get the sense that she runs this joint."

"Joint." I wouldn't have called this *that*. But this could be the . . . Holy crap. "The Red Queen."

Jamal's shoulders sagged, and his bald head fell back as he closed his eyes. "Well, damn."

"Why is your rabbit leading you to her?" Ryder asked, her shoulder brushing against mine.

I didn't feel startled by her touch anymore. Maybe I was even slightly reassured by it now? Comforted? Safe? "I think I need to go in."

Ryder shook her head. "I don't like it."

"I agree with her," Jamal said, jamming his thumb at the Valkyrie. "Dannika Love is bad news."

The floating playing cards went past us, and the thread of threat unraveled in my gut. "You know the Red Queen?" She was just one of several factions growing in the city making a mess of things while trying to gain power.

"I've had a few run-ins with her," Jamal hedged, his eyes narrowing daggers at the tent.

"Does it make sense Matt'd be here?" April asked.

Jamal nodded, his lips flattening. "Unfortunately, yes."

"Okay. Then we're all going," Julie said, blinking as if not quite believing she was saying those words out loud.

"No," I said.

"Agreed." Ryder nodded at me. "She and I go in. The rest of you stay here in case we need an escape. Or a distraction."

Jamal nodded, his expression saying he didn't like it. "Go. Go-go-go-go-go."

I took in a breath to steady my nerves. Not knowing what we were walking into, I was hoping my gift wouldn't just leave us in the lurch because I didn't have my cards on me.

Ryder shot me a look. Then, with a grave nod at the tent door, she ducked in and disappeared.

I followed and was greeted by a woman with red hair and heavily kohled ice-blue eyes.

The rabbit was up on his hind feet, stretched toward her as if talking to her. She was stooped over as if listening to him in return.

So, not a vision?

She straightened and appraised me, then Ryder. "Jupiter was just telling me about you." She gestured to a seat. "Come, sit. We have much to discuss."

Chapter 5

I didn't know much about the Red Queen. I knew she collected paranormal people, and they were rarely seen after that. Occasionally, they returned healthy and not broken. She did, however, seem to be waging a single-woman war against the government, so I mostly tried my best to stay off her radar. In my mind, she was almost the mafia, though I didn't really know much about what the mafia was either, outside of a government of thugs.

Jamal had known her name, though, and it didn't seem as though his past experience with her had been great. If Jamal was wary of her, then I took that to heart. I wasn't going to bend my moral backbone for her if that was what she demanded.

"Who are you?" I asked, knowing the answer, but needing something to break the ice with.

The woman wore a skin-tight skirt with a high slit below a blouse that accentuated her impressive figure. Her long, slender fingers were tipped with perfectly manicured nails. She had every quality of the super-sexy business executive. "Dannika Love. Who are you?"

How much did I want her to know about me? "October Blaze."

Her icy eyes narrowed. "Blaze." Her eyes went flat as if she was acknowledging something I didn't understand, and a snarl twisted her lips. "Did you choose that name?"

"It belonged to my father." Did she know something about him? I'd only taken the name to hide my pre-Wipe identity, not because I had any loyalty to the man who'd abandoned me.

She tapped her lip with a finger. "And were you two close?"

The hunger in her eyes led me to believe my answer would mean the difference between life and death. "I never met him."

She gave a long, single nod, her expression shifting into a contemplative appreciation as she leaned forward in her chair, resting her elbow on her bare knee above the tops of her black boots. "Won't you sit?"

"Who are you?" Ryder demanded. "More than a name. What are you doing here? Why did your rabbit bring us?"

"Can you all see him?" Dannika asked, giving Ryder a pleased once-over.

"No," I said, feeling a pang of jealousy ride up in my gut without reason. I'd already told myself I wasn't going to do anything with Ryder. If someone else thought she was sexy—or worth using—then I had no right to be upset. "Just me."

"Interesting." Dannika assessed me as well but without the same hunger. "And the rest of you joined because . . ."

She knew about the rest of us? "Our friend was taken."

"And that led you here."

"Your rabbit appeared when I was looking for answers."

She narrowed her eyes, a single eyebrow rising. "You have visions. Like your father."

"I have visions." But not like my father, who was renowned for being quite the prophet.

Dannika tipped her head to the side as if I'd just now become interesting. "Who's your missing friend?"

"Matt. Matt Macky."

"Oh, the wolf courier." She pressed her lips together and then lifted a finger with a nod that was more of a command.

It wasn't for me, so I ignored it even though I really, *really* wanted to twist around and look. That gave me some hope, at least. She knew who he was, and she didn't seem upset or villainously thrilled, so there was the possibility that he was safe.

"We caught him before he tripped the sensor at the gate," she continued.

Relief hit me like a fist and then held. Could we trust Dannika Love? "We understood he was captured *at* the gate."

"Oh, he was. I assure you. However, I was the one who caught him."

Was she a good guy? A bad guy? A little bit of both? How would we know?

Dannika leaned back in her chair, letting her knees fall to the side, exposing a considerable bit of thigh as her red leather skirt hitched up.

A slight smile of appreciation lit Ryder's face.

Well, I mean . . . the Red Queen *was* sexy, but now was *not* the time to appreciate it. "Is he safe?"

"He is now. He wouldn't have been if the checkpoint had caught a whiff of him." She folded her hands over her slim abdomen.

What sort of power did this woman have? How would *she* use me?

"I require a courier."

So did everyone in the city. "And how is he going to courier for you when you had to save him at the gate?"

"I have my ways." She studied me for a moment.

A wispy glass elevator rose beside her head.

My mind scrambled. First off, seeing visions without my deck was weird. Second, trying to interpret visions that were just random symbols was hard. There was a reason I preferred my decks. Anything could be a symbol, but if I limited my interpretation to the cards, that was less than two hundred to understand.

The elevator flashed as if telling me to stop whining and listen to what it was telling me.

I didn't know what an elevator meant. It'd never come up in any of my symbol studies before.

It blipped down and then rose up a few times in quick succession, but on the final rise, a person appeared in the cab. Someone was . . . rising in . . . uh, status?

The elevator flared a bright white, then disappeared.

Jeezum, so now my gift worked like charades with snark? That was going to make using it without getting caught marginally easier, at least, because I wouldn't be carrying around my deck, but if I had to question the visions this much, I'd just be in another type of danger.

Someone was rising in status. Who? The figure in the cab hadn't been clear enough for me to tell.

"Watch the earring, you moron!" Jamal shouted as he was shoved through the tent door.

April followed with a squeak as Julie and Noah joined us, followed by the man who had ushered them in.

Dannika raised her chin to the man, then gestured around the tent with a wave of her fingers.

He nodded once and disappeared.

He was a ten of diamonds, ten cards circling his head.

Circling his head. Uh, he was one of the leaders in her security?

Maybe. My gift was showing connections. Dannika's white rabbit threw me a bit. But the playing cards had appeared right around the same time I'd seen the rabbit, so it was possible that my gift had been letting me know they were connected in some Red Queen kind of way.

The woman had probably set this up to fit the moniker she'd undoubtedly chosen for herself. "You brought me a Blaze. Well done, Jupiter."

The rabbit's ears twitched as he stood on his hind legs and stretched forward.

"Yes, yes." She flicked her fingers over his ears and then dismissed him.

Dark, red smoke swirled around the rabbit. His long, white ears slid away and tucked behind a head of curly black hair. His hind legs elongated into a pair of jeans. April and Noah squawked, apparently able to see the rabbit for the first time. Julie frowned, glancing at me and then back at the transforming, now visible man.

Jamal crossed his arms over his chest and glared. Within moments, a tall man stood where the invisible rabbit once stood.

"Two hours," Dannika told him. "Don't waste them."

He darted out without a single word.

Jamal just frowned and leaned back, then righted himself again, slow-blinking in agitation.

The ten of diamonds came in with four folding chairs.

"Won't you sit?" Dannika asked again, her tone laced with a hint of danger behind her tight smile.

I swallowed and sat. "Who's Jupiter?"

"Your visions aren't telling you?" Dannika tsked.

"I'm a Martinez."

She narrowed her eyes. "But a Blaze first. You *are* a seer, aren't you?"

That was what she was after? "Not like my dad."

Disappointment filmed over her expression, but then a light filled her blue eyes as if she'd just realized something. "You see in signs."

Why did she seem so excited about that? "Who is Jupiter?"

She chuckled and then bit her bottom lip, looking at me through her thick black lashes. "He was a man who did something he probably shouldn't have. So, I cursed him."

"You're a witch, then," Ryder growled.

"As if he is not?" Dannika smiled warmly. "Jamal, darling, it really has been too long."

He grunted at her as he sat. "Not long enough, *darling*."

"The times have not been kind to you."

"I'm doing well enough in spite of you."

"Hmm." She looked around the group of us like she'd just opened a treasure chest. "What a delight. I needed couriers, and here you are."

I wouldn't forget that she'd "saved" Matt, who really shouldn't have been caught in Rockrage Park in the first place. Matt had that route because they had the lowest tech at their gates. Had she known she'd get the rest of us?

No. Nothing gave me the impression that she'd been expecting this.

"Jupiter finds intriguing people," she said, "and shows himself only to them, and then brings them here."

"For what reason?" Ryder demanded.

"Oh, so fiery. What are you?"

She didn't answer.

"A mystery then. Yes, yes. Delightful." Dannika released a tight breath. "I'm the reason for the Wipe. I'm the reason paras aren't being killed on the streets. I'm the reason you're safe."

"Great," Ryder said. "Then you can tell me where you took the bus."

A flash of frustrated patience swept over Dannika's features. "I haven't ridden the bus in a very long time."

Knowing she was the Red Queen, it would make sense to ask her. She was one of the factions rising from the darkness of our society. "There was a bus with some para kids that disappeared," I explained.

"Kids, you say." She looked at me with interest. "You've been hired to look for it?"

"I'm looking for my neighbor's son." I didn't know why I lied, only that I felt it was necessary.

"Hmm. Interesting. Well, that bus was mine, and I can assure you, there were no kids on it."

Maybe we were talking about two different buses, then.

A flash of yellow along her neckline flared.

I sincerely hoped my gift did better than that, but the yellow had flashed when I'd been in Senator Armstrong's office, so I assumed this was the same connection. Which meant that one of them was lying. Either Senator Armstrong had lied to me to maybe get me to agree, or the Red Queen was lying to get me to back off.

"I'm orchestrating the transport for those trying to flee."

She was taking credit for a lot of things. "Where are they going?"

"Well, that's the rub, isn't it? Nowhere, now."

Because the person instrumental for creating the underground system had been on that bus. "Are you hiding them here, in your city?"

The beat changed outside the tent.

Dannika touched a dial on the small table beside her, and the sound of the music dimmed as she watched me with interest. "We're still working on the way out."

"How?" Jamal demanded.

"A girl can't give away all her secrets, Jamal darling. Not on the first date, anyway. And we both know you don't like to play with the likes of me."

Jamal glared. The woman just tightened her eyes and crimped the corners of her mouth.

I didn't get the sense that she was talking about the fact he was gay, but maybe more the fact that she was evil.

The tent flap rose, and the music blared in again as Matt stumbled inside.

Julie rose to her feet, glancing at Dannika.

April plowed into Matt and gave him a wild hug.

"Hey," he said with a grin, taking the hand Noah offered him without letting April go. He looked stronger, more wolflike without his red-framed glasses and goofy stance. "It's good to see you guys."

"You good?" I asked.

He met my gaze, his own solemn. "I'm good." His tone said that things hadn't been entirely pleasant, but nothing told me he was in danger.

A wispy safety vest formed around him. That one was fairly easy to interpret.

I turned back to Dannika. "Well, we were just here to get Matt." And to see if my visions were working, which they were—except that hadn't been what'd led us to Matt in the first place, so maybe they weren't. I didn't know what else to do but to get out of there.

"I need to find that bus," she said, swaying slightly from side to side as she watched me like I was dinner trapped in a cage.

"Good luck." She'd already told me what I needed to know. She didn't have it. I didn't need to dance with her any more than that.

"I want to hire you." She emphasized the word "hire" with a smirk as if doing so would strike at my father. How, I didn't know.

"No thanks."

"I have resources."

"Then you can find it on your own."

"Oh, kitty cat," she mewed, sounding quite pleased with herself.

"Why would we agree to help you?" Jamal asked. "You're not someone I—*anyone* can just trust, Dannika."

"Water. Bridge. I'm over it."

"You are. I'm not."

What sort of bad blood did they share?

"Oh." She released a breath that seemed to deflate her, but the look remained in her eyes. "After everything *you* did? I didn't realize you'd harbor such hatred from your own actions. Really, Jamal, there is such a thing as too much self-love."

He chuckled dryly, one eye twitching. "We're not helping you."

Dannika grunted and then released a breathy chortle of surprise. "What if I gave you something back?"

Jamal raised his chin and bared his teeth.

"Would you help me then?" She smirked, victory overlaying her expression as if she already knew she'd win.

"You always extract a heavy cost."

She leaned forward and said in a loud whisper, "But don't you want it back?"

Jamal's knuckles went white, and he began to breathe harder.

The Red Queen turned a pleased smile to the rest of us. "I have power of several kinds that can protect you. The Wipe, for instance."

"That was *really* you?" Alice asked in excitement.

The woman beamed. "It was and is. They're continually trying to recreate the electronic world they once had, and I keep them in the dark. I keep you safe."

"You took their money," Jamal said, his tone colored with a hint of his guess.

"Oh, I did." She took in a deep breath and settled into her chair, pleased with herself. "And I use it, as I need to keep this place running." She held her hands out to her sides, indicating the underground rave outside.

"What is this place?" I asked.

"We call it Sunnyvale."

"A little over the top, don't you think?" Jamal asked with a growl.

"I felt calling it The Underground might be a little too on point, and I didn't want to give the authorities a roadmap on where to find us." Dannika slid her gaze back to me. "Here, we're safe. No drones. No PPE."

"And you're working to create more tunnels to get us out of here?" I asked.

"Mmm." She chuckled as if she'd gotten what she'd been fishing for. "Yes."

Then the air around her darkened into a grey so deep it was almost black.

She was lying, but it wasn't a complete lie. The person she needed to complete those tunnels had been on that bus. Which also meant that whoever had taken that bus was against both Senator Armstrong and the Red Queen.

The air around her brightened. That had to mean I was right.

Jamal turned to us. "I don't like working with her."

Indecision lanced Dannika's expression as she let out a breath, meeting his gaze. After a long moment, she jutted her jaw forward, bringing her bottom teeth in front of the top as she gnashed them together, then relaxed again. She reached forward and took his hand.

He tried to pull it away, but her grip was firm. His grunt turned into a whimper.

Matt jumped to his feet. April's seven tails flashed into existence as electricity buzzed through the room. A song of obedience filled the small space of the large tent as Julie sang. Darkness enveloped Jamal as Noah dissolved to protect him.

Ryder began to move forward, but I placed my fingertips on her arm to hold her back.

She turned, narrowing her eyes at me.

I raised my chin and shook my head.

A unicorn rose from the bright white power in Dannika and Jamal's clasped hands. She wasn't hurting Jamal. Not on purpose, anyway. Power flowed from her, from the air surrounding us, piercing my friend as he glowed brighter. Light flowed in, and Jamal quivered where he stood.

Finally, the pair broke free from each other.

Dannika sat back in her chair, glancing around the tent with some interest, but her attention remained on Jamal.

The white light whirled around him like something out of a Disney movie, as though Dannika was his fairy godmother and he was Cinderella needing a new gown for the ball. His blue jacket gained a twinkling, gemmed fringe. His pumps lost the scrapes of wear and tear. His eyeliner cleaned itself up and turned into an intricate lacework of lines and swirls around his eyes. His missing eyelash appeared in place.

The shadow surrounding Jamal pulled away, and Noah regained his human form, wincing in pain against the power of the light.

Dazzling tattoos floated into place and then seared to Jamal's dark brown skin.

When the white light disappeared, none of us dared break the silence, including Jamal, who raised his arms to study the tattoos as if he couldn't believe what he saw. "You gave it back."

The Red Queen sighed as if bored. "Don't go after me again."

"You were stealing power," he said, dropping his arms, his words lighting up the air around us.

"Yes. From those who were trying to stop me—stop us."

That sounded like a cycle. "Well, thanks for giving him his power back?" It was a night for that, apparently.

"Like I said, I want to hire you to find my missing bus. I may be willing to do more." Dannika reached into a pocket on her skirt.

I hadn't realized there was *room* in that skirt for pockets.

She pulled out a set of white and blue disks and held them in her fingertips.

I went still. What was the likelihood that both Senator Armstrong and Dannika Love had hired me to do the same job and had offered the same payment? "Where did you get those?"

She eyed me speculatively. "You know what they are."

I probably shouldn't have admitted to that.

"Senator Armstrong." Dannika chuckled softly. "So, it's you she wanted. Sneaky, sneaky."

Were they working together or against each other?

Julie's jaw went slack. "You're kidding me. You're working with *her*?"

I held my hand up. Now wasn't the time.

"She's playing a dangerous game," Dannika said with a shrug of respect. "But she's the woman for it. These will get you through any gate, through any sensor, and they're regularly updated with the latest technology."

"How?" Noah demanded.

"She owns the companies creating the sensors at the gates," Jamal said with a low growl.

He had to be kidding.

Dannika smiled and raised her eyebrows in challenge.

"You're *hunting* us?" I asked incredulously.

"Don't be so naïve. I'm controlling the situation. Someone was going to do it. I just made sure *I* was the one in charge."

"So you could collect people?"

"So I could protect them. Do you honestly believe every para who gets tagged at the gates goes to the government? They don't. Most are lost in transit or 'die' unexpectedly. I make sure of that."

"Death?" Jamal asked, but his tone only demanded further explanation. It held no recrimination.

"Faked, of course." Dannika winced. "Well, most of the time. Sometimes a real loss *does* happen."

"You know my mother works with her," Julie said, her voice quiet, as if she was trying to hide the revelation even as she spoke it.

Senator Armstrong was the type of woman to use whatever tools she could in order to remain on top, and a siren was definitely one way to stay in control.

Dannika watched us with intrigue, but when no one continued, she pinched her lips with smiling annoyance and turned to Jamal. "I'd like you to be my couriers. I can alter the logs. I can get you through the gates. I will give you free rein of Sunnyvale."

"How extensive is it?" Noah asked Matt, whose eyes widened.

"It's extensive," Dannika said. "You help me find the missing bus, and I will make it easier for you and yours to do your job with more efficiency. Working together is better, no?"

Jamal studied her for a moment. "What's on the bus that you need so bad?" His aura darkened with a red passion. He didn't trust her in the slightest.

But she'd stolen his power, so maybe that was understandable.

"A man who's invaluable."

The question remained—could I get into business with not one, but two powerful women who were okay with playing with fire and letting others burn in order to get ahead?

The one thing I knew with absolute certainty was that Dannika was dangerous, and we'd lit the match ourselves.

Chapter 6

W e were escorted back up to a manhole that dumped us directly between the lockers of Speedy Couriers.

Jamal put his hand on one of the lockers with a quiet click, looking a little rattled.

Noah turned to the group. "What the hell was that?"

What were the chances that Dannika Love, the bringer of the Wipe and the controller of tech, was teamed up with Senator Armstrong, the one person who'd used my abilities the most during the Para Wars?

Actually, it seemed pretty likely. The senator was the type of person who collected useful people and then, well, used them, guiding them along their own chosen paths to get what she wanted.

The surprise when Dannika had figured out that I was the person Senator Armstrong had been looking for had been genuine, which meant that the senator had kept my identity a secret. That, at the very least, made me feel a little better.

"Can we trust these?" Julie asked, holding up her chip and studying it.

I didn't know.

"If Dannika Love has this much control, she can use it *against* us as well," Jamal said, kicking off his heels and heading to the counter, where he grabbed a bottle of something amber and poured himself a drink. "She is not a woman I'd ever feel comfortable having much control over my life again."

"What happened between you two?" I asked, sidling up to the bar. We were well after curfew, so there was no going home—unless we went through the underground, but none of us knew the tunnels, and I didn't have a white rabbit leading the way.

I recalled how she'd admitted to cursing Jupiter, turning him into a rabbit except for two hours a day. She'd also stripped Jamal of most of his power for standing up against her. That was the type of person she was.

Jamal shook his head and pulled his lips tight to his teeth, then out in full display. "She's just not a woman to trust."

Noah gestured at the new white tattoos. "That?"

Jamal flicked an eyebrow, his jaw jutting forward. "Yeah. This." He shook his head, obviously not willing to volunteer information.

Well, Jamal had magic. Duh. That'd been obvious, but was he more powerful now? What were his limits? Did he have to be more careful now that those tattoos were on full display? Would the PPE hold him because of them? "Are you in danger?" I asked instead.

He looked at me and shrugged. "A bit more so, yeah. But I'll be fine, baby girl. Don't you worry about me. What sort of mess did we find ourselves in?"

I went to the backpack I'd stashed next to the undelivered packages and retrieved the box from Senator Armstrong's office. "Apparently, Julie's meeting with her mom was a way for Armstrong to get me to see her. She wants this bus, too, and for the same reason. Someone on that bus is very important to their underground railroad."

"I *thought* they were working together," Matt grumbled with conviction.

"Dannika doesn't work *with* anyone," Jamal bit out.

"I don't think Senator Armstrong does either," I said, setting my pack on the counter.

Ryder chimed in, her voice like smooth gravel. "You must be careful."

I tipped my head to Captain Obvious, wondering how the senator was using her.

"How do you know her?" Julie asked with a frown, her heavily kohled dark eyes narrowing at me as if trying to put the pieces together.

I sighed and leaned against the bar. "Senator Armstrong used my gift pre-Wipe."

Jamal reached for the packet of papers and thumbed through them. "What's this?"

"What the senator gave me so I could track down the missing bus." Skimming through myself, I couldn't immediately determine what I was looking at.

"It's all the intel I could get on the groups collecting people around the city," Ryder said.

Jamal put his hands palms down on the counter and turned to her. "Who the jeezum are you and what are you doing mixed up in all this?"

She was silent for a few seconds. I wanted to hear this too, so I gave her my full attention.

Ryder rolled her jaw, then sighed. "Senator Armstrong worked with my family through the war. I was given Kins City. I failed, and in so doing, we lost Michigan."

"*You* lost Kins City," Jamal said.

I snorted. There'd been a lot of us losing.

She closed her eyes and her mouth for a moment and shook her head. "Valkyries guide through conflict. I. . . strayed from my teachings. I've been assigned here to clean up my mess."

"You're a Valkyrie?" A light of dawning understanding blossomed over Jamal's angled features. "Oooh."

I wished I had that bead of understanding, but I'd figure it out. Later.

Ryder frowned at him and turned her face to the file, pushing things around. "There are seven groups outside of the government targeting paranormals."

April crossed her arms. "And we don't think this is the government because . . ."

"They're exceptionally incapable of capturing us." Ryder raised a blond eyebrow and pulled out a photo. "Killing, yes. Capturing, no. These guys"—the photo she held up showed a woman in a tight suit and a cape—"probably have the best record, if we were keeping score. But they then release the paras back onto the streets, and no one from the bus has turned up again."

The Supes, who ran around in masks and costumes like this was a comic book.

"I know all about them," Matt said, his normal excitement curbed. He had a pair of his lensless eyeglasses in his hands as if trying to decide whether or not to wear them.

"Good." Ryder shook her head as if to say she didn't really care because she'd already dismissed them. "The Red Queen and her Cards are the next two groups, which I hadn't realized are connected. However, we now know she's looking for the bus, same as us."

I frowned. "Senator Armstrong didn't tell you she was working with the Red Queen?"

"She did," Ryder said. "She kept the Red Queen's identity, to herself though."

Almost as if the senator saw Dannika as some sort of masked hero whose true persona needed to be protected in the same way she'd protected my identity. I had to remind myself of that part.

Ryder rubbed her temple. "The Card's movements have been hard to track. They could be anyone, and they don't leave much of a trace."

Except I could find them now through my gift. "Why do *you* call them the Cards?" I hadn't heard anyone on the streets call them that.

"They leave them at the locations they hit. Always diamonds, but a playing card each time."

Interesting. And that hadn't hit the streets?

"What locations are they after?" Jamal asked. "Not just kidnappings." His tone said that his information on Dannika filled in a lot of blanks for him.

Seriously, what had happened between the two of them?

"No." Ryder sighed and glanced at me. "And that's what threw me off. They're involved in all sorts of criminal activity. Thefts, extortion, murder. Until now, I just hadn't been able to make the connection."

"So, we just have to figure out what Dannika wants," I said.

"Power." Jamal's voice held a dark thread of doom to it.

Ryder shrugged and continued. "The Alliance has been collecting people, though not kidnapping. Lady Dun is inviting people to live in a sanctuary somewhere that they're protected."

The Alliance was a group of paras who had found a new place to live in peace. I'd thought it had to be a fairytale, but maybe it wasn't. "Do you think we saw that tonight? Is Dannika the Alliance, too?"

"Oh, Sunnyvale isn't run by Dannika," Matt said. "She has to play by a set of rules that aren't hers."

That wasn't what I'd seen. "Who would have rules *she* would play by?"

"Lady Dun," Jamal said.

Who was Lady Dun? And why did Jamal's tone hint that they knew one another?

Matt shrugged. "Maybe. No one knows anything about her, only that she's powerful. Maybe."

"Interesting, blah, blah, blah." Julie narrowed her near-black eyes and threw up her hand with boredom.

April tossed a picture from her fingers to the table. "Yeah. Endlessly. Interesting to see how amazingly whoop-fucked we are."

"You've got the card of protection just like the rest of us." Julie scrunched half her face into a frown. Maybe she didn't quite believe it herself.

April wasn't going to go down without a fight. "Yeah. So, now we're *expected* to jump into danger."

"Don't forget, baby girl," Jamal said, his tone rounded with reassurance, "that Dannika wants couriers. We're likely only going to be delivering messages and packages."

"Which could be bombs. Body parts." April rested her head on her fingertips.

I didn't want to get sidetracked even if April could be right, and it really felt like she could be. "Who else is on the list?" I looked over at Ryder, studying her face. How had she "lost" Kins City?

"The Resurrected," Ryder said, her husky voice hardening. "They see the person behind the Wipe as their savior, even though they don't know who she is. They give her all sorts of credit for all sorts of things. They're headed up by a man, but I haven't been able to figure out who. He's collecting people for the Red Queen's army."

"Does Dannika know about that?" I asked.

"I'm sure she does," Jamal grumbled. "What about the Witnesses? You think they'd be in on this?"

"That was my first thought," Ryder said, giving me a glance. "And if they are behind the disappearance of the bus, we can almost be assured no one is alive."

The Witnesses were a group of mercenaries who had "witnessed the destruction of the world" and had decided that their anger would be best served ridding the world of paras. They took out entire families to eradicate any sort of para line, even if the kids were adopted or a genetic anomaly.

"But," she went on, "we'd made sure there were no seers on the bus, to keep them under the Witnesses' radar."

"What do you mean?" Jamal asked before I could.

"Only that he seems to be targeting seers. Sometimes, their bodies turn up afterward. Most times, they don't."

Her words coursed down my spine like cold water.

Jamal looked at me in alarm.

"That leaves the Sect, which is the group I think it might be." Ryder exhaled and closed her eyes for a moment. "They collect paras for experiments. Not the good kind."

"Like the government?" Noah demanded.

Ryder snorted and shook her head. "The government takes most of the credit, but they haven't captured paras since the war ended. That's when the groups started, and everyone else got better at it. They're trying to discover what makes a paranormal person paranormal."

"Why?"

"To turn it off?" Matt asked angrily.

"For the sensors," Jamal growled.

Which was only worse, because we now knew who was behind those sensors, and we now understood the lengths Dannika Love was willing to go to. If she wasn't directly behind the Sect, she was at least benefiting from them.

The more I thought about it, the more I realized she probably backed the Sect, the Resurrected, the Cards, and possibly the Alliance all at once. "So the only group not controlled by Dannika, who also hired us, is the Witnesses."

Ryder grimaced.

Jamal ran his tongue around his lips.

"No bodies yet," the Valkyrie said finally.

"Why would they still be alive?" Matt said, clenching his fist.

This was the first time I'd seen him like this. He was normally goofy and good natured. He was almost primal now, his voice coming out in a consistent growl.

"They want something else," Jamal said, raising his head until he studied the ceiling. "If he's targeting seers, it might be because he's using them, and if he's using them, then he might be setting a trap for someone else."

"Like the senator or Dannika?" I asked.

"Or Sunnyvale."

Silence fell around the group.

Jamal took in a breath and straightened. "He might be trying to draw Lady Dun out."

"What do we do?" Noah asked, leaning on the counter. "Dannika just asked us to track down the Witnesses, and that's going to get us killed."

"*We* keep our heads down," Jamal said firmly, pounding his well-manicured fist against the stack of folders, his white tattoos flaring.

"And do nothing?" Julie asked as she pulled out a chip and held it between two fingers. "These will be used against us if we do that."

April glanced at her, her freckles standing out against the sudden whiteness of her pale skin. "It's the Para Wars all over again, isn't it?"

No. It wouldn't be, because we didn't have an over-powered para stirring the world to war. Or fighting for us. She'd won what she'd gone out to win, and now it was up to us to deal with the crap hand she'd left us. But was Dannika taking up Paige Whiskey's mantel and stirring the embers? "Can we just sit and do nothing?"

"We're not fighting this fight, October," Jamal said, sliding his gaze to me. "The Witnesses are the strongest and if they're targeting seers, they're targeting you."

My fire had been lit, and I didn't know how to unlight it. I couldn't just sit by and wait. Jeff was still missing; others were too. This person so instrumental in the creation of the underground railroad could end up killing the mission if he ended up dead. "We can gather information as we're delivering packages. Maybe it's not the Witnesses. You said it yourself. New groups keep coming up."

"I didn't say that," Ryder said.

"But they do." Jamal frowned.

I didn't want to fall into a trap and wind up dead, but I couldn't stand the person I'd become—too afraid to stand up, wanting only to curl up under my bed. "We can help in other ways."

"And when we get caught?" Matt asked, pushing his glasses to the side before looking up at me. "Because I did. I thought I was goners. So, what then?"

We hadn't gotten caught, but my heart raced with the stupidity of that thought. "We have the chips."

"Those will only work until we piss Dannika off," Matt said.

Jamal nodded in agreement.

She did have an insane amount of power. I didn't know how we were going to be able to do anything about her, or if normal people trying to just survive could do *anything* about someone like her, period. But maybe with Senator Armstrong's help?

That was a dumb idea, because she might be working with Dannika too. Okay. So, maybe Dannika had her hands in a lot of cookie jars. "We have to figure out who the real enemy is."

"Anyone trying to kill us," Matt said forcefully.

"Or worse," Noah mumbled.

"That *was* the government." Who could be worse? The leader of the Witnesses, Lord Shadow, which was a stupid name.

"Still is, baby girl," Jamal said, tossing back another shot as his words gained a slight slur.

Matt nodded, not looking entirely pleased with the answer. "We have the underground tunnels. But, again, those only work as long as Dannika's happy."

"As long as we keep Dannika *happy*," Julie repeated, her eyes darting around the group.

Dannika might have been the real person in charge up here, but she wasn't down there. "We need to find Lady Dun, warn her, see if she's really the one in charge of Sunnyvale." Something to remember about bad guys was that sometimes they were necessary to do good things. I'd learned that from Vance Young, who kept the streets safe during the day as a detective and at night as a masked vigilante. "We should divide and conquer."

"That's a terrible idea." April shook her head. "You never split the party."

"You're not an elf druid." Julie frowned and nodded at almost the same time. "I could take the tunnels, look for Lady Dun."

Jamal raised an eyebrow and saluted her with a shot glass as if wishing her luck and toasting her death before knocking it back.

Had something happened between him and Lady Dun, too?

"Will you be okay on your own?" I asked. We had no idea what we were facing.

Music notes surrounded Julia, reminding me that her superpower was making people do what she wanted them to.

"July, baby," Jamal slurred, "we can't go anywhere alone." His frown said we couldn't go together either.

"I'll be fine," Julie said.

"We're couriers," I reminded everyone. "We never buddy up."

"You're not leaving my sight," Ryder said in a low, husky voice, her words dangerously close to my ear.

Shivers traveled up my spine. Did Valkyries have a seduction ability I didn't know about? Did I really care? "You're not even working for us, so what reason are you going to give for moving between the towns?"

She frowned. "No one questions me."

But they might. It wasn't that we weren't allowed to move between sections yet, but I had a feeling that would change. I had no visions to back me up, but it was somehow a fact in my mind, like knowing that the sun was going to come up the next day. "It's coming. It's something we need to prepare for."

Jamal narrowed his eyes. "Dannika controls the gates."

"She controls the *tech* at the gates," Matt said.

"Senator Armstrong controls the gates and the flow of people," I said, trying to figure out what her reasoning for stopping the flow of traffic would be.

A picture of a dam swam in front of my vision, the water trickling out giving off vision wisps.

She was trying to make the flow manageable?

The water behind my vision dam rose, creeping up the landscape.

And to build a ready resource behind the dam?

The rising water halted, then settled. I'd guessed correctly.

A *para* resource? One she had access to and controlled with impunity?

The dam flashed a brilliant white light and then blinked out of existence.

If that was the case, then where was she intending to build this para reservoir? And why?

Ryder narrowed her eyes at me, watching as I worked through the puzzle.

I didn't want to tell anyone the vision, didn't want to scare them if I was wrong, but Ryder needed a job.

She nodded once as if coming to a decision, then turned to Jamal. "You will hire me."

He licked his lips and crossed his arms over his chest. "No, I will not."

"Yes," she said with a tone that asked why.

"There is no month starting with *r*, fire girl."

"Jamal," Matt said, holding his hands out. "Seriously? She's tight. We need her."

"You could make up a month," Julie said. "Like . . ." She rolled her eyes. "Rebruary?"

Silence settled around us as we all stared at her.

Then we all burst out laughing.

Jamal shook his head. "Fine. Fine. Rebruary, my girl, you'll tag team with October. Fill this out and we'll make it official." His hand missed the application cubby twice before he grabbed a sheet and pulled it from the stack. He shoved it and a pen across the table to Ryder.

"I'll look for signs of the Cursed," April said. "I've been hearing about them all through Sweetwater."

Jamal nodded. "March, I'm moving you—"

"Nope." Matt frowned at the chip in his hand and then shoved it back in his pocket. "I'm keeping Rockrage Park. That's mine, and I'm keeping it. I only got caught because Dannika needed me—well, all of us, I guess. While I'm there, I'll keep an ear out for the Resurrected."

The Cursed and the Resurrected were flashy, so they'd be the easiest. "I'll see if there are any clues that will lead me to the bus."

"No, you will not," Jamal said. "You might be the one his seers are trying to find."

I snorted. "No."

He gave me a look that begged me not to be this stupid. "You had not one but two powerful people ask you to find this bus for them, and he's after seers. And you don't think he might be setting the trap for you?"

I stared at him. I wasn't that powerful. My gift was weak, and it was a cypher gift. It didn't tell me actual information.

"So, what route are you giving us?" Ryder asked.

"Floater." Jamal licked his lips again, as if weighing the options of keeping me out of this and keeping his couriers safe now that Dannika had her claws in us. "If you see *any* sign of the Witnesses, you leave. Immediately. I'll send someone else to Lista Point. If you get something you need to track, you come here, grab a package closest to that area, and we'll send you there."

"And how will we explain Ryder going with me?"

"I'll work it out." He released a breath. His slurring stayed light, but his eyes were definitely glassier. "Be careful."

If things really were as complicated as Jamal thought, I was going to do my utmost best.

But I knew what a complete moron I could be when the bit was in my teeth. And my druthers were up. I couldn't back down now even if I wanted to. I just had to hope I'd be smarter this time.

Chapter 7

T he letter *x* flashed in the sign behind the reception's head as she smiled up at me and handed me the signed slip. "Thank you."

"You, too. Have a great day," I said, stashing it in my backpack and turning to leave. I bumped into a man in a blue suit with a name tag, the *x* in his name flashing. "Sorry."

He grunted on his way by.

Was this some message telling me to check in with Senator Armstrong? I still hadn't been able to run home for my cards, and chasing nebulous signs was still a work in progress. Part of it was that I was afraid to look into the Witnesses any further. Having Ryder with me gave me more confidence, but the Witnesses were still terrifying. If they had Senator Armstrong and Dannika's underground route maker, then he might be gone.

Yet the thought of just giving up made my skin crawl. I had to find a way to fight back, to find this person and not get us killed.

Ryder and I had been delivering packages all morning, looking for clues, but so far, my gift wasn't giving me anything more than exceptionally efficient delivery routes with careful heads-ups on what dangers lay ahead. So far, I'd avoided being mugged twice, and being run into once. Of course, with Ryder with me, the muggings might have turned into self-defense killings.

What did it mean to be a Valkyrie? What role did she have in the wars? And how had *she* lost Michigan?

She waited for me on the curb, handing me a black helmet as she climbed back onto her motorcycle. "Where to next?"

I didn't have any information to share with the senator, so there was no use in following the helpful "x" clue. So, I dug out the next package and read off the address, then stashed it back in the pack as I sat behind her.

She put her hand on my knee, waiting for me to fully settle.

I wanted to fidget a little more, to give her a reason to keep her hand there a little longer, but that was just . . . silly. So, with a sigh, I ran my hand along her arm and squeezed gently so she could feel the gesture through her leather jacket.

Her helmeted head nodded once, her hand left my leg, and she brought us smoothly into traffic.

I was attracted to this woman. That was a fact. I needed to stop fretting and just figure out what I was going to do about it instead. I wasn't a romantic person. She didn't seem to be either, and this wasn't a great time to even consider romance in the first place.

That didn't mean my mind, heart, and soul didn't want to find time for it. Surely, if the Vikings could find time in war to have babies, I could make time to have a meal and get to know Ryder.

What type of food did she even like? I hoped she like pho, because that was the only thing I could really afford. Few people could buy actual groceries anymore. They were all outrageously expensive. There was no such thing as cheap frozen anything. Ramen was still a thing, and we were getting creative in making it "fancy" by adding freshly grown herbs. Most of us could grow basil, even me.

I didn't want our first meal to be ramen and Spam with fresh basil, though. What a way to say, "I'd like to get to know you. I'm poor."

I had to admit that riding a motorcycle was a lot easier than a bicycle. The distance we traveled was incredible, and we didn't have to stay in the vehicle lane. When necessary, we bipped over to the bicycle lane and slid through.

We didn't trip any sensors, maybe thanks to the chip and maybe thanks to the fact that she was a celestial and there wasn't anything about me that should have tripped. Our courier passes got us through a lot faster, but there would come a time when they wouldn't. I could feel a cloud rising over the guard shacks as we blew through in the pedestrian lane. They would find a way to stop us.

That didn't seem right, not if Dannika controlled the gate technology while Senator Armstrong controlled the actual gates themselves.

Maybe they didn't have as much power as I gave them credit for.

Or maybe I was seeing things that weren't there.

Less traffic clogged Littleton, and the smell of garbage was down. The trash trucks were still making their way through the city, and the weather was pleasant. Not too hot and not too cold, though I could tell this summer would make things uncomfortable. We weren't allowed to talk about global warming because that was all a lie, but these summers were definitely getting hotter and longer and dryer.

I really needed air-conditioning if I was going to survive this. I wasn't in dire straits yet, but I would be. I could practically feel it.

When we got to the gate, Roger stopped us. He came up, his gun slung across his body, his shoulders tight but his stride loose.

I took my helmet off. "Hey, Roger."

"New ride?"

"It's temporary." I flicked my eyes to the guard shack, then back to him. "What's going on?"

He glanced around before leaning in closer. Swallowing hard, he took a breath. "You might want to go to the Double Cross."

I didn't know why he said it or what he thought I would find, but I nodded.

He licked his lower lip and swallowed, as if kicking himself for having passed on the message. Then he took a step back. "I just—" The corners of his lips flicked downward as he continued to retreat toward the gate. "They might have a package."

"You got it. Thanks, Roger. Say hi to your daughter."

"Yeah." He waved us through. "Stay safe."

"What was that?" Ryder asked, her voice coming through the helmet loud and clear.

"Oh my god! You're telling me we had this the entire time?"

She took us around a corner, leaning the bike so far over I thought my knee might drag on the pavement. "What kind of threat are we facing?"

My gift hadn't shown anything. "I think . . ." I didn't know what to think. I'd buddied up to him—and by "buddied up," I just meant I'd learned his name and a few things about his life and had kept being nice to him. But I'd done that to stay safe, not because I thought we'd ever become friends.

"Can we trust him?"

I didn't know that either. "He's not a para, but he seems . . . nice?"

She grunted and went quiet again.

I shoved my hand in my jacket pocket and realized there was a note. Where'd that come from?

Then I remembered the guy with the x on his name tag. Max. He'd bumped into me . . .

And after that, no more x's had been highlighted.

Huh. I pulled the note out and read it, gripping it tight in the air pocket behind Ryder's back. It was an address and a time. The Double Cross at noon.

Ah, yes. Two *x*'s. Double cross. How was I supposed to have figured that out? I sincerely needed my cards. There were too many symbols. Too many things to interpret, and this wasn't working.

The Double Cross turned out to be a pub, or at least what I'd always pictured a pub to be like. A long bar went the length of the left side with a wall of mirrors behind it, and the rest of the space was filled with tables. All the tables were full, the air buzzing with conversation.

The woman behind the bar lifted her chin in our direction and then tipped her head to the side as if pointing.

That wasn't ominous or anything, but my gift was quiet.

Did that even offer me any comfort? Was it even *on?* My fingers twitched to have my cards.

I forced myself to relax. My gift had worked all morning. I just wasn't in danger—I hadn't needed it.

But when I saw who was waiting for me, I knew I might be.

The table toward the back, in the direction the bartender pointed out, shone with a soft orange glow that then settled into a brilliant brown radiance.

Orange represented warmth and change, while brown offered grounding and safety. Interesting.

But I wasn't buying it. I knew Detective Vance Young and the danger he brought during the day when he had laws to obey, as well as at night, when he enforced moral rule with a vigilante fist. I blamed him to no small degree for what had happened before. I still blamed myself more, but he'd pushed me past where I'd said no more. He'd egged me on, pushed me harder. I could have said no. I had said no. Several times.

Together, we'd killed at least three of my friends and hadn't seen eight more since.

He looked up from the papers strewn across his small table and motioned me over with his head.

Ryder raised an eyebrow and took the lead, gesturing for me to remain behind.

I knew the dangers he posed. I wouldn't allow myself to be pushed this time.

Vance looked up at our arrival and frowned at Ryder. His eyebrows shot up as he reassessed her. "Bodyguard. Good call, but on whose dime?"

"Who are you?" Ryder demanded. The general buzz of the bar drowned her voice down to one of many.

I put my hand on her arm. While I appreciated her help, some things were my own to take care of. "Vance."

"Sky."

"October," I corrected.

He narrowed his eyes, then blinked with a shrug. Of all my pre-Wipe friends, he was the only one who'd known my full name. "Okay." He leaned back in his chair and crossed his arms over his chest as he assessed Ryder. "Battle para." The corners of his lips pulled down. "Fey?"

The people at the tables around us weren't paying any attention. The words "para" and "fey" should have attracted at least a little worry because there wasn't music to drown them out.

From what I could tell, he'd been a Supe since before the aftermath of the war had made it cool, so I didn't doubt he had some way of maybe dampening what was said around the table or making it so the people around him didn't care about us.

As if reading my thoughts, he nodded toward the surrounding crowd. "We're safe." He pushed a chair out with his foot and leaned forward. "Sit. Before you really *do* get people to look."

Ryder chose the chair that put her back to the wall while monitoring both doors—the one in the front and the one leading to the kitchen.

I took the only remaining seat and caught sight of a picture of a bloody woman on the table in front of him. "I'm not doing this again, Vance." My heart reached out, though, wanting to help. Who was she, and what had happened?

"Please, October." He reached out for my hand and pinned me with his melted-chocolate eyes. "I need your help."

I didn't feel a thing from his touch except old camaraderie and an empathic tug for how much he cared, and he *did* care, which was how he'd been able to push me so hard the last time. Thick black lashes surrounded puppy-dog brown eyes. His dark hair was cut short and neat, and his face was. . . pretty.

Ryder leaned forward and put her hand next to mine, her fingertips resting lightly beside his.

His lips rounded, and he nodded as he withdrew.

She slid her gaze away and took her hand back.

I wished she hadn't, but it'd been an awkward position. She shifted slightly, and the heat of her leg seeped through my jeans.

Ease filled me. She glanced at me with accepting acknowledgment and returned her attention to our surroundings.

Something so simple as a look made me feel sturdier, lighter, more capable of being my foolhardy self without killing people. What was it with this woman? I turned to Vance with more confidence. "People died last time. Friends."

"What happened to Gina was an accident."

"It wasn't just Gina, Vance," I said, my voice rising. "Sheldon died. Oscar died. Val and Toni were captured. Eva went missing."

He waved me off. "I know the list, Sky."

"Stop calling me that."

He bowed his head. "I slipped. October." He paused to swallow, his sharp Adam's apple bobbing. "I won't make the same mistakes this time."

"Like following my visions?" That's what'd gotten us into trouble the last time.

"That wasn't—"

"You're going to tell me I'm not the one who got us killed or captured."

"No!" He gritted his teeth. "We got too close last time."

"To what?"

"To whom," he corrected.

Oh my god. "Okay."

He took in a deep breath and met my gaze. "Lord Shadow."

Everything inside me went still. "The leader of the Witnesses?"

Vance nodded slowly.

"How do you know this? Why?" If Lord Shadow had captured them, that meant my friends were dead.

Everyone except for Parker. Dannika had said the Witnesses had been targeting seers. Maybe she was alive still?

He shook his head, then looked over at Ryder.

She met his gaze with an eagle sharpness that made him flinch.

He turned his chocolate gaze to me. "I won't use you like I did last time."

I snorted, not believing him, but with a bigger thread of that-had-been-a-lot-bigger-than-I'd-thought tripping my heart.

A wispy green fairy appeared above the picture of the dead woman, the fairy's pointed toes resting on a crime scene photo, her moth wings fluttering and sprinkling vision dust over the table as her yellow-petaled hair emitted a soft glow.

I almost took in a sharp breath of surprise. This was straight from my oracle deck, and her meaning was instantaneous and crystal clear.

She looked at me with a smile, continuing to balance on one foot and flutter her wings, vision dust flying everywhere.

Gratitude swarmed within me, knocking the cold dredges of fear from the main chambers of my mind.

The fairy shrugged with an embarrassed smile as if saying, *You're welcome, now focus.*

I relaxed a little and took in what she represented. Her message was that I was balancing a fine line and that it might be a good idea to listen. I bit back my urge to yell and instead asked, "What's this?"

Vance pushed a couple of pictures around, his brow furrowed as he kept himself a good distance from me. "People are being murdered or going missing."

"That's not news."

"I need your help to stop it."

He'd offered me a position on his Supe team before everything had gone pear shaped. "The answer's still no."

Ryder nodded and moved to stand.

The green moth fairy stomped her foot on three stars, lighting them up on the crime scene photo and shooting glowing wisps at me.

I sighed and kept my seat. Ryder bowed her head, upset, but took a heavy breath and regained her chair.

Vance flicked his gaze between the table and my face as if trying to see what I saw.

The green fairy stabbed me with her gaze, balancing on the toes of one foot like a ballerina, tipping her head to the side in a way that implied significance.

A sense of finding a new balance warmed through me. I needed to be here. I could try this again and figure out a way to not be targeted or get my friends killed. Again. The real issue the last time had been the fact that we hadn't known just how big an opponent we'd been facing. If we had, my focus would have been better. I would have asked the right questions, led us on a safer path.

The green fairy shrugged and disappeared as if she'd carried her message and was needed elsewhere.

Ryder leaned in, her gaze like a sword. "Are you a threat?" she asked Vance.

"Well," he said, nonplussed, "I could be. I really could, but . . . no. I'm just trying to do my job. I've got a city with a lot of people going missing."

"You already know who's going missing," I said low, anger rising inside me, but was it at him? The situation? Or myself, for sitting it out until just now?

"Paras." He nodded and grabbed his soda.

This was another reason he'd been able to pull my strings. Because *I* cared.

"They're still people I swore to protect. When I gave my oath, I didn't say I'd protect everyone in this city except for. . ." He let his voice trail off. "No. I said I'd protect everyone."

"So, she's para."

He nodded.

"Witnesses?"

"Most likely. I can't tell if this is Lord Shadow or the Mind Eraser, but I'm beginning to suspect they're both the same person."

Things clicked into place for me. "You want to go after him." Lord Shadow.

He didn't say anything.

"For revenge?" For what we'd lost the last time?

"He's dangerous," Vance said, staring at the photos on the table. "He's always one step ahead of me. He knows how to play us. He knows the rules of the game, what we're capable of."

"Then go after him as your alter ego."

Ryder didn't react.

"I did. I've tried." Vance flared his fingers in vexation. "He's smart."

"Or able to see the future."

The look he gave me was soft, quiet, telling me he already knew Lord Shadow was targeting seers.

"What's going to make this time different?"

He cleared his throat and tipped his head to the side with a chagrined expression, and he lifted one hand in a stalling gesture. "We've learned a lot since then."

"Since when?" Ryder demanded.

"Like what?" I asked, ignoring her.

He pulled his head down, stretching out his neck. Then he straightened, leaning forward. "Someone in your group was being targeted. It was either you or Parker."

I didn't say anything. I hadn't had a chance to put the pieces together after Dannika had told me about the leader of the Witnesses targeting seers, and I'd just learned that Vance thought he'd been after us when we'd lost so badly. "Targeted."

"That's why we couldn't shake him."

"But my visions were off. They weren't working."

"If you remember," Vance said, keeping his head low, "neither were Parker's."

My heart stopped. I hadn't put those two things together yet.

"I don't know how, but the Witnesses have something that keeps seers from finding him."

"Then what do you need me on this for if I'm no help?"

"I didn't say you weren't helpful." Vance bowed his head even farther. "Someone in the Witnesses is on the Force."

That made sense, but it only made them that much deadlier.

"That's why I'm handling everything differently now. My investigations are on a need-to-know basis."

"Your partner?"

He shook his head. "Dreven doesn't even know."

This all brought something bigger to the table for me. This wasn't about finding Jeff—no hope there—or the bus with the guy who was helping with getting paras out of Kins City.

This was about finding Parker, who might be alive, but not safe.

And who might be using her very real and very powerful abilities to find me.

"These three were nabbed out of their triple-decker." He pushed three photos toward me and Ryder.

The three-story buildings with apartments on each level were supposed to be safer. "How?"

"We don't know because the report was never filed." He pushed two more pictures toward me, both of dead people. "These two were taken from the library. These eight from their homes." He shook his head. "They're nabbing people where they feel safe."

"You want me to help you find the Witnesses, but you just said I can't. What do you want?"

"Don't . . ." He shook his head, thinking about it. "Don't focus on finding the Witnesses or Lord Shadow. Focus on what's different in these pictures. What's out of the ordinary. What might lead me to something useful, a clue I can use."

Ryder rolled her head on her neck like she wanted to punch someone.

I turned back to Vance. "What if I don't want to help you?"

He gave me a smoldering look that should have melted my heart, soul, and bones. "You don't want to help people in need?"

"It's not that simple, and you know it."

"It is. I need you to go through and tell me if you see anything with any of these. That's it. We—I do the rest."

The waitress came over with three large sandwiches and drinks, which were expensive. A full food voucher would get maybe half of this. "Vance—"

"Don't," he said, not even looking up from the photos as he bit into his sandwich.

"We can't owe you anything."

"And you won't." He set his sandwich down and looked at me, hard. "Did you feel like you owed me last time?"

Yes. The man had money. I didn't know his story or why a wealthy man was a police detective, but he'd showered us with gifts and food, and it had always made things feel easy.

Ryder leaned back, looking through her narrowed eyes between me and Vance.

"I'm going to find him," he said, "and I will bring him to justice."

I didn't know how we'd bring someone like Lord Shadow to justice.

"I'm getting close," Vance said. "Just give me one clue. That's all I need."

The part of me that always needed to be the freaking hero begged me to look. That was all I had to do—look. See if another green fairy popped up, or maybe those stars. The stars had flared. Maybe they would lead somewhere or mean something.

It wasn't asking a lot. "Fine. What do you have?"

Chapter 8

"Hey, what's this?" Torrez asked as she sidled up to our table, right as we were finishing our sandwiches.

Vance looked up at her in irritation. "Just trying to see if they know anything."

"And why would she?" she asked, looping her thumbs in her belt loops and leaning into her hip, her body weight shifting toward me.

He slouched in his chair a couple of inches and shrugged, gathering the pictures. "Be careful." He gathered his case files and left, giving the other officer a dirty look.

I'd been able to point out a few things, like the stars on the wall in the one photo and a brown bag in another, but it wasn't much. I didn't feel confident I'd given him anything further to go on. A part of me was glad—the Witnesses were one mess I didn't need to get into.

The other part of me, the growing part of me, was upset that I was willing to back down from this fight.

A lot of information had been given to me in a very short period of time, and I still hadn't gotten a chance to figure out what it all meant to me. The leader of the Witnesses might have been targeting me—probably not, but likely had targeted Parker.

We'd barely escaped, and only thanks to me being able to see a path out. It just hadn't been enough, and not in enough time.

He had a way to make it so we seers couldn't see him, blinding our third eye somehow.

And everyone wanted *me* to somehow find this guy.

Torrez took the seat he'd abandoned and picked up the remains of his sandwich, giving it an assessing once-over before taking a bite. "You good?" she asked around pastrami and rye.

I nodded. I didn't know how much I trusted Torrez, but she'd always been good to me.

A bald eagle with a big blue eye made bigger with a magnifying glass in front of it appeared beside the cop's head.

I nodded, the meaning resonating inside me like a bell had been rung in my soul. She was the type of person who saw everything—the good, the bad, the in-between. She didn't judge. She just protected those she could.

Torrez flicked her dark eyebrows at the sandwich and tossed the remaining three bites in the basket. "This was a lot of food vouchers."

"That's what I said."

She looked at me and tipped her head, the warm light from the window reflecting off her dark brown hair. "Does he have something on you?"

"Nah." Of course he did. He knew who I was and what I could do.

"Look," Torrez said, leaning in, putting one hand on her knee and pushing her elbow out as she lowered her voice.

I pulled myself closer so I could hear what she had to say.

She glanced at Ryder, who hadn't moved but watched with interest. Giving the Valkyrie a whatever look, Torrez glanced at me again. "He's tracking someone pretty bad. I warned him off dozens of times, but he isn't listening."

"He listens best when he's speaking," I said.

Torrez grunted. "Yeah, well, the last time things came to a head like this, I was mopping up bodies."

I bowed my head. I'd almost been one of them.

Her right eye twitched and she clamped her lips shut, nodding once. "Okay, well, if you need anything, you let me know."

"I will."

She craned her head forward. "I mean it, Sky. You need something, you let me know."

I licked my lips and then nodded, raising my hands in defense. "Okay."

"Okay." With another glance at Ryder, she picked up the remains of Vance's sandwich and stood. "And keep your distance from that guy. Bad luck follows that trust fund like a magnet." She saluted me with the sandwich and left.

"You ready?" Ryder asked quietly.

"Yeah. Let's go."

By the time the sun started slipping, we still had two packages in Ryder's saddle bags. I leaned back on the seat, putting my hands on the sissy bar, enjoying the heat of her body between my thighs. She was a solid motorcycle driver, though I'd never really ridden with anyone who wasn't. There was always that fear, though, that someone would be driving and unable to handle a bad situation.

Ryder wasn't that kind of person. She seemed like someone who could handle literally anything that came her way.

That comforted me more than I'd realized I needed. I'd been living in a constant state of fear ever since we'd lost the Para Wars—well, before that. Since the war began, really. I knew what living with that daily felt like. Constant cold. Constant alert status. I couldn't rest, not even in my home.

But sitting behind Ryder on her bike, taking in the warmth she offered, I felt like I'd finally found a lull in the storm, a place to rest, to regain my strength.

A wispy dove rose into the sky, turned in midair, then barreled down on me, shifting into a younger and younger bird until it landed on my knee as a baby.

Even knowing that this was a vision, my heart still pounded. I didn't like seeing a bird falling from the sky. This meant something, though. It wasn't one of my cards, so I had to scramble for the meaning.

Birds represented transformation and freedom, mostly because they could fly. For me, a dove meant peace, but it could also mean a longing for peace. Also, the dove had been flying, which represented rising above the oppression. Why, then, had it shifted into a baby bird and fallen from the sky?

My gift was trying to tell me that a relationship was shifting into something I could build peace with, but that it was currently in a stage of new growth? Or that I was in danger?

The head morphed into that of a fox, the body remaining small and tiny as it wobbled on my knee while Ryder wove through the thin traffic of Littleton.

Foxes represented cunning and diplomacy. I got the sense that we were supposed to talk to someone who was possibly in danger.

As far as visions went, this one wasn't super helpful.

The fox-dove sighed at me, then changed into a glowing blue dragon curled around a bright white light.

That was a card from my oracle deck with a meaning I knew well. The dragon was wrapped around the egg of the future, protecting it with its body and will. I was being called to help protect our future by finding someone who needed me to help protect something precious to them.

We pulled up to the gate separating Littleton from New Kins. From the rev of the engine, it was clear Ryder intended to go through like she normally did, without stopping, barely slowing down. Roger wasn't in the guardhouse, and we were waved through.

The dragon air-swam off my knee and led us through the gate, then turned right.

"Hey," I told Ryder. "I might have something. Turn here."

She didn't say anything, just followed my directions, winding us through the city like a drunk person.

The dragon stopped at a park and shifted into a dove again, flying toward the setting sun before disappearing in a wisp of light.

Ryder shut off the engine and I disembarked, putting my helmet on the seat. The park was pretty busy. Lots of kids, and people with their kids. Not a lot of dogs, but that made sense because it was expensive to *have* a dog.

"Give me a sec?"

"Yeah," Ryder said. "Need anything?"

"I have no idea."

She grunted and planted her feet on either side of the bike, prepared to leave in a hurry of we needed to.

Who was I supposed to meet?

The dove flew downward and shifted into a fox that gave me an exasperated look. It sat beside a man on a bench, and as it settled, the head turned into a dove.

Visions. It really wanted to hammer home the point that this person was the key, somehow, to building a peace.

I headed toward him, trying to work out what I was supposed to say. The man on the bench shifted, and a familiar face appeared.

"Roger?" I said without thinking.

He turned to me, surprise flitting across his features. Glancing toward the park, he moved to stand.

I held out my hands. "Sorry. I didn't mean to startle you. I was just out on deliveries and saw you. I thought I'd stop and say hi." What the jeez was I doing here?

It looked at me, cocked its dove head to the side and shifted its fox body into the glowing blue dragon again.

Okay. Well, if Roger was intent on protecting the future, then that gave me direction. "Are you working with Detective Young?"

He settled back onto the bench. "You met him?"

"I think I might have helped. I mean, I hope so."

Roger nodded, not looking comfortable as he stared into the park, where a group of girls played soccer.

"One of them yours?"

He nodded. "Miche."

I'd never gotten a name before. "Cool. I never liked soccer. There was always too much running."

He chuckled and then sobered with an almost guilty look on his face, as if he remembered we weren't friends.

But we could be if the dragon-dove-fox vision was an indicator. Now, that didn't mean that it'd just automatically happen. I still had to work for it. I could still mess this up, but Roger was an opportunity. "Vance—Detective Young is interesting. How much can we trust him?"

"Trust?" Roger leaned back onto the bench and shook his head. Then he frowned as if a sudden thought had hit him, and he gave me a quizzical look.

I sank down beside him. The fox was an interesting totem to present at this point in our relationship; the animal had an innate understanding of when to come out into the open and when to remain in hiding. They were cunning, having almost a sixth sense about things.

I needed to know what that meant. I needed to know what would make Roger feel comfortable enough to come out of hiding, per se. "What don't *you* trust about him?"

"About *Vance?*"

So he'd caught that. "Yeah."

"Old boyfriend?"

I shook my head. "We used to work together. Right after the Wipe."

"And then you stopped. Why?"

I bowed my head and took in a long, deep breath, using it to straighten myself. "Things got dangerous."

Roger raked a hand over his close-cropped black hair, his fingertips going pink. "How blunt are we being?"

He was asking *me* if this was a test? He was the guard. "Be brutal."

Roger turned to me his brown eyes filled with desperation or something like it. "Is Young para?"

"No." Probably not. "I actually don't know."

He shook his head. "Then what's his stake?"

In this game? "He gives a shit."

"That could get him killed."

It had already gotten others killed. "They're dying anyway."

The girls playing soccer crowed. Someone must've scored a goal.

"Are you?" he asked, his voice barely above a whisper. "Para?"

My heart ratcheted in my chest. Every survival instinct in me told me to shut up, to not say anything. But the fox-dove-dragon had led me here. In fact, it was still there, offering me guidance and support in a way I hadn't realized I'd missed. "Yeah."

He dropped his gaze, his chin jutting to the side as he turned his attention to the girls. "I think Miche is, too."

I hadn't seen that one coming, but a lot of things were making sense about him. "How?"

He shook his head. "It's like a witch being born to muggles."

Harry Potter had fallen onto the banned reading list, so I didn't know if we could even use the pop culture slang in conversation anymore.

"If the Witnesses find out—" He cut himself off and shook his head.

They would kill her and then his entire family, just to be sure the para gene was eradicated. "Why haven't you moved to Lista Point yet?"

"I'm afraid."

"Afraid she'll set off the wards?"

He nodded.

I didn't know him well enough to tell him about the underground city where paras were welcome. This could be a trap for all I knew. The fox was cunning, and peace could take on many shapes. Our government thought our current situation was a peaceful one.

"Detective Young is going to help me find a way to protect her."

I didn't know what kind of strings Vance really had, but I knew his heart was in the right place. Without the actual backing for that, all he'd be doing was luring Roger and his daughter into a false sense of safety that could get them both killed. "Is she safe here?"

"As long as we don't move."

"Then don't."

Roger licked his lips. "I feel like you're good."

"I feel like you are, too. Mostly."

He shook his head.

So he didn't know what line he'd draw, what line he'd cross to protect his family. We were in dangerous territory.

The dragon-dove-fox shifted again, this time flickering between a golden retriever and a raven.

Those were two very different—well, subtly different symbols. Loyalty and protection versus healing and protection.

Jeez. I wasn't going to offer Roger the keys to the castle. I couldn't. I still didn't know if this was an elaborate trap. My gift sometimes got it wrong. It wasn't often, but there were people who were really good liars, and then there were the people who didn't realize they were being played. For that matter, there were people who didn't realize they were freaking lying. Roger could have been one of those. I didn't *think* he was being false, but that didn't mean he couldn't be played right now.

He needed to heal, and I could gain a little loyalty by helping there. "What do you need? For her? What does *she* need?"

Roger shook his head, then took in a shallow breath and released it. He fidgeted with his hands before rolling his head on his neck.

I could tell he was fighting something inside, and that told me a lot. Maybe more than my visions did. Nonverbals, if you listened hard enough, could reveal a ton about another person.

I just watched the girls play soccer, letting him fight it out on his own.

Then a girl's aura flared a raging red, embers falling away from her like she was on fire. She was the one who'd been smiling the most during the game, laughing the hardest.

That girl was pissed, and she was hiding it brilliantly.

"Visions," Roger said, almost at a whisper. "Miche has visions."

Maybe *this* was the reason I'd been brought to him. If the Witnesses were targeting seers, and if their leader collecting them . . . I didn't know what to think. Was he imprisoning them? Then why not just outright kill them? Was he using them? If that was the case, then that would be how he was able to target them. "I do, too. That's—that's how I was brought here. I didn't actually see you from the . . ." I gestured to the parking lot behind me.

He flicked his eyebrows as if saying he'd already figured that out—or maybe realized this was a trap.

Oh, crap. I hadn't even thought of that. "I could . . ." Teach her? Where? When? How? Show her a few things? If she practiced even in the comfort of her own room, and someone just happened to walk by and saw, PPE could be called, and she'd be hauled away.

Or we'd trip the Witnesses' radar and she'd be taken, while he'd be killed.

"Can you teach her how to shut it off?"

No, but that might be the only way to keep her safe. I mean, now that I was thinking about it, maybe that'd been the only way *I'd* remained safe for the past year. "I know someone who can."

Roger nodded and met my gaze.

I could almost feel the terror rising from him.

"When?" he asked. "Where?"

"Let me talk to them first and see if this is something they'd be interested in. I'll get back to you."

He nodded.

I got up to leave.

But the anger rising from the one girl was getting crazy. She was a white girl with red hair and freckles, so not Roger's daughter, who I assumed had to be Black because he was. She could have been adopted, sure, but I didn't think so. "You see that girl with the blue shirt and pink shorts?"

He glanced out into the field. "Kitty?"

"Yeah? Sure. Be careful of her."

"Why? She's safe."

"She's pretending." That girl was anything but safe. "She could be a Witness." So much anger. It made sense, but they were mercenaries. Then again, mercenaries could be recruited young.

Roger raised his chin as he watched the girls finish up their game. "I'll watch out."

"If I see anything else, I'll let you know." I turned to head back to Ryder.

"October," he called.

I stopped and turned back to him. "Yeah?"

"Can we trust him? Detective Young?"

In his position? "Carefully."

Roger nodded and waved me goodbye.

As I approached, Ryder crossed her arms. "Anything else?"

I looked around, trying to find any other visions or symbols. This bus full of people, wherever they were, had been taken twenty-four hours ago. Time was of the essence, and it upset me that we hadn't made any more progress. Why had my visions led me to Vance, Senator Armstrong, Dannika, and Roger, but not anywhere else? Where were these people?

For that matter, where was Jeff? Was he okay? Was he safe?

Ryder bit the corner of her lips and nodded. "Well, come on. We've got two more packages."

The second package put me in the reception area of what looked like a third-world health clinic but sounded like a dentist's office. I needed the signature of a Janet Olfgood, so I waited.

Three stars glowed in the mural on one of the walls, growing larger. Several more were sprinkled throughout the community paintings, which were faded and chipping off the CMU blocks, but those three were the only ones glowing.

Stars were symbols of success, or sometimes guidance. Well, frankly, there were several ways to look at them, but I'd trained myself to see them as success indicators, and on rare occasions, a guide toward a successful end.

I didn't get the sense they meant that this time. I felt like I was standing in a dumpster filled with rotting garbage.

Janet Olfgood came in, her lab coat covering her light blue scrubs, her brown hair pulled back in a tight bun at the back of her head. She didn't offer a smile as she signed for her package.

I offered one anyway and handed the box to her.

When our hands touched, she flared with an intense blue-white light.

That meant intelligence, and that she thought she was acting in purity. I could taste blood in the air as she disappeared toward the back.

I turned and left, pushing down the bile in my throat and the fear in my chest. I didn't know what was going on there, but something was bad. I acted as normally as I could, even opening the door for the older man with the scar over his right eye who growled a low, "Thanks," as he walked past.

Ryder waited until my helmet was on and we were on our way back to Speedy. "What happened?"

I had to stop being surprised that she noticed me and how things affected me. "That place is . . . gross."

"Missing-people gross?"

I didn't think so. I mean, I didn't get any . . .

Clues! The stars. "I need to contact Vance. I think I found one of the locations he's looking for."

The three stars had been on the walls of two of his crime scenes. That was where I'd seen them, and probably why they had enlarged for me.

"Okay. I'll send the message. But then you and I are going to talk."

That sounded ominous. "About what?"

"About us," she said, and revved the engine.

Chapter 9

Ryder's statement made me nervous, and I tried to work through that on the relatively short ride back.

It wasn't that I was scared.

No. I was.

It wasn't that this was a woman-on-woman relationship.

No. It was.

Jeezum. Was there anything about this relationship that didn't frighten me? And with the realization I'd just made earlier about how my fear made me smarter, why was this a bad thing?

Because fear felt bad.

Okay. Why would a *relationship* frighten me?

Because I'd never had one. Well, at least not one that had succeeded.

Not with my mom. Not with my dad, or my sister, or the people who'd raised me. I mean, I kinda had with my aunt, but I'd kept her distant, knowing that one day, she'd abandon me too. Everyone did.

I didn't exactly have a lot of dating experience.

Speedy Couriers was a beehive of activity as all the riders came in, dropping off the packages they couldn't deliver before heading back home.

"I'm close," Julie said with a triumphant grin, her black hair up in twin pigtails, her goth attire more blue than black.

"To what, Miss July?" Jamal asked, his hands busy checking in packages which had to be difficult around those extremely long, yellow nails.

"To finding Lady Dun," Julie crowed, leaning backward and balling her hands into fists with a scrunched "yes" face.

Someone shouted out a goodnight. A few of us turned and waved back.

Ryder disappeared to send Vance the message about the location.

How much would Lady Dun be able to help? Well, if she could keep Dannika off our backs long enough to focus on one person, that would be helpful.

Gods bless it. I was actively searching for the man who might have almost killed me six months ago.

A horned cactus rose from the tabletop and snorted at me in a female empathic *feel* that went against the male features of his cactus face.

Wow. My gift was on fire, but I *liked* how it was relating to me now. I was really enjoying not to have to pull my decks out to get guidance.

The cactus represented resourcefulness.

Okay. Well, all right. Yes. It still made sense to find other resources, though, so we weren't pinned down if things went bad.

Meanwhile, Julie and Jamal had continued to talk.

I was debating whether or not to go with Detective Vance to check that place out, but I wanted to kick myself for thinking that thought out loud. Wasn't I the person who'd been getting down on myself for being the stupid, reckless hero type? And here I was going, "Hey, let's be the stupid, reckless hero type with no fighting skill whatsoever, and hope I don't die. Doesn't that sound like fun?" It was like putting a sword in Emma Swan's hand, calling her the hero, knowing I was going to be upset with her when she didn't win with her complete lack of skills.

I could see clues no one else could. That wasn't a fight skill or even a survival skill. That was a support-person skill.

I went up to Ryder, my insides twisting a little with nerves, not sure how I wanted the next conversation to go. I waited for her call with Vance to end.

When it did, she looked up.

"He gonna check it out?" I asked.

Ryder nodded.

"What else can we do?"

She shook her head and studied me, leaning up against the red lockers.

The Moon Maiden floated between Ryder and myself, lighting Ryder's blond braid and filling me with the promise of something new.

That was a little exciting, if ill-timed.

She scoped the area. "Is there something going on between you and Vance?"

"No."

"Was there ever?"

She didn't seem jealous; she was just clarifying. "No."

"Are you attracted to him?"

I heard a raven caw behind me, offering me courage. I took what the spirit animal offered—or the real one, I wasn't sure—a little amazed that I was getting so much help in such a small amount of time. That could only mean that this conversation had weight and that I needed to be honest. "No."

She looked at me and said nothing, her expression calm and waiting.

I searched for the courage to just tell her how I felt. "I should be."

The edges of her expression relaxed by millimeters. "His eyes are very nice."

They were. "And he's very charming."

She shrugged. "If you like that." She crossed her arms over her chest, and her expression softened as she frowned.

This was why I didn't do relationships often. Well, no. The real reason was that I could see into the other person's psyche, and I usually didn't like what I saw. I didn't get that with her, though. I mean, I didn't know her. I didn't know her history or her story. I didn't know how she'd *lost Michigan*, which seemed like a lot for one person to do. "I find you incredibly sexy."

Her lips flashed a smile before she stashed it. "Same," she said, gaining a huskier tone.

Her voice sent heat flushing through me. "I've been acting differently since you arrived in my life." It was like the fear had just fallen away in the blink of an eye. "Is this a Valkyrie thing?"

She narrowed her eyes again, but this time with interest and intrigue as she shook her head. "Kind of." She flinched and blinked, then winced and continued. "I lead."

Ryder said that as if the word meant something more. "Okay?"

Taking a few breaths, she studied the room behind me. "Valkyries take warriors to their final resting place. That's the myth."

"Valhalla or something?"

She shrugged. "Whatever you believe. Dead is dead."

So, celestial but not connected to any god. Okay. Interesting.

"We inspire greatness from those around us."

So, she *was* the reason my fear had subsided, and it had nothing to do with my attraction to her or a connection we had.

She nodded with a grimace as if seeing that thought on my face. "My sister—half-sister—inspires *in* battle. She's a fierce warrior. Very capable. And . . ." Ryder let her head fall back slightly so that it almost rested against the lockers. "She got the sword." Anger flashed across her face for a brief instant.

"That sounds . . . important."

She rolled the anger off her shoulders with a sigh, her lips stiffening. "I wanted it. I've known I was meant to have it since I was a girl, and Frey got it instead. Just like everything else. But—" She shook her head. "What's important is that I've never inspired like that. Our mother said I'm the lighthouse and that I need to be content with being the lighthouse."

A few things settled into place for me, but mostly because I understood where she was coming from. I was support with a hero's personality type. "You lost Kins City because you tried to be more like Frey."

Ryder's chin dropped, and she nodded slowly.

Well, that made sense, then. This was her redemption arc. But . . . "What I'm feeling for you isn't real, is it?"

She rested her head against the lockers, unfurling her arms. "I don't know," she breathed. "I never know. I—" She took a sharp inhale and released it slowly.

I waited, getting the sense that she needed time to work through her emotions.

"I was hoping, with your abilities, that you could . . . see what's me and what's this"—she sneered—"lighthouse."

I'd never in my life had a proposition like that before. "I could try."

Ryder pushed off the lockers, pressing her top lip to her teeth with her tongue. "Don't get too hung up on what you feel toward me. It's probably not you."

Having my feelings invalidated like that stung a little, even though I'd been asking that question already to myself and had just directly brought it up. "Okay." I didn't know what I felt about that.

"Good. Well, we need to find that guy. Without him, everyone's trapped."

"What about Sunnyvale?" An underground city sounded good, but I had to admit I wasn't interested in moving.

"And living under Dannika's thumb? No thanks. We've scoured the city and found no clues."

Scoured wasn't really the right word for it. We'd gone in several random directions and found nothing. "It might be time to put it up for the night, give it a rest." Mostly, I didn't know that I wanted to go up against the leader of the Witnesses again. I'd lost a *lot* the last time.

"You got a couch?"

"If you want to call it that."

"Fine. Let's go."

We headed toward the counter. Most of the couriers had left or were leaving. Julie, Matt, April, and Noah had stayed behind, helping Jamal and talking to each other quietly.

He looked up with a sassy eyebrow raise. "Did you get done with all you needed to discuss?"

How could I tell him it wasn't going to be like that? Ever. "Yes."

He widened his eyes, pulling his head back. His tone didn't reflect the shock on his face from what my face must have managed to convey. "July's getting close to finding Lady Dun. April found where a lot of Cursed are hanging out. March struck out with the Resurrected, and November found nothing. Tell me you and Rebruary found something."

"We were enlisted to help a detective," Ryder said, leaning on the counter and frowning at Noah.

He grinned and gestured toward her, raising his eyebrows suggestively toward me and nodding.

She frowned at him, glanced at me, then shook her head, closing that nonverbal door.

Noah looked perplexed, then glanced over at me like it was my fault.

Which it *wasn't.*

He rolled his eyes.

Jamal stabbed me with his honey-brown gaze. "Tell me it's not Vance."

I opened my mouth to say something but then stopped and just clamped it closed.

"There's a story here," Ryder said, pulling off the counter.

"He nearly got her killed the last time," Jamal said bluntly.

"We were up against Lord Shadow last time," I cut in before he could get riled up.

Jamal swallowed, his round Adam's apple bobbing. "What?"

I was kicking myself for not catching this sooner, but it all made sense. Too much sense. "Remember how our visions went wonky, Parker's and mine?"

Jamal nodded, his expression pensive.

"It's as if he's using the seers somehow to see in front of us and to keep other seers from seeing him."

"The seers. . . Hold up." Jamal took a step back, then staggered back again, his fingertips finding one of his tattoos. His expression was haunted, as if he'd just learned a lot more than I'd told him, as if there were puzzle pieces falling into place for him too.

"He's looking for people," I said, watching Jamal with interest.

"He was the last time, too." His voice was thin.

"I'm not getting sidetracked." I wished I knew what he knew. "Vance is trying to track Lord Shadow down in other ways."

Jamal looked up in alarm, his brown eyes flaring. "Seers?"

I had no idea what part of the conversation he was latching on to.

He flapped his arms as if he were waving down an incoming plane, then walked toward the door. At the wall, he grabbed a roll of sage, lighting it with a word, and chanted. I couldn't tell what he was saying. Lines I'd never seen before flared a bright burgundy before cooling to a slightly dimmer burnt-sienna light until it was as if we stood inside an electric dome.

"What the hell?" April asked, her tails out and twitching in nervousness.

Jamal turned to us, his eyes giving off a honey glow. "Don't say his name."

Lord Shadow's? "Why?" I asked. Again, this wasn't Harry Potter.

"Imagine these seers pooled together. What would it be like?"

I had no idea. I was still wrapping my head around the idea that Parker might still be alive.

"He's building a search browser," Matt said.

Ryder glanced at me in concern. "And each time we say his name, it's like shooting a flare onto the battlefield."

"Or," Jamal said, regaining his place at the counter, "like running a search—"

"—in Google," Julie finished, her nearly black eyes distant. "Huh."

"Gotta admit," Matt said. "That's pretty fucking smart."

"Language," Jamal muttered.

"Shit," Matt said, his words falling into the old banter, but his tone lacking the zeal. "Hell."

Jamal waved him off. "What's Vance's plan this time?"

I shook my head. "It's not what Vance is doing." I looked around at the pale orange cage. "Are we okay to talk about this?"

"Not really." Jamal clenched a hand into a fist and let it go, his tattoos flaring. "But I'll do some more and by tomorrow, yes. For now, it should at the very least make it harder for them to understand what we're saying."

So, speak in code. "Okay. Well, everyone I've talked to—"

"Which has been a lot," Julie said with a look that showed she didn't understand how that was possible.

I agreed with her. Senator Armstrong. The Red Queen. Vance. Two was a coincidence. Three was the world reminding me I had skin in this game. "They're all looking at different parts, chasing this from different angles. If we can *keep* this multifront—"

"I like this plan," Ryder said with quiet interest, taking a step forward.

Noah straightened, tipping his head to the side as if intrigued because she was.

I still didn't know if this would work. "We *might* have a chance."

"Okay," Jamal said. "What's the plan?"

Why was he asking me? "Sleep."

"Obviously."

But more than that. I realized in that moment that I wanted to go back to my apartment to retrieve my deck. It was great that my gift was working without needing to pull out my cards, but it was almost as if I was drawing from them somehow, even from a distance. What would happen if PPE found them and destroyed them? Would my gift still work? I liked this, and I hoped it would continue working this way. And maybe I was being dumb. I'd already determined I was. But what if?

Jamal nodded. "I'll work on some protections that should allow you to target douche canoes no matter how crafty they are."

Lord Douche Canoe. I could get behind that.

"But before I get the protections up, no one does anything." Jamal looked around the group. "Do you understand me?"

We all nodded. It'd been a really intense couple of days anyway. All I wanted was sleep. Boring sleep.

We got on the motorcycle and headed back to Littleton and my apartment. We weren't dangerously close to curfew, but if we got tied up at the gate in either direction, we could be in trouble.

I was trying to figure out what we were going to do for dinner, since I was poor and my kitchen was empty, when something large and glowing rose over the tops of the New Kins skyline.

What had Jamal just said? Don't do anything until the protections were up?

I couldn't quite make it out. It looked like a large, new billboard, and as we drew closer to the gate to Littleton, I realized that this sign was glowing. Wispy pink neon lit up what might have been a jacket, and a peach neon color outlined a face. More pink gave him what I could now make out was a hat. And in his hand was a neon-green . . .

Sword.

The Knight of Swords.

The card for someone filled with hate, violence, and courage.

Could this be Lord Shadow? The guy we couldn't find using a seer's ability? Here, before Jamal had been able to put up any protections?

The sign flickered out and disappeared.

Yes. But if I was able to see it then . . . how?

I hadn't been *looking* for Lord Shadow. I'd been thinking about dinner with a quiet worry stirring in the back of my head, wondering if we'd ever find this guy Dannika and Senator Armstrong wanted so badly, and what would happen if we didn't find him before his body showed up, and if we would still be protected by Dannika's chip if that happened . . .

The neon sign lit up again.

Interesting.

Keeping my thoughts away from—

The sign flickered.

Keeping my thoughts focused on the underground maker guy—whatever he did, I kept my eye on the sign, trying to determine where it was.

And if we should follow it. The likelihood was that this was . . . *him*.

The sign remained lit.

If this was him, then there was a good chance I would be in danger. If that was the case, then I should just go home.

The neon sign turned to me, and a pink glowing line curled into a smile.

Or not. Anger stirred inside me. I hated this man for everything he'd taken from me, and I wanted revenge. I wanted my friends back. I wanted my *life* back.

The neon sign tipped his head to the side as if signaling me to join him.

Knowing this was a bad idea, I gripped Ryder a little tighter. She was a fighter. If we could get the underground guy back, we'd be that much closer to making it safe for paras again. And that mattered. All I had to do was get information. I could stay at the back, remain hidden.

Except I wasn't that person. I never had been. I really needed to learn how to fight if I was going to keep making stupid decisions.

"Hey, we need to head that way." I leaned forward and pointed. Stupid as it might be, it was the right one.

Chapter 10

Ryder signaled to the traffic behind her and made a move in the direction I'd indicated.

The neon-lit knight moved, stooping over and heading down the top of the building where I'd seen him.

"We gotta hurry. He's on the move."

Ryder applied some gas, and we sped through the streets with me giving her directions that were a bit hard to follow at times. All I had was a floating light to guide me, so I did the best I could.

We were in a super-sketch part of town. Like it was dark even though the sun was still up. That kind of sketch.

The neon light disappeared behind a building, but the glow was still there.

"Cut your lights. I think we're here."

With a switch, the street went even darker. She slowed to a stop and cut the engine, rolling the bike forward on her feet. "I see it."

Around the corner of a wide alley that ended at a dock, and with another street entrance to the left, a group of six men had surrounded a grey van.

"I was following the trail of the guy Dannika and Senator Armstrong wanted us to find," I murmured into the headset in the helmet.

"So, you think that's the man we're after."

A single light on the side of the building flooded the area, showing the driver's hands with a death grip on the wheel as he looked for a way out. He flared with a bright white light and then went back to normal.

"Yeah," I said.

"How many?"

What? People in the van? People around the van? The windshield was pierced on the passenger side, blood splattering the immediate area and the driver.

Kids shouted from the back, crying for help.

"I don't know."

Ryder took off her helmet and swung her leg over the front of her bike. "Stay here." She flexed and pulled two knives off her belt as she advanced.

The situation was rather obvious, and one I had experience in. With Vance, Parker and I would lead the way with the visions, then find a place to hide while he and his Supes fought the bad guys. I wasn't going to become a magical overnight ninja assassin warrior just because a fight presented itself.

Ryder punched one blue-dressed guy in the face and threw her dagger at the other. He staggered and grunted, fingering the knife in his chest.

Blue-dressed. I looked at these guys and realized that they were all wearing the same uniform: blue pants, blue-belted tunic with a cowl, and a blue mask over the top half of their face.

"Well, well, well," a dark voice asked from behind me. "What do we have here?"

I turned and saw man in a matching suit walking toward me. He wore a blue mask over the top half of his face, too, making it hard to see who he was. He was white, I got that much, and he had a solid jaw with a slightly pointed chin. His hair was covered by a piece of material coming off his mask, which was a good idea. In movies, superheroes couldn't get ID'd by their hair. In real life, connections were connections.

I hoped this wasn't . . . him.

"Nice costume." No one knew anything about Lord Shadow, which was how he'd gotten his name. Vance had dubbed him that because no one was ever left alive to say what he looked or sounded like. He was a ghost, a shadow in the city.

So, what could *I* tell about him? Who was he? What did he stand for?

The Knight of Swords was stooped over, looking angry.

How could I still see that if I was trying to figure out who he was?

The glowing knight bowed his head and appraised me. Got it. Because I wasn't trying to figure out specifics. I was trying to figure out what made him tick, which was indirect.

"Take off your helmet," the man said, raising his chin.

He didn't look like a puncher, but I wasn't about to take off the only protection my head had, and my brain was the only weapon in my arsenal. "We're gonna be leaving soon. So . . ." I shook my head, glancing back at Ryder.

She was busy.

He eyed me, looking intrigued, and smiled. "I said, take off your helmet."

"And you're obviously used to getting your way." Wait. "But not today." That had to be his superpower. Right? He could manipulate people. Get them to do what he wanted. Maybe? Jeezum. Should I pretend to do as he said?

Or was this helmet protecting me somehow?

Something clanked hard, metal against metal, as someone swooped in.

The guy in blue growled and bared his teeth. "War Hawk. What a nice surprise."

The neon knight behind him snarled.

Vance wore a dark grey suit with a gadget-filled belt and a combat vest that held a few more, with a cowl and an upper-face mask to protect his identity.

He flicked his wrist, and a metal string flew back into the gadget, which he then stashed on his belt. He walked forward. "Lord Shadow."

With Vance and his team here, I was free to get out of danger, so I scurried out of the way as the detective—the vigilante, now—stalked forward.

"Not so fast," Lord Shadow said, grabbing my arm.

A part of me wanted to punch this man in the face and demand to know where my friend was, but another part knew I didn't know how to throw a punch. The only thing I could do was find a safe place to gather information. This was the first time I'd come this close to the man who had—who might have—killed my friends and taken Parker.

He smirked. "Take your helmet off."

I slammed the heel of my hand into his elbow and pulled out of his hold.

Surprise flashed across his face as I slithered away and hid behind a trash dumpster.

Vance could handle himself, so I left the fighting to him, Ryder, and the two masked people with him—one in all black with cat ears, the other wearing white, with real fur sprouting along his exposed scruff.

I didn't think that Vance had had a chance to fight this guy directly before. At least, that was the impression I'd received at lunch. Hopefully, he'd be able to capture Lord Shadow this time.

That name was still so supremely stupid.

With Ryder still punching blue-clad bad guys and Vance and his team dealing with the man in question, I went to the van. I didn't have to sit around and find things out about a guy we were hopefully going to capture, but if the guy in the van was who Dannika and Senator Armstrong were after, we needed to get him out.

The kids had stopped screaming, which was nice, but that also could mean that things weren't great inside. Like they'd all been knocked out. Or . . . I couldn't bring myself to think it.

When I got to the front, the driver I'd seen before was gone, and all the kids were now in front, trying to figure out how to drive.

Where'd he gone?

I rapped on the window, then tried the door. It was locked.

The kid in the driver's seat looked at me, his eyes wide as he gripped the steering wheel.

The boy beside him screamed. "Move the stick!"

The gear shift? "I'm here to—" I took off my helmet so they could hear me better and shook my hair out of my face. "I'm here to help. Let me in."

Wild Eyes shook his head, but he paused for a half second.

Ryder rammed a guy into a wall behind me.

The kid stared at her with even larger eyes, then returned to messing with the steering wheel.

"I'm with her," I shouted to get his attention.

"Let her in," a blond girl squeaked. "Get us out of here."

That was something I could do.

The boy in the middle reached over Wild Eyes and opened the door.

Wild Eyes screeched, but he scrambled out of the way as all the kids piled toward the back to allow me room to maneuver.

"Where'd the driver go?"

"I don't know," the boy who'd let me in said with a grunt, moving the original passenger to the floor. "He got dragged out."

"By one of the guys in blue?"

"Yeah." He gestured to the wheel. "Can you talk *and* drive this thing?"

With a chuff, I locked the doors with a button and started the van. It didn't want to go, which explained why it was still here and the other guy hadn't been able to drive away. If I couldn't get this thing to move, we might have to get out and walk. I pressed the gas twice, waited a second, then tried it again.

The engine roared to life.

I threw it into drive and mashed the gas, hitting two blue-clad people on our way out.

I didn't feel too bad about that.

With no idea of where to go, I stashed my helmet on the dead guy's legs and followed the wide alley out from between two buildings, then turned sharply to get on the road.

The thing drove like a friggin' lumber wagon. It was top-heavy and felt like it was going to tip over every time we went around a corner. The kids were busy yelling at each other in the back, but I couldn't make anything out.

A pair of headlights appeared in my side mirror after the second turn.

Dang it! Where could we go? As a courier, I knew all kinds of areas, but Littleton wasn't my route, so I didn't know anything *here*. I lived here, of course, but all that meant was that I knew where my apartment was, where the local grocer was, and where the nearest pho place was. None of which was where we were going.

We made it around three corners. The sound of gunfire abated, which was good, but the headlights were still behind us.

They weren't gaining on us, just following.

Crap. I took a sharp left, another right, turned off my lights as I passed a parking garage, then ducked into an alley behind my apartment that I knew had another entrance similar to the one we'd just escaped from. Dropping the van into second to keep my foot off the brake, I ducked around the final corner, put it in first to slow down a bit more, and coasted to a natural stop as we went up a slight hill, hoping I didn't happen upon something bigger like a trash can or something.

I sat there, listening to the kids bicker as I watched the mirrors.

Nothing.

I put the van in gear again and crept forward, careful to keep all the lights off, which meant not using the brake still. We were in the lived-in part of the city now, so I also had to worry about drones, even if I did manage to shake our tail. This van was going to get attention, being this beat up with bullet holes and broken glass. Plus the blood all over the inside. I was sitting on blo—

Wait. Bullet holes. "Is everyone okay?"

"Amy's shot," one of the kids said.

Not good, because it wasn't like I could just take them to a hospital. "How bad?"

"Uh, bad."

Great. I threw out a line to the universe. *Hey, we could really use some guidance. I have no idea where to go and no idea how to help these kids.*

The air directly in front of me was dark.

I took a careful right onto the next street, looking for any traffic. *Can you send Jupiter our way, or guide us to Lady Dun? If she can help?*

A wispy white rabbit immediately appeared in front of me, driving a bunny-sized motorcycle. His white ears poked through the top of the helmet, then lay flat as he mashed the throttle and jetted in front of us, vision wisps trailing behind him.

He reminded me more of Ralph from *The Mouse and the Motorcycle* than Jupiter, and he had the wisps of a vision.

We had a direction I could trust.

The rabbit jogged us around the city, but only along dark streets, and he was careful not to use his brakes either, slowing cautiously as if using his transmission too.

He led us to a dark neighborhood. No overhead lights. No lit, occupied apartments.

That meant no surveillance. This was the kind of neighborhood Jamal kept us out of. There was no way of knowing if we'd come out the other side alive.

The rabbit stopped at the dead end of an alley and got off, his helmet disappearing, a red conductor's cap taking its place. A red vest appeared over his rippling torso.

Okay. Vision. I trusted that a little better than if it were an indentured servant to another potential villain.

He thumped his foot on top of a manhole cover and waited.

Right. And here we were without Ryder, who could lift that lid. Well, we'd just have to figure it out.

I twisted in the seat. "How many do we have?"

Wild Eyes looked up at me, blood on his face. "Who are you?"

"Eight," a girl said with a soft voice. She gave off a slight pink glow over her afro puffs.

"I think I have somewhere we can hide and hopefully get your friend looked at, but we need a prybar and to move."

"We need help with Amy," Pink Puffs said.

"'Kay. Can you guys find a pry bar?" I climbed into the back but couldn't really see much of what was going on with the girl—Amy—bleeding on the bed of the van. I wasn't a healer, nor much of a medic. I knew we needed to stop the bleeding, but so did they, judging by the wad of bloody material on the girl's stomach, which meant they had probably seen just about as much medical TV as I had.

"I got the metal stick."

How many kids had actually been taught how to use a prybar?

Not that I had either.

It turned out to be the cross-bar thing to take your tire off with, and that didn't work because the knobby thing at the end was too big to fit in the pry-it-up hole on the heavy lid. My fingers weren't strong enough to get in there, grip, *and* lift, even with the help of the kids.

However, we figured out how to eventually lift that lid and gently get Amy down into the hole. Leaving the body in the van I parked a little ways down the street, I closed the lid over us and climbed down the rung ladder.

That kid wasn't going to make it if we made everything last this long.

The rabbit waited for us at the bottom, tapping one foot.

I carried Amy, even though my muscles were now tired. It wasn't like I'd been biking all day and *then* had wrestled a fifty-pound lid, but the girl was heavy. She'd been shot in the stomach, which . . . all the shows I had watched told me this wasn't good. I couldn't just leave her behind, though.

"Do you know where we're going?" Wild Eyes asked in the glow of his flashlight.

"What's your name?"

"Eric. Do you," he said, emphasizing each word, "know where we're going?"

The dry, wide tunnel was pitch black, but at least it was dry with large pipes strung across the top. "I do," I lied. "It's just a little farther down the way."

Worry started to build because I wasn't stupid. I was just desperate, which frankly was sometimes worse.

A golden mushroom popped up beside the wall, its head bobbing in a breeze I didn't feel, golden wisps trailing off it as it moved.

A water bead of relief welled inside me, pushing at the worry as I took in the message my cards were sending me. We were safe and heading toward a community that would offer us safety.

More golden mushrooms raced outward, trailing in front of the rabbit.

He flicked his head this way and that as if seeing the mushrooms himself.

A yellow mushroom fairy zipped in, leaving wisp-motes behind her, and booped his nose.

He jerked back indignantly and frowned at me.

I just shrugged at him, not sure what to make of my visions interacting with each other.

With a final scowl, the rabbit turned back to leading us, sneezing at the mushrooms and fairies as he passed them.

These visions were progressing in ways I'd never imagined possible.

"Where are we going?" Eric asked.

The rabbit had appeared after I'd asked for specific help. "Lady Dun."

Eric stared at me with surprise. Seriously, his eyes looked like they could bug out of his head. "You're kidding."

"No. But I'm not—that's where I'm trying to take us."

"Trying?" Pink Puffs asked.

Amy moaned in my arms, and I shifted her around as a nerve in my shoulder pinched. "Yeah. Well, I've never actually been here before."

"Then . . . how?" the brown boy who'd tried to help Eric drive demanded, his slim face telling me just how insane I was. "We're in tunnels, and we could be getting lost up in here. How do you know we ain't about to get dead?"

"She's like us," Pink Puffs said, her eyes trailing movement I couldn't see. "She can see things."

"And what are you seeing?" the brown boy asked.

Pink Puffs rolled her eyes.

"It's fine," I said. The rabbit disappeared around a corner that was glowing with an intense golden light. "I'm following a rabbit."

Eric groaned. "I'm not eating the cake."

"You had to drink the potion first," the girl with the blond hair said.

This was the second reference to *Alice in Wonderland* in two days. I had to hope I wasn't being led to Dannika again. We needed real help, not assistance wrapped in a dagger. "What are you seeing?"

Pink Puffs looked up at me and then back to what was ahead of us as we rounded the corner. She gave a little wave.

The rabbit was waiting for us and waved back. He glared at me again, then continued on.

"You can see him too?" I asked.

"The rabbit?"

I nodded, shifting Amy again.

She groaned louder, and her muscles bunched, making her heavier.

"She's starting to come to."

Eric put a hand on my arm, as if wanting me to set Amy down.

That wasn't going to happen. This kid needed help, and fast. If I set her down, we'd be that much further from maybe saving her life, and I really didn't know if I'd be able to get her back up again.

The mushrooms were thicker here, which was the reason for the brighter glow, and there were a lot more yellow fairies buzzing about.

Pink Puffs only had eyes for the rabbit.

That meant this really could be Jupiter, which also meant we might be headed toward Dannika and not Lady Dun.

But my decks wouldn't lie to me.

We—my cards and I—were speaking an entirely new language here. It might have interpreted my request differently, answered the question I should have asked instead of the one I actually had. That was something my decks did often.

A few of the fairies buzzed around me, making moves to help me carry Amy.

I realized it was all in my head, but it seemed like she got lighter. "We gotta move."

Hurrying as much as my tired legs would allow, we followed the mushrooms and the rabbit around another corner.

There, we were greeted by a short Black woman with cornrows, her braids pulled back in a loose tail. She leaned lightly on a cane and was surrounded by eight other people, all carrying weapons or brandishing magic. "You better be for telling me why you're here."

Chapter 11

W e didn't have time for this. "We need help."

"Really," the woman said, moving her cane to the front and leaning a few inches forward. "And how did you find us, pray tell?"

"The rabbit," Pink Puffs said.

"What rabbit?"

"If it wasn't Jupiter," I said, "then it was my visions."

The woman narrowed her eyes a bit and studied us both. "And the girl?" she asked, pointing to Amy with her chin.

"Shot," I said crisply. "Do you have a doctor?"

The woman grimaced, then glanced at the tall man beside her and gestured toward me and Amy.

He sheathed his knife, letting it hang around his neck as he came to gather Amy.

Phew. Carrying people around—even smaller people—was hard work.

The woman with the cane motioned to the rest of us to follow her, while the man disappeared down another concrete corridor. The bunny disappeared after Amy and the man, but a pink mouse with a crown appeared in its place, his nose moving as if he was talking to me.

Pink Puffs looked at me with a frown as we moved to follow the woman and her entourage.

"You're telling me you can see that."

"A mouse," she muttered, "with . . . a gold crown?"

Okay, now this was getting weird. "Yeah."

"I don't get it."

I kept my voice low and my lips close to her ear. She was nearly my height, so it wasn't hard. "My visions work in symbols."

Pink Puffs nodded.

The mushrooms kept appearing, lighting the way, and the fairies buzzed around us like they were working and having fun. At least that wasn't changing. "I bonded with a deck when I was first starting out."

"A deck?" She narrowed her eyes and shook her head.

"Of cards. Oracle cards. Like tarot."

"Oh. Ohhhhh."

Right. "Well, the mouse with the crown says that the efforts we've put out there are about to come back to us." That was crap, of course, because I'd been hiding for nearly a year, helping Jack and jeezum. "Good things are coming our way."

"So, we can trust her."

"Pretty much." Hopefully.

"That's . . ." Pink Puffs frowned. "I wish mine worked like that."

Mine didn't always. "I had to train."

"How?"

I was more intent on where we were being herded into, so I waved the girl off and focused on our surroundings.

The woman with the cane continued to lead us as we talked, through a few more tunnels that eventually dumped us into a large room with several chairs, though not enough for everyone. She turned to us and gestured toward the silver chairs. "Please, sit."

I got the feeling we were about to be interrogated, which wasn't something I was going to enjoy. *If* she was really Lady Dun, though, I felt better knowing she didn't just invite everyone in with a smile and a chip to the city. I took one of the offered chairs and let the kids figure things out for themselves.

The woman took one as well, resting both hands on her cane as she studied me. "Who are you?"

Air bubbles surrounded her head as if she'd just dived under water, which was an invitation from my deck to dive in. I might not be able to see everything or where we were going, but now was the time to swim in dark waters to find the mystery waiting for me on the other side. Fine, then. If my deck told me it was okay, I was going to trust it. "October Sky Martinez Blaze."

The woman raised her chin and straightened. "I've been hearing quite a bit about you."

That couldn't bode well for me. "Who are you?"

"Lady Dun."

Relief washed over me. We'd made it.

The woman smiled at Pink Puffs. "I need to know how you found us."

We filled her in as quickly as we could. The kids had been on their way home from school in a group because they'd all been getting visions to varying degrees that they were about to be taken. They'd evaded a few of the attacks they'd seen coming, but earlier that evening, they'd been unable to, and had been shoved into the van.

The van hadn't gone anywhere afterward. It'd been parked in the alley we'd found them, just before the driver disappeared.

Then Ryder and I had shown up, saving them with the help of Vance—whose name I kept quiet.

That sounded like it'd been a trap, using the guy Dannika and Senator Armstrong had wanted me to find as bait. Which meant the seers were watching.

Jeezum.

"And *you* were led here by visions," Lady Dun said.

I nodded.

As did Pink Puffs. "A rabbit."

"I see. And who might you be?" She tilted her head to Pink Puffs.

Pink Puffs looked away, appearing shy but her eyes came back up and locked on Lady Dun. "Shay."

"Is it Jupiter?" I asked because I had to know.

The woman met my gaze. "You've met Dannika."

"I did."

She grunted thoughtfully. "And your thoughts?"

"She's not a woman to be crossed."

"Or trusted."

"Agreed," I said. This woman was sharp. I felt like I had to be on top of my game with her. "Can we trust you?"

"What do your visions say?"

The air bubbles receded, and golden mushrooms and fairies slipped under the door, inviting me in and offering me sanctuary. "Yes."

The woman nodded. "As do mine."

She had visions too?

"Wait," Shay said, asking the question before I could, looking around, her finger raised. "Which ones are yours?"

The woman narrowed her eyes at the girl.

"She can see all of our visions," Eric offered.

The woman raised her head and then leaned back, gesturing to the room. "Tell me what you see, then."

Shay flicked her uncertain gaze toward me, then took in a deep breath. "Well, um, there are mushrooms coming in and filling everything. There were air bubbles around you, and now they're gone. There's a dolphin swimming around, and there's a yellow dog by the door."

The woman looked at me with her eyebrows almost up to her hairline.

"The mushrooms and air bubbles are me," I said.

Lady Dun narrowed her dark eyes. "The dolphin is me."

Shay frowned. "Then, who's the yellow dog?"

"Mine," one of the girls said. "I'm scared."

The woman frowned, but she looked inquisitive, and soon a slight smile slid into place. "Interesting. Well, then." She looked up at the man guarding the door. "Guy, can you please make the kids comfortable, and have Bethany reach out to them. And we need to get instructors for them." Lady Dun gestured with her hand as she stood and led the way out the door.

The mushrooms were still there, but they dimmed in the darkness and thinned out as stars filled the corners and darkened doorways. A soft lull of people talking to one another reached my ears, and a heaviness filled the air as if we were heading somewhere with a lot of water.

Hopefully we weren't headed toward the sewers. I understood needing a new home that was safe, but at what cost?

A bug buzzed around my head, something that looked like a dragonfly but with a much larger head. It paused to hover in front of my eyes.

"You're not going to ask?" Lady Dun asked.

"Ask what?"

"Anything, really."

I'd gotten a little distracted. "My gift is telling me a little, and I want to ask more questions . . ."

Yet none were coming to mind. My gift was too busy literally heading off all my anxieties and concerns. "But I'm not sure how far to push for answers or if I'll piss you off." I'd just handed this woman the kids I'd saved. However, we had been looking for her to see if she was someone we could trust, if she could help us fight against Lor—the Witnesses, and I'd completely forgotten that in all the chaos with the children.

"What *are* your visions telling you?" she asked.

The stars weren't lighting the area. They weren't strings of lights someone else had put up. They were visions. Stars could mean. . .

Oh, right. This was a card in my deck. It really didn't come up often, which was the reason I wasn't more familiar with it, and the card itself focused more on a rock bridge and a glowing person. However, it told me to figure out what I really wanted and to look at it like a guiding star as I moved forward.

My immediate need had been to find a safe place for the kids—all of whom had the seer ability. My next need was finding the man targeting them. "There's someone hunting people like us."

Lady Dun nodded as she slowed her steps.

"Do you know him?" I asked.

"I know of him, but we haven't met."

I stopped and turned toward her. "Lady Dun, I'm in a mess."

Taking in a deep breath and releasing it, she stopped and faced me, pushing her shoulders back. "You may call me Pearl. Why? What mess are you in?"

I connected her name internally to her superhero moniker, and looked around, not really seeing the people moving through the space as I put all the pieces together. "One person is using me as she did before the wars. Another is using me because of my father. And yet another is using me because he used me after the war."

"And you've allowed this."

Hearing her say it out loud felt like a slap, but it was true. "I believed they were right and that what we were doing was for a good reason."

"Except for the one using you because of your father."

I shrugged. "Yeah."

"Who is he?"

Was this something I wanted to admit to her? Would she be upset as well? "Elias Blaze."

"Oh. I see. So, Dannika, again." Pearl nodded, letting her gaze drift. "If you're seeing in signs, you didn't get your gift from him."

I shook my head. "My mother's people."

"Good. But the others. You trust them?"

That was a heavy word. "Not fully."

"You have to ask yourself what you want."

My heart didn't hesitate. "I want to find this guy." Which was dangerous and stupid. "He's terrorizing us. He's hunting us. He makes us feel like there are no safe places. He has my friend. I want him stopped."

"Then, already, you're in a place of power," she said. "You're no longer waiting to be used. You can use them equally."

Except that if this guy had a team of seers and was using them, he'd found a way to use this ability to lead with.

The voices outside my head grew louder, and the vision stars soon had nowhere to shine in a place filled with light. More bugs flitted around my head and hands. Bushes and trees pulled out of the concrete. The hard, cold floor was replaced by softer earth dampened by rain. The large space didn't have concrete walls, but ragged rock ones, and what should have been a ceiling was a sky filled with sunlight and white clouds.

I spun around in a slow circle, staring. "What is this?" It wasn't a sewer, that was for sure.

She smiled up at the blue sky. "I call this place Paraden."

"This is amazing."

Pearl grunted.

Wonder filled me as I took in the trees and the absolute lack of concrete. "How?"

She chuckled. "We've stepped onto a different world."

That didn't make sense. I mean, I understood that magic expanded the limits of reality, but there were still limits to reality. "You're kidding."

"I'm not. The elves allow us to remain here with certain conditions."

What did this even mean? That we were safe somehow? That we couldn't be pursued?

"One of them is that we will have to find a way to reside in our world and soon."

What were some of those other conditions? Did we all have to be worried? "And you're working on that?"

She nodded. "That's been . . ." She let her words recede as she paused to sigh, one black eyebrow rising in quiet vexation. "Stalled."

"You're looking for the guy the Witnesses took too?"

"Is that who they sent you after?"

I nodded. "Yeah."

"Ah, I see. Dannika and Victoria. I should have known."

Did they all know each other? I got a sense that these three women had serious history—maybe all with Jamal, too.

"October," Ryder shouted, her husky voice carrying through the crowd.

I searched the huts nestled in the trees. People milled along stone paths, talking to one another or working together. It was hard to believe that we'd come through sewer tunnels to get here. The farther I stepped into this area, the more it looked and felt like a forest. The air was heavier, more damp, as if it'd just rained recently. The smell of spruce filled my nose.

Magic was weird, but more than that, if Paraden was safe. . .

Then why didn't we send more of our paras here?

I spotted a bright head over the top of everyone else—Ryder was pushing her way through the milling crowd.

She saw me, and relief washed over her face.

An answering relief warmed me as well. "How is it that no one is able to find you?" I asked Pearl.

She clasped her hands over her cane as she waited for Ryder to join us. "There are protections at the doors, of course. We can't just let anyone walk in all willy-nilly."

That was a term I hadn't heard often.

"Are you okay?" Ryder demanded as she reached for my arm and inspected me.

I relaxed with her near, and only at her words did I realize I was probably covered in blood. "It's Amy's. I'm hoping she's getting taken care of?"

I'd left my helmet in the van, too. Dang it!

Pearl nodded, her face pointed toward Ryder while her eyes remained on me. "She's with healers and should be fine." She turned her attention to the newcomer. "Welcome to Paraden."

Ryder bowed her head slightly. "May the heavens protect you."

Pearl gave a soft hmm.

Before I could be derailed again, I cleared my throat. "Jamal sent us to find you."

She let her eyes drift closed and turned to me, her pink-tinged, brown lips gone flat.

I was right. They did know one another, and there was history there. "He wanted us to warn you that the Witnesses are targeting seers, and to see if there was a way you could help us. Right now," I said, charging on before either Ryder or Pearl could interrupt me, "Dannika holds a lot of power. If we fail to provide the guy she's after—"

"Fred Drake," Pearl interrupted. "He's an earth mage, of a sort. He's helping us burrow a tunnel to the nearest free border."

"Which isn't that far away. Canada is—"

"We're going underground, and there's a very large lake between us and any freedoms we may hope to find." She shook her head. "Without him, we have no road."

That was bad news. "If the Witnesses have him. . ." I let that thought trail off.

"You think they do?" Pearl asked.

"I—" Oh, jeezum. "He was in that van. I'd been following his trail." I looked to Ryder. "Tonight was a trap."

"I agree," she said.

"For me."

"Yes."

I licked my top lip, trying to figure out how to figure out a winning solution. "He knew I'd be looking for the—for Fred. And when I was there, he took Fred again before I could free the kids."

"So you almost had him," Pearl said.

I nodded. "I was able to track him."

Pearl raised her chin and squinted, reassessing me. "You may have received something from your father yet." She frowned. "Interesting."

Her expression said that interesting wasn't necessarily good. I turned back to Ryder. "How's War Hawk?"

She rolled her eyes and shook her head. "Bringing who we caught to the station."

I opened my mouth to speak, but then a glowing white bridge spanned the village, running through huts and lighting the area, making the dew and water droplets on the leaves sparkle. A weight slid off of me, a sense of sureness replacing it. I was where I needed to be. Here, I could strip away all the masks I wore, all the barriers I'd erected around myself. I could just be me.

With a wink that felt like a soul hug, the vision dissipated.

Why had this card presented itself to me just now?

Because I'd been tempted to lie. I'd been tempted to hide, to keep things to myself in order to . . . protect Vance? Myself? The couriers? I didn't know.

I wasn't entirely certain what I'd been about to say, but I pushed away all the curtains I'd erected around myself. "Pearl, just how safe is Paraden?"

She gave me a frank look, then tipped her head to the side. "There are people looking for us."

"Is Lord—" Would his seers hear me on another planet? "Is he after you? Is he hunting us to get to you?"

She bowed her head, tossing it lightly from side to side. "Perhaps."

That information didn't change anything, I realized.

"Do you know either of their identities?" Pearl asked. "War Hawk, or this Lord—"

I held up my hand to stop her. "If he's using the seers he's collecting, we think he's using them to stay ahead of us by listening."

"Ah," she said, understanding lighting her dark eyes.

It felt wrong to tell, but I'd just been told I could trust Pearl. "War Hawk is Detective Young."

Ryder looked at me like I'd betrayed him.

It was the right thing to do.

Pearl pondered that a bit. "That's helpful. I knew there was something about him, and I hoped . . ." She shook her head, not filling us in on the rest. "Nothing on . . . the other man?"

"He's somehow attached to the PD. That's all we know. He seems to be able to manipulate those he talks to, though."

"How so?" Pearl asked.

"He tried to control me, and he acted like I would do what I was told." I glanced at Ryder, wondering now if she was even safe. Had he had a chance to speak with her? "I don't know how I was able to fight it. I did have my helmet on?"

"That is a powerful observation." Pearl's tone was thoughtful.

"He also thinks he's protecting something, that his actions are just."

"The older you get, the more you realize that every villain is simply a hero for a people who aren't yours."

That didn't make him any better in my book. If anything, it made him marginally more terrifying.

"Well," Pearl said, "this is certainly a good start. Let's see what else I can get from you."

Chapter 12

"You're certain you can keep this safe," Pearl said, and it wasn't a question. She stood beside the wooden door of a small tower room, the stone covered in moss and a strange, yellow-spotted ivy.

"If it's only opened with that ring," I said, gesturing to the gold she still held clutched in her hand, "then there's no way anyone can get it."

"Unless you're taken."

"And if that's the case, then anyone on the outside could be a danger." Anyone could be broken eventually.

Pearl looked around as if waiting for someone to remind her not to do this. "You must guard this entrance with your life."

I didn't want to be the person who brought Paraden down. We needed sanctuaries like it. "You don't have to give this to me. I can use the sewers, like I did to get here."

She shook her head and straightened, glancing at me as if reminding herself that this had been her decision for a reason. "If he is hunting you, you will need a place to hide quickly. And I cannot have you leading him to us through the less protected ways."

"Okay." She'd given me a fresh shirt, one that wasn't covered in blood, and had allowed me to wash up a little. I'd somehow gotten blood in my hair, which was gross. I'd need to take a shower when I got home. "Are you going to get in touch with Jamal?"

Pearl clamped her lips shut and clenched the top of her cane in agitation.

"I trust him."

"You should not," she said, almost to herself, then shook the words off. "I'll have someone come by."

I was so over all this back history intrigue. "Whatever this is between you two, stop it. You seem to be the only two who actually care." And who weren't willing to sacrifice countless people in order to get their way.

Pearl nodded, rolling her jaw in thought. "Agreed." She gestured to the woman who'd created the portal between Paraden and my apartment.

That woman stepped aside and motioned with both hands that it was safe to proceed.

Ryder looked bored, as if portals were a common thing where she came from and we were all spending too much time jeezing around with this. Her expression said, "It's just a door."

Pearl narrowed her eyes but handed me the ring.

The piece of jewelry looked normal, but it felt heavy in my hand, as if the weight of keeping the portal safe rested inside the metal.

"Be safe, October," Pearl said, giving my fingers a squeeze. "We will provide what support we can but do not depend on us to save you."

I remembered Miche. "There's another girl. Uh, my guard's daughter."

Pearl shook her head and frowned in confusion, not understanding what I was saying.

I waved that off. "She sees visions, too. I had thought of taking her to Jamal to see if we could put her abilities on hold for a bit, but if I can send her here instead?"

"Give me the details, and I will look into her."

Breathing a sigh of relief, I gave her all the information I had.

"Thank you," I said when I was finished.

"I make no promises."

Great. So it would be a race to see who managed to get to the girl first.

Jeezum. Could I warn Roger? Get to him? Get to Miche?

I didn't know where he lived. So, no. I'd think of something.

And hope I was leading *him* straight to Miche?

Jeezum in a basket!

"Go," Pearl said, with a slight push.

Stepping through the portal felt just like walking through any door. I really thought there'd be more . . . moreness. Instead, the temperature just changed from Paraden to home. It was hotter here, and the sun was down, which was dumb. The air conditioner idea was going to be a reality sooner than I'd hoped.

Ryder exited the bathroom, putting the towel back on the rack on her way through the door. "I need to get my bike."

"It's past curfew." She wasn't getting anything, but I definitely needed a shower.

She shook her head as if that didn't matter, then headed toward the front.

I stopped her. I didn't want her to get herself killed just because she thought she was invincible. Or, I don't know, whatever. "Don't be stupid."

The Valkyrie raised a pale eyebrow at me, then looked toward the windows with a scowl.

"Or, you know, reckless." Now that I was here, and before I could take a shower, I needed to just get my cards out of my apartment and into a safe place, which I now had access to. Before, they'd just been a bomb waiting to go off. But now? I had a way to defuse it before it potentially blew up in my face—which could happen at any time. From the looks of things, we were going to be doing some pretty stupid stuff. I didn't know if my decks would continue to be tied to me in this new way if they were destroyed, or . . . shielded away?

Crap. I really had no idea how they were interacting with me right now. But I had a feeling—just a feeling, not necessarily with any basis in reality whatsoever—that I needed to make sure they were safe.

Roger and Miche were tugging at me too, though, like I had a bit in my teeth and was being led. I fully understood—No. I had a better understanding of the danger she was in now. I'd met Lord—*him*. If Vance had caught him, I was fairly certain Ryder would have mentioned that, which meant he'd gotten away. Again. Not that I'd expected any different.

What was it going to take to get this guy? And how was I going to keep Miche safe?

Not that it was my responsibility to—

Oh, cut the crap. There was no way I was slipping this off onto someone else. It was my responsibility because I could see the situation, and I wasn't running from it. Not this time. Not again. I was done hiding.

Dana. As I closed my eyes, my heart hurt, knowing that I'd wasted too much time. That boy hadn't been found in two days now. There was no way he was still alive.

"What are you doing?" Ryder asked as I shoved the small brown couch to the side.

"Getting my cards out of here."

She grunted. "I don't need to be here for that."

I knew I couldn't stop her as I knelt down to open the door in the floor, but . . . "Just"—I released a disgusted-at-her-stubbornness sigh and continued unearthing my buried treasure— "be safe."

She nodded, her lips flat in thought. "Yeah." Then she headed for the door.

I grabbed my deck, which was wrapped in the silk shawl, and pulled it out. I desperately wanted to do a reading to get better details into what was going on.

Before I could even think about starting, though, someone knocked loudly on the front door.

We both went still.

A golden mushroom fairy slipped under the door and buzzed about, leaving vision-motes around.

"It's safe," I said. I put the lid on the floor compartment, stashed the cards under a seat cushion on the couch, and scooted it forward again.

Ryder frowned at me and gestured toward the couch with a shake of her head. Clearly, she didn't believe me.

I didn't know *who* was out there. I just knew that whoever it was, they were a part of our community.

She went to the door and opened it.

Vance stepped through wearing street clothes. "I—" He peered around Ryder to see me. "I just wanted to see if you were okay."

"We're fine," I said with a smile, wanting him out of there so I could stash my cards in a secret world and then take a shower.

"Where's my bike?" Ryder demanded.

"Out front." The detective rubbed his forehead. "I brought it."

"Great," she said with a sigh.

"Not great." He opened his mouth and twisted his head on his neck as if trying to figure out how to say what he wanted to.

"Just tell us," I said, not wanting to hear what more he had to add.

He flicked his fingers. "You two were caught on surveillance drone. I told the cops that you were my CIs and that you were helping with a case."

"And they bought that, right?" I asked.

He winced. "Maybe."

A flashing red light lit over Vance's head. There was danger there.

"Okay." We were out of time. I needed to get the death sentence out of my apartment. I wasn't ignoring the red flashing light again. "Get out of here. Thanks for bringing Ryder's bike."

If the police were on to us, the PPE could be here any time, and they couldn't find my cards. And if they showed up right then and there, there was absolutely nothing Vance could do to stop them, and I couldn't just pop them through the door to Paraden with him standing right there.

"What were you even doing there tonight?"

"Later." I put my hands on him and pushed him out of the apartment.

He blinked, his expression telling me he had something else he wanted to say, but the flashing red warning light wasn't getting any dimmer.

"Have a good night."

"October, wha—"

I closed the door in his face.

Ryder stared at me with a question in her eyes, but she wasn't impeding me.

She obviously had no idea, which kind of made me angry. How could she live in our world and not know how much trouble we were in? I'd watched PPE come in and take entire families for nothing more than possessing books they shouldn't have. An actual deck of cards would get me killed on the spot. I snatched the cards out of the couch and headed back to the bedroom.

She followed close on my heels. "Are we in danger?" she asked, her breath husky on the back of my neck.

"Yes," I whispered, and pressed the ring I'd just received to the door, stepping through.

Paraden was exactly as we'd left it except that it was nighttime now. Time obviously didn't flow the same, which was going to make things difficult. A fleeting thought had passed through me that we could just sleep here, where we were safe, and go back when it was time to head to work. A good night's sleep wasn't something I'd experienced in over a year.

Pearl had shown me where I could safely stash my cards. It was a nook in a stone wall behind a large cooking area and several stools.

I wished I could pull them out and do a reading, but I didn't know if I had time. PPE might be beating down my door, and I didn't want to have to explain why we weren't there—if we hid—or where we'd been if we arrived when they were inside.

So, I stashed my cards, told them I'd be back, hoping that the distance—being on another world, jeezum—wouldn't impact how they performed. I turned away to get back to the portal. .

.

And stepped through the eye of a needle and directly into the orange eye of a dragon.

Calming my heart, I listened to what my deck was telling me. I had to walk with intent and stay true to myself. The dragon was a blending of opposites, and they were fierce. The color orange represented energy and encouragement.

I took in a quick breath and released it into the stillness around me.

The eye disappeared, leaving only Ryder's face.

I stepped past her, glad that she was there but understanding that I couldn't appreciate much more than that in this moment. I hurried to the living room.

Loud voices sounded on the other side of the apartment door. Vance was doing what he could to keep PPE away, but he wasn't going to last much longer.

Ryder stopped me and ripped off my shirt.

Desire rippled through me, but so did a massive amount of fear. "What are you doing?"

"Just trust me." She mussed up my hair and unbuttoned her pants, kicking off her boots.

I sincerely wanted to see more, to touch her skin and feel how soft it was, but we didn't need to go through all this. We just needed to answer the door.

She gripped my face with both hands and stared into my eyes. "Trust me."

Every inch of my soul demanded I obey.

Then she claimed my lips with hers.

A wildfire unlike anything I'd ever felt before swept through me, and all I could do was melt to her touch.

I tried to fight her at first. There were PPE agents at my door, after all. But her kiss ignited a fire inside me, warming parts of my soul that had never seen light before. A startled sound escaped my throat as something euphoric and painful hit me like a stinging arrow of desire. I didn't know what she wanted in that moment. It was too chaotic to really think, but the one thing I knew for certain was that I didn't want her to stop.

She pulled away from me, her blue eyes smoky as she breathed heavily. "I needed you flushed." Her voice was much huskier than normal, which I wouldn't have thought possible.

This wasn't just her trying to make me flushed or whatever. Maybe it'd started that way, but . . .

I swallowed. "Ah." That was the best I could do.

She closed her eyes in frustration as the noise outside my door rose. Then she stomped toward it, nearly ripping it from the hinges. "What the hells do you want?" she roared.

Vance turned with his mouth open as if to speak. It closed as he looked at her, then at me, then back to her again, taking us in.

The lead PPE agent didn't look like she was used to being addressed this way. She straightened her black suit jacket and raised her chin. "We're here to search the premise."

"For what fucking reason?"

Oh, jeez, if that woman didn't watch it, she was going to get us both killed. I searched for my shirt. She'd thrown it across the room. I rushed to grab it and scurried back. "Sure. Sure, yes. You can search. It's fine. It's fine. Just—she's, uh . . ." I had to hope we'd get back to what she'd started. "Grumpy."

"I'm busy," Ryder growled low in her throat.

The lead PPE agent raised an eyebrow over prim lips and flexed one hand before stepping around Vance and Ryder to get in.

The other three agents, all dressed in riot gear, remained in the hallway.

Vance widened his eyes at me, then rolled his gaze to Ryder, then back to me.

First of all, we weren't *that* good of friends. Second of all, well, we weren't that good of friends.

I had never felt the same reaction with a man as I had from one kiss with Ryder. Did I care that this might be nothing more than her gift? Maybe? I knew I probably should.

The lead agent walked to the couch and looked down. Tipping her head to the side, she flicked her hands out. "What am I going to find in the hole in your floor, Ms. Blaze?"

Ms. Blaze. Well, it was nice to see that at least one person didn't know my pre-Wipe identity. "Nothing, Agent . . ."

"Rosa Spike." She narrowed her brown eyes, her dark brown hair pulled back in a French-braided bun. "You're certain."

"I used to keep my weed in there before it wasn't legal anymore."

"It was never *legal*, Ms. Blaze."

"Actually, it was. Quite legal, in fact. We were the first Midwestern state to legalize it."

She hmmed softly to herself and moved the couch, stooping down.

I wanted to demand how she knew about the compartment. I wanted it confirmed that their drones used invasive tech.

But who cared? The point was, we weren't safe. We weren't allowed privacy.

She opened the door to the compartment with a triumphant smile, then froze. "Ms. Blaze," she said, her voice quiet but dangerous, "where did they go?"

A cold chill raced down my spine, and acid rolled in the pit of my stomach as the heat from Ryder's kiss disappeared like a ghost in the chill of terror from that one question.

"The joints?" I asked as calmly as I could. "I smoked them. A long time ago."

Agent Spike swiveled her face toward me and rose like smoke from a dying fire. "It's not wise to lie to me."

"I'm not." I clearly was. I didn't know how she knew my cards had been in there, but she wouldn't be bluffed. That didn't mean I wasn't going to try, though. She hadn't arrested me, and she had come here to "catch me red-handed," which said that she had rules to follow still. That was oddly comforting.

Agent Spike raised her chin with a sour smirk and tapped her ear. "Search it all."

The three officers from the hall spilled in. For the next thirty minutes or so, they tore my apartment apart, even going so far as to stab my seat cushions. They broke three plates and a mug as if I'd somehow be able to hide my cards in porcelain.

At the end of it, Agent Spike was pissed.

"Where did they go, Ms. Blake?" she asked me, her voice barely maintaining its cool.

As if I was just going to tell her after it was obvious they weren't going to find them on their own. "I already told you," I said, my heart racing despite the fact that I knew we were safe. They were tucked away on another planet—a place they couldn't access. The reality was, though, she didn't *need* my cards to take me in. She could just do it because she wanted to. She could trump up a charge, even plant something on me.

Ryder stalked up to the woman, seeming to get taller as she approached. "Get out."

The three PPE officers stopped what they were doing and scurried to Agent Spike's defense.

I scrambled to stand between, my hands raised. "Whoa, whoa, whoa! She's just really . . . horny." Dear gods. "She's not thinking straight. It was just weed in there. I swear it."

"I wouldn't believe anything you said," Agent Spike said, her tone all ice now. "I have half a mind to take you both into custo—"

"What do you think you're catching them doing?" Vance asked, pushing his way around the wall of riot shields behind Ryder.

Agent Spike advanced on me. "I happen to know there wasn't weed in this compartment, Ms. Blaze."

Ryder shouldered me out of the way and glared down at the agent.

Then Vance moved in with his hands palms down. "Ladies, ladies."

The Valkyrie wasn't backing down and neither was the agent.

"What do you think was in there?" he asked.

"Magic supplies," Agent Spike said, watching me with lazy eyes.

I didn't for one second believe she was calm. She was just waiting for me to slip up, waiting for me to react in some way I shouldn't. I snorted. "Magic supplies. I'd rather have pot."

"Cards, to be exact."

I pulled a long face and shook my head. "None here."

"I happen to know they were."

"And how's that?" Vance asked, crossing his arms over his chest as he came to stand in front of Ryder.

Agent Spike glared at me.

Had something changed that I didn't know about? Were there actual protections for us now?

"There's still such a thing as a right to privacy, Agent. It was reinstated just this morning because of PPE's abuse of power."

Well that had happened quietly. Still, it was a huge relief.

"Situations like this," he continued. "Without proof, you can't bring her in. Without solid evidence, you're leaving empty-handed. So, unless you were invited in or she personally showed you something, you have no right to actually be here."

The agent turned her glare to Vance. "Whose side are you on?"

"Unlike you, I swore an oath to protect the people, and I intend to honor it."

Agent Spike raised her chin, then nodded at the people behind us. "I'll be back with a search warrant."

"I'll be interested to see your chain of evidence on this one," Vance said with a smug smile as he moved out of her way.

She leaned into him on her way by and bared her teeth. "This was a mistake, Detective."

"I doubt it," he quipped back with a smile.

But as the door slammed shut, I knew that it had been. Vance had just put himself in the eye of the target.

Chapter 13

Sleeping was nearly impossible for me that night. I kept thinking of Ryder's hands on my body, of feeling her beneath my own, imagining how she would taste, feeling her lips exploring me.

I woke up with a restless energy and took in the roughed-up look of my apartment, anger mixing with my high emotions and creating something uncomfortable. As I stepped into the living area, I prepared myself to be even angrier.

Things weren't one hundred percent put back together yet. The books that should have been on the now-broken bookcase were stacked neatly, though in a completely random order I could see from across the room. The cushions were duct-taped together where they'd been cut. The side table was rigged to stand, though it looked like anything might blow it back down.

Ryder sat at the breakfast nook, a cup of tea in hand as she read a book, fully dressed.

My nerves settled, grateful she was still here. Plus, the tidying was a nice gesture. "Hey," I said, morning-stomping to the counter and flipping the switch on my electric kettle.

"Morning." She looked at me without raising her head, then dropped her gaze back to her book.

My skin tingled where her gaze caressed me, my mind recalling her dream lips against my skin. "What you reading?" I asked, my voice a little hoarse.

Ryder looked at the cover, then shook her head with a shrug. "*The One and Only Crystal Druid.*" She shrugged again, this time accompanied by a smile. "It's pretty good."

"Annette Marie's a good author. I like her work." That was one of my favorite series. I was a little surprised I'd been allowed to keep it and that they hadn't used it or my other urban fantasy books as a reason to take me in when they couldn't find my cards.

What right did they have to barge in after spying on me?

"Hey," Ryder said, putting her book down, using a fork as a bookmark. "Let's grab breakfast."

I looked at my tea kettle. It was hissing angrily, but the water hadn't even had a chance to bubble yet. So, I clicked it back off and dressed quickly, able to find most of what I needed, and followed her to the bike. She had a replacement helmet for me, and we rode toward Speedy Couriers, taking a slight jaunt to stop at a bagel shop.

"I can't afford anything here." Well, a food voucher would get me a bagel, but it seemed like a waste since it was only one food group.

She took off her helmet, setting it on her seat. "I can. Come on."

Ryder ordered me an egg and sausage sandwich that was worth four food vouchers, then chose a table toward the window. She chewed on the inside of her lip as if she was nervous. "Last night was interesting."

Wild energy coursed through me like fire. I recalled my dreams of her, of seeing her splayed on my bed, reaching toward me. Was that the part she'd found interesting? Or the fact that we'd found Lord Sha—*him* and had almost been caught or the fact that we'd found Lady Dun or the fact that we now had a portal to a secret para city?

I hoped she was talking about the kiss. Well, more than a kiss. She'd ripped my shirt off. I still didn't know if this was *her* or if this was natural, but I didn't care.

Shaking myself, I focused on the fact that she was likely talking about the agents who had invaded my apartment. I had to quell this attraction. Reminding myself that this was probably her gift, that it wasn't real, wasn't helping.

I knew what I felt. And I wanted her.

The green fairy from my deck danced on one foot and then the other, staring up at me.

Everything was a balancing act, indeed—I had to figure out how to handle all of this and not fall down.

The fairy tipped her head to the side and gave me a disgruntled look.

Right. Right. That wasn't the only thing she represented. She was reminding me that there was a difference between readiness and preparation. That made sense in terms of what was going on around us, but I wanted to address the need coursing through me.

The fairy stomped her foot and flung dust in Ryder's direction.

She was telling me to be prepared for Ryder?

She rolled her eyes and regained her balance on her one foot.

My throat went dry. I was used to my cards telling me what others needed, not what I did, not to follow what I wanted. And I wanted this.

Except that Ryder's brash, no-one-can-tell-me-no attitude was going to get us both killed, and I wasn't a fighter. Being with her could be dangerous. Was that something I could address with her?

A girl surrounded by roots appeared beside Ryder's bagel, shivering and brown.

The green fairy tiptoed toward her and sprinkled green vision dust on her.

The torn girl's roots perked a bit, but she looked up with her haunted dark eyes and shook her head, curling deeper within herself, her roots shrinking.

The green fairy turned to me like a whimsical ballerina constantly dancing on her toes. She held her arms out, her moth wings shiver-fluttering.

Ryder's reaction last night had something to do with her past failures, or at least her perception of them. I mean, the woman claimed to have lost Michigan in the war, which was dumb because a few states had lost. Like both of the states that actually touched our borders, so, I mean, what had she thought we could be? A peninsula of ParaWest surrounded by nothing to protect us?

The fairy nodded as if to say I was finally paying attention.

"How do you like your bagel?" Ryder asked, her blue gaze flicking toward the window for a moment.

"It's good." It was *really* good. "What happened? Last night?"

Ryder blinked in confusion and then frowned. "With the kiss?"

A shiver rippled through me, and I expelled a breath I couldn't control. "That was cover."

Her gaze remained on my lips for a long moment.

Was she fantasizing about kissing me again? Could this be more than her gift? Could my need be reciprocal, and if so, then was that bad?

She closed her eyes for a moment, then met my gaze. "This is what I am."

"Meaning what I feel for you. . ." I shook my head.

"Isn't real," she finished, as quiet as she'd ever been. "Unless you can see that it is?"

The green fairy just shrugged at me, continuing to sprinkle her sparkle on the Root Girl.

"Fine. What I'm feeling isn't real." Except that it was. "You could have gotten us killed last night."

"That's not what—"

"Ryder," I said, leaning in on the small, round table so the other patrons couldn't hear me, "those were PPE agents, and they have full and complete control over this city. They *are* the law."

She shook her head and rolled her eyes but ground her jaw at the same time. "They shouldn't have even been there."

"I agree with that. But they were. And your reaction only made things worse. Agent Rosa Spike is never going to forget me now."

"You got free."

"Because of Vance, who is also now in danger. Not you."

She pulled her head back and looked away, clearly upset. "I would have kept you safe."

Frustration welled in me. She was like a freakin' immovable wall. The comparison only brought up memories of Uncle Ramon putting one on and getting belligerent in his drunken state. During those long-ass nights, I'd thought I'd never get out of the kind of rut he was determined to keep us in.

But thanks to my visions and my deck at the time, I'd been able to find a path to freedom.

Ryder wasn't an alcoholic, but she was still just as determined to keep us in a rut.

Root Girl curled in deeper.

I stopped and thought about that for a minute. Root Girl represented the little unwanted forgotten girl buried deep inside, begging for attention. When she acted in jealousy, she just wanted to be noticed. When she acted in anger, she just wanted to be protected.

"Someone tormented you."

Anger flashed in Ryder's blue eyes as she snarled, slamming her hand down on the table.

Several people around the busy bagel bar looked in our direction.

I smiled at them to show that we were okay, and they turned back to their lattes and smears without a second thought.

Ryder glared at me. "You're reading me?" she asked, low in her throat.

No. Yes. Was that a problem? "I'm just trying to figure out what happened."

"Then we talk about it."

"That's what we're doing right now."

"Last night was—"

"Saved by Vance. Not you. You made it worse. Why?"

She stared into my eyes, anger rolling off her with an almost visible heat, but as she searched my soul, her anger dimmed and her body deflated in a long exhale. "I overreacted." Surprise pinched at the corners of her blue eyes.

"You did," I said, not reaching toward her, feeling like that would be a bad move. "Why?"

Ryder looked around and then shook her head, rising to her feet. "We're going to be late."

Root Girl smiled up at the green fairy and moved to Ryder's last bite of bagel, stuffing a vision version of it in her mouth happily as Ryder picked up the actual bite and shoved it in her own mouth.

That seemed like a good sign, even if the silence didn't feel like it.

How did other people talk to each other without their ability to read cards and signs? If it wasn't for my tarot deck, I'd think she was blowing me off again and I'd be reacting to that, probably making the situation worse.

We drove up to the gate, and my heart pounded. We had the chips, and Ryder was a celestial, but we'd put ourselves on Agent Spike's radar, and there wasn't a chip in the city that would help me against that if she made it an issue.

She had known about my deck. She must have been in my apartment. She must have gotten her hands on it, seen it with her own eyes.

My timing had been impeccable. If I'd been just one hair's breadth slower. . .

I didn't want to think about it.

Roger stopped us, looking around carefully. "You pissed someone off last night."

I flipped my visor up. "Yeah. Am I okay?"

"You are. She's not." Roger shook his head and took a step back. "Be more careful." He waved us through.

A red warning light similar to the one that had been above Vance's head the night before now appeared above Roger.

"Hey," I said, pressing my fingertips into Ryder's waist without looking in her direction. From the corner of my eye, I saw her pause, turning her head.

"Be careful," I told Roger. I didn't know what the warning might—Jeezum. I knew exactly what the warning was about. "Where's Miche?"

"At school?"

"Get off early and go get her."

Alarm crept over his face. "You're sure?"

"No, but I've got a feeling."

He nodded just once and ducked into the guard shack.

I'd done what I could. I tapped Ryder's waist and settled back on the seat.

Jamal was his normal high dystopian overlord self with silver rings, bones in his piercings, and chains connecting his ear to his nose and eyebrow. He grabbed my hands and pulled me close to whisper in my ear, "I heard there was trouble at your place last night, boo. You good?"

I nodded.

"Because I also heard them people could turn others to turn the rest of us in."

Did he honestly think—

Of course he did. He had to. We lived in a world where that kind of thing happened all the time. "No. Between Vance and Ryder, I'm good. We're safe."

"Safe?" he asked derisively.

I rolled my eyes.

He nodded and let me go, acknowledging my eye roll with one of his own. "What happened last night?"

"I found Pearl."

His expression froze in a smile as he worked through packages. "Is that so. And how is Lady Dun?"

It seemed like there was bad blood there, but he was awfully respectful for someone who might have a beef with her. "She's good."

"Good."

I wanted the story, but I wasn't going to ask right then. "She's going to send someone to you. I told her she needed you."

He snorted.

"She does, Jamal. And we need her. She also said she'd think about helping us." Kind of. Not really, actually. "She's got her own people looking into Lord No Name."

"She would be able to do that. Yeah."

"You know Pearl, don't you?"

He clamped his mouth shut, smiling as he handed me my packages. "Be safe out there, baby girl."

I huffed a smile, tucked my packages into my backpack and headed back to Ryder.

Everyone else I cared about was already gone, but the area had a slightly red tint to it that didn't feel good. Red was bad. It was a warning. I *knew* it had good qualities too, but I attributed it to bad things. When it showed up, bad things followed.

I walked back to the counter and leaned in. "Be extra careful today. 'Kay?"

Jamal sobered up and nodded. "Yeah, baby girl. What do you see?"

Nothing that provided any sort of answers. "Just. . . a lot of red."

"With the stir-up last night, I don't doubt it. But I've got protections up. I'll keep this place quiet."

"Thanks." It was the best I could hope for, given everything else going on.

I headed back out to where Ryder was waiting for me.

A man with a ten of diamonds strolled down the other side of the street.

A woman with a matching nine hovering over her head was talking to a guy at a blue car further down.

A kid with a two card over his heart, also in diamonds, ran past, shouting up at me to get out of his way.

Either Dannika was enlarging her ranks, or she'd put a protection detail on me.

Did that make me feel better? Or more scared?

We went on our delivery, heading into Sturwood. I hadn't been there since just before the war ended. None of us really had been. It wasn't a no-go zone, there just weren't a lot of calls to go there.

I was totally using one of my food vouchers today, though. I might even spend a few and just shove the leftovers into the saddlebags. Sturwood was where Little Mexico, Little India, Little China, and so on were. Every suburb had their own Chinese restaurant. We weren't that dystopian, but this was where the good stuff was.

And I had a hankerin' for some rellenos and barbacoa.

A cat darted out into traffic ahead of us. A few people slammed on their brakes and honked their horns.

Not everyone. The streets in Sturwood weren't busy, anyway. This wasn't one of the richer suburbs. As we wound through rundown single-family homes in varying colors of the rainbow, we shared the road with a handful of other vehicles. One of them blared music, the bass thumping inside my helmet. Men and women guarded the corners in clumps and groups, weapons strapped across their torsos. Guns had been made illegal a few weeks into the new government. They had invaded homes and confiscated them, along with ammo. I remembered rolling my eyes when the conspiracy theorists had blasted anyone who would listen about how that would happen. Of course, the government at that time wouldn't have done that. It had taken a dystopian state for it to occur.

Guns or no, the people of Sturwood were still prepared.

There also wasn't a huge cop presence here, and absolutely no PPE.

"'ey, Momma," a man from one of the corners shouted at us, waving his hand machismo style.

Three cats sat at his feet.

I waved, not sure what was going on with the felines, but I got the sense that he was literally looking out, guarding, not meaning anything rude. He was just saying, *Hey, I see you. I got you.*

His smile told me I'd read him right as he raised his chin in a nod and turned away.

As we made two of our stops picking up packages, we were called out to by several of the people guarding the corners. I waved back to each of them.

There were a lot of cats. I'd never seen so many of them in my life before, not in one place anyway. It was almost as if they'd all left the other suburbs and headed here. They stood with the human guards. They escorted people from their homes to the store and back again.

I tried to remember what cats represented. Aloofness. Sensuality.

Guardianship.

That realization hit me hard. The cats were guarding this town.

Was there a higher para presence here?

"Gracias," an older woman said as she gave me her package.

"Yeah." I smiled and tucked the small box into my backpack.

She snatched my hand, turning me around. "Stay here."

"Huh?" I looked up at her in surprise.

The woman sighed at me and sat down on her front steps, motioning me to join her.

I glanced at Ryder, but she wasn't paying any attention to me. "I'm on a route."

She just nodded. "I know. We gave you that route. Now, sit."

Great, just what I needed. Another woman trying to get to me. "Look—"

She held up her hands in surrender. "We heard what happened last night, niña."

Why would they even care?

"We look out for our own." She put her hand on the step beside her and looked up at me again. "We're offering you a place to live in safety. That is all. We do this for a lot of people."

"And you requested packages be picked up today so . . ."

"So that one of us could talk to you. Let you see what we have to offer. That living here is maybe not so bad an idea. Okay?" She shrugged and got up. "What you do now is up to you." She disappeared back into her house.

For someone who was used to being not seen, this was getting weird.

Three cats ran up to me, mewling. The tabby stopped at my legs as I got back onto the broken sidewalk along the street, and he reached up to my knee.

I wasn't about to just pick him up. I had never been a cat person. Well, I had never been a dog person either. I'd always been a neither person. They didn't speak a language I understood. "Meow" only sounded like "meow."

Ryder pulled off her helmet and frowned at them. "Are you the cat whisperer now?"

I had no idea. "They're everywhere."

Twisting on her bike, she nodded, and then her eyes widened in surprise and alarm. "Uh, O?"

Warmth wrapped around my heart and gave it a little squeeze at the nickname. "Yeah?"

I looked around to see what she was reacting to.

Dozens of cats were converging on us.

Ryder brought her helmet to her head.

"They're not after us. They're guardians."

She paused, frowning at the approaching animals. "They're not attacking us."

Claws found my leg, but not enough to draw blood. I looked into the glowing yellow eyes of the tabby. "Yeah?" I asked, not knowing how in the world I was going to understand what this cat was trying to tell me.

"Something's happening, chica," a man called from the street.

I waved at him with one hand. "Know what?"

He grabbed a shotgun, walking into the street. "This many cats?" He shook his head. "Something big."

People spilled onto the streets, various weapons in their hands—or their hands becoming weapons with claws. One man took his clothes off as he walked and shifted into a bear. Another woman shook like she was a dog sloughing water as black fur sprouted along her neck and over the back of her head, her hands turning into large panther paws.

I realized in that moment that *this* was the reason there were no cops and no PPE. What I didn't understand was how this suburb existed.

That thought was going to have to wait.

I followed the herd of cats, more interested in seeing how this neighborhood handled situations like this than anything else. I wasn't going to join the fight—that was certain. However, several of these cats were clearly visions, so my gift was trying to tell me something.

A large cat with wispy eyes stood at the mouth of an alley, meeting my gaze and crouching, prepared to pounce.

"Here," I called to the people and the cats.

The bear stopped at the mouth, walking through the large vision cat who evaporated and sniffed.

Ryder stepped toward the alley mouth.

A large arm stopped her as the man who'd called to me, telling me something was going on, stepped closer to her. "This man is very dangerous." He shoved orange plugs into his ears. "He controls minds with his words. Without these, you don't go in."

Ryder narrowed her eyes but raised her chin. "Okay," she said, raising her hands in surrender. "We'll stay out here until you need us."

"We won't," he said with a smile, holding his shotgun in both hands and squaring off with the alley mouth. "Stay safe."

I tucked myself close to the concrete building, looking into the alley. Eight people, all wearing blue cowls and masks, guarded a green van with a red rear door, as if readying it for prisoner transport.

The blue cowls were the Witnesses and if they'd gotten into Sturwood to collect people—

The man beside me fired his shotgun, exploding the world with noise. A blast that close to my ears in an alley wasn't a good mix. I really wished I had ear plugs.

The people of Sturwood converged on the people in blue. Soon, it was next to impossible to use a gun, which was good.

Everyone here seemed prepared as if this wasn't the first time Lord Sha—the first time *he* had been by.

"Why do I get the sense something else is going on here?" Ryder asked in my ear, leaning over me to see around the corner.

Why would they extend the invitation? Because it was safer for them, or safer for me? "Someone contacted Jamal to ask me to live here."

Ryder gave me a frank look out of the corner of her eye. "There are too many people using him to get to you."

"Two people." I had to agree, though. "But look at this place." The Witnesses' forces were down to three. "Do you have any idea what it would mean to sleep in peace?" Or were they hoping my abilities would help them stay one further step ahead of the Witnesses? This could be a good thing.

She sighed and shook her head. "You *just* got a door."

I'd forgotten about that. "Maybe we can bring it with us."

My very large vision cat reappeared and yowled, a sound I felt in my soul rather than heard.

"What?" Ryder asked, on alert.

"Something's ha—"

A door opened and more Witnesses spilled out from one of the buildings, adding themselves to the fight, as another group escorted people into the alley and toward the van. The rear door of the vehicle opened, and two kids were shoved inside.

"Why are they taking them?" Ryder asked. "They're Witnesses. They kill paras. Why not just kill them?"

"They're seers?" I didn't know.

"How many damned seers have you met in your entire life?" she asked heatedly. "How many were there last night? Before that? No. I don't know what this is, but this isn't seers." She moved around me to enter the fight.

I reached out to stop her. "You don't have ear plugs."

"I'll be fine," Ryder growled.

The only thing I could add to the fight was visions. What was the point of this attack?

Eight glowing black swords appeared over the van, and a sticky, oozy feeling filled my chest as if I was stuck and couldn't find a way out.

This was a trap. For who, though?

I swallowed, my throat dry.

How would he have known I'd be here? I hadn't known—

Until Jamal had made the decision to send me on this route. That was the point where this moment had been born and a seer could have seen it.

A flute trilled over the noise of the fight as if congratulating me on making the connection.

"October?" a familiar voice said beside me.

I looked down into Jeff's face, surprise ripping through me. "Hey."

"What are you doing here?"

I hadn't been looking for him, so he couldn't have been the bait in *this* trap. "Working. You okay?"

"Yeah," he said. "Until just now."

"You've been *here* this entire time?"

He nodded. "They got Mom here this morning."

I hadn't known, but I was glad. "That's awesome."

"Yeah, well, I think you need to get out of here. So, um, can you go?"

I nodded. "That sounds like a great idea." I pushed away from the corner of the building and took a step.

Someone stopped me with his body. "Hello, again," a familiar, pleasant voice said. "I was so hoping to see you."

Chapter 14

I recognized the voice through the howls and yowls of attacking cats. This was Lord Shadow. But why wasn't he wearing a mask? He just looked like a normal white guy with red hair.

Ryder body-slammed a blue-cowled man into the brick wall of a building to my left as a tabby cat leapt on him and clawed at his face. One of the shifters roared and slammed into another Witness, the pair crashing into a dumpster a few feet away from me.

A cat leapt at Lord Shadow.

I took that as an opener and turned to Jeff. "Get out."

His eyes were wide, and his face was filled with a why-didn't-I-think-of-that look as he turned and ran away.

If Lord Shadow was here and this was a trap for me, then I needed to get out. I also had to hope that whoever he'd been trying to shuffle away in the van—probably Fred Drake, the guy I'd been looking for?—could escape as well. Then, I needed to figure out how to stop being so seer-ably findable.

"Stop," Lord Shadow said, grabbing my arm with his hand.

I didn't acknowledge him. I just pulled away and ran.

"I have Fred," he called.

A smarter person would have kept running.

"I won't keep him around forever. His ability has to be stopped."

Those words got me better than a lasso. I turned to him, the sound of the fight filtering onto the street, but not much more. "What do you want?"

Another cat attacked him with a wild howl.

Lord Shadow grabbed it by the scruff of its neck and growled, "Don't."

The thing yowled in shock as if it'd been stepped on, then ran away as soon as it got out of his grasp.

Three more blue-cowled people stepped out of the shadows beside me, almost literally. It was as if the shadows were doors.

Who was this guy, and what was his ability?

He narrowed his violet eyes as he closed the small distance between us, the cats giving him a wide berth. "Come to me."

"No," I said, stumbling a step back.

The blue-cowled woman on my right looked at Lord Shadow, shook her head, and then moved toward the alley, the other two men following her.

He gave me a slow blink and raised his chin. The challenge seemed to excite him. Then he leaned in as if getting closer to my ear would help. "Come to me," he commanded again.

This time, my feet jerked to obey. I fought the urge, tried to regain control, but it was as if my mind had disconnected from my legs. I stumbled toward him until I was within arm's reach.

He narrowed his gaze. "I recognize you from somewhere."

"I wish I could say the same," I said, backing up, my heart racing. I didn't know how I was able to resist his voice control in general, or why it was that when he made enough of an effort, I couldn't.

I could see into the alley now, though. I wished I could see Ryder in the mayhem, but at least there were more blue-cowled fighters to keep her and the protectors of Sturwood busy.

The cats were staying clear of Lord Shadow. Whatever he'd done to the one had left all of them unwilling to move on him. What else could I use against him?

I waited for my visions to help me.

Meanwhile, Lord Shadow studied me as the fight went on beside us, acting like he had all the time in the world. He steered us to the side as if it were a dance, blocking the view of the fight again.

A flash of memory hit me. This had happened once before, which was what had led me, partially, to hide my abilities for the safety of everyone in my life. My gift had glitched, getting people killed, kidnapped, and maybe worse. I'd thought it'd been me, my fault.

I was better armed now. I knew he was somehow blocking my ability to read him. The only reason I'd found him before was because I'd been looking for Fred—and then, today, I'd followed the cats.

But I *had* been given information on him. My gift was fighting him, trying to skirt around his protections to give me the insight I needed.

Maybe that was the reason he was looking for me. Or maybe he was looking for me because I was one of several who had the seer ability.

The world flashed red as if to tell me that line wasn't correct, and a flute played a rally of low notes.

I didn't know what the music had to do with anything, but red was bad. In my book, it meant that I'd made the wrong guess.

He was targeting me because I could get around his protections.

The red filter turned green.

A smile grew on his lips. "You are so intriguing. You're trying to read me right now, aren't you?"

It had to be like seeing the stars. When I looked directly at them, I sometimes couldn't see them, but I could see more if I looked slightly to the side. I didn't need to know *him*. What did he want?

A rumble filled my soul, echoing off the faces of the buildings around us. A chunk of one of the buildings to my right broke off and crashed beside him. A fire escape screeched beside me, coming undone.

He craned his head forward, unfazed. "What do you see?"

That hadn't been real. He hadn't seen it, so . . .

The Tower. He was seeking demolition, to destroy the world in order to make way for something new.

"Tell me," he commanded.

"The Tower," I whispered, unable to stop myself.

Lord Shadow had the ability to make people do what he said. Not like a siren, but—

Or maybe *exactly* like a siren. A male siren? Had I even heard about that?

Monument pillars rose on either side of him as three golden, interlocked circles glowed at his feet, the single one pointing up.

The reversed Hierophant, tradition turned on its head. He was. . .

The vision disappeared.

I shook myself and tipped my interpretation to the side again. He was a person who didn't believe in following tradition, or felt the need to rebuke it.

The golden rings appeared again only to fade as the upside-down pillars replicated around us like a prison.

"Male sirens aren't allowed, are they?" I asked. It made sense. I hadn't heard of any, and if he was kicking tradition aside, it might be because—

The pillars receded.

This was frustrating! I pulled back again. It could be that any male siren who had been born would have been treated poorly, or in such a way that tradition felt more like a prison than anything else.

"No. They are not."

"Why?"

"Because we are too powerful. Tell me who you are."

"No," I said, feeling the tug of his voice pulling at me, demanding I do as I was told. The last time we'd met, I'd been led by the Knight of Swords—highly intellectual and a champion for justice, but that didn't make sense. "Are you . . ." This didn't look like justice. "Are you protecting these people?"

"*These* people?"

"Paras." Who needed protection.

Lord Shadow snorted. "No."

"Then you're protecting others from us?"

"Yes." He tipped his head to the side and bounced it slightly as if to say, *Kind of.*

"Why? This," I said, gesturing to the world around us, "didn't happen because paras tried to destroy everything. This started because people tried killing paras off and we defended ourselves."

"And this is what your defense looks like." He shrugged. "How many of us have we lost to this fight?"

"Us?" As in norms?

"Is it even worth it?"

"*You're* one of us."

"My point exactly." He shook his head and took a step closer to me.

I backed away from him with each step he took.

His smile flickered with excitement, anticipating the chase. "I know what we're protecting the city from."

How was I going to get myself out of this? Grab a knife and stab him? What would stop him from just telling me not to?

His eyes tightened as he continued his advance.

How was I going to get out of this? I wasn't smarter than him in this instant. I didn't know what his weakness was, but I also wasn't going to just allow him to take me. "Are you protecting the city from people like you?"

His ears pulled back as he hissed an acknowledgment.

Ryder screamed in pain.

A burning need to go to her aid ripped through me, but the best way to help her was to keep Lord Shadow away from her and to not get captured by him at the same time. "Then do the world a favor and take yourself out of the game."

"I was created so I could handle this situation."

Seven irregularly shaped glass cups formed around him, most of them right-side up, one upside down, and each seemingly filled with a liquid that was the same color as the buildings. That was nothing more than an illusion.

The Devil appeared, poking a clawed finger toward one of the cups, giving it a tinging sound and smirked at me.

It only looked like Lord Shadow was succeeding, but the man was easily tempted in other directions. How could I use *that* to my advantage? The vision disappeared, but I didn't need it to come back.

"Messiah complex much?"

"Who *are* you?" he asked.

"I thought you said you recognized me." If he'd seen me the last time, but hadn't known who I was, that was a clue I didn't know how to connect.

Who was he, though? And why was he showing me his face? The Knight of Swords was cunning and smart.

Because he didn't think I'd make it out of there?

Three of the cats around me grew dog faces as they stopped in their fight and looked at me.

A vision in answer to a question directly about him. Now, that was interesting.

But if cats were wearing dog faces, then . . .

His face was a mask, and I hadn't been focused on who Lord Shadow himself was, just who his face belonged to. "Nice mask. Makes me *think* you're showing me your face. Making me a little scared because now you've got to kill me. Nicely played."

He stopped and assessed me. "Your abilities are exactly what I'm looking for."

"For what? To root out more paras? To kill them?"

"To protect our city from them."

"That's not going to happen." What if I asked for guidance to save Ryder and me *from* Lord Shadow? "I'm not going to help you."

How was I going to get out of this situation? And why wasn't he pouncing on me yet?

A golden wheel appeared to my left, large and impressive, divided into sixteen different slices with varying markings on each. It rolled and wobbled, the diamond in the center catching the afternoon sunlight.

A tall, silver woman whose hair flowed around her as if she were underwater steadied the Wheel of Fortune, turning her face toward me.

The Mother of Swords wore my face.

The future was within Lord Shadow's grasp. He was dangerously close to getting what he envisioned, what he wanted, but to get it, he needed my ability to see through situations, through lies and fronts. He needed my singular visionary strength.

The wheel and the mother disappeared and were replaced by a glass man, hanging from one foot.

And he needed me to come of my own free will. It had to be by my choice.

That wasn't likely to happen.

"Think about it." He leaned forward, his hands out, entreating. "Once we clear our city, we can have our freedoms back."

"You mean they can have their freedoms back. Humans."

He winced as he dropped his hands. "Yes. Exactly. Humans can have their freedoms back. The city will be safe again."

If he needed me to come of my own choice, then he wasn't going to attack me. I was safe.

Those around me were not.

Lord Shadow's face shifted into that of a Black man in blue robes, a matching mist expanding around him. A bright golden light warmed his right hand as he stared at me, blinking slowly with his bright, glowing blue eyes.

Was my deck kidding me? The Stranger? I was supposed to see how the darkness of our world had shaped this monster and find a common path? Was my deck freakin' *kidding* me?

Lord Shadow advanced on me, pushing me farther from the fight, and the Stranger disappeared, his own bare face filling the space again. "I need you."

"I know." The sound of the fight had receded. I had to make sure Ryder wasn't captured. I cared about her, but I wasn't sure Lord Shadow knew about that.

"War Hawk and his Supes aren't going to come save you this time."

I had to warn Vance about Lord Shadow's ability to control people with his voice.

I could also get a message to Julie to talk to her mom, because *she* might know Lord Shadow's real identity.

"I know you two are connected somehow. But is it through War Hawk, or Vance Young? I wonder."

I tipped my head and gave him a confused expression. "Who?"

"Mmm." He didn't seem convinced. "You certainly don't disappoint."

"Get to the part where you offer me something I want in exchange for my help."

"Cutting to the quick. How refreshing." His wince said it wasn't. "I will ensure the safety of everyone you care about."

"Oh, thank goodness. I was so worried, what with you not knowing who I am and all."

The street flashed yellow as if warning me to not goad him.

He gave me a smug smile. "I know more than you'd like."

Because he had Parker? "You have nothing to offer me that I want."

"Fred."

"Someone else wants him."

"And you'd willingly let me keep him."

To save us from the future he wanted and keep me out of his clutches? I was his Mother of Swords righting his Wheel of Fortune. In no world was it a good idea for me to willingly go with him. "They'll just have to find a different way to get what they want."

He raised his chin. "Do you know what that is?"

"Do you?"

That earned an impatient sigh, and he looked away, vexed. "If you did, you'd want to agree to work with me."

I had to believe there'd be another way if he decided to kill Fred or if I'd be unable to get him freed. The Wheel of Fortune was a powerful card, and if it was in *his* hands, I had to be careful.

"*He* knows who you are, doesn't he?"

So he could find out about me. "Who?"

Lord Shadow tipped his head to the side. "War Hawk."

"He knows my code name." I didn't actually have one. We'd test driven a few, but none of them had stuck.

"Join me, and I won't have to dig your name out of his head."

"Hey," Ryder barked, advancing on us.

Dang it! I did *not* need him to get his hands on her, but I also didn't need to give him the impression that she meant anything to me.

Lord Shadow sighed petulantly and turned to her. "Yes?"

"Leave her alone," Ryder growled.

He chuckled.

The bear and the panther followed her.

Lord Shadow turned back to me with a growl of his own. "You don't want to make this hard."

"I really don't want to make this easy." I just had to hope I could outsmart him.

The Mother of Swords appeared beside me.

We were facing off against him together. There was hope.

Lord Shadow turned in a flash and grabbed Ryder by the arm. She jerked to defend herself, but he said one word and she stopped. He wrapped his other hand around her throat and whispered something in her ear.

I froze in horror as reality crashed around me louder than the gunshots and sharper than the knives I'd been dodging.

Ryder went still.

Lord Shadow smiled and turned to look at me over Ryder's shoulder, raising a dark eyebrow over his glowing violet eyes. He returned his gaze to her and said something I couldn't hear.

Ryder relaxed.

The bottom of my stomach dropped. I prepared to run.

He gasped and let out a startled sound of pain. I turned toward them again. Lord Shadow's eyes were wide as the purple glow receded. He stared at Ryder in surprise.

She grabbed his arm and pulled it away from her throat, raising her blade.

Almost as one, the blue-cowled men and women pulled away from their fights and knocked Ryder away, surrounding Lord Shadow and moving him back toward the door they'd all flowed from to get here.

Ryder walked toward me, her attention on the escaping army, her knees bent as if ready for anything.

They were no longer interested in us.

Then she gave me a cocky smile and shrugged. "Easy-pe—"

She fell to the ground.

Chapter 15

I had no way of waking Ryder up or getting her out of there, and I had no idea where to even go.

Checking her body, I could only appreciate just how much damage she'd taken in the fight. There were cuts all over her arms, torso, and legs. She had been shot three times—once in the thigh, once in the upper arm, and once in the abdomen.

That one looked like the worst. So, with my heart racing and my hands shaking, I did what I could in the darkening street, trying hard not lose my shit. I'd just had a wit battle with someone who was almost literally holding the city hostage and had managed a draw. The fight was still going behind me, though it was hard to think about them with Ryder's blood warming my hand.

People moved all around me, but they were worried about their own friends and family, trying to get *them* taken care of, pulling them away from danger. No one called out. No one screamed for help. We lived in a world where helping others was a weight no one else could carry if they wanted to survive as well.

Holding the wound, I searched the street for any sign of Lord Shadow. This trap had been for me. I had to assume he wasn't going to just give up because he'd been stabbed. His people were still in the alley, but I didn't see another sign of the great leader himself. Hopefully, he'd been wounded pretty badly, and he'd be down for a bit. I needed time to regroup, to think about how to stay a step ahead of this guy, or at the very least to stop falling into his traps.

I couldn't do that without Ryder, though.

No. I could. If I had to, I absolutely would, but it would be so much easier if Ryder was with me. I'd feel better. I'd be more confident.

I focused on sounds as I held some cloth I'd found pressed to her wound, trying hard not to think about the infection I was likely introducing to her system, fighting to ignore how the blood warmed my cool fingers.

I heard the cats continuing their fight.

I heard people shouting.

I heard a bicycle pedal in on fresh rubber, the buzzing clickety-clack of the tread giving me a sense of ease that didn't belong.

I heard no drones.

I heard no cars or motors of any kind.

The streets in this area were pretty much cleared, and it was probably thanks to the sound of the fight. People had likely cleared out because any threat of danger was something to be cautious of.

I pushed myself through the mechanics of keeping Ryder alive. Rummaging through her saddlebags, I got some actual rags and bandaged the other wounds with one hand, never letting the pressure up on her abdominal wound with the other.

I didn't know what else to do.

"Are you okay?" a woman asked from behind me.

I twisted around in surprise to see who she was. She seemed normal—Hispanic, older than me, though not by much. Her jeans were comfortable looking, her shoes were worn, and her blue-and-white button-down shirt was open to show a plain, white T-shirt beneath. "Who are you?"

Several cats surrounded her feet, some real, some visions.

So, I could probably trust her.

"Melinda Gomez," she said politely but briskly. "I'm a nurse. Do you need help?"

Relief rattled my words as I spoke with a slow exhale. "She's been shot and stabbed."

Melinda reached up and tied her curly, greying hair back into a loose ponytail as she knelt opposite me. "Looks like she put up one heck of a fight."

"We need to get you out of here," another woman said in a thick, lower Kins accent, a jack of diamonds floating over her head as she rolled up on us from down the street.

"Do you have a hospital?" I asked the nurse, wondering where the jack had even come from.

"You, nitwit," the jack said, grabbing my arm roughly. "I'm getting you outta here."

I pushed her arm away. "He's gone, right?"

She nodded, then shook her head and shrugged. "Who the fuck knows?"

"Well, Ryder needs my help," I told the jack. "So. . ." My thoughts were starting to get really sluggish, or maybe they already had been, and I was just then realizing it. I didn't know. But one thing at a time, and Ryder was that thing.

"Mel's got it." The jack of diamonds grabbed my arm. "We're getting out of here."

I twisted from her grasp. "I'm not going anywhere without her."

"She's in pretty bad shape," Melinda said with a frown. Something was going on that she didn't understand. "Suzi, I need help to get her to my clinic."

Suzi shot Melinda a pained look and then turned her attention back to me. "He was after *you*."

I grabbed one of Ryder's arms, not sure exactly what the jack was there for. Was she my other *other* bodyguard? Had Dannika sent her? And could I trust her? No. Dannika only wanted Fred, and Lord Shadow had just admitted he was using

Fred to lure me in. One thing at a freakin' time. "You helping or not?"

The jack glared at me but then gestured to some people behind her.

Three men came in and picked Ryder up, one of them grunting, "She's heavy."

"Muscle, man," Suzi said. "Use it."

I followed Melinda and the three men as they carried Ryder down the street. As we got farther away from where the fight had happened, more and more activity surrounded us, until we reached a gathering of people at the clinic doors.

A man came out of his pawn shop with a black bag that had a red cross on it. He gestured with his head to Melinda.

She gestured behind her to the alley. "Bring the ones that need me. Patch up the rest."

"You got it, lady boss."

Three kids looked around, then darted into the street armed with brooms. A woman stepped out with her dog on a leash, her eyes darting around. The cats were everywhere, prowling, protecting the streets.

It looked like the people in this neighborhood had this system down.

Melinda didn't spare me more than a glance as we got Ryder settled in the run-down but clean clinic, taking up one of the empty beds. I didn't know how to help, so I got out of her way.

Down the hallway and near the nurse's station, the other rooms were filled. People worked together on the wounded like this was an average day.

And maybe it was. If Lord Shadow knew about Sturwood, that the paras were congregating here, and his mission was to rid the city of paras, then Sturwood wasn't a safe place. It was a one-stop-shop for all those who wanted to end para-kind.

Except that Lord Shadow *had been* here and had left empty handed, as far as I could tell. So, maybe it was safer than I wanted to admit. I was rattled. That was evident.

Once in the hallway and in the relative quiet of the clinic, the calm I'd had disappeared. It was like the pressure in the hallway was turned up to block out the noise. My shirt clung to me. My skin was starting to itch where the blood had dried.

Ryder'd been hurt, might even have been killed, all because Lord Shadow had been after me.

My stomach roiled. I stumble-ran to the bathroom and locked the door behind me, leaving breakfast in the toilet as the sounds and visions of the last time I'd lost friends crashed around me. The gunfire. The shouting.

The feel of Gina's blood on my hands as I tried to keep her alive but had to watch her die instead.

Using the coolness of the tiled walls and floors to ground me, I pulled myself out of my memories and into the present. Ryder wasn't Gina. Ryder wasn't human. She was a Valkyrie. I didn't know exactly what that meant, but I had to wager that they were damned hard to kill, being battle angels and all.

I hoped so, anyway.

Pulling myself to my feet, I walked slowly to the sink and washed Ryder's blood off my hands and the door. I surprisingly hadn't gotten all that much blood on my shirt. The knees of my jeans had taken the biggest hit.

By the time I was cleaned up, my hands had stopped shaking, and anger was slowly warming my frozen veins, filling me with a need to strike Lord Shadow down.

Suzi grabbed my arm and pulled me to the side as soon as I was out the door. "Got nothing on pants." She handed me a fresh shirt. "We're getting you outta here."

Where had she gotten this? I didn't ask. I just replaced my shirt right there with no one caring. "I'll be okay." The waiting area filled with cats.

"My ass," the jack said, rolling her eyes at the felines as they meowed and mewled and raised a general fuss. "You get killed, it's my butt on the line."

Now that I had space to breathe, I took her in. She was shorter than me, heavyset, and dressed in men's jeans and boots along with a leather jacket. Her dark hair was pulled back in two buns behind her ears, but it didn't look cute on her. It looked like her hair just wasn't long enough or thick enough to go in a ponytail. She carried a gun at her hip, and knives peeked out of three of her pockets. "Well, you can tell Dannika that Lord Shadow has Fred and he's using him to get to me, so I'm done."

The jack snorted, looking around and shifting uncomfortably. "You tell her that. I'm not gonna."

"It's not worth it."

"Sure, I get it. One horrible person hunting you versus another but remember which one knows who you are. Right?" She leaned in, her arms swaying at her side. "Sky." Tipping her head, she took a half step back, looking around as if she'd just said something that could get us both implicated in a felony.

She wasn't smooth, that was for sure, but she wasn't wrong either. Dannika might not have known who I was when we'd first met, but she'd admitted she'd been the one behind the Wipe and that she was still working actively to keep that information hidden.

Which led me to believe that maybe, just maybe, that information was still around.

Help Dannika find Fred—who was in serious trouble, having been kidnapped by the deadliest person in the city—or remain hidden from said deadliest person and become the target of the second-deadliest person in the city, while allowing an innocent person to be killed or worse.

That last part didn't sit well with me, at all. It chafed at me like someone petting me with a nail brush.

I headed back into Ryder's room to see how she was doing.

Melinda met my gaze, her eyes telling me to leave.

Ryder was breathing.

Without making a fuss, I turned and headed out.

"O," Ryder called to me.

I turned at the door.

Her bloodied hand reached toward me, and her blue eyes blazed. "You're not safe."

I knew that, but what she was really saying was that I needed to actually do something. "On it."

She nodded once, then relaxed onto the blue bed.

A wispy greenish-gold woman with wings along her head appeared in front of me and pressed her cheek against a glowing timepiece before handing it to me. It was a twenty-four-hour clock, but the hour and hand minutes were on the six.

Normally, when this card came up telling me I needed direction, it talked about limiting my decisions to the next twenty-four hours to keep myself from getting too overwhelmed with trying to figure out what to do.

A lot could happen in twenty-four hours. A lot *had* happened. What was I supposed to do? Who was I supposed to go to? I couldn't face Lord Shadow on my own, even though I'd managed to hold my own against him pretty well today. But to take him down, to keep him out of Sturwood, I needed help.

People had already asked me to get involved. Would they make ready partners? Could I trust them? Pearl, I probably could, but would I bring more danger to her doorstep than even she could handle? I had a suspicion that Lord Shadow was hunting me because of her. I didn't know that, but I was no one. Pearl had made a name for herself, and she hadn't done that by being a person on a couch complaining while scrolling social media—even though that wasn't a thing anymore. Senator Armstrong knew her. Dannika did too. Even Jamal, and I was starting to get the idea that maybe he was more involved in all of this.

The wing-eared woman shook the timepiece and the second hand wobbled along the six, twitching as it was forced to stand rigid with the hour and minute hands.

Six hours. I had to focus my view of what I needed to do in the next six hours.

The green-gold woman nodded, her dark wings flexing along her ears.

Okay. Okay, I could do that.

Rolling my head on my neck to pop it, I let my mind run down the overwhelming list of options. What did I *need* in the next six hours?

Well, the man I'd been sent to find had been found. Kind of. At the very least, we knew who had him. All I really had to do was set my mind to finding Fred, which would tell the seers, which would give Lord Shadow the trap to set. Again.

And hopefully this time, we'd be ready for him.

With ear plugs and a small army? Fear flared on a thin thread through me.

Lord Shadow. He'd found me. Twice. He'd killed my friends. Twice.

I glanced at the door, willing Ryder to live.

Okay. Not killed. Wounded my friends.

I needed protection.

Dannika Love. Her jack was here, acting as my bodyguard, though how much longer would that last for? When would Dannika be tired of me? How far could I trust her?

Not far.

Okay, fine. Vance, then.

No. He had his own vigilante thing going on that I'd already gotten mixed up in once before, and nearly died as a result. Well, no, I hadn't even come close, but others had. I'd done that. I didn't doubt that he meant well, but I didn't think I could risk trusting him with my life.

Senator Armstrong?

We'd worked together before, and we'd done okay. At least I knew where she was coming from, but the work we'd done before was the reason I was on the fence about her. When would she be done with me? In her game, when would I be a piece she was willing to sacrifice?

What did I want to do?

The woman with the timepiece popped up again, the clock hands still twitching on the six, fighting to be released.

What did I want to do in the next six hours?

A bright white globe started as a speck of dust and grew big enough to block out the glass front door. A sword swung out of nowhere and stabbed into the globe.

Right. Every action had a consequence. I had to be careful of what I decided. Action could be bad. Doing nothing could be bad.

But the time to do something new was now.

It was time to make a decision. Shit or get off the pot. It was go time.

What exactly did that look like for a person whose greatest skill was seeing things no one else could?

What could I do in the next six hours that would make a glimmer of difference?

Melinda came out, tossing her blue gloves in the step-open metal trash can beside the door. "She heals fast."

Relief welled through me. "Good."

"You should move to Sturwood," Melinda said matter-of-factly. "Most of us are here for obvious reasons."

"But you were attacked."

"He chose one of our few blind spots and deployed tactics to keep our guardians from being able to see him. It won't happen again."

"He's after me."

She shrugged. "All the more reason."

"He will attack here again if I move here."

"And we'll be ready. Look," she said, putting her hands on her hips and breathing like she was recovering from a light workout, "when he first started attacking us, people died, but we're getting smarter. We might not be five steps ahead of him, but we're taking out his people faster than he can strip their minds. And he didn't kill any of us. Wound us? Plenty, sure. Kill us?" She shook her head, her mouth turning downward. "We're safe."

"You're not worried that they'll trap you here?" Senator Armstrong's dam still worried me.

"We're stronger together."

And easier to take out.

What could *I* do in the next six hours?

I needed trust.

I couldn't trust Dannika. I couldn't endanger Pearl, even inadvertently. I didn't believe Vance wouldn't push me.

Could I trust the senator?

I knew what I needed to do—I felt it in my gut. I needed to talk to her, tell her what I'd found and figure out what she meant to do with all these people living in Sturwood. Were they in danger? Were they safe?

"Keep her safe," I told Melinda.

"Of course." She frowned deeper but stepped out of my way.

The feather-eared woman dispersed as I walked through her to the door.

Then the jack stopped me with a hand to my chest, not quite touching me. "What the fuck are you doing?"

"I have an errand to run."

"On my ass."

I didn't know how to respond, so I just kept going, the cats moving out of my way like water to Noah.

"Fucking, shit," Suzi cursed before her stompy boots thudded after me. She took the lead through the glass doors and stopped when we were on the sidewalk, the sun glinting on her dark hair and making it almost red. "Where are we going?"

I opened my mouth to tell her I didn't need to go anywhere with her.

She pulled out keys and dangled them off her hand, which was covered in a black leather fingerless glove. "*You* got a car?"

I didn't like allowing Dannika to know what I was doing and who I was doing it with. What if this jack was here not to protect me but to keep tabs on me?

The asphalt of the street shimmered and turned a light beige, rising and taking on the shape of a rock bridge. A glowing portal shone to my right.

With a sigh, I accepted the message offered and pushed my fear aside to build new bridges. "I need to see Senator Armstrong."

She didn't flinch. She didn't wince. She just nodded and led the way to her rust-ridden blue sedan. The interior smelled like old cigarettes and must. "Not a word," she said as she started the engine.

Holding up my hands, I kept quiet.

She drove in silence, and I was okay with that. There was no resistance at the gate, which made sense if they were controlled by Dannika and Suzi worked for her. Well, technically, so did I.

As I stared up at the tops of the skyscrapers of Lista Point, a bridge appeared, wispy orange light dancing away.

I had nowhere to retreat to. I couldn't go back. I could only move forward.

The message did make me feel better, more confident. I didn't want to go backward. It didn't matter if knowing that Dannika controlled the city made me feel better or scared—it was just what it was. All that mattered was that I was now connected to this world, to Dannika's and Senator Armstrong's. For better or for worse, this was where I needed to be.

Suzi didn't get out when she stopped in front of Senator Armstrong's building. "I'll be here when you're ready."

I nodded and exited the vehicle.

The receptionist out front waved me in. "She's expecting you," she said with a smile as she answered the phone.

I'd forgotten how nice that felt, to be recognized and allowed in.

When I reached her office, I was greeted by a sea of people crammed into the large space.

"Go," Senator Armstrong said. "What are you waiting for?"

They trickled out.

I waited before going in, not wanting to fight the current. "What was all that?"

Senator Armstrong flicked her dark eyebrows before getting a drink. "Want one?"

"Sure?" Now that I was here, though, what was the plan? I needed to see if I could trust her. How did I go about figuring that out?

She shot hers back before pouring two more and handing me one. "You did good, Sky."

"You—"

"Found the van? Yes. They're safe. Most of them. We're still missing one."

"Fred. The real person you're looking for."

She looked at me in surprise. "Yes."

"I know who has him."

She took in a deep breath. "The Witnesses."

"Yup. The leader is using him as bait."

"For what?"

"For who."

She was quiet for a moment, then shook her head. "Oh."

Did that change things for her? Was she still going to use me even though it was endangering me?

"You know Fred's name."

I nodded, and she latched on to my gaze. "Tell me where she is, Sky."

"No."

She pressed her fingertips to the desktop and bowed her head. "I really wish you hadn't said that."

Chapter 16

"**S**enator—"

She narrowed her dark eyes. "Victoria."

For as long as I'd known her, I'd never called her by her first name before. What did she think? That with that familiarity, I'd suddenly think we were friends and I'd give her the secrets of the city? "I can't tell you."

She ran her tongue along the front of her teeth. "Can't or won't."

Can't, really, but now that she was asking . . . "Both."

She glared at her glass.

"Senator—"

"Victoria."

Was she threatening me or offering me friendship?

An onyx scythe sliced through the air between us, leaving a ghostly trail of dark vision smoke in its wake.

Death. That could be ominous, except that the person holding that blade was a buxom woman in an *I Dream of Genie* outfit with the planet Earth floating behind her. She stared at me in challenge.

Death being wielded by The World. Interesting, but that only meant that the old ways were gone. That door was closed, and there was no opening it again. The way Senator Armstrong and I had dealt with each other in the past was over. We were both masters of our own parts of this new world that we'd helped build, and if Death and The World were riding together, then it was time for us to move forward differently than we had before.

A white sphere with a sword stabbed into it appeared beside Senator Armstrong's head, letting me know it was time to make a choice, but that this choice—choosing to use her given name and walk down the path she was offering—would be a decisive one.

A second sword slid into place, glowing orange with warmth. This one challenged me to find courage.

Courage wasn't my problem, though if anyone had met me in the last six months, they would have disagreed. I just didn't want to be stupidly courageous. Again. Taking the direction my deck offered, I pulled on my determination and focused on the success I needed. Could I trust her? That was what I needed to learn.

Biting both lips, I faced her. "Victoria."

Her eyes widened with a curious yet hesitantly pleased expression as she faced me, picking up her drink. "Sky."

"October. For real."

"Duly noted. For real," she said, her tone open and inflecting upward.

"Why did you want me to find that bus full of people?"

"You know about Fred."

"I know what I've been told."

"By Dannika."

I nodded.

The Stranger appeared beside Victoria, but as a woman this time, still black, still swathed in robes, still bald, her face blank, waiting to guide me through to the truths I needed to pay attention to so I could get a better understanding of the real woman sitting across from me.

Victoria leaned back, assessing me and the situation. "You're reading me, aren't you?"

"I have to." A thread of guilt rose inside me, but I pushed it down.

She nodded, looking away, biting the inside of her lips. "Fine." She kicked off her heels, went to the office doors and locked them, then returned to her desk and rang her admin. "Joy, I'm not to be disturbed."

"Of course, Senator," Joy said.

Disconnecting the call, Victoria took one of the chairs in front of her desk and moved it so it faced the other.

I mirrored her actions so we sat opposite each other.

She cradled her drink for a long moment, then nodded. "I'm afraid of the world we're creating."

The Stranger folded her hands in front of her teal robes and nodded solemnly.

Victoria was being honest, but she was dancing a tight rope with the truths she offered. "What are you planning to do with the paras in Sturwood?"

Her eyes widened as she looked up at me, startled.

The Stranger's robes flashed magenta, then a purple-ish blue, before returning to a silvery teal.

Compassion, justice, and then a glamoured open communication.

"What do you mean?"

"I mean, Victoria, that I know you're using Dannika's security gates to move people from certain burbs to Sturwood."

"Where they're safe."

The Stranger's robes flashed blue in trust.

"Until when?" I asked, because I didn't buy it. Not a hundred percent.

Now the robes darkened until they were nearly black.

Victoria sat for a long moment, planning to hide something based on the shade of the Stranger's robes.

"That's what I thought." I hadn't realized until that moment how desperately I'd wanted to be able to trust her, to believe that the work we'd done together in the past hadn't been a complete waste of time.

She closed her eyes, her shoulders tightening.

The Stranger held up a hand, a frown furrowing her brow as her robes shimmered with a rainbow array of color before settling with a dark purple. Wisdom.

"I want to free Kins City," she said finally.

Shock hit me like a fist to the chest. "What do you mean? Like war? Like what we—"

She held up a hand to stop me. "No. Just—" She swallowed and tried again. "What we're doing is wrong. How we're treating everyone is wrong. The Confederate States are able to keep paras in their own towns, and everyone's safe. If *they,* of all people, can figure out how to live with paras, then we certainly should be able to as well."

"This isn't the eighteen hundreds, Victoria, and we're not talking about simple segregation." We were living in a prison state.

"Do you *really* think we've evolved since then? We haven't." She looked away. "You might have grown up mostly white—"

I recoiled from the obvious insult, and it hurt. It did. I knew I was hiding from my heritage, but it was just so much easier that way. I could live my life without the weight of a second language or . . . you know, being the "Mexican" of the group.

"I wasn't that lucky. There's no way to hide this." She gestured to her brown arm. "So, I owned it. I see the world around us. I've felt it. And I'm—" She rolled her eyes and gnashed her teeth as she looked away. "I'm not going to stop trying to make it better, to make it easier on me."

"It?"

The World woman appeared on the other side of Victoria, walking in place as if on a treadmill, an unfelt wind blowing her blue-and-white, multipaneled dress around her long legs and bare feet as her dark hair danced around her head.

Victoria was trying to change the world.

I didn't want to be a part of that. *That* was a fight we couldn't win. I rose from my chair.

"Stop," Victoria said, her word firm, her tone soft, nearly a question.

I went still in midmotion.

Death's scythe appeared in The World's hands again.

Running was the approach of the version of myself I didn't like. I couldn't keep walking that path, but I wasn't going to stay here if I knew I couldn't trust her. No way was I going to lose my new friends this time. I wasn't going to endanger everything Pearl was building, either. I needed help to go up against Lord . . . yeah. I had to move forward with people I could trust.

"I know why you ran the last time, October. I don't agree with it, but I understand it."

I'd gotten three people killed, eight people taken never to be seen again, and three more had been gravely wounded, one of whom was now in a wheelchair. And I was fairly certain that Parker was in Lord—his control, which meant I could save her.

Maybe. Hopefully. Maybe.

I'd been confident in my ability to see things before they happened the last time, and that hadn't helped us. My gift wasn't great for what we were facing.

"There's something bigger going on," she said. "You were always good. There was a reason I kept you on staff. You could read people better than anyone I ever knew. But something happened the day you disappeared."

How did she not know? "I was out with some vigilantes."

She nodded like that was something she knew.

"I went up against the leader of the Witnesses. He lured me into a trap. Killed some of us, took more, crippled one of my friends."

"I didn't know." She gave a disgusted look and sipped her liquor.

It hadn't made the headlines. Para crimes never did. Without social media, there was no way to get the real story out. And she wasn't para, so no one would have told her.

I took a sip of my drink. I didn't really like it. It was bitter and burned all the way down my throat. But, you know, whatever. It numbed a little, so that was okay. I'd had a . . . tough day. To put it mildly. My nerves were strung tighter than a harp string.

"The leader of the Witnesses has a protection over him that keeps people like me from being able to find him."

"That's why he's targeting seers."

"Maybe."

She flicked her eyebrows and looked away, taking in a deep breath and releasing it. "Fine. Yeah, well. That makes sense. I've thought the person I'm tracking down has that ability. To see the future."

"And what does any of that have to do with Lady Dun?"

"She's got a safe harbor, and that's good, but how safe? What kind of protections does she have?"

"Is that really what you're after?"

The Stranger studied Victoria for a moment, her robes shifting to a gold color.

Maybe Victoria was being honest in her concern. Maybe she really did care.

"Yes."

Alarm slammed over The Stranger's face as she turned angry eyes to me, her robes flashing into a nearly glowing dark red.

"Are you sure about that?" I asked, telling her in my tone that I knew she was lying.

She bared her teeth and flexed her fingers around her glass. "You've gotten better at this. Dangerously better."

I shrugged.

The senator released a tight breath, clamping her lips to her teeth for a moment. "No."

The Stranger didn't relax, though her hackles lowered. Her eye still twitched as she stared daggers into Victoria.

"Pearl was supposed to help me rebuild something for paras to live in here in Kins City. She has. . . an ability that's very. . ." She took a ChapStick tube off her desk and opened and shut it, the pop-click-pop-click filling the space between her pauses. ". . . beneficial in creating things others don't want you to build."

I wasn't going to tell her that Pearl had created a place where paras were safe. It just wasn't in New Kins. But knowing her ability and her connection to the senator, I now wondered if this was the reason Lord—his name was so dumb—was hunting Pearl.

Nah. That was a stretch.

"We had a plan, Pearl and I. I gathered the people. Dannika would relocate them. Pearl would keep them safe." Victoria raked her thigh with her fingertips. "In every group, we had a seer to keep them one step ahead of dangers."

"It wasn't enough that you and Dannika controlled the gates."

She released a surprised breath. "You have been busy." She ran her tongue along her lips as if forgetting she had the ChapStick. "No. That's how we discovered what the Witnesses are really after. When some of the groups go missing and their bodies are found, the seer is always gone."

"Gone?"

"We haven't recovered a single one of them."

That wasn't telling me what she really wanted with Fred, though I supposed that was a moot point by now. Fred was likely dead, and that avenue was gone. She'd *said* she'd wanted to take back Kins City, but she couldn't do that if paras were fleeing and finding sanctuary elsewhere. It didn't make sense that she'd need someone with Fred's ability to meet her true intentions.

My focus had been to see her intentions behind Fred, because that was who she'd hired me to find. Her focus was on finding out where Pearl was. Had that been her intention all along?

"I need Pearl's help in finding the missing seers."

"Not Fred?"

Her eyes dodged, searching for something in the space over my head. "And Fred."

The Stranger's robes flared red.

Lie. "Why Pearl?"

"She's the most powerful seer we have. She's more powerful than you. She was able to create a place and hide it."

Using portal magic, and I didn't understand how reading signs could have helped her create a door between two worlds. "Stop looking for her."

Victoria glared as she looked away.

The Stranger robes remained a seething red.

"I'll help you find the missing seers."

"Out of the goodness of your heart?"

Not even. "Because Lord Shadow's hunting me."

An alarm sounded in the room with a high-pitched flute trill.

Oh, crap! I shouldn't have said his name. But I should be safe here. Right? How? What was I thinking. This was a huge mistake.

She sat up straighter in her chair, concern settling in her features. "Where's Ryder?"

"Injured and healing."

"And you're here alone?"

"He's injured. He's licking his wounds."

"And not alone. He could strike out against you."

"I'm being careful."

Victoria studied me as she sipped her drink.

I wasn't going to have any more of the whiskey. It just wasn't that pleasant. I liked the effect, kinda, but not the taste.

"Did you get what you needed?"

I didn't know. "I needed to know if I could trust you."

"And can you?"

"Nope."

The Stranger nodded her agreement, keeping her gaze fixed on the senator.

The look on Victoria's face shook with surprise. "I—" She gave a ghost of a chuckle. "I don't understand."

"I don't know what's going on with you, but you're not being honest. You're herding paras into Sturwood, and they're going because it's easier to live there. There aren't any drones. No PPE. And no other choice."

Victoria nodded with a shrug. "I made it safe for them."

"Great. But what's your real agenda? Because it isn't to protect them. I asked if you meant to protect them, and you lied. Badly."

"I didn't—"

The Stranger's hackles rose.

Victoria closed her eyes and tipped her head to the side, twisting it around as if popping it. She looked up at the ceiling before turning her gaze to me again. "I'm tired of the world we're in."

The stranger's robes shifted to blue, but her face didn't relax.

Well, at least she was being honest. "Is Sturwood your army?"

She didn't answer.

"Do they know that?"

Victoria's eyes pinched with worry and concern as she turned to me.

The Stranger frowned, the anger erased from her face.

"We're not a tool to use at your whim, Victoria."

Silence filled the office as Victoria's expression shifted minutely, the concern fading into angry fear.

I couldn't believe I'd almost wanted to believe I could trust her. "Pearl made a good decision in separating herself from you."

The Stranger shrugged at me and folded her hands in front of her, calm radiating over her.

So, I waited. I raised the glass to my lips, smelled the burning alcohol and set it back on my leg untouched.

"What do you need from me to gain your trust?" Victoria asked finally.

The Stranger tipped her head as if to tell me that if I pushed any harder, I'd be pressing my luck.

I agreed. "I don't know." I set the glass on the table. "I can't."

"Trust me," she clarified.

I shook my head.

"You could use me."

"Is that what you offered Dannika?"

Her head wobbled in an absent nod. "We have a bond of mutual use." She met my gaze unapologetically. "Sometimes, that's the best you can hope for."

Silent as always, The Stranger agreed.

Victoria pressed her fingertips to her forehead. "This Lord Shadow seems to be the person I'm after."

The flute trill shrilled through my head again.

"Don't use his name out loud. Seers."

Victoria waved me off. "Give me what information you can about him, and I'll give it to my guys."

The Devil crawled out of the senator's computer screen and preened on her desk.

"Be careful who you tell." The Devil was pretty much what you'd think he stood for. Duplicitous and deceitful. If he was crawling out of her computer, Lord Shadow was a part of her inner work situation, someone she trusted.

She glanced at her desk and frowned, then nodded slowly. "Okay. I will only tell those I trust."

The Stranger held up her hands as if to say she was done here, then disappeared in vision dust.

That meant I should be as well. "Are you an ally we can rely on?"

The Devil looked between us, interested and intrigued to hear what she had to say.

She nodded, biting her lips. "I really want to be, October. I really do."

The Devil shrugged, looking bored.

She opened her mouth to say something else, but the door burst open, and Suzi plowed through.

"You're not answering," the jack said, five wands glowing brightly on the door beside her.

"Suzi?" the senator asked.

"Vick. Hey," Suzi said uncomfortably before turning to me. "PPE." She grabbed for my hand and dragged me out of the room. "We're leaving. Now."

Chapter 17

F ive swords floated around the elevator door.

"Take the stairs!" I shouted.

Suzi didn't hesitate. She darted to the right, expecting me to follow.

Which I did, because I wasn't dumb, and I didn't have a death wish.

Victoria followed, shouting over the office, "Why are there PPE agents here? Get Henry on the phone. Now!"

I wasn't going to wait. Hopefully, the senator would be able to provide some sort of distraction.

"October," she called after me.

I paused at the stairwell and glanced back.

"I didn't know."

I believed her, but I darted down the stairs after Suzi without further pause.

"They'll be in the stairwell soon enough," the woman shouted up to me over her stompy boots. "We need a strategy."

The Five of Swords appeared again at the next door. "Keep going."

That wasn't a strategy though. The Five of Swords held a special meaning. I'd won, and this was the defeat I was facing for *having* won.

What the hell had I—

Lord Shadow. I'd defeated Lord Shadow—I mean, kinda. He'd been forced to retreat, and that was good. That was a win. Right?

It had to be.

And this was the defeat that came from winning?

Fuck. We'd both said his name in that meeting, tipping off the seers, and instead of sending the Witnesses, whom we'd already defeated and who probably couldn't gain access to Senator Armstrong's building, he'd sent someone who *could*.

Lord Shadow had connections to the PPE.

Fuck my life.

As we came to the fourth-floor landing, the door lit up with a golden-geared wheel.

I ran to it. "Here, here, here."

Suzi stopped midway down the next flight. "You sure?"

The wheel dimmed and hummed in a way my soul felt but my ears couldn't hear. "Yeah." Why was the wheel dim? This was the sign of luck and . . .

Right timing. It was telling me to hold.

I pressed my ear to the door.

Someone shouted on the other side. A few moments later, a ding came from the elevator.

The geared wheel glowed a bright gold.

I nodded at Suzi and opened the door, slipping inside and easing it closed behind us.

The door to the stairwell somewhere below opened, and boots stomped upward as men shouted.

Damn.

The Fool tripped through the closed stairwell door and looked at me with a lopsided smile. He brandished his top hat and bowed, gesturing to his right.

Yeah. Sure. We needed to get out of there, not have a freaking tea party. I just had to hope that he wasn't going to tell us to jump off a ledge. Literal leaps of faith weren't something I wanted to entertain, since this wasn't the Matrix. Physics still applied in this reality.

He skipped ahead of us at a somewhat leisurely pace.

Suzi widened her dark eyes at me, silently pushing me to move faster.

I wished I could, but The Fool was going at his own freaking pace.

The golden gear wheel appeared on the elevator doors, glowing, and The Fool stopped at them and gestured grandly.

The office was cordoned off into cubbies. The people inside were on computers and phones. It looked so pre-war, it was eerie. However, with everyone busy, no one noticed us.

The elevator doors opened, The Fool went in, and I followed.

Suzi gave me a pained expression as if asking me if this was the way I wanted to die.

It wasn't. But . . .

I shrugged at her.

She got in, and the doors closed. The elevator went up.

Well, crap.

I glared at The Fool. Was this really his big idea?

He just grinned at me and pointed to the panel of buttons.

One button glowed a bright gold. The button to the top floor.

Of course it was.

I closed my eyes, ruing the day I'd decided to awaken my gift. Then I pressed the button for the roof.

"Oh, fuck off on my ass, seriously?" Suzi demanded.

I shrugged helplessly and shook my head. "I'm sorry." I really, *really* hoped The Fool wasn't going to tell us to actually step off the side of the building. If so, I was seriously ignoring him. There was no way in anywhere I'd do that. Ever.

I trusted my gift and my connection with my decks, but no. Not ever.

The Fool meant for me to trust my gut, not to take a physical leap.

However, as we continued toward the top floor and probably the roof, with only the sound of the cables lifting us to our inevitable doom to break the silence, I questioned my devotion to my gift. It was *so* much stronger now than it had ever been before. And that was probably due to the fact that it'd been shut off for a long time, which was good. Really good.

But was I really okay with putting this much faith into something that could get me killed?

A rainbow-colored winged monkey appeared, grabbing Fortune's Wheel off the button to the roof and sticking it in his mouth, biting down on it.

I scowled at him. The Dream Thief gave me a wide-eyed monkey look that told me to stop listening to the old doubt. I wasn't the same person who'd turned off her gifts out of fear. I was different now. Stronger. The only way I wouldn't make it out of this situation was if I fed the fear and allowed my actions to be guided by it.

Fine. I pushed my fear back—though not away, because it was like a fire raging inside me that refused to be put out—and told myself to just keep my eyes open. It was the best I could do.

The Dream Thief morphed into a raven, Fortune's Wheel still in his beak. He looked around the elevator cab with glowing golden eyes that exuded a wisdom I wished I had. But I took the courage the raven offered and prepared myself as the elevator slowed and then settled.

"So," I said, breaking the silence. "Vick, huh?"

Suzi grunted. "Sometimes, women like her like to slum it with women like me, and I ain't afraid to make a buck."

I struggled to picture Suzi as a prostitute. Maybe I was interpreting that wrong, but then again, maybe I wasn't. "Okay."

She pulled out a knife that had been sheathed at the small of her back, then pulled on her head to stretch her neck. "This is gonna suck ass."

I hoped it wouldn't. "They might not have made it up here yet."

She grunted.

The elevator doors opened to a wide hallway with doors along either side. A bulletin board with room numbers showed that there were mostly lawyers on this floor.

Great.

The Fool went to the left, pointing with a skip to the brown sign that read *Roof Access*.

Suzi growled but took the lead. "You better not get me killed."

"I will try my best."

The Fool stumbled to the side as she pushed past him. He looked affronted and shook himself, giving me a comical stare as if asking me if I was going to just let her do that to him.

Of course I was. She couldn't even *see* him.

The corridor continued to be empty as we found the door to the roof and stepped into another stairwell.

The booted feet of the PPE stomped their way up.

I opened the door labeled *Roof Access* and met another half flight of stairs. Suzi pushed past me as I closed the door behind me, separating us from the approaching boots. She tried the next door.

It was locked.

Oh, great. "Can you open it?" I whispered.

She gave me a do-I-look-like-I-have-a-key look, then rolled her eyes, stashed her knife, and pulled out some tools and started working on the lock.

Well, I guessed she *did* have a key to the lock. Sort of.

I needed a lookout but didn't want to offer myself up, so I sent The Fool.

His shoulders slumped, but he moved to the corner, where he could look down into the stairwell, his head and shoulders slipping through the closed door.

Oh, closed door.

I went back down the stairs as quietly as I could and flipped the deadbolt back, pushing the doorhandle lock in.

The Fool poked his head back in, looked at what I'd done, and nodded, pointing to the door and gesturing at it with his fingers splayed.

Then the door to the main stairwell banged against the wall right next to me, and I nearly let out a startled exclamation.

The Fool motioned for me to be quiet as his clothes morphed into a long cloak. His hair receded until he was bald, and an I-want-to-suck-your-blood mustache appeared on his upper lip with a thin triangle pointing toward his chin.

Thank goodness.

The Magician was adaptable and could get us out of there. I'd be much more willing to follow him to the roof than The Fool. The Magician was calculating, present—he made plans.

Right now, he gave me a look with his bright eyes that told me to stop.

I held up my hands in surrender.

Someone tried the handle. "Locked," a male voice said on the other side. Footsteps headed away.

I'd bought us time, but I didn't doubt that they'd be back. Probably. Hopefully not, but in all likelihood they would.

I crept back up the stairs.

"Nice," Suzi said, glancing at the door below us, still working.

"Doesn't this usually go faster?" I whispered.

"On TV? Sure."

It wasn't a skill of mine, so I just backed off.

The Magician stepped through the door at the base of the stairs and disappeared.

Suzi made a noise and smiled, putting her tools away quickly and pulling her knife back out. "Let's see where we can go on the roof."

Closing the door quietly behind us, I made sure to lock the door again. With the locks on this side, I had to guess that people weren't supposed to be up here, which meant there wouldn't be a fire escape or, well, anything that could help us. But we might be able to hide up there for a bit and then slip down after the PPE were gone.

We just had to stay out of drone sight until then.

The Magician appeared in front of me and motioned wildly toward the right, herding me to hide.

I grabbed Suzi's arm and dragged her behind me.

We'd barely managed to cram ourselves into a cranny between the wall and some big rectangle thing before a drone buzzed into the area.

Suzi and I went completely still. Most of the drones were fitted with motion sensors, which allowed them to track people better. I didn't know if this one had the ability to read heat signatures or not. If that was the case, we were in trouble.

Suzi pressed something on her wrist.

The drone turned away from us, paused for a moment, and then flew away.

Suzi maneuvered out of there and stood on the roof.

"You can control the drones."

She shrugged and looked around. "Okay. Now what?"

I didn't know. Getting out of the small space was harder than getting into it. The concrete wall kept gripping my clothes, and I wasn't entirely sure I'd make it out of there without more than a few rips and holes.

The Magician held up a finger, his dark eyebrows raised.

Was he pointing to the sky, or was he telling me he needed a moment?

The sound of something rippling in the wind hit my ears.

I looked up.

And saw an angel dive bombing us.

I raised my arm to cover my face—for what reason, I didn't know—and tried to keep my scream to myself.

Ryder landed with ease beside me. "Are you all right?"

My heart was still beating wildly, but yeah. I was fine. Much better now— a wave of relief washed over me at the sound of her voice. Was that her Valkyrie affect? "You were shot."

"I heal quickly." She appraised me with a quick up-and-down. "You left without me."

"You're the one who told me I wasn't safe, and I didn't go alone. I took Suzi." I hooked my thumb over my shoulder.

Ryder leaned over to take Suzi in. Then she stepped to the side and walked toward the other woman, her posture making it look like she was going to kill her.

"Whoa, whoa, whoa! Ryder! We're cool. We're cool."

"You're on the roof, and your heart rate states that you are not *cool*."

"PPE showed up," I told her, moving to stand between Ryder and Suzi. "I'm pretty sure it was *him* who heard us talking about him."

"The seer trap."

"Yeah. And now we know that he is connected to the PPE, because they came instead of the Witnesses."

"And we're standing here because?"

"There are two locked doors between us and them."

Ryder tipped her head. "Who led you to the roof?"

"My visions. I'm guessing because of you."

She turned and looked at me. "Do you trust her?"

"She saved my life." So, sure. For now. "But she works for Dannika."

"Hey," Suzi said. "Girl's gotta eat. I'm not sayin' I have expensive tastes, but even the poor tastes cost money I ain't got without a paycheck. And Dannika pays."

Clenching her jaw and breathing out of her nose, Ryder bowed her head to stretch her back. Then she tossed her hair back and shook out her shoulders, white wings sprouting out of her back. She wrapped an arm around my waist and drew me close with a sharp tug. "Hold on tight."

"You've got to be fuckin' kiddin' m—" Suzi said, but her words were cut off when Ryder grabbed her waist and tucked her close as well. Suzi looked at me with wide eyes, then grabbed fistfuls of the Valkyrie's shirt.

Ryder leapt into the sky, her wings pumping the air in powerful strokes.

I wrapped my arms around her neck and tried to get one leg around her waist, but I ended up just kicking Suzi in the knee, so I stopped and held on with my arms alone.

I couldn't breathe. All I saw was the tiny, tiny buildings of the big, big city shrinking far, far below us.

And then clouds—literal clouds—wrapped around us, cutting off the view.

I closed my eyes and buried my face in Ryder's shoulder. I knew—I *knew* she was strong. I knew she could fly.

But I had never flown like this a day in my life—well, the one time when we'd flown to the roof and back, but that'd been nothing compared to this. I didn't even like going on ladders with more than three steps. Heights were not for me. Being in the clouds outside of a plane? This was freaking nuts!

We began our descent, and I didn't let her go. I didn't peek.

Our feet touched the ground, and I still didn't move.

After a minute of shaking, I let her go and took a step back.

Suzi did too, looking over at me and giving me a flickering smile. A chuckle escaped her lungs, choked off by a sob, followed by another chuckle.

I joined her, feeling a bit wavy emotionally and physically. "We're safe."

I heard Jamal sigh. "No. We're not. Baby girl, we need to talk."

Chapter 18

I thought I'd been handling things pretty well for the most
part, but I was done. I'd had my fill. I was ready to go
back to my apartment with the empty refrigerator that I paid
to power for no good reason and just sit in a chair in the
candlelight and relax. Heck, for that matter, I was ready to step
through my closet door and just hide for a minute or two in a
place where I knew I was safe. Even people gung-ho to change
things and make life better for others needed a jeez-dang rest.

But I pushed my weary irritation aside and turned to Jamal.

His white tattoos blazed a little brighter as he stepped out
in dark slacks and a tight-fitting vest that covered his figure
with finesse. Silver chains adorned the lapel and a pocket on
his vest, and his bald head was painted with eyeliner in designs
that added to the white tattoos already there.

"What's going on?" I asked.

He gestured to me to follow as he stepped back through the
blue door that led from the alley.

"I gotta go," Suzi said crisply. "You good?"

"Yeah," I said. "Thank you."

"Yeah, whatever pays the rent, you know." She turned and
left, grumbling. "Wish I had my damned car."

I followed Jamal through the door.

He glanced at me, rolling his eyes dramatically under long,
double-layered lashes. "Whatever hornets' nest you shook, you

brought the PPE down on us. They tried to shut us down. Again."

Lord *Him* had to be getting closer to finding my identity. First the senator's, and now here?

Jamal shook his head. "They didn't have your name."

"The protections aren't good enough." I was still upset with myself for slipping up earlier today. "He can hear us when we say his name."

Jamal blinked, and then he nodded, looking thoughtful. "Okay."

"What happened out there?"

"Did you know about Sturwood?" I asked.

He shrugged, his hands busy pulling out candles and bags from underneath the counter. "You're gonna have to be a little more with the details than that."

"That paras are gathered there."

"Oh, that." He placed a chicken foot on the counter and lit a black candle, muttering something under his breath. "Yeah. That I knew."

"They were attacked," Ryder said grimly, coming up behind me. "By him. It was a trap for her."

Jamal looked at me in surprise, his eyebrows raised. "That is twice in as many days, baby girl. Why you?"

I shrugged, but I knew. "I can see through his protections."

His hands went still. "You can what?"

Ryder leaned on the counter, the heat of her body warming my arm.

Resisting the urge to find more of her warmth, I nodded. "Things are different now that my gift is back. It interacts with me. I can ask it questions, and it gives me answers."

"Still seer-ing symbols, though, right?" Jamal asked.

"Yeah. Still that, but they're giving me insight that I wouldn't have had otherwise. Like, with Victoria—"

Jamal snorted and returned to his spellwork. "You do not want to get on a first-name basis with that snake of a woman."

I really wanted to know their history, but this wasn't the time. "I was able to read her, and I got a lot more truth out of her than she wanted."

Ryder rolled, leaning on both elbows against the counter. "What did you learn?"

"I can't trust her."

"I could have told you that, baby girl," Jamal said, sounding particularly derisive.

"Yeah, well." I shrugged. "I also discovered she's intending to use Sturwood."

"That doesn't surprise me." He set out several more candles and lit them, pausing to focus on the flame, as if his lighter needed the assist. "So, he's hunting you because you can find him."

"He's hunting me because he's seen I'm the key to getting the future he wants."

"What?" Ryder asked.

I flicked my eyebrows at her.

"All those seers," Jamal said, "and he still needs you. Interesting."

"Yup." I scrubbed my face, feeling tired and wanting to change out of my blood-crusted pants. "I don't know how we're going to stay ahead of this guy. He's . . . too much."

"It's all a bit much." Jamal rubbed under his eye, pressing the lower lid up, his fingernails parting his lashes, the gemstone at the corner flashing in the overhead lights. "Okay. Well, your day just keeps getting more exciting." He turned away from us and pointed through the banks of red lockers to a dark-haired woman standing beside the hanging bike racks. "You got a visitor."

I stopped dead in my tracks, as I looked upon the face of a woman I'd really only met a handful of times.

"Who is she?" Ryder asked quietly.

"My sister," I answered in a hushed voice.

Jamal shrugged. "Well, that's only part of what you got goin' on. So, you go take care of her, and then you need to be explaining to me what I'm supposed to tell Mr. Pamoule about why he never received the package I guaranteed he'd see."

Ryder glanced at me with a question on her face, as if wanting to know if she should stay or go.

I shook my head and gestured for her to follow Jamal.

She moved away but didn't look pleased about it as she told Jamal about what had happened and how she needed to figure out how to retrieve her bike from Sturwood.

I took in a deep breath and walked over to my sister.

She raised her chin when she saw me, then met me halfway. "Sky," she said, her soft voice clipped.

"Calypso."

Her face twisted as she bit back what she was about to say.

She'd never liked me, and I didn't know why. We didn't share the same mother, and that was fine. I kind of always wondered if she was the reason our dad had never claimed me.

"I wouldn't have come if I had another option," she said.

I didn't have to ask how she'd been able to find me. She saw actual visions, sometimes of the future, but mostly of the present. It was as if she could astral project but in a way that was unique to her. It was more like she borrowed the eyes of people, looking to see what they saw, feel what they felt. "What happened?"

"Someone took Jimmy."

This was stupid. An insane number of people were being taken. "He had the ability?"

She nodded. "Do you think he was taken because of it?"

"Yes." There were way too many seers disappearing in the city. I hadn't even realized there were so many here to begin with.

Calypso gripped the straps of her denim purse.

A golden man materialized in front of a forest behind her, his hands over his head, holding a wand in one. His smiling face morphed into Calypso's as he turned as if on a wheel and inverted, the smile slipping away and turning into a fear-filled frown.

She was afraid of change, something I already knew. If the Son of Wands was here, she'd lost her confidence and was being devoured by her fears. "Do you have a safe place to stay?"

She shook her head.

I didn't have to like her to help her though. "Go to Sturwood. Ask for Melinda. She's at the clinic. Tell her I sent you."

Staring at the floor, my sister pulled her lips against her teeth. "My son?"

"I'll look for him."

"You don't need anything?"

"To track him with?" I shook my head. I had a feeling I knew who had him. If I tracked down our bad guy and found the seers, I'd be able to release Jimmy, too.

"Let me give you something." Calypso rooted in her bag and pulled out a small stuffed animal. "Take this."

"I don't—"

"Just take it. Where he—He could be hidden. He could be hard to find. Just . . ." She took my hands and wrapped them around the worn bunny's single ear. "Find my son, Sky."

"I'll do what I can." If my hunch was correct, though, finding him meant putting myself in the kind of danger that could destroy the city.

She swallowed hard and then headed to the front door. Stopping there, she turned back to me. "He's my son."

"I know." I also knew she wasn't just telling me that to say it. What she meant was that it mattered.

"He's your nephew."

Except he really wasn't. He was just another boy in a sea of people, but one who was doing okay. "I'll do what I can."

"I hated you for the longest time." Her lips curled slightly. "Did you know that?"

"You didn't hide it." Was now the right time for this conversation? It felt like one of those movie moments with lots of action, and then the characters stood around and talked all heartfelt for a good eight minutes when they only had four minutes left to win.

"Dad said you were important. Not me."

"Yeah, well, he stayed with you. He couldn't be bothered with me, so I couldn't be that important."

"He wasn't the man you thought he was."

Past tense? "When did he. . . he died?"

She made a disgusted face. "Last year."

"During the war."

She nodded, her pale brown eyes turned to slits. "You were the only thing he could talk about. He kept talking about how you were the only one who could save us from what was coming."

"Well, he was wrong." He had to be because, yeah, my gift was better now than it had been a year ago, but I was still seriously only one woman seeing visions and trying her best to interpret what they meant.

Calypso pursed her lips together and strangled her purse straps again. Then she turned and left.

Five wands glowed a dark turquoise on the door she closed behind her.

Five of Wands.

It had been on the door in Victoria's office when we were fleeing. It could just be a coincidence. It stood for defeat, which was what I'd originally thought it meant in the moment as we ran.

It also meant competition and natural enemies. It could represent people who were equally matched in a fight, which Calypso and I were. And it represented someone who could push the limits with bitterness.

Dark turquoise wasn't good either. It could mean secrecy.

Could I trust Calypso? I'd just sent her to a sanctuary for paras. Not Pearl's, so at least I hadn't breached that, but had I just endangered Sturwood?

The Five of Wands shifted into the Lost Compass, which signified someone who was lost and was trying to find their way back.

How much of a second chance did I really want to give a sister who'd never given me a first chance? With the way I'd grown up, I didn't hold a lot of value in blood or what that meant. But in the family you built? Sure. I felt a lot of value there.

The area around me darkened, and bright stars popped out, a cloudy glow rising up from my left to showcase the Milky Way.

Limitless possibilities. Where? In the idea of letting Calypso into my family? Of helping her? Of bringing her closer?

Or in doing what I needed to protect the family I already had? Because those, to me, seemed like two different directions.

The stars reduced back down into a compass again.

I didn't know if I was interested in entertaining the idea of letting my sister into my life.

I went to the counter and leaned on it, setting the rabbit down, trying to push Calypso and her son out of my mind. I'd try to find Jimmy. I wasn't being spiteful. I just didn't want to give a sister who'd fought to keep me out of her family the emotional energy she didn't deserve. "Did you need to get your bike?"

"I'll get it," Ryder said. "That looked intense."

"Yeah." I twisted around to look at the Lost Compass again, remembering everything that had happened that day, all the symbols I had, all the ways they could be placed together, but the most important was the Five of Wands. That card had shown itself twice. "I think she was behind the attack at Victoria's."

"Your sister," Jamal asked, his tone disbelieving.

I shrugged. That was the other side of symbols. They could be interpreted in several different ways. "I don't know."

"What's the beef between you two, baby girl?"

I didn't know that either. "It's a long story."

"Okay." His wide-eyed, pinched-lip look informed me I'd be spilling the beans to him later. "What did she have to say?"

"Her son was taken."

"Your nephew," Jamal clarified.

"A seer?" Ryder asked at the same time.

"Yeah," I told them both. "And we know where he probably is."

Ryder leaned back, closing her eyes. I felt shut off from their blue comfort.

How were we supposed to get ahead of him if he kept taking all the people capable of seeing ahead?

Why couldn't *I* start gathering those people? Have a war of seers?

Because it wouldn't make any difference. Seers couldn't find him. I was the only one who could.

But that didn't mean that they couldn't look elsewhere, for other seers, get to them before he did.

"The PPE were here and didn't have your name," Ryder said evenly. "If your sister was really behind the attack, then wouldn't they know who you are?"

Maybe. Or maybe she was hiding part of the information? Or maybe it really was a coincidence, because the same card could show up in different readings and have different meanings each time. And it wasn't like I was doing actual readings. I was asking questions with no real layout-intent and just seeing random cards.

The Fool appeared beside Jamal and looked affronted before disappearing in a cloud of glittery smoke.

Jamal waved his hand over the candles. "You can't see the future when he's around?"

It took me a second to figure out what he was talking about. The lord who shouldn't be named. "I don't see the future."

"She sees symbols," Ryder said, crossing her arms over her slim chest. "But you were able to find him. You took us right to him. Twice."

"It's all about looking around him." Was that something I could tell other seers to do?

Ryder let her head fall back. "So, you think he can't be found if you're looking for him directly?"

"That's exactly what I think." So what was I going to do with that? "If he's targeting people like—"

"October," Roger called out, the blue door slamming open. "They took her."

Chapter 19

"Roger?" I was confused for a hot minute. I didn't think he knew where I worked, but of course he did. How would he not have? Still, I never thought this would be a place I'd see him.

"I didn't know where else to go." His hands were shaking.

Okay. This was genuine. "Miche? When was she taken?"

He nodded as he walked toward the counter. "Like, an hour ago? I tried calling the authorities. They. . ." He shook his head.

I could just imagine. He'd all but admitted to them that his daughter was para. They didn't care if this was a "real" kidnapping or not. "Did you call Detective Young?"

"He's not answering."

"Answering," Jamal said with a snort.

It was hard to remember, but less than a year ago, everyone had phones. "Do you know who took her?"

"Women. In white."

Relief hit me like a lead balloon. "Not people in blue."

"No. It's not him. It's—I've never heard of these people before," he said, panic lacing his words.

"Nor have I," Ryder said with a frown. "Someone new?"

"Who are we talking about?" Jamal asked, narrowing her eyes at Roger.

With all the things that'd happened, I'd completely forgotten that I hadn't had time to talk to Jamal about doing this one favor. "His daughter. She has the gift, and he was thinking it might be a good idea to turn it off. I hadn't had a chance to ta—"

Jamal turned to me in shocked outrage. "We shouldn't have done that for—"

I held up my hand. "It's dangerous for—"

"Of course it is. It is for all of us, but that doesn't mean—"

"If she hides, she lives," I shouted.

"At what cost?" Jamal demanded, slamming one powerful hand on the counter and making all conversation around us stop.

I hadn't even realized others had been talking until the quiet hit.

Jamal straightened, looking a bit uncomfortable. He used his fingers to gesture slightly toward himself, then shrugged. "Hiding might be breathing, sugar," he told Roger, unable to meet the man's gaze. Then, he raised his bald head and daggered the man with a courageous set of his shoulders. "But it isn't living."

Roger's jaw twitched. "I'll take breathing, if it's all the same to you."

It was time to diffuse this. I reached inside and tapped a part of me that felt. . . open, I guess. It unfurled like a fairy blossom in some cartoon, only I didn't see it. I just felt it.

Directing my thoughts toward it, I focused my question. *Who took Miche?*

A little mouse with a crown appeared before me, sitting on a mushroom. Another mouse with Miche's features—which was weird because it was still obviously a mouse—crawled to the mushroom top via a branch of apple blossoms, and the two little mice snuggled close.

"She wasn't kidnapped," I said, relieved but still confused. "She went willingly." But was she safe?

"She what?" Roger demanded.

"What are you seeing?" Ryder asked, her words feathering across my ear and sending a shiver up my spine.

I caught my breath, glancing at her lips, and for one insane moment, all I wanted was to be reminded of how soft they were when crushed against mine, and how good it felt to be what she wanted.

She ignored me, focusing on Roger.

I didn't know what signals she was giving me. "The Benefactor." But how? The Benefactor was a card that meant all the hard work you'd put into helping others was coming back round. It showed that the generosity you'd put out into the world was being returned.

Jamal shook his head and shrugged. "I don't speak symbols, baby girl."

"Was Miche helping others?" I asked.

Roger released a breath and raised his face to the ceiling. "Yes. Helping people stay out of trouble and under the radar at school. I told her to stop, that it was only going to get her arrested—or worse. But she didn't listen."

"Okay. Well, that's good. It's good. But. . ." We'd narrowed down the players in the field. "Who are the women in white?"

"How would we know what—" Ryder stopped herself as realization flashed over her face. "Oh." She shook her head and raised a hand in apology.

The two little mice morphed into a tall and graceful, light brown colored horse that seemed to shimmer in the light.

A pearlescent shimmer.

The horse represented a strong person who put in a lot of work to help others. Match that with a pearlescent sheen to her dun-colored coat, and I could deduce it was. . . "Lady Dun."

"Ballsy," Jamal said with respect.

Ryder tipped her head to the side. "Then she's safe."

The horse nodded, tossing her long, curly mane as she stomped one hoof.

"Yeah." I had just thought about gathering seers before *he* could. I was glad to see someone else was doing that instead, someone bigger and stronger than me.

"Where?" Roger asked, his hands out as if trying to catch the information I had.

"I can't tell you and I can't take you there, but I will—" I continued, talking right over as he tried to interrupt me. "I will talk to Pearl and see if we can't change that."

Roger's shoulders sagged. "She's safe."

"Yes."

"Without me."

I had no idea what it meant to be a parent. I could only read the additional sag in his shoulders, the look of defeat and grief on his face. I vaguely recalled what Pearl had said when we'd brought in the other kids. Had she mentioned sending someone to their parents? I wanted to say she had, but I was spending a lot of my retention on storing and understanding symbols. Real-world conversations that didn't have a direct impact weren't sticking.

"That's good." He shook himself, then tried and failed to plaster on a happy smile. "I was so scared when she and Kitty were taken. I feared the worst with all the stories—"

"Kitty was taken too?" The redheaded girl who seethed with anger? That little punk? "I told you she was bad news."

"You're wrong about her," Roger said, the whites showing stark around his irises. "That girl's been nothing but sweet to Miche."

"Since how long?"

"Since forev—well, since the beginning of the war, I guess."

I wanted to throttle him. I turned and grabbed Ryder's arm. "She wants to harm someone. Badly." Returning my attention to Roger, I growled, "You might have helped bring down the *only* person trying to keep people like your daughter safe."

His mouth fell open as if he intended to speak.

I didn't have time for him. I had to tell Pearl. With no idea how good *her* seer-ing ability was, I couldn't trust that she'd see the same things as me. "You good?" I asked Ryder.

She nodded once, but her expression held a question.

I hoped like hell that when she'd said she healed fast, she really meant it and wasn't just trying to be the tough chick. I had no idea what we'd be facing when we went to Pearl's.

"She's good," Roger said, his words softened by the lack of conviction in his voice. "She's good."

He wasn't talking about Ryder and hadn't caught on that I wasn't talking to him. He was talking about Kitty, probably because Miche was all he could think about.

That was something I could kind of understand.

No. Not really. I didn't have family in the truest sense. I just had people who wandered in and out of my life, people I cared about for the time they were with me. When they left, they were gone. I didn't mourn them. I was just me without them after they left. So, no. That wasn't something I understood.

But it was something I'd seen.

I hoped for his sake that he was right, but I knew he wasn't. I looked to Jamal and gestured with my head to the manhole cover that led to the underground.

He rolled his eyes and gestured for Roger to follow him to the back. "Come on, sugar bear. I got something in here that'll sooth that tortured soul of yours."

I had two issues that I needed to deal with. Calypso, who might very well get Melinda in trouble, and Kitty, who could blow Pearl's entire operation into explosive danger.

And I still had to deal with the Lord *Him* situation.

As Roger disappeared toward the back with Jamal, the front door opened again. "October," Vance called.

Fuck. Fuck! Fuck my life. "What?"

Ryder stopped and gritted her teeth as if chewing on a bit.

He frowned at us both. "Are you in a hurry?"

"Yes," I said with a frown. "What's up?"

"I heard about what happened in Sturwood. I wanted to see how you were."

"Busy."

"I. . . see that. Look." He grabbed my arm and pulled me to the side. "I'm sorry I wasn't there to help."

He didn't pull me far enough away so that Ryder couldn't hear what was going on. "We can talk about that later." However, I had to tell him about the connections I'd made. "Does the police have a connection to the PPE?"

"Yes."

"How?"

"It's more of a tip line, I guess. They look in on our reports. They act on what we put in there."

I tried to remember what'd happened a year ago versus what was going on now. "Lord Witness knows who you are, how to track and keep you busy, and how to tip off PPE to do his dirty work for him."

"Lord. . . Oh."

"He was after me today, but he doesn't know my name. He knew enough to send PPE to Senator Armstrong's, though, and to here. And he knew how to keep you busy so you couldn't help out."

"Oh." He pressed his tongue to the roof of his mouth and narrowed those pale brown eyes of his. "He's gotta be on the PD."

The Devil had presented himself from Victoria's computer. She worked with the PD, not the PPE, at least as far as I knew, but I didn't have time for that at this moment. "Okay, well, be careful until you can figure out who he is. Also."

He frowned.

"He saw my face."

Vance flinched.

I wished that was all, but it'd been a very busy day. "And he didn't wear a mask today, which means he doesn't have to hide."

Surprise flooded the detective's expression. "He's a shapeshifter?"

"And a siren."

"And a . . ." Vance let out a long sigh. "Shit. He really could be the Mind Eraser."

I hadn't even really heard about that one and couldn't care. "I gotta go." I turned and walked away.

"What is this?" He called at me as if inviting more details.

"None ya," I flung over my shoulder as I continued to the back. I stopped and turned back to him, not wanting to leave while he was still there.

He shook his head with a confused look, but eventually he turned away.

Noah plowed into him at the door. "Hey—hey!" He sounded a bit upset to realize that a detective was here.

I didn't have time for him to stall Vance any more than he already was. We needed to leave through the manhole that he didn't know about. "Let him go, Noah!"

He glared at the detective and rolled his bike through the door. "Why's the garage doors closed already?"

Jamal came out from the back. "November, baby, stash that bike and come to the back. I gotta catch you up on some things."

Noah frowned at me as he followed orders, the front door closing behind Vance. "You okay?"

"Will be." We were now that the coast was clear. "See ya."

"Yeah, okay."

Ryder opened the manhole cover to the underground and waited for me to head down first, closing it again after we were in. "We could have gone to your apartment."

Truth. "This is closer." If Lord *Him* was someone on the police department, then he could track me with video surveillance. He'd seen my face. He already guessed where I worked. He'd be able to track me to my apartment—

Had that been him too? If it had been, then why didn't he know my name yet? No. No. The invasion of my apartment had to be someone else, but still. I couldn't use the door Pearl had given me, especially if I was being watched. This might seem dumb, but this was the smarter move.

Ryder grunted as she waited for me to lead the way. "You're worried."

"Yeah." I waited patiently, asking for help. I didn't know how to get to Pearl from this hole.

A fire dragon appeared before us, writhing in the air with his finned, serpentine body. As the orange light of his eyes pierced mine, I was filled with courage and the knowledge that whatever happened, we'd be able to find a way to overcome what was thrown at us.

I hadn't realized just how heavy the anxiety was piling on until he appeared and soothed it with a look.

I nodded my thanks and gestured for him to lead the way.

He twisted around and roll-flew through the air, lighting the dark tunnels.

Ryder frowned. "How are you able to see in this?"

"See in what?"

"It's pitch dark."

We'd traveled down some tunnels that had no light whatsoever, and I hadn't realized it. "Uh, the fire dragon is emitting light."

"Huh."

"What about you?"

"I can see in the dark."

That didn't exactly feel right, but when I looked back at her, she shone with a white-golden glow. "Are you part angel?"

She snorted and dodged the question. "You said you could see things about him."

It took me a minute for me to realize who she was talking about. "Kind of."

"Anything we can use to figure out who he is? You said shapeshifter and siren."

"Yes."

She released a puffed breath. "That's going to make it hard to ID him. He showed you his face?"

I nodded. "A face."

She groaned. "What do you think with the pieces you have so far?"

I tried to put them all together. "He, uh—I don't know. He has a messiah complex, but in a weird way. He thinks he's protecting humans from people like him."

"Interesting. So, maybe abused as a child."

I hadn't done a lot of psychological studies. "Maybe?" Trying to put myself in those shoes, though, that didn't quite make sense. "Maybe, you know, like, if someone kept telling him what a bad person he was and how dangerous he was all the time and beat him for it?"

"But why fight to keep him alive if that's all they were going to do?"

"What do you mean?"

She looked at me sideways as we turned a corner. "Male sirens are killed at birth. Usually before birth."

"Why?"

"They can't be controlled."

"Julie's mom seems pretty out of control."

Ryder shook her head. "Kalindi has a lot of rules to follow. That she's using her abilities on high-ranking people doesn't mean she's out of control. She works for the betterment of society, and so those are the rules she follows. Males take what they want for themselves."

"How many male sirens have been allowed to exist?"

"I don't know."

It sounded like a terribly short-sighted view of things, and a bad reason to kill people before they'd had a chance to prove the need for it. "So, you know Julie's mom by name?"

"I've worked with her."

"Is she part of how you lost Michigan?"

Ryder didn't respond. "Is he on the PPE, do you think?"

"Police department, probably."

"Is there anyone you can trust? Besides Vance?"

I nodded. "Torrez. She's always been good and someone I can trust. She's a guardian."

"Maybe we can talk to her."

The fire dragon turned to us with an expectant expression as if telling us . . . something.

Fire dragons were needed in the face of danger or opposition.

"Maybe be ready for a fight," I muttered, concern blossoming inside me.

Ryder nodded and pulled out two knives.

Taking in a steadying breath, I continued to follow the dragon until he disappeared in vapor.

By that time, I could see a steady stream of light and hear the voices of several people. So, I just followed that.

We weren't even greeted by anyone until we'd made it nearly to the clearing.

A guard in a flak vest with a rifle strung across his front turned to us. "Hey, what are you doing back here?"

"We're here to see Pearl."

He rolled his eyes. "Get in line."

I moved to push past him.

He didn't budge. "No, seriously, she's busy. Like . . . busy."

Ryder put a hand on his chest and calmly moved him aside, allowing me to move forward.

A crowd had gathered round. A soft popping sound hit my ears as if I'd changed in elevation. That had to be the veil between the two worlds or something.

"What's going on?" I asked a woman next to me.

She shrugged, just as confused as I was.

Ryder pushed her way ahead of me and then *made* a hole in the crowd in a way I certainly couldn't. People seemed to just sense that she was there and moved away from her like a school of fish in water.

When we got to the center, Miche was standing over a prone Kitty, her hands out, her human teeth bared.

That wasn't what I'd been expecting.

Chapter 20

P earl emerged and came over to stand close to Miche. "What is the meaning of this?"

"She's not good," a woman said, pointing a finger at Kitty.

I was glad I wasn't the only one who understood that.

Pearl looked to me and raised her chin. "October, what do *you* say?"

I hadn't realized she'd seen me. "That's why I'm here, actually. I heard you'd taken Miche in *with* Kitty, and I came to warn you." Which she obviously didn't need.

Pearl narrowed her eyes and then gestured for me to follow.

Guards came for Miche and Kitty, bringing them with us. Miche didn't seem happy about it.

"I'm not going to profess that I can read the future," Ryder murmured in my ear, sending gooseflesh down my spine, "but I can read the room. Are you sure Kitty is bad?"

I nodded. "You didn't see her aura, Ryder. She's pissed."

"You can be pissed for a lot of reasons. Were there other symbols with that?"

I had to think back. There'd been symbols leading me to Roger, but none, really, around Kitty. I shook my head.

"Well, if Miche can see things and she's protecting Kitty, then maybe you're not seeing the bigger picture here."

I appreciated the fact that Ryder was trying to help, I really did, but she hadn't seen the anger. This wasn't something I

could just be casually wrong about. And if there were others
in Paraden who could see things like I could, if there were
others who believed she wasn't good, then I couldn't ignore
that either.

But Ryder wasn't wrong either. Symbols had many
meanings and sometimes you had to look at them from
different angles to see how they applied to the given situation.
Like tarot readings and interpreting cards depending on their
card position. There was a lot of room for error.

What did Pearl see?

She led us down a corridor.

"Hey, um—" A part of me didn't want to take on my sister's
quest, but her son was young and didn't deserve to be ignored
because I was mad at his mom for not allowing me to be a part
of her family when we were kids. "You haven't by any chance
brought in a young boy, have you?"

"I've brought in a lot of people." Pearl looked at me with
narrowed eyes. "Who are you looking for?"

"My nephew, Jimmy."

"Jimmy Blaze?" Pearl asked as if that name meant something,
then shook her head, her shoulders riding up as if she'd received
a chill. "No. You're lucky I allowed *you* in."

What did that even mean?

Pearl led us into a room similar to the ones we'd been
brought into the first time we'd shown up. She stashed Kitty
in one, Miche in the next one, and then led the me and Ryder
into yet another. She turned to me, her hands resting on her
cane, some of her braids falling over her shoulder. "You came
down here."

I didn't know what she was asking. Was she asking if I'd been
followed? If we'd betrayed the location? If we were in trouble?
Or was she asking about Kitty?

Probably all of that.

"When we heard you'd brought Kitty down here with
Miche, I knew I had to warn you."

"Even though I'm capable of seeing the future."

"No one sees the same future or the same things. When I first met Kitty, she was very angry, and her anger was directed at Miche."

"You didn't think that maybe it was because they'd had a fight?"

"No. Not for one second. It seemed bigger than that."

A wispy blackbird winged in, singing a song that hummed at my soul before disappearing through the wall leading to the room Kitty was being held in.

There was something here I wasn't seeing. "Maybe I was wrong."

The blackbird flew back through the wall, shifting into a raven and perching on Pearl's shoulders.

It was showing me who my teacher was and telling me to open my mind.

I nodded, embarrassed. "What did I miss?"

"Why do you say that?" she asked.

"Because a blackbird just came in and disappeared into Kitty's room before coming back, changing into a raven."

"And what does that signify to you?" She leaned against the table behind her, setting her cane to the side, and watched me with eagle eyes, the raven beside her turning his head to look at me better with one dark brown eye.

When I'd first started this journey as a person who could see things, I'd studied spirit animals, thinking they were the coolest thing since warm butter. After I'd gotten my tarot deck—which didn't last long—and then my oracle deck, I'd stopped seeing them as much, so I was a bit rusty. "I'm being called to be more self-aware. I got something wrong. I need to look deeper."

She nodded and turned to the wall that hid Kitty. "Do you know what I see?"

I didn't, but I wanted to know.

"Bigfoot."

I snorted. I couldn't help myself.

Ryder told me to shut up with her pale eyebrows.

Pearl shook her head, her small gold earrings quivering with the movement. "What that says to me is that she's hiding herself to remain protected, and that she's being hunted not for food or protection, but out of sport."

That would explain the anger, maybe, and why my initial reading had been wrong. "Well, she's also very angry about it."

Pearl gave a solemn nod. "If you were hunted, wouldn't you be angry about it?"

I was. "Yup."

She looked at something over my shoulder that wasn't Ryder, then focused her gaze on me once more. "Come with me to question the girls."

That was an invitation I hadn't been expecting. "I don't know what good I can do." She seemed to have this under control. The best thing for me to do was probably head back to the top and try and find my nephew.

She shrugged and glanced at the thing over my left shoulder again. "Neither do I." She moved toward the door, barely using her cane. "Let's find out."

Once we were outside, she headed toward the right, going to the room where Miche was being held. Entering, Pearl smiled at the girl and gestured to one of the chairs. "You can have a seat, child," she said as she took one of her own.

Miche glanced at me, her eyes filled with fright.

I raised my hands to tell her she was okay, then motioned for her to settle down and sit.

She swallowed, nodded, and then practically fell into the chair, gripping the edges with her fingers. "Where's Dad?"

"He's safe," I told her. "Worried about you, but I told him you were okay. He's just eager to see you is all."

"But am I?"

"Are you?" Pearl asked, quiet as an echo, studying the girl.

She shook her head, her mouth opening like a fish as her dark eyes danced around the room.

"Calm your breathing," I told her, a mirrored panic rising in my chest just from watching her. "You've got the gift, right?"

She stared at me, asking with her expression what the heck I meant.

"Your dad told me. You're safe here. You can *talk* about it."

She snorted and sank back in her rigid chair, crossing her arms over her chest.

Golden mushrooms crept under the door and spread around the room, golden fairies with dandelion hats buzzing around them.

I had to show her that she was part of a community now.

Right. How did I do that, though?

Pearl watched me with a face that was all patience.

Was this a test? Well, that was fine. I excelled in performance tests. "You know what I see?"

Miche's look that told me she didn't care.

"I see golden mushrooms and fairies. And the fairies have dandelion hats that start yellow, but as they buzz around tending the mushrooms, their little hats become seeds, and the seeds are flying away to create more mushrooms."

"Dandelion seeds are growing mushrooms," Ryder said with derision.

"It's symbols, Ry."

She raised an eyebrow, the corners of her lips rising slightly as well.

The name had been a slip, but I liked it and really liked how she'd reacted to it. "The color is gold. That's important. The mushrooms are all over, and they're growing in darkness to provide light as we talk. There's a bush of dandelions and mushrooms growing under your chair, growing brighter as the ones under Pearl's—" I frowned as I watched the mushrooms shrivel. I met Pearl's gaze, startled.

With a heavy sigh, she nodded, telling me to continue.

I licked my lips and shook my head, my heart twisting inside me. "As the ones under her get weaker."

Miche shook her head but relaxed. "What does that mean?"

It meant Pearl was dying. Or getting weaker? "It means that you're in a community now. One that's safe, and you're safe in it as well—but more than that, your presence helps us build it stronger. You help make it better and happier and healthier."

But what was going on with Pearl?

Miche looked around. "That's what it really means?"

"Yes."

She rubbed her forehead with two long nails and a stubby fingertip. "How do I trust you?"

Pearl clicked her tongue and rested her chin on the back of the hand on her cane. "Do you want to know what I see when I look at your friend?"

Miche straightened in her chair, her back and shoulders going rigid.

"I see a scared girl trying to keep herself alive and doing what she has to in order to do that."

Miche relaxed just a bit, looking back at me.

Symbols weren't like reading words with only one meaning. "Hey, I see someone who's pissed and very, very angry and she's hiding *that*. I assumed she was angry at you."

Miche shrugged and rolled her eyes. "She was."

"And she's not now?"

The girl looked up at me, expressionless now. "Will you give her a chance?"

"Tell me why we should." As soon as those words were out of my mouth, I realized I was stepping on Pearl's authority. I had no room to talk here. I had no power. I had no say.

The old woman quirked her lips at me as if understanding all that was going through my head at that moment and telling me to focus.

Fine.

The fairies continued to putter around the room, spreading mushrooms and glowing glitter until the entire room was filled with a golden light.

Miche glanced at something we couldn't see and then nodded. "She's a part of the Witnesses."

I felt like my heart had suddenly disappeared. "What?" And she was *here?* The Witnesses, who destroyed entire families in order to eradicate the para gene so that the "horrors" they'd witnessed would never be felt again. The Witnesses, led by the very guy hunting *me?* And they'd been invited into the only safe place for paras?

Pearl didn't seem distressed.

Was this why her mushrooms were withering?

A golden fairy fluttered into my face and bopped me in the nose with a blue, star-shaped aster flower, glaring at me as if I'd deeply insulted the entire fairy nation.

I took the wisdom she offered—because she'd hit me upside the head with the aster flower, which literally meant wisdom—and put a pin in my question, giving the fairy a defiant look.

She glared, bopped me in the nose again, and flew off.

Miche frowned at me like I'd lost my mind.

"I just got hit in the face by a fairy." Oh, dear gods. "I sound insane."

Pearl rubbed her head and then gestured with that hand as she shrugged. "And who's to say the insane aren't touched like we are?"

Right. I turned back to Miche. "Why are you protecting her?"

Miche looked at me and then at Pearl, then shook her head. "I told her I wouldn't tell."

"So . . ." What was I going to say? Tell her to tell? Like that'd work.

"Just listen to her? You know, if that's something you're capable of doing." Her tone said it wasn't.

Teenagers.

Pearl rose to her feet. "Is there anything you need? Drink? Food?"

"Safety."

I grunted. That was what we all needed. Ryder led the way out of the room and let Pearl take the lead once we were in the hallway, but I stopped her outside Kitty's door. "What's the deal with the mushrooms?"

"What do you mean?" she asked, looking up at me as if I were simple.

"They were shriveling under you."

She shrugged as if it made all the sense in the world. Then she opened the door. "As am I."

Ryder frowned at me. "Is it bad?"

I shook my head. Everyone died at some point.

Pearl turned to me and then looked down at my feet before turning back. "Are you comfortable?"

A mound of golden mushrooms and daffodils blossomed where I stood.

New beginnings and safety. At my feet. Yeah, that wasn't terrifying at all.

That was what *I* was seeing, though. What was *she* seeing?

In the new room, I closed the door behind me.

Ryder took a position in the corner, leaning against the wall, her arms crossed over her chest, looking bored.

Kitty glared up at me from the chair. "What are you going to do to me?"

I recalled what Pearl had said about Bigfoot and pulled myself back, looking at her instead and asking myself what I was missing.

Round, grey stones filled the room as Kitty's hair turned to gold. The gold spread over her body as if she'd been touched by Midas.

The Daughter of Stones? There was a reason I'd given up the tarot deck and had switched over to the oracle deck all those years ago. Tarot was intense and filled with deeper meanings than I could keep track of.

The golden woman came toward me, stepping away from Kitty like an astral projection, her stones rolling with her, but each one left a path of newly sprouting growth, and they all led to her feet. She gave me a golden stare.

I wasn't sure what she was trying to tell me. "You've got options, Kitty."

She looked between Pearl and me, then shook her head. "I really don't."

Pearl narrowed her eyes and pulled her head back a little as if looking around the young woman, her chin never leaving the backs of her hands. She wasn't offering anything.

Leaving me to take lead? Fine. I looked around the Daughter of Stones to get a better view of the scared and angry redhead sitting in the interrogation chair. "Why are you so angry at Miche?"

Kitty's eyes went wide. Then she blinked a bunch of times and looked away. "I don't know what you think you know, but you're wrong."

"Am I, though? You were seething with rage."

The raven winged in and stood beside Kitty on one of the stones, the largest one. Then it shifted into a crane, completely still as it stared at the ground.

I took the patience it offered even though it didn't feel quite right, like the patience wasn't meant for—

Me. Someone working with and behind Kitty was playing the long game. "Are you working with Lord . . . the leader of the Witnesses?"

She barked a laugh. "No one works *with* him."

Oh. "But you know him."

"Yeah, sure. We've met face-to-faces."

So, it wasn't a suspicion.

Kitty watched the understanding fill my face. "Now you're catching on."

How were we going to catch him if he could be anyone? "What's your connection with Miche?"

The girl chewed the air angrily, her eyes twitching as she looked at Ryder and then back at me. "I was supposed to bring her to him."

"How?"

She shrugged. "How do you bring anyone along? That was the easy part."

"What was the hard part?" Pearl asked.

Kitty looked down and then shook her head. "He let me see where he was taking them all and what he was doing with them."

"Them?" I asked, my heart skipping.

"All you who see stuff and things." She shook her head and shrugged.

So, he *was* collecting us. "What's he doing with them?"

She bit her bottom lip, then jiggled her jaw from side to side, stretching her neck, visibly uncomfortable. "He had them tied to chairs with wires injected into their brains feeding some pool or something."

That sounded horrific. "Why?"

"I don't know." Kitty looked up at me, her breath thin. "But he's looking for you."

Chapter 21

My first reaction was to crow. I'd been right. Kitty was dangerous. She was working with the man who could easily be labeled as the worst person in the city.

Ryder pinched her lips and tipped her head to the side. Something in her eyes silenced my personal victory and reminded me there was still a girl inside this redheaded villain.

So, I turned back to Kitty and fought to keep my emotions in check. "What happened? How'd you fall in with him?"

She looked at me in surprise, as if shocked I cared enough to even ask. Then she looked around and shook her head. "Same as anyone else, really. Lost everyone in the war. My mom, my dad." She frowned and glanced at her lap. "My brother."

One of the dandelion fairies who had been buzzing around the room stopped in midflight and frowned at Kitty, then turned her confused gaze to me.

"I was on my own out on the streets, and, I don't know. He just found me. He was nice at first, you know. He . . ." She released a long breath, and her shoulders stooped as she bent forward.

The golden fairy didn't look any less confused.

"He gave me a sandwich that first day. A good one. It was right after we'd been hit the first time."

Our city had never truly been hit. There were other cities that had been, looking as if they'd been blown up. Instead, we'd been blockaded, more or less. The news hadn't died right away. We'd been able to get stories on social media and on TikTok. But that'd stopped shortly after the first "attack." We'd lost communication first, food second. I still wasn't sure that was due to an outside attack. It had felt more like a controlled move to root out paras within the city.

"Then he—" Kitty swallowed, her green eyes shining brightly as the rims reddened. "He gave me a . . . home." She choked on the last word. "He gave me a new mom. A new dad." She dipped her head in shame, then shook it. "Another brother. I was okay." Her voice cracked as she closed that statement.

My heart hurt for her. I mean, poor kid. I remembered what it'd been like for me during all that. Things had gotten bad. A lot of us had been hunted. Shortly after that first attack, the Wipe had hit, and a lot of us had gone to ground. We'd been a different kind of homeless. This kid had been on her own way too soon, unprepared for this dystopian event. "I understand."

She snorted.

I didn't want to tell her. I didn't want to open up to her.

The dandelion fairy stared at me with a plea in her full black eyes, begging me to reach out to this girl.

Jeezum cripes. "I grew up without a family who actually cared about me. I know what it feels to have no one. My mom died. Not in the war, but when I was a kid. And, uh . . ." I hated telling anyone about my past.

Pearl tipped her head to the side, an open invitation, no judgment in her eyes, and the look on Kitty's face said it might not hurt.

I took in a deep breath and continued. "I bounced around from one home to the next after that. I had a lot of family, but no one that wanted me. When I got to Aunt Sere's, I was horrible and she wasn't. She seemed to care and was grateful to have me in her home and eating her food and making a mess in her bathroom." She'd been the one to help me connect with decks, to give me a language I could understand. "I'd thought I could make a home with her, that I could just belong to her and she to me."

Kitty blinked and nodded, staring at the floor but with an expression in her eyes that said maybe she was seeing her new family and memories she wanted to keep.

"I woke up one morning, and she was . . ." Pain twisted my heart, and I closed my eyes. I hadn't actually talked to anyone about this. I'd just been shuffled off to the next family who hadn't wanted me. "Gone."

Kitty's head shot up as she stared at me.

"Heart attack," I whispered around the knot in my throat. "And I was alone again."

The girl's lips curled in on themselves as she pulled them to the side, blinking quickly as if to stop tears.

"I understand the fear you must be feeling to lose this family."

"They're good to me," Kitty whispered.

"What price are you willing to pay to keep them safe?"

She stared at me like my gaze was a rope in the emotional battle raging inside her. "I don't know."

I didn't need visions or symbols to see where this girl stood. I felt it. I felt her pain inside my heart as if it was my own. What would I do? What could I have done? What would I have promised to keep Aunt Sere alive?

"Could you take us back?" Ryder asked, her husky voice puncturing the silence that had filled the room. "To where he's holding the seers?"

I shook my head, turning to look at her.

Kitty stared at Ryder in horror, tears sliding down her cheeks. "No."

I could see her wanting to want to help. The horror might have been twisting her lips, but her eyes were fighting to figure out a way to do what was right.

"We can't ask this, Ry," I said, keeping my voice as low as possible.

"We need to get them back," Ryder said just as quietly, staring at me with her arms still crossed over her chest, her stance firm as she leaned against the wall. Her brows were furrowed, though. She understood what she was asking.

This was her power, pushing people to do what needed to be done, past what was right for them.

Her gaze landed on mine before sliding back to the girl. "If we take out his power, we make everyone safer. He's the leader of the *Witnesses*."

The way she put the emphasis on that last word reminded me of the horrors they'd inflicted on my neighbors. On Dana, who was actually going to get her son back, but how many others hadn't?

So many, and I didn't even know their names.

She needed a solution. We all did. "What if she just tells us where to look?"

Pearl frowned and sat up straighter, bringing her cane to rest against her chest.

"He'll know," Kitty said, her green eyes going vacant, as if she'd already lost her new family and was already grieving them.

"How? The seers?"

"He's not dumb. He only allows a few of us to live free. And if any of us goes quiet like—" She stared down at her lap as if realizing something. "Like I did. Oh, god. They've been trying to get me to tell them something. They know there are paras at the school. We can't *not* know. Abigail put out the fire in Home Ec the other day, and Dingo's making all the animals go nuts with the change. I mean, they know. And they know I've gotta know something, and if I don't—oh, god." Her breath came faster.

Pearl reached for the girl and touched her knee.

Kitty went still, her breath ratcheting in her chest like ammunition. "They're dead."

"Not yet," I said.

"How?"

I didn't know exactly what Kitty was asking. How was Pearl going to save her family? How weren't they dead yet? How were they going to remain alive if she gave up Lord Shadow's location?

Pearl leaned back in her chair and twisted to look at Ryder, her lips tight as she thought about what she wanted to say a moment. Finally, she said, "If I gave you ten fighters, what could you do?"

Ryder let her head thunk against the wall, thinking before answering. "It depends. What kind of defenses are we going to run up against?"

"It's a pool of seers," Kitty said. "They don't need defenses. They'll know you're coming."

How did Lord *Him* prevent people from seeing him? "Jamal's working on something to keep us safe from his spying, but I don't know that he'll be able to do anything about his ability to keep *us* from seeing *him*."

Pearl opened her mouth to chastise me, then pursed her lips instead as her dark eyes saw things I couldn't. "A cloak."

"Sure." I didn't do magic. I didn't understand it. I didn't know how it worked. I saw things—that was all I had. But Paige Whiskey had had magic. She hadn't performed spells or anything, at least not what I'd been able to see. It'd almost been like she had a similar relationship to her abilities as I did with mine. Except, she could punch people with fire. I just read things.

Pearl nodded and got to her feet. "I think I might have something. It'll take me a moment." She paused at the door and turned to me. "Let the girls see each other. It really couldn't hurt. We don't hold prisoners."

That last statement was phrased like a promise, but it had a sharp edge to it like a threat.

I got up and followed her out of the room, Ryder not far behind me. Then, I closed the door and just stood in the hallway. I'd been getting some weird signals, and I wanted more information. Nothing came up.

"Are you okay?" Ryder asked.

"Yeah." I shook my head, needing to address something with her. "You said that you inspire people, like a lighthouse. What did you mean?"

She looked around uncomfortably. "If they're normally good people, they do what feels natural to them when I'm around."

"Even if that puts them in danger."

Her bottom teeth jutted forward as she chomped on that, studying the ground in front of us for a moment before looking up at me. "Do you think I'm putting people in danger?"

I leaned against the wall and let my head fall back. "Maybe, but do I think it's a bad thing?" It felt *good* to be doing something besides hiding. "I don't know."

"And us?"

What was she even asking? "You've been pulling away."

Her mouth opened and her shoulders rose as she looked around us. Then she shook her head, flicking an eyebrow. "Yeah. I guess." She took in a deep breath and released it slowly. "I see you being more heroic."

"I've always been that. That is quite literally my personality."

She shook her head.

"No. Listen. You know how some people create their entire lives around astrology? I found my personality type, and it fits not quite a hundred percent, but a lot. I am the Protagonist. I'm the stupid hero."

"But you—" A blip between her eyebrows. "You weren't."

I cleared my throat. "No. I was hiding."

"Why?"

Part of being a hero was owning up. "Because the last time I went up against this guy, I lost a *lot* of people. Because of me.

Because I sincerely and blindly believed we'd be okay and we'd make it and we had this and . . . we didn't. So, a lot of this is me being me again for the first time in months."

Ryder nodded and took a step back as if taking me at my word. Then she frowned and took a step closer, her body heat feeling more like a blanket than an intrusion as she hesitantly caressed my cheek, lifting my gaze to hers, which blazed with strength. "Are you okay?"

I couldn't tell if she was offering me strength or showing me where I should be, but staring into those eyes, I couldn't hold off the storm raging outside the protective prison I'd built for myself in order to keep everyone else safe. It was like a force of zombies were fighting to break down my door and shatter my windows. "No," I whispered with a ragged sigh.

She nodded, her thumb brushing my eyebrow. "I want to help, but I'm afraid I'll do more harm than good."

"Same." Lord *Him* might have Parker, but I was still free. I was still alive, and she might have been captured and had probes jammed into her head connecting her to a pool. Guilt rode me like a horse. I didn't want to be the person who hid again, and if it meant keeping Ryder beside me so I could. . . be me? That sounded so dumb. "We need to get her parents to safety."

"Agreed."

That one word was like a building block to a column I could construct a better house around. My fingertips settled over her heart, wanting desperately to touch more.

Her free hand wrapped around mine, her breath harsh.

"How do we do that?" I asked against her lips which were so close, certain I wanted to kiss them, but not sure if that was because of me or her effect on my reactions.

She smiled tightly and stepped back, releasing me, her game face sliding back into place.

A cold blanket enveloped me. I wished I'd given her another reaction, any reaction.

"We get her family." Ryder shook her head and shrugged. "And then we go for the seers. We find this place. We take it down and kill Lord—"

I held up my finger to stop her from saying his name out loud. "And if that doesn't work?"

She looked around. "Then we try something different."

Sounded like my kind of half-assed plan. "How are we going to get Kitty's parents?"

Tipping her head, Ryder let out a shallow sigh. "You let me worry about that. You're the only one who can see him."

Elation and trepidation marched side by side within me. "I know."

"Okay." She reached for me, pulling my face to hers. Her lips settled over mine, demanding and giving.

My soul unbound like a corset being unlaced. I stepped into her embrace, wrapping my arms over her shoulders and rising on my toes to deepen the kiss, answering with a need that had to be my own.

She pulled away, her breath heavy against my lips. And then she was gone, slipping into the crowd in order to fulfill her part of our hasty plan.

Chapter 22

I desperately needed what I felt to be real. I needed to know that these emotions were me because it certainly felt like they were.

"We cannot do this on our own," Pearl said, leaning against her cane in the jagged-walled room.

Of course, I really did have bigger problems to be hyper-focusing on.

"Then we get help," a woman with wildly curly hair said beside the ruined, ivy-covered column.

"From who?" a tall, thick man demanded, a tattoo of a swastika gleaming on his bald dome.

What was a white bald man wearing a Nazi symbol doing in a place where outsiders of all colors and norms lived?

The dandelion fairies buzzing around us didn't seem to care or to notice, so I kept that little pebble of a question to myself. "There are other people we could ask."

"Dannika?" Pearl asked.

Her tone said it was a dangerous idea. I didn't like it either, but we needed to put Lord *Him* on a multifront battle to divide his attention. "She has a lot of power in the city, a lot of people at her disposal. She could keep him busy in a lot of places."

Pearl looked away, her pinched lips letting me know what she thought of that idea.

Still, she didn't immediately say no. "And Senator Armstrong. Victoria . . ." I trailed off, not sure what I even wanted to say here. "We can trust her about as well as Dannika, but she has people we can use."

"We need power to fight power," Ryder said from the other side of the room, her face to the door. "After we've dealt with . . . this guy, *then* we worry about the other two. Until then, we ally. Enemy of my enemy."

The bald man sighed, his heavy shoulders barely moving with the effort, but he nodded, looking over at Pearl in agreement.

The woman with the wild hair shook her head. "Sturwood."

"Isn't ready for something like this," I said.

"But they are allies," Ryder said.

"No." Pearl's voice was firm. "They're a sanctuary, and as such, they're vulnerable. To think anything else is a good way to get them killed."

"Or worse," the bald man said under his breath.

Pearl nodded to him, her gaze going distant with thought.

"I doubt they'd see it that way," I said into the quiet.

With a growl, Pearl released her frustration.

We all took a moment as the silence gathered around the half-cave room.

"We just need him divided," I said. "We just need him in many places at one time, and if he doesn't fall for that—"

"Because he's listening to us right now," the woman with the wild hair said.

Exactly. "Then we all rally together at the point he's at." Which, hopefully, wasn't where the seers—and Parker, if we were lucky—were being kept.

The dandelion fairies just kept working as if my decks had given me all the answers I needed.

Maybe they had. After all, my decks were just cards. "I'm going to Jamal to see if there's something he can do to put up blinders. Maybe something in an amulet or something?"

Pearl nodded. "It's a good idea. That *is* something he should be able to do."

"I'll get Kitty's family," Ryder said.

"I'll go with her," the wild-haired woman said.

"Ryder, I want you with Earl." Pearl glanced over at the bald man. "Let's get a plan together to rescue the seers." She raised her chin, her lips tight.

He nodded, caught the tone of her look, and winced. "Yeah. Okay."

I didn't need a translation from my deck. I knew what she was saying. If we couldn't save the seers, we'd have to end them. Parker, maybe my sister's son? They were people. Real people.

"Make your plan," Ryder said, "but I'm getting the kid's parents."

We needed Kitty to find the seers and for me to let people on the seer recovery team know if Lord *Him* was coming.

Flashbacks to how the last time a team of friends and I had gone out against this guy with me and my visions leading the way hit me, but less hard this time, because this was a feeling that just kept coming back. I didn't know how to face it outside of what I was currently doing. Would the feeling go away after we'd done this? Would it get bigger if we failed? Again?

Except this time, my gift was more active. I asked a question, and it showed itself—when it could—in the form of a true vision, something I hadn't had before. Plus, I knew what, or who, I was up against this time. I knew he was shielded from direct visions. I knew I could see around them as long as he hadn't developed something that took that away, too.

I could have taken the shortcut to my apartment, but my bike and everything was at Speedy, so I headed toward the tunnels that would lead me back there.

Rolling my head to pop my neck, I managed only to jam it up instead, making the area right between my shoulder blades tighten further. I shook out my shoulders and tried to work it out as I walked down the sewer tunnels, following dandelion fairies to the manhole under Speedy.

Shifting the cover to the side a little, I stopped to listen. I didn't need anyone catching me, and I didn't know what time it was.

Not hearing anything, I pulled the cover completely off and climbed out, which wasn't as easy as others liked to make it look. There was nothing to hold on to, nothing to pull myself with. But I finally managed it and stood there looking around an empty garage.

Jamal's apartment wasn't far away. If this was early morning, all I needed to do was to stay low and out of sight of drones. Well, and wish I'd had a chance to sleep. I should probably leave him a note telling him I needed the day, though. Going out tonight without sleep was going to be stupid.

"October, baby girl, is that you?" Jamal asked from the back, his voice sleepy.

"Yeah."

He was still wearing yesterday's clothes, but he'd put on a purple vest. "What happened?"

I shook my head. "False alarm. I thought—everything's fine."

His face crumpled as he shook his head. "Come. I'm making breakfast in the back. Fill me in."

Slipping around the back of the counter, I followed him to what had once been a storage room and small break area. Now, it had two rooms closed off farther back, plus a small kitchen with a cook top and a mini fridge. "You've been busy."

"Sweetie, you're unobservant as fuck. I've had this for a good while."

I grunted, trying to count how many times I'd even been back here.

"Fill me in."

I did, without giving him too much information, and as the smell of hot cakes filled the small space, Julie came out of one the back rooms and started a pot of coffee.

She listened but didn't add much.

Matt came out with a yawn that overtook his entire body. "When are we going to meet this Lady Dun?"

"When she allows it," Julie said into her cup and sat down, her brown eyes droopy.

"Which reminds me," I told Jamal's back. "We came up with an idea to help *him* not see us as we're doing our things. Amulets? Is that something you could do?"

"And Lady Dun was okay with this?"

"She said it was something you could probably do."

He grunted. "What did she want?" He flipped some cakes into a stack on a plate and slid them onto the table.

Noah and April came out of the other room, bumping into each other as they both tried to get out the door at the same time.

"Hey," Noah said.

April grumbled and gave him a why-do-you-get-to-go-first look, but she stepped back.

Same room, huh? Could be normal. Could be they were sleeping together? "She agreed to it," I told Jamal. "What happened between you two? There is history and she doesn't like you."

"She doesn't trust me. There's a difference." Jamal glared at me out of the corner of his eye. "What do you want it to do?"

What had he done to break her trust? I had a hard time seeing my version of Jamal doing something bad. "To blind a seer's eye."

He turned away from the sizzling pan to give me an incredulous look. "And Lady Dun approved that."

When Noah got to the table, he grabbed a plate and handed it to April.

I held up my hands in surrender. "Why wouldn't she?"

Jamal turned back to the hot cakes. "She knows what's involved."

I was collecting more clues as to what had happened between them, but still not quite understanding. "The stakes are high."

"And the price is finally worth it," he grumbled. "My, how the mighty have fallen. As it happens—"

The front door crashed open, and people shouting commands slammed into the garage out front.

Jamal stared at me in alarm.

We all froze. This wasn't the first time we'd been hit, but they were after me. Lord *Him* was after me.

"This could be something else," Julie reminded us. "He's not the only one getting close to finding you."

Agent Spike's unpleasant face filtered to the top of my mind.

"Hide," Jamal commanded, pointing behind him. He killed the heat on the burner and headed to the door with the flipper still in his hand.

Matt moved to the side and opened the lid to what I'd thought was a seat. He gestured for me to climb inside.

My reawakened instincts demanded I stand and fight, not hide like a coward, but Noah grabbed my arms and propelled me forward. "I'll keep her hidden."

Matt nodded, his eyes on the door.

The noise out there was getting louder and more intense, which meant that people were getting closer.

"Don't be stupid," Noah said.

I didn't like it, but I scrambled inside the long box as Jamal exited the room.

"Agents, agents," I heard him say. "What brings you by again so soon?"

Noah slipped in over me, turning weightless almost immediately. The lid closed and created near darkness. I turned to my side and found a small hole to look through.

April stacked a few boxes on top of the one we were in and then headed toward the door as if nothing was out of the ordinary.

Two PPE agents burst into the room, looking around. "No sign of her, sir," one said.

April took a step back. "Her?" she asked, her voice small.

The other PPE agent shook his head. "Not you. Where's the other one? We know she's here."

"Like I said," Jamal said, entering the room. "I don't know what you think you know, but—"

"Stop," the second agent said, sounding irritated.

Agent Spike walked in with an air of confidence, wearing battle gear instead of a suit.

The first agent lifted her shoulder in a shrug and pointed her gun at April. "You'll tell us where she is on a count of three."

My heart froze. Hearing stories, seeing people disappearing was one thing. This—this was another.

"One."

Matt scrambled to the front. "What are you doing?"

Julie shook out her hands and opened her mouth. "This is *not* what you want to do," she said, the air vibrating with the power of her voice.

The female agent looked at Julie and smiled. "Two."

I needed to get out of that box. Now. I scrambled.

Noah's weight sank down on me. "No," he whispered directly in my ear.

"But—"

"No."

"Three." The agent raised an eyebrow and pulled the trigger.

A large blast punctured the room, followed by silence.

April's face practically glowed in surprise, right before she slipped to the ground.

Chapter 23

J ulie screamed, "Get out," with so much siren ability, the walls vibrated.

Agent Spike moved next to the woman who'd shot April. "Where is she?"

Matt growled low, his voice rising to a howl as he shifted, his clothes ripping. He launched himself at the woman who'd shot April.

She looked bored and pointed her weapon at him.

Another explosion of sound shattered the room.

Matt's howl only turned darker. He landed on her and snapped at her face.

She let out a screech.

The male officer looked around and shook his head, backing toward me, his gun hand shaking.

Agent Spike's lips twisted as she cursed, bringing out her own gun and trying to aim at Matt.

Jamal's lips twisted as he said something low, his tattoos glowing.

Matt had shifted in front of a PPE agent, which meant he was going to be arrested. Jamal was showing them that he had abilities, which meant *he* was going to be arrested, and our little haven was going to be shut down.

I flailed against Noah, who fought to keep me in the box. If I got out, if I showed myself, they'd leave.

Except I knew—I *knew* they wouldn't leave my friends alive.

The male officer's eyes shot over to the box we hid in. He scrambled toward us.

Julie launched herself at the door as more agents burst through the door, singing a song of leaving.

Jamal's tattoos glowed brighter, but there was no indication that his spell or whatever he was doing was going to be finished anytime soon.

The male agent moved all the stuff that had been piled onto our box.

"Stay quiet," Noah hissed as his body weight lifted.

I fought myself, struggling to remain still when the only thing I wanted to do was to leap out of that box and punch the guard in the throat, even knowing that I didn't have that particular skill.

The lid rose on our box.

"What is going on here?" Senator Victoria Armstrong barked.

The lid fell with a bang.

The fighting stopped.

Except for Matt, who was still tearing at the female agent's face.

Agent Spike grabbed his scruff with one hand and threw him off. "What are you doing here?" she demanded, holstering her weapon and pulling something out of a pouch at her lower back.

I opened my eyes in surprise and peered through the small hole.

Victoria stood in the doorway with two more agents at her back.

Jamal breathed heavily, his tattoos fading.

"It's set?" Victoria asked him.

He nodded once.

The senator sighed and gestured to the two behind her. "Gather them."

Agent Spike finished handcuffing a now naked Matt and turned to Victoria. "Let me repeat, what are you doing here?"

Victoria's frown softened. "Stop," she commanded, her tone quiet.

The fight fled from Agent Spike like someone had released air from a balloon.

The two men who'd arrived with the senator collected the PPE agents and taking them out of the room.

"Is she here?" Victoria asked Jamal.

He didn't say anything.

"October," she called, "you're safe."

I watched Jamal, waiting for him to tell me it was really okay.

He took in a deep breath and nodded once.

The darkness enveloping me disappeared. I climbed out of the box, staring at Victoria, wondering what her next move was and why she was even here. I inched toward April.

Her shaking hands were covered in blood from a shot in her abdomen. "Hey," she said, her voice quivering. "Is it over? Did we win?"

I nodded and found something to put over her wound, replacing her hand. This was my third stomach wound in the same number of days, and I was getting tired of the blood. "Tell me you're a fast healer."

April giggled, but it came out shaky. "I wish."

Victoria picked up her phone. "My location. Now." She hung up. "I'm glad you called."

"Like I had a choice," Jamal said.

"He's getting close then."

I didn't care what they were saying. I just took April's hand and gripped it. "I'm sorry."

She smiled. "Don't be. We knew the risks."

"You're going to be fine." I didn't know that for sure.

Julie dropped to her knees on April's other side, lifting the towel I'd just pressed down. "You probably didn't hit much." She looked over at me, her eyes full of pain.

Someone unshackled Matt. He rose to his feet and pulled on a pair of pants, blood seeping down his arm. "That looks bad."

None of us knew. There were a lot of things in the abdomen.

Someone pushed us aside.

It was Melinda from Sturwood.

"Wait. How'd you get here? And so fast?"

"I was en route when Victoria called," Melinda said succinctly. "How many bullet wounds?"

"One," Julie and I said at the same time.

"In her," I added. "There's Matt, too."

"I'm good," he said with a groan. "I'm good."

"Good," Melinda said. "Go away. We need to work."

Two other people came in, taking over.

Jamal and Victoria weren't even in the room anymore.

After we finished washing our hands, Julie handed me a clean towel. "Will she be okay?"

"I hope so." But there were no signs to tell me one way or the other, so I couldn't say for certain.

She nodded. "Do you know her?"

"Melinda?" I nodded. "She helped patch Ryder up after the ambush."

Julie stared at the door. "They were prepared to fight against me."

That had registered for me as well. They must have been wearing protective ear plugs or something, because Julie's voice hadn't made a difference. How much *did* they know about us? And if they knew this much, why hadn't they taken care of us sooner? I mean, *really* taken care of us?

I wanted to stay with April and see if she was going to be okay, but I had no idea what Melinda and the other two were even doing. It wasn't like on TV when they just talked a bunch of really smart-sounding words and did some heroic stuff. They barely even used full sentences with each other as they hooked an IV into April's arm and then put her on a stretcher.

Melinda came over to me on their way out. "Is she a fast healer?"

I shook my head. "Kitsuni."

Melinda winced. "Okay. Good information. I'll do my best."

"Thank you," I said quietly, fighting off the feeling of despair. This wasn't like the last time. This time *was* different. I was closer to figuring out who he was.

At the same time, he was closer to finding me.

Melinda nodded, understanding aging her face as she turned around and followed April and the two guys taking her out.

I wanted to know what was going on with the PPE agents. Were we safe? What was Victoria doing there? Was she helping, or was she putting us in a vice and keeping us in her control?

Jamal stood behind the counter, his tattoos flaring occasionally under his purple vest. He glanced at me as I came up to him, then turned his attention back to the PPE agents.

They were on their knees in the middle of our garage.

I walked up to Victoria.

The man beside her in the black flak vest stepped back and went to talk to some of his other teammates.

"The director will hear about this," Agent Spike said with a sneer.

"I doubt that," Victoria said, her voice calm and quiet and had almost a hint of regret.

A chill spread through me. "What's the plan?"

She looked at me and then all around, her hands spread below her waist. "Protect you."

"And these agents?"

"Do you care?"

"If you plan on killing them when their last known locations were here, yes."

"Do you think I'm that dumb?"

A sizzling pop filled the air, and the kneeling agents bent over, their hands going for their ears.

The man who'd been talking to Victoria nodded.

Victoria knelt down in front of the fallen agents. "You entered the garage like you were ordered and ransacked the place. But you didn't see the woman you were sent to find, and there was no evidence of other paranormal activity. You forced the situation, trying to get them to reveal themselves, and you shot a girl in the stomach to do so, but found nothing."

Agent Spike sneered. "And what about Shelley's face? How am I going to explain that?"

Victoria tipped her head to the side. "What about Shelley's face?"

The woman turned to the agent in question and her expression fell with shock. "His face—"

"Everyone here is fine," Victoria said. "And so is Shelley."

I didn't understand. The woman's face had been bitten and clawed at by Matt. He hadn't killed her, but he'd done significant damage.

"I don't understand," Agent Spike said, blinking in confusion.

"What are we still doing here?" another agent demanded. "There's nothing here, Serg."

"I know there's—" The woman's head lolled, and she fell to her hands.

"There is nothing here," Victoria said. "This is a simple messenger shop, and it's time to stop looking into it. It has been a dead end, it's still a dead end, and it will always be a dead end."

"Stop wasting our time," a man said, staggering to his feet and heading for the door.

Victoria stood and held out her hand. "Don't forget these."

"How'd those fall out?" He grabbed two violet, glowing balls and shoved them in his ear. "Thank goodness we didn't need these."

"I don't feel great," the bitten woman said. "My face feels like it's on fire."

"Your face feels fine," Victoria said, and handed her a purple set of ear plugs.

"That's weird. Yeah. Huh." She shoved them in. "Must have been something I ate or something."

Victoria handed plugs to the rest of the team, leaving Agent Spike for last.

"I know something weird is going on here," she said.

The senator knelt in front of the woman and placed the earplugs in her ears, then cupped her face between her palms. "You need to listen to me very carefully, Rosa. This is off limits. You are not allowed here."

"Victoria?" the woman asked, as if coming out of a sleep. "What are you doing here?"

"Doing what we said we were going to do. Leave this place alone, and work to get closer."

"This isn't working," Rosa said, her voice thin.

"It is. You just have to keep trying."

Rosa's hands gripped Victoria's. "Are you putting me back to sleep?"

"Yes." Victoria pressed her lips against the other woman's forehead. "Everything will be fine."

Rosa shook her head. "No, Vic, it isn't."

The senator pulled back a little. "You came here. You did your job. Your agent shot a woman in order to show how serious you were and still found nothing. This is a dead end."

Rosa's eyes went blank as she nodded. "This is a dead end, but I know I'm close." She got to her feet and stumbled like a drunkard to the door.

Once the door was closed, Jamal stomped over to it and threw the lock.

"What was that?" I demanded.

"Can't you read me?" Victoria asked, her face set in a dark mask of upset.

The Stranger appeared, her bald head gleaming, but she only raised her eyebrows as if she'd been trying to tell me this all along.

How had *this* been what she'd been trying to tell me? "You're a para."

"I am."

"And you never told me."

"You never asked."

"You talk like you're on the other side of the line."

"In a lot of ways, I am."

"But you're a siren."

She shook her head. "I can change people's memories with my voice. That's not what a siren does."

"And that agent's face? How'd you heal him?"

"I didn't. I changed everyone's memories of what happened to him."

"So . . ." Shock rocked me. "He's still wounded."

She nodded with a cool mask of resolve.

Her wounds, which no one else remembered seeing, were going to get infected, unless she took to the infection. In that case, she'd be a shifter like Matt. "What are you?"

"Capable of doing this job."

"And Agent Spike?" It looked like they'd been close—lovers close. Was that what Victoria did to her friends?

"She knew what she was getting herself into." Victoria folded her hands in front of her and put her weight on one high-heeled foot, leaning back an inch. "You're getting close."

"To who?" I still couldn't wrap my head around who Victoria was showing me she was, or the fact that I'd gotten April shot.

"Lord Shadow," Victoria said in a flat voice. "He's enemy number one. Find him. Dannika and I have the resources to take him out."

"You and Dannika?"

"I'm capable of making the alliances needed to stay alive," Victoria said harshly, her stance remaining the same, but anger crept around the edges of her expression. "I realize you can't with your high morals."

"High morals?"

Victoria shook her head and looked away, straightening. "Just find him, and I'll do the dirty work. Like I always have."

Whoa. Whoa, whoa. "Always have?" She'd never told me she had a problem with my morals before, but I realized in that moment that she obviously had, because there had been several times in the past when she'd asked a question, I'd given her the answer, and her careful mask had slipped into place right before a major vote that hadn't gone our way.

"You helped the votes that didn't go our way."

"I'm creating a world we can survive in," Victoria hissed. "I knew we wouldn't make it to ParaWest. We're surrounded by the Federalist states. I knew what survival might mean for us, so yes, Sky, a few of those votes, I went the other way to make the inroads that are keeping us alive right now."

Bile rose in my throat. "The same laws that make us outlaws."

"But living outlaws, safe and outside of prisons. Yes."

"Are you the reason there are so many people trying to kill us?"

She shook her head with a slight roll of her eyes. "I'm not that powerful, Sky."

"Her name," Jamal said, coming up behind me and taking my shoulders, "is October. Now, you saved our pretty little asses, and I'm grateful, but it's time for you leave."

Victoria daggered Jamal with her gaze. "Find him so I can end this." Then she hard heel-clicked her way out of Speedy Couriers and slammed the red door shut behind her.

The moment settled over me like a scratchy blanket. "You called Victoria?"

"Wasn't my first choice, but turned out, she was the *only* choice." Jamal turned me around and gripped my head. "You look at me, baby girl. This isn't your fault."

That wasn't even what I was asking. "You called Victoria?"

He leveled me a hard look. "Without her, we'd all be in some form of very much worse."

I accepted his answer for what it was. He needed to stay alive, and to keep us alive, and he was doing the best he could with the resources he had. "What does she want?"

"She's a complicated woman." Jamal shook his head and looked away, his jaw tight.

April was being taken care of by someone I barely knew, but someone I trusted. I had to. I couldn't afford to waste energy on not trusting everyone. I needed to sleep.

"Where the hell is Rebruary?"

"Taking care of something else so we can get closer. Wait." Something Victoria said hit me. "She used his name."

"Yup. Protections are up. What are you doing?"

I was so jeezing exhausted. "I need sleep."

How could I sleep after everything that had happened?

"You will, baby girl," Jamal said, wrapping an arm around my shoulders. "Trust me."

I didn't know how that was going to happen, but one way or another, Lord Shadow was going down. Tonight.

So, I'd better figure it out.

Chapter 24

It was almost afternoon by the time I woke up. The blood on the floor had been cleaned up, and breakfast had been cleared away.

Noah stopped me. "Matt and April are doing okay."

"Good." That was a relief. I reminded myself that this wasn't like the last time. Things were going to be different. They already were.

"Are you mad at me? For keeping you hidden?"

I wanted to be. He'd protected me from discovery and had kept me quiet, kept me from showing myself. I shook my head.

"You sure? You seem pissed."

Maybe I was. I didn't mean to be. I knew I *shouldn't* be. He was the reason I was alive. "Maybe," I said aloud.

"I did what I had to."

"And that's why I'm trying not to be mad." Still, I was angry with the fact that I'd needed to hide again.

Noah bowed his head. "I'm sorry."

"For doing the right thing?" Maybe that was what Victoria felt like being on the other side of me. Now that I thought back, there'd been many times she'd told me what she needed to do and I'd stood steadfastly against her. I'd thought I'd been doing the right thing, and I still believed I had been, but . . .

The hard truth was that Victoria wasn't wrong. We were surrounded by Federalist states. We couldn't be like New

York, Vermont, and Maine, bundled together, supporting one another. If we separated to ParaWest, we'd be an island sharing a border with the enemy.

"Why doesn't it feel right?" he asked quietly.

I reached for him, my heart twisting. "Because April was shot to keep us hidden and Matt was shot protecting us. That's a heavy guilt sandwich."

"Hard guilt sandwich." He shook his head with a confused frown.

"It feels heavy for me."

"It doesn't feel like a sandwich to me."

He looked so spent. I stepped toward him and wrapped my arms around his waist.

Noah sagged into me, pulling me closer. We clung to one another for a long moment before he pulled away. "Okay. Now, I'm just angry."

Me too. The hug—touching or sharing my pain with a friend—had helped more than made sense to someone who hadn't had that type of support.

Jamal looked up when we came through the door. "You better, my babies?"

I didn't understand how he thought that calling us babies was a good thing, but the way he said it made me feel protected and wanted and comforted. I nodded.

"Good. Collect the calendar. It's time for a meeting."

Noah went to the bike shop in the back.

I went to the lockers where Julie was working on reorganizing the lost-and-found pile. "Hey."

"Hey," she said, her voice soft.

"Jamal's calling us."

"They knew about me." Now it was a whisper. "They were prepared."

That's what I'd initially thought too, but then . . . "They were armed against the senator."

Julie looked up in surprise.

I knew I was right. It was the only thing that made sense in that moment. "She knew exactly what to do. And they seemed pretty relieved to get their ear plugs back from her after she wiped their memories. It was her. And think about it—she's the perfect person to clean up this stuff. You know?"

"Then they don't know about *me*," she said, sagging with relief.

I shook my head. "They still don't know."

Julie thought about that, then released a short breath through her heart-shaped lips, closing her eyes.

I threw an arm around her shoulders and walked with her toward the break room. "They were here for me, anyway. Keep that in mind."

A ghost of a chuckle issued from her. "This is fucked."

It certainly was.

"A messenger came by from the clinic," Jamal said as soon as we'd entered the room. "April is out of danger and should be fine. Matt is a fast healer and is biting to come back. They're both good."

I sat down, finding a seat, and pinched the bridge of my nose, glad.

"So," Jamal continued, "what do we want to do?"

I already knew what I had to do. "Ryder's getting someone so we can find Lord—"

Jamal held up his hand abruptly.

I knew. "His lair. Can you create amulets or something that keep us protected from his seers?"

He raised his hands in protest. "There are limits to what I can do."

"Pe—Lady Dun seemed to think this was in your wheelhouse." I had no idea what the saying meant. "And can we even discuss this? With the. . ." I gestured around the room to ask about the seers who could be watching us.

He shook his head and waved me off. "I put protections up. They're not going to keep someone powerful out, but as long as we don't push the limits, we should be fine.

"Okay. Well, what can you do?" It was high time I found out, so I could determine our abilities.

His expression tightened. "I'm an abjurationist."

I had no idea what that was. "Is that voudou?"

"Catholicism," he said bluntly. "It's protection magic."

"But with the Catholic Church?" Julie asked, confused.

"My spells . . ." He took in a deep breath, the silver chain on his ear widening as he dipped his head to the side. "I suppress the ability of others."

So, that was how he'd been able to take my abilities.

"I'm good with barriers and protections. That's about it."

"What were you going to do in the fight?" I asked.

"Exactly what I did do, baby girl. I took away their abilities with the use of the protections I already had in place, and I protected the area from all seeing eyes."

"Why did Dannika take your abilities?"

"She didn't take them. She suppressed them."

So, she was like Jamal?

"We had a disagreement on how things should be done. She won because she's willing to cut corners I won't."

"Why is Pearl upset with you?"

"Because I bend rules she believes should remain unbroken."

That sounded like a group of people unwilling to work together.

"What are we going to do?" Noah asked.

"We can continue to hide," Julie said.

"Or we can fight." I rubbed my eyebrow. "Look, we have a partial plan. Between Pearl, the senator, and Dannika, we have enough people to divide his forces, keep him occupied on as many fronts as possible. Then, when he's distracted, we find the seers and relieve Lord *Him* of his greatest strength."

"What are his other strengths?" Noah asked. "He can hear us when we talk about him. What else?"

"He's a shapeshifter," I said, then glanced at Julie. "And he's a siren."

"He's a what?" Julie asked in surprise. "No, he's not."

I nodded. "He can make people do what he wants to with his words."

"So . . ." Her dark eyes went distant as she thought. "They could have been looking for him, too."

I hadn't thought of that. "I think he's on the police department."

"But not PPE?" Noah asked.

"I don't think so, but I don't know."

He took in a deep breath and nodded. "'Kay. 'Kay, 'kay, 'kay, 'kay, 'kay."

"There hasn't been a male siren in . . . generations," Julie said.

Jamal grunted. "There are more than you think. They're not all bad." He shrugged. "But the ones that are . . ." He shook his head and flapped his hands around as if he was flicking away motes of misinformation.

"If we fight," Julie said, her eyes still distant as she worked through the siren issue, "we die."

"How much worse would that be?" Noah asked. "Do you enjoy *this* life?"

How much worse *would* that be? That simple question hit me between the eyes. I didn't have anyone relying on me. If I died, the only one affected would be me. I didn't have family that cared. I didn't have friends who would grieve a ton. I had these guys in this room.

Noah glanced at me and then over to Julie, his expression saying he was making a similar realization.

"Well, darlings, I'd be missed, so I'm not dying today," Jamal said. "But I'm not hiding, either. If the three queens are rallying together, then it's a fine kettle of a day. I say we join October to find a way to locate this seer place and take it down. We're not fighting a war. We're just freeing some sleeping beauties. I like this idea."

It felt good, for sure, but I didn't think it'd be *that* easy. "We've got someone who's been there who said she'd help."

Jamal's eyes widened. "October."

The way he said my name carried surprise and a question of caution. "Ryder's collecting her parents right now to keep them safe."

"Which is what *he's* using to use her." Jamal pulled the corners of his lips down as he nodded appreciatively. "Crafty."

Julie shook her head, her eyes narrowed. "And if that doesn't work?"

The vision of the Five of Swords flashing along the door closing behind my sister rose in my mind. "I may have another way."

"Okay." Jamal took in a deep breath and released it. "Well, since we need all our allies, should we bring your lover boy in on this?"

"She's into Ryder," Noah said with a wrinkled face.

"Who says the girl's gotta choose?" Jamal said. "Or couldn't bring that lovely piece of meat back with her?" He batted his full lashes at me.

Going to Vance wasn't a bad idea except for the fact that his office was in the police station and Lord Shadow had actually seen my face. If he was on the police force, I couldn't just walk in.

"Baby girl," Jamal said, giving me a frank look, "We need all the help we can get."

We did. I just needed a way in.

Torrez.

He handed me a baseball cap and an amulet on a silk string. "Wear this. It should . . . help. Stop him from hearing you, yes. Seeing you? No. So, be careful what you do."

I slipped it over my head, grabbed a bike, and headed out.

The ride cleared my head a bit, trying to figure out how to find the beat cop. She was typically just around, but I didn't know her routine.

I went to Littleton, where I knew she worked. As I looked for her, my mind settling into our plan, my fear and hesitancy took a back seat with the knowledge that this really wasn't like the last time. We had faced him a couple times now and won. Kind of. That was a very definite step up.

I stopped at the grocery store by my place.

Johnny came out as I propped my bike against the light pole in front of his produce stand. "I saved you one of those apples."

I smiled and followed him into his small shop. "Thanks. Hey."

He reached over and grabbed an apple, handing it to me. "On the house."

I wasn't going to let him do that, so I reached into my pocket and pulled out a food coupon. The fruit wasn't worth the entire thing, but he did stuff like this for me often. "Have you seen Torrez?"

"Yeah, yeah," he said, taking the coupon with a thankful smile that promised more apples and possibly a banana if a shipment came in, then stashed it in his cash drawer with a ding and a bang. "She was just here. You find her down the street. Not far. Slow check today."

"Thanks, Johnny," I said, waving to him with the apple.

"Keep safe, October," he called after me.

"Always."

I ate as I rode down the street, searching for Torrez's cruiser, though she didn't always use it. Sometimes, she used her personal vehicle, which was blue maybe? Or silver? I didn't quite remember.

The apple was delicious, though not the best I'd ever had. The big bruise on the back mushed in my mouth with a bland flavor, but it didn't make the enjoyment any less. Fruit was hard to come by, and I hadn't eaten an apple in almost a year. I tossed out the skinny core in a nearby trash can and continued on.

"October," Torrez called to me.

I looked around, spotting her as she stepped into the nearly empty street. I waved and headed her way.

She frowned but made her way to the sidewalk and waited, leaning against a no parking sign, one thumb in her belt loop.

I slid off my seat and straddled the bike. "Hey, can you do me a favor?"

"Depends on the favor."

Uncertainty hit me. She wasn't involved with any of this yet. I hesitated. Did I *really* want her help with something she might be better off not knowing?

"Do you need help or not?" she asked.

"I do." This would be a wasted trip if I bailed, and I didn't have another way to get into the police station and grab Vance. "Can you get a message to Detective Young to meet me?"

Torrez's eyes and mouth both tightened, but she nodded. "Are you in trouble?"

I let out a small puff of air and shook my head. "About to be."

"What do you need?"

"I don't know that you want to be a part of this."

She tugged at my arm.

I got off my bike and set it against the sign then followed her to the building, each of us taking a side of a small alcove.

"Tell me you're about to take down the Witness—"

I reached out and stopped her, my hand close to her mouth. Hoping the amulet actually worked, I stepped closer to her and whispered, "He's listening to us."

"How?" Torrez asked, even softer but with daggers in her eyes.

"Seers."

She looked around the street, her mouth set, and nodded. "Makes sense. A lot of it, actually. Okay." She dropped her gaze back to me. "What do you need me to do, then?"

"Just get a message to Vance."

"Just." She snorted and searched my face, wanting to push. "He's being watched."

"I know. The leader is close to him. He's a part of the department, I think."

"Shit." Gnashing her teeth, she pulled her head back, the dark bun of her hair almost touching the pale brick wall behind her as she nodded. "Yeah, okay. That's all you need?"

I didn't need my cards or my gift to tell me that she genuinely wanted to help. "It'll be going down tonight, hopefully. We're waiting on one thing." The rescue of Kitty's parents. "Once that happens, we have to move fast."

"Are you not telling me because of the seers?"

Partially. "Because I don't know if I can trust you."

She closed her lips and pulled her jaw down as she ducked her head. "Yeah, okay. I buy that. This something you can survive?"

I really hoped so. "Sure."

She snorted again. "Be at the corner outside the precinct in fifteen."

The police station wasn't actually that far away, so I took my time, enjoyed the sights for the first time in a year.

A lot had changed, something that I'd known but hadn't really noticed before. A lot of the old stores were gone, and in their places were meeting halls and play group hangouts. One entire building had been ripped down, which I remembered—and hauled away, which I didn't—and a community garden stood in its place with multiple tiers and small pathways.

More people walked or rode bikes. There were fewer dogs, more cats. People were slimmer, but still wearing the clothes they had when they'd been larger.

Kins City and her suburbs had changed a lot in the last year.

I didn't have to wait long outside the precinct before Vance came out, slipping his business jacket on, his dark tie fluttering in the wind. He looked both ways and crossed the street, having to sidestep the one car that went by. He made eye contact with me but didn't even pause as he walked by.

I waited a little bit, then turned my bike around and walked it after him, meandering through the light pedestrian traffic as unobtrusively as I could.

The detective stepped into a sandwich shop and disappeared.

I locked up my bike on the rack outside and followed.

He was sitting at a table with two sandwiches, waiting. The man was fast.

Unless that other sandwich wasn't for me.

He smiled at me as I sat down. "What's going on?"

"We're finally making a move on Lord"—I didn't want to push the amulet—"on him, and I thought I'd fill you in on it."

He nodded and unwrapped his sandwich.

"This for me?"

Vance shook his head. "But you can have it. Dreven'll just have to order a new one."

If he was okay with that, so was I. I unwrapped it and dug in, not quite remembering the last time I'd had a bite. It had to have been the day before. I filled him in roughly on what had happened and what we were planning as I ate.

He listened without adding much. "How'd you get out of PPE custody after the raid?" he asked when I was done.

"I can't tell you, but we're safe. For now."

He sat back in his chair. "You know the Mind Eraser."

I frowned at him, trying to remember where I'd heard that name before. "Who?"

"Don't play coy," he said, leaning forward again on the table. "I've been trying to figure out who he is for a while now. We all have been. All law enforcement agents go out with special ear plugs, but now that we know those are useless . . ." He shook his head. "I want to find that person and stop him."

We could tackle that later. "I don't know about that." And I didn't know who *he* was.

Vance tipped his head to the side, his expression droll.

"But I just wanted to let you know," I said, "because of your side job that we might need."

He frowned and sat back. "Is this you asking or Jamal?"

"Jamal."

"What is it going to take to get your trust back?" He leaned forward another inch.

"Why would I want you to have it?"

"Because, together, you and I do great things."

I coughed.

His jaw worked for a moment, and then he looked down. "Someone was hurt. Weren't they? At the raid?"

I looked at him and then fell back in my chair, closing my eyes for a long moment. "April and Matt."

Vance licked his lips and leaned back in his chair as well. "Are they okay?"

"For now."

"People," he said, rubbing his bottom lip and then his chin with his finger, "are going to get hurt if we have the courage to make a change."

"I know that."

"Was this your fault?"

"Yes." I swallowed. "They'd been looking for me. April got in the way. Matt defended her."

Running his tongue along his teeth, he nodded. "Okay. And if people get hurt tonight or tomorrow or whenever this is going down? What then?"

I knew I'd continue fighting. That's just who I was. "I'm still going to feel bad about it. You can't stop that."

"Please don't let that stop you. Because this city needs you. I need you. We need you."

I looked up into his chocolate eyes for a long moment, taking what he was giving me. "'Kay."

"Okay. Well, this has got to be planned. How are we doing that with . . ." He gestured around and sighed.

I held up my amulet. "Plus, Jamal has protections up. Might not work completely, but it'll help some."

"Sounds good. When and where do we meet?"

"This afternoon at Jamal's."

"I'll be there." He opened his mouth to say something, then stopped and smiled at someone behind me. "Hey, Drev. You'll have to order another. I gave yours away."

"Of course you did," a familiar voice said, and a wave of dread washed over me.

It was Lord Shadow. And Vance knew him.

Chapter 25

"Who's your friend?" Lord Shadow asked.

Vance smiled and looked at me.

I widened my eyes in alarm and tried to shake my head as little as possible.

He frowned slightly and then waved Lord Shadow off. "A CI."

"A CI I don't know about?"

"You've got some too, partner. Can you give us a minute?"

"Sure. Sure," Lord Shadow said good-naturedly. "I'll go reorder my sandwich. You didn't use my voucher, did you?" He turned to the order queue.

"Of course I did," Vance called after him jokingly, then leaned forward. "What?"

"That's Lord Shadow," I whispered.

"Dreven Black?" Vance looked over my shoulder and back at me, his expression saying he didn't believe me. "Detective Dreven Black?" His face flashed into a smile, and he laughed, shaking his head. "How do you know?" he asked, barely moving his lips.

"His voice."

He thought about that for a second. "Shit. Shapeshifter and a siren?"

I nodded. "He could be using his siren ability on you, and you wouldn't even know it."

"Not likely." He raised an eyebrow. "Get out before he comes back. Take your sandwich. He can use it to run DNA."

He could do that? I popped the last two bites in my mouth and got up, keeping my back to the monster.

"Can I offer you anything else?" Lord Shadow asked, coming up behind me.

I shook my head, gathered my trash, and snaked my way to the door.

"What spooked her?" I heard him ask from behind.

"You know how it is," Vance said, his tone showing no signs of excitement. "Lots of things. How's our case?"

I ducked out of there and slid to the side where Vance and his partner couldn't see me.

He'd come so close to figuring out who I was. I was lucky to get away.

But this also gave me a chance. I could follow *him* for once. I could track *him* for once.

The Devil appeared beside me and wiggled his eyebrows with a mischievous smile, nodding his approval.

That wasn't necessarily a bad thing, but what he really represented was distractions. I didn't know how *this* could be a distraction. Following the man I knew was Lord Shadow couldn't be a distraction when we were trying to take him down.

The Devil nodded his agreement and gestured toward a shadowed corner for me to hide in.

I was divided. Here we were, ready to take this very man down. He was right here in my grasp, and . . . This was what we needed. This was the lucky break we'd been waiting for. His identity.

So, why didn't it feel like that?

Because he had to know who I was. He had to know I was the person he'd been trying to track down, and he'd be waiting for me. He might be able to use his voice on me.

Damn it!

A car pulled up at the curb in front of me, and the passenger-side door opened. "Get in!" a female voice shouted.

"Suzi?" I asked incredulously.

She nodded, her head jostling from side to side as she continued to lean over.

"Dannika send you?"

"No," she asked like I'd just called her an asshole. She rolled her eyes and nodded. "Yes. Just get in."

Dannika, I didn't trust. Lord Shadow, I definitely didn't trust.

Suzi? I kind of trusted her. I walked to the door, keeping an eye on the table Vance and his partner sat at. Lord Shadow's back was still to the door.

Of course it was. He didn't have to worry about anything. His seers could see what he couldn't.

"Would you get in already?"

"Why are you here?" I asked, trying to decide if I should grab my bike and ride, or hop in the car, or stay.

The Devil gestured to my hiding spot again and grinned, light gleaming off his pointed tooth.

"Your name popped up on a lot of radars, sweetie, so you get your tight little ass into this car right now or you're meat."

"Meat?"

"Probably not the dead kind. Seems pretty bad, in my opinion, which you ain't askin' for and that's fine. But get your ass in this car right now."

Sirens sounded to my left, but that was the direction of the police station, so it might not be for me.

"October," Suzi said with a hedge of warning.

"Fine." I got in the car and shut the door. "Where?"

"I was going to ask you that," she said as she ground the car into gear.

"Where'd you get this thing?"

"Do you really want to know?"

"No. Fine. What radars?"

"I got a network of strange people." Suzi nodded with her entire body, glancing at me. "None of Dannika's, I can tell you that."

"Great." That still didn't illuminate what her sources were.

"Jesus H. Christ," Suzi said, slamming us around a corner and slowing down. "Do you really think Dannika's the only person who knows a person who knows people? I grew up in the network. I went to school and shit with these people. I know more about their bowels than most people know coffee orders."

"I don't understand how that relates to . . . anything."

"It means that when shit gets real, your real friends push up like daisies over dead people and start helping. Now, look, I'm not sure what you did, but it wasn't great. APB went all over the cities searching for Sky Martinez. Now, you and me know that October Blaze *is* Sky Martinez, but whoever popped your ID doesn't. Great for us, but doesn't make for a lot of wiggling room to save your ass."

That could have been Torrez. Except that she'd known where I was. "Why are you here?"

"Well, first of all, Dannika was there when Shorty told Bobo that Sky'd been popped. Then Bobo wanted to know if your brain had painted a wall, and Killa—gotta love Killa, but I don't know why. That girl's bat-shit and kinda dumb like a box—asked if clouds had brains. That's when Bobo informed her that clouds had more brains than she did—which might actually be legit, you'd have to meet her, you'd probably agree—and that the Martinez chick was lighting up the wires. By name. You know, which means a lot around here. Even with the Wipe, a name's a lot."

"Sky Martinez doesn't exist post-Wipe."

"You gotta somewhere, sweetie. I was already fixin' to find you, but Dannika told me to, which gives me more resources. I mean, with my crew—which, okay. It's not much of a crew, I gotta say. You wouldn't. . . Okay. Okay. Yeah. Not a crew.

More like. . ." She paused her discordant ramble and turned the corner, slowing down, the sounds of sirens fading behind as she ducked into an enclosed parking garage. "Yeah, I don't know. Anyway, I would have found you. Probably your body judging by the dumb look on your dumb face, but. . ."

I stared at her in disbelief as she took us two levels down and parked. "This is the most you've talked since I met you."

"Yeah, well, to be fair," Suzi said, putting the car in park, leaving the keys and getting out, "there were a lot of bullets last time."

"How long ago did my name . . ." I didn't know how to finish that without sounding narcissistic. I closed the door, hiking my bag higher on my shoulder.

She brisk-walked down the line of randomly parked cars and went to another, this one shiny and black. Opening the driver-side door, she looked at me over the roof, though only barely. She had to kind of reach to see over, her dark eyes and hair the only thing I could see. "Long enough for me to drive over from Kins City."

She ducked into the car.

I didn't know what slip I'd made, but it didn't matter. Vance's partner was a police detective. He had access to video surveillance. The Wipe had cleared a lot of information away, but obviously not all of it.

No. It could have been anything. It could have been the decision to go after Lord Shadow. It could have—

He had a pool of seers who could see things. It could have been a butterfly having sex in the park while getting squished by my bicycle tires. Seriously, I had no idea what had drawn his attention to me.

"Sky Martinez," I said in the passenger seat as she took us lower in the parking garage.

"That's what I said."

There were two people who knew my old name. Torrez and Victoria. I'd already figured out it couldn't have been Torrez.

What about Victoria? She could be purchased. Maybe not with money, but with a vote? Though I had no idea what Lord Shadow would do to—

Then it hit me. Calypso. She knew my name, and if she was trying to get Jimmy back and I hadn't found him yet, maybe she'd been forced to give me up. Or maybe Jimmy's life was being threatened?

A golden chariot appeared upside down, the dragon and the Pegasus pulling it fighting each other to right the vehicle.

Defeat.

Jimmy?

That didn't feel right.

Calypso?

The chariot glowed.

Crap. Did Vance's partner have Jimmy?

The chariot disappeared.

"Do you know anything about Vance's partner?"

"Vance?" Suzi asked.

"Detective Young."

She flicked her eyebrows and smacked her lips. "Well, you shoot high, that's all I'm saying. Yeah. Detective Dreven Black. Not a great guy. He's a real piece of work. Got the voice, you know? So, careful there. He speaks, and next thing you know, you're dancing. And he don't care. He's a man what gets his way."

"That makes sense."

"Why?"

"Because . . ." I closed my eyes and took hold of the amulet Jamal had given me. "He's our big bad guy."

"Lord—"

I held up a finger to silence her.

Suzi pulled into a tunnel from the parking garage. "Okay. How bad is this guy?"

I'd forgotten she hadn't been a part of *any* of those conversations. "He's the leader of the Witnesses."

"You're shitting me."

"I'm not."

"Well, if that don't blow it all. Okay. How do we take that guy down?"

"We take out his seers."

"Sounds smart. How we do that? You guide, I follow."

"Right now, let's get to Speedy."

"You got it." She mashed the gas, and we shot forward toward Kins City.

We got to Jamal's in the early afternoon, when most of the couriers were already out. Julie and Noah sat at the table in the breakroom shoving ingredients into bags and tying them up with string.

"Tell me that's not what's protecting us," Suzi said. "A bunch of weeds?"

"Oh, you dear girl," Jamal said, walking in behind us and brushing his fingers along her cheek.

She jerked back and glared at him.

He didn't notice. "Weeds are but a conduit." He picked up one of the bags. "It could be filled with dirt or trash or whatever nonsense. As long as it's something I can connect to. The magic is in me." He gave the bag a squeeze, and a soft white glow filtered through his fingers.

"Yeah." Suzi held up both her hands, her fingers flared and then let them drop to her sides again as she shuffled her weight uncomfortably. "Makes me feel a smidge better."

"Good. Now then." Jamal settled us both with a fierce smile, leaning on the back of Noah's chair. "If we're protecting an army, we need a lot of these made up."

By the end of the first hour, I'd stopped caring how much of which herb went into each bag. We'd run out of some of them, though the names I didn't know. Well, one was dandelion.

"That's the most powerful herb in the world, baby girl," Jamal said. "You can't *keep* a dandelion down."

At one point, however, I was fairly certain Jamal was just throwing in kitchen spices because we'd run out of everything else. He was down to scribbling notes on scraps of paper and having us shove those into the bags with basil. The first bags had been leather. Then cloth. By the end, they were made out of scraps of brown paper bags.

"I hope this works," I muttered, not sure how bags, shoestrings, notes, and basil were going to protect us against seers who could see our every move.

"The real ingredient is me," Jamal said, but with a lot less confidence than when we'd started.

"I didn't know," Vance said as he walked through the door to the break room.

"Well, hello to you too," Jamal said.

Vance stopped, assessed the room, and took a breath. "Tell me we're protected here."

"We are," I told him.

"He's a shapeshifter *and* a siren?" he asked.

I nodded.

"And how can he hear us?"

"The seers he's gathering."

"Fuck." Vance closed his eyes and let his head fall back. "I fucking gave him that fucking idea," he said quietly, pulling his hands through his hair.

"Uh, there's been a development." Jamal injected himself into the conversation. "What happened?"

I raked my top lip with my teeth and breathed for a moment, feeling like saying it out loud would make it not real or too real. I didn't know which.

Vance popped his neck and met Jamal's gaze. "Lord Shadow is my partner."

"What?" Jamal asked, stunned.

"Dreven Black. I've known him—" He stopped, pressing the tip of his tongue to the roof of his mouth. "I went to his wedding."

"He's married?"

"He was. He lost his wife and son during the war."

That made a lot more sense. I'd been trying to figure out what was driving this man. And now? Grief. That was big and ugly, and even though there were many in the city who could relate, it wasn't something that eased when shared. Not really.

I shrugged at him and pressed Vance. "What do you know about him that could help us stop him?"

"He's just a guy."

"He's more than that. He's a lot more than that. He's Lord freaking—"

"Darkness!" Suzi shouted, shoving her hands in her pockets with a decisive nod to the group. "Code." She gestured to the bags of basil and scraps of paper with her fist still in her pants. "Protections or not."

"Right," Julie said. "I told my mother about him. She seemed to already know."

"Of course she did, July, my dear," Jamal said, clicking his tongue and heading to the table. "As soon as she heard that a man could control others with his voice, she knew. That's not something that would fall under *her* radar."

"Wasn't Ryder immune to him?" Julie asked.

"She was not," Ryder's husky voice said from behind me, "immune. I have two parents out front wanting to see Kitty."

"How did you fight him?" Julie asked.

"Kitty should be here shortly," Jamal told Ryder.

She nodded, then turned to Julie. "I can fight siren calls, but it takes some strength."

I narrowed my eyes at Vance. "Why didn't *you* think you were being controlled?"

He sucked in a breath through his nose and shrugged. "I'm immune to magic."

"Like . . . all magic?"

He made a noise with his tongue. "I don't know, but it doesn't seem to have an effect on me."

"Do you break it?" Jamal asked, glancing at the walls.

"No. Just if it's applied to me. Your protections are still fine."

Ryder narrowed her eyes at him. "This could work in our favor. If we know who he is, then we can direct him. Put him where *we* want him."

I liked this. "And as soon as we know where he's hiding the seers—"

"We distract him," Ryder said.

"And keep him distracted," Vance added.

"And I free the seers," I finished.

"Seems simple." Suzi clapped her hands. "We're gonna die." She made a clicking noise with her tongue and let her hands fall to her side.

Vance shot her a look, then turned to me. "You can't go off on your own."

"I'll go with her," Ryder said.

"You most certainly will not." Pearl's clear voice filled the room. "You have your mission, and you know it."

Ryder pulled her head to the side and kept her back to the door, her face filled with frustration.

My guess was that she didn't like being told what to do. "I'll take Suzi."

"I've got October," Suzi said, her gaze skirting the room as she nodded in more of a chicken-head-bob than a true nod and snap-slapped her hands together. "We'll be great! Me, her, and the kid? Yeah. What could *possibly* go wrong?"

I ignored her and focused on Pearl. "You're bringing aid, or just Kitty?"

"What we can afford. It's not much. Kitty's with her parents." Her eyes landed on Jamal, and her expression shifted, softening around the edges though her shoulders remained tight. "Jamal."

"Pearl." He dropped his gaze for a moment, then brought it back up, throwing his shoulders back.

She took in a deep breath and nodded, her hands closing around her cane. "Do you have points around the city you want to focus on?"

Jamal walked to the city map on the wall. "Now that we know who and where to target, Vance here can give us some direction on how to do that."

"I have a couple ideas." He blinked and looked to the group as if to say his ideas weren't great ones.

I didn't want to get into the details. "Do we know a general idea of where they're being held?"

"Downtown Lista Point," Pearl said. "Kitty will give better directions when she can. She was brought there, so she'll need to use landmarks, but she should be able to get you there on foot."

"That slows things down for us," Vance said.

"We'll just have to keep him interested longer, is all," Ryder said, grit in her tone.

"How do people win against you?" I asked Julie.

She shrugged and crossed her arms over her chest. "Ear plugs. After that, it's pretty easy to kill us. We're only good if you can hear us."

"That's not all he has, though," Noah said, and his quiet voice commanded the room for a moment. "He can see us."

"Until we break the seers free," I said.

He nodded, his expression grim. "How will we know?"

"That's where Victoria comes in," Pearl said, holding up a black ball. "This is one of her special earpieces. We give these to the leaders throughout the city, and we communicate to each other that way."

"Is that the only support she's offering?" I asked.

Pearl nodded. "It's enough."

The Magician rose in the doorway and nodded solemnly.

We had the talent we needed. Now all we had to do was not mess this up.

Chapter 26

The plan was good, and it was flexible enough that *if* Dreven Black had been able to hear it, we'd still be able to change things up if necessary. I was a little frustrated that Victoria hadn't sent people to help us, but the earpieces were exceedingly helpful.

"In place," Vance said in my ear.

"Watch Tower's up," an unfamiliar voice said.

As Suzi, Kitty, and I walked down the empty streets of the high-rise district, the other team leaders called in. The occasional overhead light buzzed or flickered, throwing more shadows over the cracked road. Storefronts with apartments above them rose on either side like giants with sagging, hollow eyes.

Who was I going to find in the seer pit? My nephew? Parker? Could she still *be* alive? Was that possible? And how was I going to win against Lord—against Dreven Black this time? I knew a lot more now than I had before.

A cocoon waved at the bottom of a leaf hanging over the sidewalk.

Careful not to knock it off the leaf, I breezed by. "I don't know how helpful I'm going to be in this fight."

"Says the woman who can see things no one else can. Yeah." Suzi looked over her shoulder at me, nearly knocking into another cocoon. "I'd hate to be smarter on any given day."

What was up with the cocoons? I brushed at another one in front of my face—

Only to discover it wasn't real.

I paused and looked closer. The cocoon in question was white and had a green slitted eye on it. The whole thing shook as if the butterfly inside was getting ready to burst out.

Okay. What was the message? What was I supposed to hear right now in this moment? It seemed like an odd time for this. We were heading into battle.

A cocoon was an invitation to do something different, something I'd been thinking of testing out and hadn't. It was a reminder to step away from habit and turn toward doing something smart.

What *was* my habit?

With Senator Armstrong, I'd answered the questions she'd asked. I'd looked for the clues and indicators she'd wanted.

With Vance, I'd given his team the direction he'd asked for and then I'd inserted myself into the battle as a fighter, which I wasn't.

In both instances, I'd been following. My gift seemed to be trying to give me the chance to take more of a lead. It was giving me information before I even asked for it, providing insight before I knew I needed it.

So, maybe this time, I needed to lead instead of follow.

That's what I *was* doing, though. The trip to find the seers wasn't Senator Armstrong or Pearl or Dannika. This was me.

The realization of that hit me. This was my idea, so the repercussions of that would be mine to own. That thought might have scared me earlier in the week, but now it just felt right. This was a fight of visions, of reading the future.

On this battlefront, I *was* the right warrior.

Something floated above the buildings a few blocks away. At first, I couldn't quite tell what it was until a dim rainbow crossed underneath of it. I made out a large, floating stone next and what appeared to be a goat standing on top of it. The Ace of Stones?

What was it trying to tell me? That this was the perfect time to act?

Did that mean that the plan was going to work?

Success was likely to evolve from our actions.

Also good.

Kitty motioned for us to follow her to the right. "It's here."

I still didn't quite know what the cocoons wanted me to do. I had a suspicion that I needed to pay attention to *something* in this moment, but I wasn't clear what that needed to be. Were we on the wrong path? Should we divert?

With no clear answer, I followed Kitty down a small, clean exterior corridor lined with plants to make it appear like a covered greenway. After a cautious look around, she opened the front door.

"It's not locked?"

At Suzi's question, a chill ran over me. Was he expecting us? But then why the cocoons and the Ace of Stones? If we were in imminent danger, wouldn't there be something . . . more?

Suzi pulled out a small gun, pointing the muzzle to the floor with an air of cold confidence that had been lacking during the drive.

I tapped my earpiece. "We're in place."

"Beginning distractions." Vance's voice was strong.

Kitty walked in and slid to the side, skimming along one wall and then slinking along the next one.

Suzi and I followed.

"They don't need locks," Kitty whispered. "The *seers* are their locks."

That made sense.

The girl led the way down one corridor, and a growing sinking feeling filled me, but without further signs, it was just a sensation without direction or merit.

It was quiet here. No lights. No sounds. No movement. "Are you sure this is the place?"

"I'm sure." Kitty's voice was small, though, as if she had doubts.

"Is it always this dead?"

She shook her head, glancing at me as she went through another door.

Blue lights flashed all around us, but Kitty and Suzi didn't react to them. This had to be something only I could see. But blue alarm lights? That didn't make sense.

They flashed red for a moment, then reverted back to blue again.

I was supposed to trust the alarm? Or trust the vision sending me the alarm?

The ceiling and walls turned into mirrors, showing only the three of us. Kitty remained in the lead and headed toward a door, Suzi not far behind.

Jeezum! What did mirrors represent again? I needed to dig back into my symbols library and refresh myself with them.

Before I could try to figure it out, the mirrors shattered, crashing down, the broken shards diving toward me.

I tried to hide my shriek as I ducked down, shielding my face with my arms.

"What the hell?" Suzi whispered hoarsely, coming to stand beside me.

I looked up, my heart racing. The walls were white again. The ceiling was a grid again. I didn't—

I knew what my vision was trying to tell me. I had to break out of the vision of my life and my gift and what I thought I knew. I had to emerge, seeing what was new.

The white walls flashed blue again.

Blue represented trust and security.

The blue flashed brightly as if to tell me I'd gotten it.

I had a new relationship with my gift. It interacted with me, which meant that I didn't have to follow blindly. I could—

The blue flashed to black and pulsed angrily.

I was getting an interaction, but this . . . wasn't my gift? This wasn't my vision.

The walls flashed bright blue again.

This was someone else.

The blue sagged into an amber for a moment before returning and flashing blue again. Joy, and then trust once more, followed by a trilling flute.

Parker. She'd played the flute and would randomly play all the time. How was she—

That didn't matter. The alarm. Alarms indicated something was bad, and this looked almost like a fire alarm strobe. Someone was telling me this was a trap.

"Stop," I whispered.

Suzi froze where she stood and gestured with her hands. "And do what?"

"They're not here," Kitty whispered at a door, peering through the small window. "I don't understand." She moved to open the door.

Two swords appeared on it, handles down, blades up.

"Stop!" I said a little louder. Two of Swords meant that battle was about to begin, and it was on the door, so I had to believe that it meant that if we went through, we'd be faced with a fight.

Suzi grabbed the girl's arm.

Kitty turned to me, her green eyes filled with desperation. "I'm not lying to you. They were right here."

"I trust you." I swallowed hard, trying to wet my dry throat. "He probably saw this . . . days ago. Seers. They must have known. Maybe they moved the pool."

"They *were* right here."

"I just said I believed you."

"I'm not lying."

Suzi put her hand on Kitty's shoulder and sighed, looking at me. "Kid, we get it. We aren't gonna take this out on you or your parents or anything like that."

"I'm sorry," Kitty said, looking up at her.

I slinked along the wall, back the way we'd come. My gift *had* been trying to talk to me. The Ace of Stones wasn't just the Ace of Stones. It was trying to tell me where to start, where we'd be successful. "I think I might know where to go." All I had to do was find it.

Suzi nodded, then tapped her ear.

Right. Initiating the earpiece, I said, "Seers aren't here."

"What's the"—Vance grunted—"plan?"

I respected his ability to talk while keeping Dreven's forces occupied. "We're on the move."

"Are we scrapped?"

"No. Not yet. I'll update in a bit." I tapped the comm unit to turn it off, keeping my eyes on the big stone with the dancing goat. Cocoons hung from leaves and branches.

Then I moved toward the building with the Ace of Stones rotating over it like a neon sign.

"What the hells happened?" Suzi demanded.

"I have no idea." And I didn't. I had never *interacted* with a vision before. I'd never had an impact before. This seemed like something else. The air felt different, something I hadn't realized until I'd gotten back.

If that had been Parker trying to show me what she saw, then . . .

First of all, how?

The seer pool. Maybe it was amplifying her ability. Kitty had said that there were needles in their brains connecting them to the pool. But if this really was Parker helping us, then why was now the first time I'd heard—

This wasn't the first time.

The dark street flashed blue.

I'd heard the flute before.

A happy trill floated through the air, and I could almost hear a wild whoop.

Okay. She was helping us. Her gift worked differently than mine. It always had. Her visions were cannily on point. But if she was reaching out to me? Connecting with me? There had to be a way to use that.

The world around me flashed silver.

Jeezum. I didn't have time for twenty questions. I needed to focus on Dreven—or *not* Dreven, but his men. Where were the largest forces? Were they moving? Was our plan working?

A great silver-and-black stag rose over the buildings to my right, teal vines dripping from his horns. The stag's head shot up as he looked back in alarm.

I initiated my comm unit. "Vance, you have someone coming to you from behind."

The stag looked at me and nodded before fading.

A white falcon shot from the thin clouds, filling the sky with blinding golden light, but then broke off from the attack, opened its wings, and circled on a current, searching. "Ryder, your prey has left."

"I need a direction," she said. "I have Dreven."

Where was Dreven going? But I knew that if I asked—

The falcon's head shot in my direction, her glowing blue eyes narrowed.

"Me. He's coming my way."

"You've got him?" Vance asked, light sounds of scuffing coming through with his words like he was staying low while moving.

"He was here," Ryder said, her voice clipped with quick breaths. It sounded like she was running.

"Changing channels," Vance said. "Go get the seers. Break his connection."

I changed the channel and responded. "Keep him occupied and away from me." I didn't want to really face off with him. A war of visions was one thing, but eye to eye, face-to-face?

Bad idea. I fingered the earplug in my pocket, reminding me it was still there, just waiting to be used if Dreven got too close. I wasn't going to be stupid. I wasn't charging in blind and deaf and dumb.

I lengthened my stride. We needed to get there faster, but it didn't take long for the surrounding buildings to block out the large, floating stone and the goat standing on top of it.

Green arrows lit up the sidewalk, directing us down one street around a corner, then back up another.

This was taking too long. If Dreven was on his way here, we needed to be faster.

The green arrows stopped at a glowing green door.

I put my hand on it, but Kitty stopped me. "This could be a trap," she whispered.

"Nine out of ten it is," Suzi said.

"Are we going to stop now?" I asked, my hand still on the metal bar of the door. "Dreven's out there fighting our friends—" A flash of light in the distance punctuated my words.

"I did what I had to," Kitty whispered, her tone pinched with fear.

I took a breath. She was just a kid and I could not push her on this. Doing so was wrong on so many levels. "You did," I said, and tapped her shoulder. "Go back. We've got this."

Kitty didn't wait. She turned and bolted down the street.

"Did you happen to notice," Suzi said, peering inside the door and then giving me a look that said she agreed with me sending Kitty away and was upset about it at the same time, "not a single drone this whole way?"

I hadn't until that moment. "Dannika's helping?"

Suzi grunted again. "That's a bill's gonna come due soon."

Yeah, well, if it made this impossible mission possible, then I'd figure out a way to pay it. Later.

I opened the door and Suzi swept inside, her gun pointed to the ground. "My job," she said, shaking her gun. "Your job," she said, shaking her head from side to side. "Got it?"

"Yup." We were in danger, and Dreven was on his way here. How long could they keep him away from us? I looked around, no idea where to go first, so I asked my gift.

The way in front of us glowed white. That seemed like a solid no, but I knew things could change, especially with a guy like Dreven. I just had to hope we'd be able to break the connection with the seers. Quickly.

Suzi led the way around a corner and stopped. Her eyes went wide as she let out a low whistle. "You've gotta see this."

I turned the corner and my breath caught in my throat. In the large run on the other side of a short, wide hall was a circle of chairs with people strapped to them, IV stands beside them. Their feet rested in a large, glowing pool.

There had to be over a dozen here, all seers, all trapped, their eyes closed.

Now, I just had to figure out how to break them free without harming anyone.

Chapter 27

A light mist rose over the pool, changing color from blue to green to yellow. A wolf face snapped, teeth clamping on nothing. Then the face disappeared, leaving a bulb where the snout had been.

The mist spun as if looking, then disappeared back into the pool.

Were the seers looking for us? Were they blind from Jamal's wards and protections? "See any guards?"

"Nope," Suzi said, giving the area a wide look. "But they're in wheelchairs, so that's gotta help. Really wish that kid'd stuck around now."

I nodded, but Suzi didn't see me. "Same." It couldn't be helped, though.

I walked to the first person, peering into his face to see if he was someone I knew. He wasn't, but I couldn't help but notice the three tubes attached to a silver circle at the man's right temple. Kitty had said a needle had been jammed into their brain. I had to assume it was because she'd seen the process, but that could be an assumption. This could be nothing more than a pad.

I touched the tubes, following them into the pool. It glowed faintly at my touch. Was it reacting to me or to my power?

If that pool was connecting them, then they were working together. They could probably see me—

Except I was wearing the protection. So was Suzi. The vision wolf had turned away, but would it again? The mist rose into the wolf again, searching for me, then fell back into the pool just as quickly. He hadn't seen me.

Okay. Good. That gave me a chance to see if I could find Parker and Jimmy.

Leaving the man there, I moved around the circle, checking each person's face. I was really looking for Parker, as I had no real idea what Jimmy would look like. I mean, he'd be a young boy, would probably have our skin and hair color. He might have a family resemblance, but he might look like his father, whom I had never met. So, I kept my eye out for someone younger.

There were no children.

I didn't want to think about that. There'd been plenty of kids who'd gone missing, some with gifts. Was Dreven hiding them somewhere else? How many hadn't survive this process? Were they being held elsewhere? I stopped my mind from continuing in circles.

I looked once more, concentrating on each person before I finally found Parker's familiar face, her eyes closed, her dark hair freshly shaved. Glancing at the circle of people, I only just now noticed that they'd all had their hair removed. I didn't care, though. Hair didn't matter. She was here. She was alive.

Her arm was so small under my hand that my breath caught in my throat. She'd been here for a year. Not in the building, but here, captured by Dreven and held in stasis, unable to move the whole time.

"Nothing from Ryder or Vance," Suzi said. "I think I'll begin panicking."

"Check the other channel." I had to figure out how to disconnect Parker, how to get her out of there, to get them *all* out of there.

"Got 'em." Suzi moved to the far end of the room, chatting on the comm.

That gave me time to trace the tubes to and from Parker. How was I going to free them?

I remembered what Pearl *hadn't* said to Ryder and the Nazi-insignia guy. *If you can't free them, kill them. Lord Shadow* must *be weakened.*

A part of me wanted to start with someone else, anyone else—just in case I accidentally killed my friend while trying to extract her. That might take too much time. Dreven could be here too soon. I peeled back the white circle attached to her temple carefully.

"They still got him, but he's harder to hold down than a greased pig in an eel farm. I told them where we are, but Dreven *is* on his way here."

"Jeezum." A needle protruded from the sticky pad and into Parker's brain, right where Kitty had said it would be. My face pulled into a toothy grimace as I started to pull it out, but then I stopped. *Was this the right thing to do? Was this safe?*

I didn't get an answer. Fine time for my gift to be silent.

My heart raced and my hands shook as I braced myself, pulled the sticky off her skin, and then gently pulled the needle out.

It was longer than I'd hoped, but it was thin. She didn't move, didn't even twitch. A bubble of blood welled up after its point emerged.

Releasing a shaking breath, I scrambled to my feet and grabbed her knees, pulling her feet out of the milky pool.

Her head shot backward as she screamed an unholy noise, deep and guttural, her eyes wild and eerily pale, like the milk of the pool.

Dropping her feet, I stumbled back. What was I supposed to do?

Her eyes fell on me as her lungs lost their air and she slumped forward, spent.

"The fuck?" Suzi asked from the other side of the room.

I shook my head. I had no idea. I moved to the next person in line, pulling her feet from the misty pool. "We've got to hurry."

"Are they all going to scream like that?" she asked, coming to help.

"I don't know. Be gentle with the temple. It *is* a needle."

"Fuck me," she said, her voice somewhere between awe and horror.

We spent the next several minutes pulling the seers from the pool. No one else screamed, but their eyes were all milky white. They seemed comatose, but their eyes were open and staring.

"We've got them out," Suzi said into the comm. "How long?"

I grabbed the handles of Parker's wheelchair and prepared to move away.

She made a strangled sound, and the white and glass walls around us dissolved, becoming a corridor of blue, pulsing vertical lines. The wheelchair became a sailboat, and stars glittered from the dark blue waters beneath my feet. Turning, I saw each of the seers trapped in similar sailboats, each in different directions, calling out to each other, their faces reflecting back at them like light shadows in mist.

"They're still connected somehow," Suzi said. "This guy is still getting information."

The vision was a card from my deck, though I didn't necessarily believe it was telling *me* to go with the flow but instead showing me that they were still trapped inside the seer pool.

Or maybe that was exactly what the card was telling me. I needed to join them.

I wasn't going to inject that needle into my brain. I had no idea what type of damage that would do. But Parker hadn't reacted until I'd removed her from the pool. So, maybe there was something there. She'd already been reaching out to me, trying to connect.

Kneeling down, I stretched out my hand.

"What are you doing?" Suzi demanded, scrambling toward me. "They lost Dreven. He could be here at any time."

I met her gaze, shook my head, and lightly touched the water.

The world disappeared into comforting silence. The walls receded into a bank of white clouds, and for the first time in years, I felt peace. True peace. Closing my eyes, I allowed myself to simply enjoy this, to give my soul the rest it needed so badly. I felt the tranquility, but the press of time pulled me forward.

When I opened my eyes, the starlit river rippled around my feet, but without walls anymore, and two winged figures danced in the sky above me, one pink and one blue, reminding me I was straddling two worlds, and that I needed to move.

I didn't know where to go.

The familiar face of the Stranger appeared beside me, her dark brown, bald head reflecting the light of the shifting white clouds, streams of blue light falling from above all around us, creating walls of light and information. The Stranger—curiosity, and . . . acceptance. She smiled at me, her blue robes folding around her as a cascade of distant planets formed behind her, telling me that this was the first step of a new beginning.

Hello, October Sky, the Stranger said, her voice full and low, vibrating through me.

"Hello," I whispered, awed that I'd heard her voice and wondering at the familiarity of it. "What is this?"

These waters are the conduit and something you should destroy if you get out.

"If?"

She tipped her head to the side and folded her hands in front of her, tucking them into the billowing, gold-embroidered sleeves. *It was not wise to come here.*

"But the vision said—"

I showed you where your friend was, not that you should join her.

"She's still connected."

They all are.

"I'm here to get them out of this."

The Stranger raised one shoulder in a shrug and tipped her head the other way.

She made this sound like this was a trap—wait. Like *this* was the trap.

The Stranger raised her bald eyebrows and nodded as if I'd just caught on.

"This is for me."

Yes.

"And if we destroy this pool, will he be able to stay two steps ahead?"

You will have to see. I only show you the door. You will have to destroy the pool.

"How do I do that?"

Use fire. Light the waters ablaze.

Light water on fire. That didn't make a lot of sense, but okay. "If I get out and destroy the pool, will Parker be okay?"

The Stranger paused. *She is connected. Trapped in here with the others, unable to escape.*

That wasn't good enough. "I need to find Parker."

Choose another.

Another what? Another seer? "She's my friend."

The Stranger looked at me for a long moment, then dropped her bright gaze and shook her head. *To find her, follow her sound.*

"Her sound? Like music?" Parker rarely went anywhere without her flute.

The Stranger shrugged again.

"When I find her, how do I get out?"

I will show you when you are ready. But understand, you are unlikely to find her. You are running out of time. This trap was meant for you.

"Then why did you lead me here?"

I answered your questions. Showed you where they led.

"But you gave me no indication that I should turn away."

Sighing, the Stranger looked away and then back at me. *There are answers here that, should you survive them, will benefit you greatly.*

If I survived. I released a pent-up breath and turned my back on the planets behind the Stranger. Closing my eyes, I searched for the sound of Parker's flute. When she'd been in elementary school, her band teacher had fought for her to join band, even going so far as to lend her his own instrument. She'd used that to get her through her childhood years. She'd been good enough to get a scholarship into college but hadn't pursued it much further after that. Parker had always said she preferred the unstructured music. Many times, I'd find her lying on her bed or on her couch, just playing. She would play in the same way others talked.

How much time had gone by? Dreven had slipped Ryder and Vance. Was I already part of the pool?

A flurry of notes trilled upward through the air in an invitation.

Opening my eyes, I was greeted by a garden of violet flowers and leaves. Glowing hummingbirds flitted through the trees lining either side of the starlit river, a bright white light guiding me, coaxing me forward. I moved forward, not allowing myself to fall into the promise of a good night's rest. I needed to find Parker and get out of there.

The light grew brighter as I moved forward until the starlit river flowed upward in an abrupt ninety-degree angle. Instead of violet vegetation on either side of it, two windows appeared, one filled with the street in front of my apartment, the other filled with a street lined with silver cars and silver-faced buildings.

A pink ribbon streaked with black started from the top of the line high above my head, working to weave the two together, like the rift between the two realities was a shoe to be laced.

I realized what was going on here. To my right was the future we were living in. To my left was the future Parker was seeing, and she was . . .

She was asking the questions to bridge the two realities together in the same way I'd asked the right questions to get me here, inside the trap Dreven Black had laid out for me.

"Parker!" I yelled. "Where are you?"

A flute rambled to my left, the notes a question.

Veering from the path of the starlit river, I headed into the silver landscape, my feet touching the concrete sidewalk. The rattle of a tank track drew closer. Identical silver cars lined the clean street. The siding of each building reflected a shimmering silver sheen, the windows black, emptiness staring down at a quiet street.

The tank slowed, stopping somewhere behind me.

I caught sight of a single window that wasn't dark. A little girl in a silver dress and knee-high socks stared at me, her gaze meeting mine without enjoyment or curiosity or alarm.

A man stepped out of one of the buildings, his pants and tunic silver, his hair tied back in a neat bun. He glanced at me, then looked away without acknowledging me or showing any sort of emotion at all.

"You will move, Citizen," a robotic voice said from the tank. "Return to your uniform and your scheduled appointments."

My uniform? I moved out of the way, stepping back to see if the robotic voice might be talking to anyone else. More people streamed from the buildings, all wearing the same dress or pantsuit, their hair neat and tidy, their faces expressionless.

"Citizen," the robotic voice said again, the tank turning toward me.

"Of course," I said, heading toward a door. It opened, and a woman stepped out, not even looking at me. "Parker," I called, quieter now, not sure how or why this vision was interacting with me. It shouldn't be, and the thought of it made my soul-skin crawl. If I found her, would she even know she was in a vision? This felt dangerously real. I grabbed the door and ducked inside, listening for a flute and eyeing the tank.

It paused for a moment, so I stepped through the doorway deeper into the foyer. Eventually, it turned its cannon nose away and continued down the street.

I made my way down the hallway at a brisk walk, listening for the clue that Parker was nearby.

"Citizen," the same robotic voice said from behind me.

My heart clenched as I spun around.

A slender, white-and-silver android on wheels rolled down the hallway toward me. "You are out of uniform."

"I am lost."

"You have lost your domicile?"

"I'm looking for my friend." There was a chance this wasn't a vision, but a mindscape. I'd read about them in fantasy novels—when a reader invaded the mind of another. This android could be a defense, not necessarily the true vision Parker was seeing. "Have you seen Parker Ortiz? I think she lives near here." I didn't actually know that, but if this was one of Parker's defenses, then I might be able to get to her faster.

"She is very close, Sky," the android said, twisting her head to the side. "Follow me."

That the android knew me had to be good. It meant that Parker could hear, was coherent. I'd be able to connect with her.

The corridor widened the farther we went, and the walls shifted from standard to glaring white with silver shadows. When I peered more closely at the walls, I could make out faces, many of them.

"Parker," I called out. "I'm here to get you out. I'm here to save you."

The android turned to me on her wheels and gestured to a tall, nearly flat white mask that turned into a door. "She is through here."

"Thank you." I twisted the golden doorknob and took a step inside.

The door disappeared. No room emerged. Instead, a gaping black vortex spiraled before me, a bright white center surrounded by a ring of fire. It looked a lot like the card from my oracle deck that told me my well was empty and that I needed to replenish it.

It flared and grew, inching toward my feet, threatening to suck me in.

"Parker!" I yelled. "I'm here to get you out!"

The Stranger appeared, orange flames lighting up one half of her blue face. *She does not wish to leave with you.*

"I'm not leaving here without her."

Then you will be trapped here with her.

The sound of an electric motor surged behind me, and something pushed me forward into the vortex.

"I'm no—Parker!" I yelled, fighting as the vortex sucked at my feet. The orange flames enveloped me, imbuing me with fiery will and a strength I had never before truly felt. The bleached energy in the center pulled at me, tugging me through, surrounding me with silence I felt along every nerve of my soul.

I sensed people without sound. I was reading the intent of those around me and those around them and those around them multiplied hundreds or thousands of times or more. I fell through the center of the vortex.

My feet touched something solid on the other side, and a door made of gnarled wood and etched deep with green vines appeared before me. The door was open, a bright yellow light seeping through. The light was filled with pain and doubt and misery.

But it was familiar.

You have to leave me, Parker's voice said.

"I'm here to save you."

No, Parker said evenly, though I couldn't see her. *You're here to save everyone else. Save them. Get out. Destroy the pool. And above all else, stay away from Dreven Black.*

The light of my anguish and guilt pouring through the crack in the door beckoned me to open it and languish in the misery of it.

If he gets his hands on you, the world he will bring about with you in his control will be intolerable.

My breath quivered with the threat of tears. "I'm here to get you out."

No. Parker appeared beside me, bathed in white light, her green eyes radiant. She tugged on her favorite pink sweater and came to me. *I'm not someone you need to save. I'm right where I need to be. And you? You need to be out there.* She pointed back through the vortex.

Seeing her face brought a painful twist of guilt.

He's getting closer.

"Because this trap was for me."

And he's winning as long as this pool remains.

Swallowing, knowing what I had to do but aching not to, I closed the door, shutting out the familiar, shutting out the anger and frustration, the fear.

Darkness surrounded me. Silence filled me. My soul found the sanctity of quiet.

A crash of gunfire shattered it.

Chapter 28

Two guns fired in the small space.

Dreven and his cronies had found us. I needed to get us out of there.

A man grunted beside me, and a woman let out a noise somewhere between a scream and a growl not far away. A blue-cowled man ran by, his sword raised high above his head, only to stagger to a stop, surprise washing over his face as two shots hit him in the chest.

I pulled my hand away from the milky liquid and fumbled in my pocket for a lighter, knowing there wasn't one. I did, however, bring out my hearing protection, tied together by a blue plastic string. Shoving them in my ears, I searched the chaos for Suzi or Ryder or anyone else I might know who could help.

Suzi scrambled to my side, dumping her pistol, the spent cartridges falling to the floor. "Tell me you got a plan," she said, her voice muffled through the earplugs but not silenced.

"Do you have anything that will hold liquid?" I could hear myself better than I could hear her, but at least the sound of fighting was quieter.

She looked up from shoving new bullets in her gun, a confused look on her face. "What?"

"A canister? A bottle?" I didn't know what I was looking for, or why I was asking for that instead of a lighter.

"Jesus, O," Suzi said, handing me her pistol and a handful of bullets. "Don't die while I search my pockets for a piss can."

I had no idea what to do, but I figured the round end went in first, so I plugged the remaining four holes with bullets and slid the barrel in until it clicked.

She frowned at me, pulling a green canister out of her pocket. "Will this do, and why do you want it anyway?"

"Sure, I have to collect some . . ." I took it, exchanging the gun and two bullets, and popped the top. A whiff of weed hit my nose.

"Don't judge." Her gun went off with a barely muted blast. "Maybe hurry, though. You know?"

I dumped the bud on the floor.

"Hey," Suzi cried.

I didn't know much about marijuana. I'd never actually done anything with it even after it became legal, but it smelled good.

Suzi stooped down, grabbing the flower off the floor and stashing it in her shirt pocket. "What a waste." She aimed and fired. "What a goddamned waste, O. Goddamnit. Give me something."

I knelt between the pool and Parker, resting my hand on her knee as I scooped some of the liquid into the cup. I didn't want to destroy the entire pool if Parker and the rest were somehow trapped inside it. If I destroyed the rest of the pool and it didn't work, I'd throw this in there too, but . . .

I refused to give up on my friend.

"You got a lighter?"

"Need anything *else*?" Suzi asked. "A shirt? A cookie? How about a fuckin' chariot?"

"A lighter would be fine."

Another man in blue stumbled toward me, falling over one of the wheelchair-bound seers, collapsing over the woman's knees, his eyes vacant as blood seeped out of his open mouth, the stench of blood filling the air.

Suzi grabbed my hand with the one holding the pistol, the wood handle warm from her death grip as she shoved the lighter into my fingers. "Fix this." She stood up again, taking a position at my back.

Not knowing how this was going to work, I flicked the lighter a few times until a long orange flame rose from the extended tip. Taking care not to rush and blow the flame out, I lowered it to the white waters.

As if thinking about it, the surface pulled away from the flame. Then, within a blink, fire rippled across the surface, a roar filling the room.

One of the seers moaned low, his voice rising to a fevered scream as the others joined.

Everyone except for Parker, who remained silent.

The fighters slowly went still, heads turning back and forth at the noise.

"Well, well, well," a familiar voice said, muffled through the earplugs. "This is unexpected."

I straightened and stepped away from the heat of the rising flames, hoping the seers were far enough away that they'd be safe. "How unexpected?" I asked, taking another step away from the pool and setting the canister, with the cap popped back on, in Parker's lap. "This trap was for me."

"Yes, but I expected you to remain in it." He narrowed his dark eyes and stared at me. "Take your earplugs out."

"Probably not."

Several of the blue-cowled individuals turned to one another as if confused as to why they were there or where they even were. Two of them looked around and backed away. Another crouched on the ground, turning over a body beside them and weeping.

Dreven appraised me and chuckled. "Well done, Sky. *Well done.*" His eyes crinkled with evil mirth.

He knew my name. "Where's Jimmy?"

"Do you even care?"

"I didn't, but you used him against my sister, who told you my name, so yeah. I guess I do."

"He's safe. What do I do with you?"

All I had to do was keep him sidetracked until someone did something he couldn't see, something normal like swing in and kill him.

The room was abandoned by the cowled army; all that remained were three costume-wearing individuals I didn't know and four people in street clothes.

Torrez came through the door, her ears plugged, her gun low.

I didn't look at her—I couldn't give him any indication that someone I knew was behind him. "Give up now. Surrender."

"I will not surrender." He smiled and let out a sad sigh. "It's not that I didn't anticipate you making it this far. I just didn't think it was likely to happen." He clasped his hands in front of him, waiting.

Suzi shook her head. "Fuck this shit." She raised her gun, aimed, and shot him.

He grunted and stooped forward, wincing a little. Straightening, he laughed. "You're going to have to do better than that." He held out his hand and turned it over, dropping the bullet to the ground.

"Oh, I will," Vance said, storming in, his black suit making him seem bulkier and a little taller.

"Ah, my partner," Dreven said, rolling his eyes and turning, his lips curling in disdain. "This is unpleasant." He smiled at Torrez before looking back up at Vance with a smug air.

Torrez shrugged and shook her head. "Whatever. Can we hold him?"

"No," Vance said. "We have to kill him."

"With what?" Dreven asked, tipping his head to the side. "You have nothing that can hurt me."

If the attention was no longer on me, I was good to wheel Parker and the other now-silent seers out of there.

"Silver," Ryder said, stepping through door behind Torrez. "You're not the first shapeshifter I've come across."

Dreven growled. "How did you overcome my call?"

I pulled Parker a little farther away, looking for a place to stash her and then grab others.

"You're not that strong."

"You know I am."

"Dreven!" a new female voice shouted from behind us. "Give this up."

Parker was so quiet, so still. I knelt in front of her, checking for a pulse, and looked up. Julie and a woman who looked a lot like her stepped out of the hallway toward the back.

"Kalindi," Dreven snarled.

"You are surrounded," the siren leader said calmly.

Parker's heartbeat was faint, but she was alive. Rising, I scrambled around, taking the handles and pushing her forward.

"O," Suzi called, from behind me.

The voices of several women rose, filling the room with sound.

I turned to Suzi. *What?* I mouthed through the noise.

She shook her head and shrugged. She drew her finger across her throat and pointed to the man in the wheelchair beside her.

I jabbed a finger at the next one in the line and then pointed in the direction I'd been going. I was looking for a room or something. I didn't know. I just wanted to get them out of the way of the fight as quickly as I could. They were helpless.

Suzi rolled her eyes, but grabbed the first wheelchair and followed.

I found another room that had a door we could lock if things got bad. It wasn't great. There wasn't another door. We'd be trapped, but I didn't know what else to do. "I'll be right back," I told Parker, skipping out of Suzi's way as she plowed past me at the doorway.

The siren song rose in pitch, clawing past my ear plugs. The need to relax and stop fighting made my legs heavy.

Dreven clamped his hands over his ears and screamed with the power of his own voice.

I stumbled as I moved back to the pool, pushing off the floor again as I almost fell. "We gotta get them out of here and then be done." I didn't know if Suzi heard me, but she watched my lips moving.

"Yeah, yeah, yeah," Suzi said, her feet slipping on the floor as she pushed a woman whose head had fallen forward, her hands dragging the wheel.

I looked down at the floor to see what she was slipping in.

The pool had only been a plastic kiddie pool. It hadn't been enough to withstand the heat of the flames, which soon wouldn't be contained within the warping brim.

Dreven knelt on the other side.

A large, wispy cat with bright green eyes stared at me from a milk-bath cocoon.

Here was the opportunity I needed.

Shoving one of the seers out of the way, her wheelchair rolling her to safety, I used my foot to push down the lip of the pool. A new hole ruptured instead, the milk water streaming out toward Dreven. The liquid flowing out was only liquid; it hadn't caught fire like the surface of the pool.

He raised his head and screamed his siren intent.

One of the men wearing street clothes turned his gun toward the female siren nearest him and shot.

I shoved my earplugs harder into my ears, but that didn't make a difference. They were foam, and in was in. I wasn't taking them out and readjusting them now. Instead, I watched the water as it traveled ever so slightly toward Dreven's knees and continued to push the seers closest to the path away.

Vance saw me and nodded, stepping toward his ex-partner and slicing the man's arm with the knife in his hand.

Dreven howled in pain.

With the nearest seers clear of the flames, I waited for the liquid that was already on fire to burn through the kiddie pool and set Dreven on fire.

But the flame never shot past the warping rim.

Ryder came in with her own blade and attacked, swinging with precision.

I didn't want to light the seer waters on fire. I didn't want to watch him burn. I didn't want to see *anybody* burn. If Vance and Ryder could take care of him, I'd let them.

With the power of the female sirens keeping him suppressed, he struggled to defend himself. He was bleeding all over—from both arms, both legs, his chest. He stumbled, then stood raggedly and laughed, blood dripping from his lips. "You can't kill me," he said, his voice quiet but powerful. "I'm too strong."

"Silver isn't the trick," Ryder told Vance.

A slice on his back healed as I watched.

"No," he said, blood bathing his teeth as he grinned. "It isn't."

Taking in several deep breaths to calm myself, I knelt, the lighter in my hand.

Vance nodded, his intention set.

Ryder shook out her shoulders and prepared for another attack.

With three flicks, a small flame danced on the surface of the milky liquid. It stood there for a moment as if pondering if this was a good idea, if it wanted to spring to life.

Dreven Black has to be stopped, I thought toward it, willing it to breathe, to grow.

Jamal stepped up behind me, putting one hand on my shoulder, his white tattoos glowing on his left arm.

The flame grew, throwing me backward to get out of the way of its fury. It raced toward Dreven Black and encircled him.

Jamal met my gaze as Dreven's siren song rose, changing in pitch to desperate screams.

I turned my back on the man who'd called himself Lord Shadow and found Parker in the next room.

Wheeling her out of the building and into the cool, dark night, I kept walking until I could no longer hear the screams of the one I'd killed.

Chapter 29

"Be careful with that," Jamal yelled as his desk was rolled through and moved into its new home. "It might not look like much to you, but that thing has gone through more with me than you'll ever know."

Matt paused and bowed to the desk strapped to the dolly. "I hadn't realized the prize I had in my wildly insignificant hands."

"Oh, piff!" Jamal waved him on. "Get on with you."

With an eye roll and a smile, Matt continued, looking a lot less like his old self. The goofy man who'd worn glasses with no lenses was gone. In his place stood a man with jeans that fit and a flannel over his black T-shirt. He looked like someone you didn't want to mess with instead of someone who could fall under the radar.

Which was probably good. Sturwood was only safe when everyone living here kept it safe.

The banks of lockers had already been installed near the back of the old garage, the place still reeking of oil and other car liquids.

April looked up as Matt went by, pausing as she painted the last of the four garage doors red.

I followed Jamal out of the shop and down the hallway that spilled into an open, glass-fronted lobby that had to have been the sales floor for the used car lot. "I'm heading to check on Parker."

Jamal stopped outside the room he'd claimed as his office and sighed at me. "There's nothing you can do for her, baby girl. I hope you get that."

I knew it, but I didn't like it. "I'm not going to stop trying."

"Well, just don't get your hopes up."

"I won't." That was a lie. This was just who I was, the person who fought to believe that things would get better if we simply tried hard enough, that everything would work out if we just applied the right pressure in the right places.

Jamal sighed and looked toward the corners. "We've got some protections going up." He shook his head as if disgusted with the cameras being installed.

I didn't like the fact that they were coming from Victoria. She could turn on us at any point. If the price of something else she needed was just a little too high—

The Stranger appeared underneath one of the cameras, calm and cool, her hands folded within the bell sleeves of her blue robe. She shook her head at me. *Stop looking for trouble where there is none.*

I blinked, ignoring her. I didn't understand why my visions were talking to me now, and I didn't think I liked it. It had made more sense when all I could do was see them. This freaked me out a little. "Well, they're fine," I told Jamal.

"That's what you said." His tone implied that he didn't quite believe it.

Ryder stepped through the front glass door. "Going to see Parker?"

I nodded.

"I'll go with you."

I shook my head and smiled at her. "I'm okay. I'm staying here. I'm *safe* here."

She looked around, her eyes wandering the open space. Finally, she nodded. "'Kay." She gave me a tight smile and disappeared down the hallway to the garage.

"Baby girl," Jamal said, his voice layered with accusation and inquisitiveness, "what in the heavens is going on there?"

I didn't know. After the fight, something inside me had shifted, and I didn't quite understand it. "I relied on her through all of this as someone who could protect me." I had no idea what I was thinking or feeling. "I just want to make sure that we build a relationship on something more than a one-way need."

"That's fine and all, but the key words were 'build' and 'on,' which implies the key words 'not shutting the door in her fuckin' face,' if you take my drift."

I did. "I'll be back."

"Oh, dear gods." Jamal disappeared into his office and closed the door.

Heading into the street, I was greeted by dozens of cats, wisps drifting off most of their tails and fur as they kept pace with me. A few of them mewed, and I wasn't certain if the vision cats were talking to me or if the real ones were.

The streets were filled with people as the sun crept up the sky, pushing around the tall buildings that kept the street in shadow. A woman with long, curly dark hair and tight pants pulled out café tables and set up the green umbrellas. She smiled at me on my way past. A group of kids ran by, laughing at each other.

One, a Black kid with short hair, stopped and pulled something out of his pocket. With a bright smile, he grabbed my hand, gave me a note, and continued running past.

I opened the paper and found a short phrase in Victoria's handwriting: *I'm here.*

I didn't know why she'd felt she needed to let me know when I was already heading her way, but I had to remember that we didn't have another form of communication and she didn't know my schedule. Granted, it was only three days old, but I'd been fairly religious about it.

I continued to watch the streets open up as the briskness faded into warmth, until I made it to the medical care clinic.

Melinda greeted me with a smile, her hands busy with a bloody bandage and a kid who didn't appear to be much older than fifteen. "Upstairs."

"Thanks." She'd been relocated to an actual clinic, thanks to Victoria. I didn't have all the details, but she now had access to more floors and more supplies. It'd been a slow work in progress, but she'd told me the day before that her intent was to put the seers who'd survived on the third floor.

The kid winced, looking at the damage on his arm.

He was going to be just fine.

Continuing down the hall, emotions rode through me that made me feel uncomfortable—anger, guilt, worry, a desire to fix something I couldn't. The elevator ride to the third floor was short. I stepped out, looking at a blue, glass-covered hallway with open doors to my left and right.

Victoria's bodyguard stood just outside of a doorway to my right, his button-up shirt tucked into dark jeans. He nodded to me once and then gestured with his head inside the room behind him.

I gave him a nonverbal thanks and went inside.

The senator stood in her brown pumps, her woven pencil skirt cutting off just below her knees. She turned to me and smiled. "Settling in?"

I wished I knew her plan and if I was falling into it, but the reality was that it didn't matter. Just the thought of moving to Sturwood had relaxed the anxious tension building in my entire body. "Yeah."

"Good." She turned back to Parker, who lay on the hospital bed, her white eyes closed. "They're all here, like you requested, and I've added staff."

"We didn't—"

"You were going to add this to Melinda's workload?" Victoria asked derisively. "Even you aren't that cruel."

"But I trust her."

"And not me."

"No." And I wasn't going to call on my gift at the moment either. I didn't need it. Not now. "Who's Rosa?"

Victoria went still, then looked at me out of the side of her eye. Clearing her throat, she ducked her head. "My wife."

Agent Spike was her *wife?*

She took in a deep breath. "I can't tell you more, but we have a plan, and that's . . . really all you need to know."

"I didn't know you were married."

"I keep her out of the spotlight when I can." Victoria raised her face, the sun streaming through the window beside her, catching one of her brown irises just right and making it glow. "That's why you don't trust me?"

I hadn't understood why it'd eaten at me until this moment. "If you're willing to sacrifice her, someone you love, then none of us are safe."

She opened her mouth to say something. Then understanding filled her face and she turned away, her full lips pushing out as she shook her head.

"What do you hope will happen?" I asked.

"Here?"

I nodded. "How are you using Parker to get what you want?"

"Hmm." She folded her arms over her chest and studied my friend. "Cutting right to the chase. Fine." Turning to me, she rested her fingertips on the bed rail. "I'm hoping to find a way to get them out of this coma, but also to figure out how he did it in the first place. I want to recreate it."

"To use us like this?"

"Not like this. Find seers who are willing—"

"To be sacrificed."

"To help us," Victoria said, leaning forward. "To get ahead. To break free. To *make* the sacrifices we've already made worth it."

I swallowed. "And if the price is too high?"

"Higher than the one we're already paying?" She closed her eyes and took in a deep breath, turning away once more. "I'm tired of losing, of going to funerals, or not even having them because paras aren't allowed to be buried."

I couldn't disagree with her conviction. She was right. What price was too high when we were already being killed or worse? "Do I need to be worried about my safety?"

"I will not use you against your will, Sky."

"October."

She remained silent.

Frustrated, I left. Parker was where she'd be for a while now, at least until she got better. I didn't know what to do about Victoria. I didn't want her to be able to make another seer pool. I didn't want to have that threat looming over my head.

But what was I going to do about it? Nothing.

I stopped in the lobby next to the elevators. What was I supposed to do? I didn't want to ask my gift. I didn't want it—it was too much. I couldn't explain it any other way. It was just too much. I'd gone from being able to see intentions with my cards with the occasional symbol vision, to having visions interacting with me at almost any time, to now being able to talk with my visions? Was this what it was like to slowly lose your mind?

One thing was clear, though. The seer water I had kept to maybe help Parker had to be taken to a safe place, and the only hiding spot I could think of was the one where my tarot cards hid. I couldn't allow Victoria to find it, even if that meant keeping Parker in her coma just a bit longer.

Exiting the medical clinic, I turned to the right and walked six blocks away to a triple-decker. My apartment was on the top floor with roof access, which was nicer than anywhere I'd been in a long time, even when I'd been working for Victoria and had a sizable paycheck. With that income had come a high cost of living, which simply didn't exist here. We didn't have real rent in Sturwood. No one owned the building I lived in. We just had to protect one another.

Pearl greeted me in my sparse living room, walking in from one of the three bedrooms as if she'd just arrived, leaning heavily on her cane. Her body seemed to be weighing her down more. She raised her eyebrows and smiled. "It's up."

"Is the other one down?"

She nodded. "Still got the ring?"

I pulled it out of my pocket and slipped it onto my finger.

"Good. Best keep it on. Rings in pockets look suspicious. Rings on fingers don't."

"'Kay. Anything else?"

She narrowed her eyes, her lips tight. Then she nodded and turned toward the back.

It seemed like she wanted me to follow her, so I did, but on the way to the closet door which she disappeared through, I dug behind the toilet and pulled out the vial of seer water. We'd transferred it from the weed canister to an actual glass jar.

What do you intend to do with that?

I spun and caught the gaze of the Stranger watching me with interest. "Putting this away, somewhere it'll be safe."

And what about Parker?

This didn't sound like the Stranger. This sounded a lot like me, like I was having a conversation with myself. "She's sleeping."

She's trapped. In a vision she is not safe in.

What else could I do? "Can I trust Victoria?"

The Stranger's robes turned to a vivid red and then reverted to blue again. *No.*

"Then this is what we're doing."

She plans something?

"You can't tell me?"

I only know her intent in this moment.

"And what's that?"

The Stranger tipped her head to the side, the bathroom light reflecting along her dark head. *To protect.*

"At what cost?"

The Stranger's robes slipped imperceptibly to a golden glow. *A high one.*

But one that might be worth it, judging by the color.

Walking around the Stranger, I moved to the closet and slipped through the portal, stepping into a cool, damp night. Moss clung to broken stones and a tree jutted through a rocky face as if it and the rock had fought to a brutal, life-changing standstill, moss dripping from its fingerlike branches.

Stepping out of the clearing of sorts, I found Pearl. "Where's the room you let me stash my cards in?"

"Just—" She stopped herself and looked down at the vial in my hand, her entire being going still. "What is that?"

It looked like she knew what it was. "Dreven Black was using it to trap the seers."

"And you brought it here."

"I'm hoping I can use it to bring Parker out of her coma."

"Parker is not here," Pearl said succinctly, raising her dark gaze to mine as fury fired her expression.

"No." I didn't realize Pearl might not want this here, but now? Watching her reaction and remembering she was a seer, I realized I'd made a serious misstep. "Victoria has Parker. I can't have this around her, even to save Parker and the other seers. She's trying to recreate it."

Pearl let her head fall back slightly in her stooped position, closing her eyes. "To create one of her own making."

"I won't let her have this sample."

The woman gritted her teeth and then took the vial from me. "And neither will I."

My world got quieter; bugs, leaves, cats, caterpillars, sun rays, rocks, and several other things I hadn't realized had even been there, disappearing as soon as the bottle left my fingers. "If I can get Parker away from Victoria, I will want that back."

Pearl breathed heavily, her hand flexing and unflexing around the slim bottle, the liquid inside glowing with each squeeze. "Consider it gone, October." She turned to leave.

I didn't understand fully what she meant to do, but I knew I'd done something wrong in bringing that here. "Was there something else you wanted to discuss with me?"

She stopped and turned, staring at me like she was brutally disappointed. "No. No, October Blaze, there is nothing I wish to speak to you about."

I took a step back from the anger of her words and the way she'd thrown out my father's name like it was an insult I'd now earned. Not sure what else to do, I went back to the tree and the stone-framed portal beside it and slipped back through, almost glad the seer liquid was gone, but upset that I'd managed to disappoint Pearl by trying to help a friend.

My apartment was quiet on the other side, but not nerve-rackingly so. Peaceful.

I went to the window, skirting the large bed I hadn't made yet. A wispy cat strolled up to me, his mouth moving without sound.

I leaned against the bright window frame, enjoying the cool glass under my fingertips and watching as people walked the street below like it was just another day. Like it was just another normal day.

And it was.

The first normal day I'd had in over a year.

I closed my eyes and let the weight of that thought settle the nerves that had been ridden raw. I allowed myself to savor the warmth of the sun streaming through the thin curtains. Though I didn't know what was to come, I'd managed to take down quite possibly the biggest threat our city faced—and I'd managed to save my friend.

There was still work to do.

But now, we had the space to do it. That was a big win.

I touched the glass again, my heart heavy but my soul glad as I watched the activity on the street.

We'd had a big, big win. For now, that had to be enough.

And it was.

Also By

London Bridge Down
Midnight Whiskey
International Team of Mystery
Slipping on Karma Peels
Eye of the Saber
Breaking Whiskey

Other Books in the Whiskey-Verse
Shifting Heart Romances
by Alivia Patton & F.J. Blooding
Bear Moon
Grizzly Attraction

Other works by F.J. Blooding:
Devices of War Trilogy
Fall of Sky City
Sky Games
Whispers of the Skyborne

Buy direct and get free books at

https://whistlingbookpress.com/
Be sure to sign up for news if you haven't already.
news.whistlingbookpress.com/whiskeywitches

About Author

F.J. Blooding lives in hard-as-nails Alaska growing grey hair in the midnight sun with Shane, her writing partner and husband, their two kids, his BrotherTwin, SistaWitch, TeenMan, and SnarkGirl, along with a small menagerie of animals which includes several cats, an army of chickens, a rabbit or two, but and three dogs.

She enjoys writing and creating with her wonderful husband, and is finally running an electrical contracting business. She's dated vampires, werewolves, sorcerers, weapons smugglers,

U.S. Government assassins, and slingshot terrorists. No. She is *not* kidding. She even married one of them.

Keep up to date on her latest works on her site:

https://fjblooding.com/

Twitter: https://twitter.com/fjblooding

Facebook: https://www.facebook.com/FrankieBlooding/

Bookbub: https://www.bookbub.com/profile/f-j-blooding

Newsletter: news.whistlingbookpress.com/whiskeywitches

Ingram Content Group UK Ltd.
Milton Keynes UK
UKHW010745150523
421757UK00004B/333